THAW

ARLAN ANDREWS, SR

WOODS
PUBLISHING

THAW
Arlan Andrews, Sr.

Thaw

This is a work of fiction. All the characters and events portrayed in this book are fictional, and any resemblance to real people or incidents is purely coincidental.

Print version by Woods Publishing

Cover art by Tomislav Tikulin

Note: Distance units used herein—miles, yards, feet, kilometers, meters, centimeters— refer to equivalent values in the societies they are used in. Those different societies will use their own names for these units of measurement.

CONTENTS

PART ONE

FREEZE

CHAPTER ONE

Snarling, the huge, black-furred *velk* leaped from behind a large stone, its massive canine body blocking the narrow path in front of Reader Thess and his steed. In an eyeblink of time, Thess saw fierce yellow eyes threatening quick death from the rows of finger-sized teeth in its open, slavering jaws. Thess barely had time to register the deadly beast before the animal leaped once more, right at him. But Thess' *two-leg* steed, an emu war-bird bred for fighting as well as riding, reacted instantly and instinctively, arching its long feathered neck and closing its pointed beak, rocking back on its long legs, then deftly stepping aside as the attacker drew close in mid-jump. In less than another eyeblink, the bird delivered a hard blow from a knobbed claw, taking out one of the velk's eyes.

In another eyeblink of time, the beast's howls of pain assaulted Thess' eardrums, the sickening fear-musk of the beast his nose, as its interrupted trajectory sent it sprawling on its back. Thess held tight to his pommel as his bird jumped backward from the force of the blow, steadying itself for another kick at its thrashing foe.

The velk, stunned at the unexpected pain, writhed on its back on the stony ground, shaking its head, blinking at the blood from its ravaged blind eye, its howls now snarls again. Shaking, it struggled to stand up, but before it could regain a four-footed attack stance, Thess' son Rist, astride his own two-leg, ran up beside the struggling creature and loosed his swinging bolo at its head. As the spiked bog-iron balls spiraled inward around the velk's head and slammed into it, the giant howled again, whimpered, then fell to its side. Rist's bird pummeled the downed animal with repeated kicks, and Rist quickly jumped off, pulled his blacknife and dispatched the twitching animal with a deep thrust through the other eye. It quivered, then lay still. Rist held up his bloody weapon and cried aloud, "Sire, will this velk's pelt make me a Tharn's Man?"

"I hope not," Thess replied, still trembling from the sudden violence of the attack, "I sincerely hope not. You are too small, too smart, you already wear black fur. And we still have business Coldward." As he watched, Rist first hooded his anxious bird with a rabskin shroud to shield its eyes from the dead velk, preventing any more deadly kicking (with an accidental kick, a frenzied two-leg could kill its rider as well as a velk). Then the boy unwound the bolo balls from the velk's carcass and began expertly skinning the huge beast from the neck down. *Three man-lengths tall, a hand long,* Thess calculated, *a truly gigantic predator. Lucky for us that our two-legs are as tall as they are, and instinctively hate them, can fight them so well.* Rist led his two-leg over to the velk, to squat over its dead opponent, shitting on it to claim a victory. Wrinkling his nose at the stench, Thess smiled at the scene. His own bird had settled down. *Let Rist's bird have its fun,* he thought. Thess just enjoyed seeing velks killed.

That thought brought back unwelcome memories; he had lost his twin, Rees, to a similar velk attack in the peat fields outside of The Tharn's Town, five hands of cycles ago, when he was just the child, Ress. But Ress and Rees had not been riding two-legs at the time and the two boys had had to fight off the monster before adults could arrive. His brother had perished horribly in the beast's jaws before Ress had finally thrust his shortspear into the creature's eye.

But in the midst of the shock and horror of that day, he had earned his man-name because of his bravery and spearskill, becoming the named adult Thess. He still wore that velk's pelt, his long furred sleeve cuffs since dyed green, proudly proclaiming his Reader status to all in The Tharn's Lands. Instinctively, his left hand—his Reading hand—slipped down into a deep pocket, finding the velk-bone totem onto which the newly christened Thess had carved the entire incident. A few light strokes brought back that day's details to Thess' mind—the time of day, the location, Rees' last words, Ress' own actions, the agony of his Sire and his birther when they heard the news. Thess shivered at what he was Reading. Perhaps it would be better to leave this totem with the Old Wen for archiving, and not relive his twin's death so many times over the cycles?

Thess' reverie was interrupted when his other son, Rusk, rode up to the scene on his two-leg, carrying a shortspear. "Took you long enough to get here, twin," Rist taunted as Rusk continued to look upward, left to right, up and down the valley trail, at the rocky hillsides on both sides of the wide, rapidly flowing New River.

Rusk ignored his twin's jeering. "I am searching for the velk's mate, Sire," he said directly to Thess, "for I have read that they hunt in mated pairs."

At that, Rist snorted. "*Read* about it? I have just killed one, right here. I don't have to *Read* it; I *do* it!"

Rusk shrugged, reining in his dancing emu to stop it from kicking the dead velk. "I have seen another one pacing us, but far up on the hillside across the river. I believe it won't come after us just now, over the river. Until it sees about its mate here." He looked down at his bloody twin, who was peeling back the velk's pelt. "Rist, if you leave the carcass behind, it will draw other scavengers, *thicks* and the like. The velk's mate will come and feast on them and leave us alone." He scanned the high walls of the valley on both sides of the flowing river. "At least until we come back this way," he said, frowning. With that, Rusk rode on ahead, constantly scanning the valley for new threats.

Thess sighed; his twin sons once again were showing their differing qualities. The same body size, they dressed alike in thickfur, though one in black and the other in gray, with similar facial features, and like their Sire, black-eyed with skin the color of brownwood. To the eyes of other People, they appeared to be identical. But inside,

Thess knew, they were as different as could be. Rist, the boy of action: competitive, athletic, good with bolos, chased after by the wen. Rusk, the thoughtful, observant; a developing Reader, a planner and far-seer. Each with good strengths, but each needing guidance to develop other necessary business and survival skills. Perhaps taking them Coldward to The Ice at the End of the World for the first time in their lives would give them—and him—that chance.

Overhead, the Misty Sky was dimming further; Dark was approaching. Thess shivered, hoping to exit the valley before then. The Ice was still a few dims away.

"THIS IS WHERE THE WORLD ENDS," THESS ANNOUNCED TWO DIMS later, waving his arms as the mist cleared in front of him, "and The Ice begins!" His two sons pulled up their steeds alongside Thess' own nervously dancing bird. Like Thess, the adolescents sat in their feathered saddles, awed by the spectacle of The Ice at the End of the World, happy to watch it safely from their stony ridge location, separated by the wide glacial lake and marshlands before them. On the far side of that body of black water, The Ice rose heavenward, blending its blinding mass into the grayish white of the Misty Sky, high up above.

To their left, Darkwise, the wall of Ice disappeared into the hazy distance; far to their right, Dimwise, in the thickening haze, The Ice encountered black mountains whose tops likewise vanished upwards into the Misty Sky. Where The Ice met the barren ground directly across from them, a slump of crumpled icy debris formed a flaring skirt between stone and Ice; where it met the lake, clumps of the melting whiteness floated in the black water.

As the three People gaped at the majestic sight, in the distance The Ice groaned, and shivered and cracked. A giant shard of The Ice, many hands of man-lengths wide and extending all the way up into the Misty Sky, began to separate and slide. Within eyeblinks, the mass of Ice slipped downward and fell forward; eyeblinks later, the sound followed, thundering, *crash*ing, a world-shaking noise like none most People would ever hear. The splash it made as it encountered the lake sounded like the gods taking a piss; the lake volume it displaced created thundering waves of dark, foamy spray that reached almost to the bottom of the ridge where the riders stood. Surprisingly, the water smelled of rotted plant life, belying the pristine white beauty of The Ice from whence it came.

Thess smiled. *This huge piece of Ice will be good for business!*

At the awesome majesty of the sights and sounds Coldward, Thess reined in his two-leg, bringing the fearful bird to a halt. Motioning for his two boys to do likewise, he stretched forward and hooded the nervous animal's head with a rabskin covering. As usual, the bird burped at him to show its displeasure, a deep, croaking, peat-induced foul stench almost as bad as Thess' own body odor. But his own smell emanated from a clear, thick layer of *beezt*-fat smeared on his face and hands, protection against the finger-sized flying bloodsucker bugs that sometimes swarmed these marshlands at the edge of The Ice.

After its odorous objection, the emu finally knelt, allowing Thess to disembark. His boys were doing the same, ensuring that their steeds were likewise hooded and no longer a threat to their riders. A sore memory arose in Thess' mind, of more than one painful pecking on his arms and face when as a boy he was learning to ride the unruly beasts. *How long ago?* His aching butt and back muscles cried out *Many hands of hands of cycles!* But he knew that he was only birthed a little over a hand more than a hand of hands of cycles before. Almost without volition, his left hand, the Reading hand, slid into the pocket of his furs, finding and thumbing his personal bone totem, his life story; the carvings there did not lie. On this very cylinder, Thess' Sire had recorded Thess' own birthing, all those hands of cycles ago.

Memories and carvings put aside for the moment, Thess called out to the boys. "This is what I was telling you about, boys! The End of the World, where The Ice extends in all directions. Where you will learn about calving, and how to tell when a shard will enter the New River. Where it becomes a berg."

Thess had brought his boys on this journey two hands of dims

Coldward along the New River from The Tharn's Town, through the vast peatlands, through the deep, barren stony valley—site of the velk attack—not only to witness the sky-filling vision of The Ice, but to begin their training, to apprentice them to Ice-watching, his family's historical business. His fathersfathers for ages had passed on the traditions down the generations, as recorded in the totem cylinders. Thess' packsaddles carried several hands of the totems, amounting to lifetimes of carved records, memories engraved in horn and bone and ivory, from many hands of cycles ago. As his fathersfather had taught him the ways of glacier-watching, so he would continue to teach these boys. His Reading hand positively throbbed as he anticipated passing on his knowledge.

AFTER DARK, THE THREE SAT AROUND A SMALL PEAT FIRE, ENJOYING beezt fare and potato brew. Above them, far up in the Mist, a pale dimness shone fuzzily through the ever-present cloud layer—*the Wen of the Mist*, Thess thought, *riding above the Misty Sky, dark after dark, for endless ages, companion to the male Pursuing Dimness who chases Her. Like all wen*, he thought, *the Wen of the Mist is unpredictable.* Sometimes appearing near the Dimwise horizon, sometimes the Darkwise horizon, sometimes overhead, sometimes too dim to distinguish, other times brighter, sometimes not appearing at all. Even the Old Wen in The Tharn's Town, who studied everything, could never make sense of Her movements.

But *Pursuing Dimness*, now, like all men, He was very predictable —every dim He appeared on His own horizon, paradoxically during the cycle moving Coldward during Warm, and Warmward during Cold, but always chasing the unattainable Wen of the Mist. Thess smiled as he remembered his own chases after wen in The Tharn's Town, until his fathersfather had finally given him his own wen, Mell, who quickly thereafter birthed his twin boys. Shaking off these useless thoughts, Thess held up a new totem, a small cylinder of horn, one he had purchased for a few coppers before this journey, from the brownsmith in The Tharn's Town.

Thess stared at the totem in his Reading hand, its outlines no less indistinct than the fingers that held it. He felt the carvings he had made, but could not distinguish them visually. When he was just a hand of cycles old, then called by the child-name Ress, he had asked the Old Wen why he could feel the edges of things close up, but could not see them clearly; and could see the edges of things beyond his reach, but could not touch them. She had explained it all to a young Ress in a way that seemed very logical at the time; an older Thess sometimes wished he could see better close up, but accepted the limitation without further thought, much as he did The Ice and the seasons Cold and Warm. He shook off the past and said, "In this piece of beezt-horn I will carve what we observe tomorrow. One of you will take the record back to The Ice brokers in The Tharn's Town. Bid the brokers come to the plaza and make offer for the knowledge therein. Old Broker Thenuss usually makes the best bids."

Rist, the more aggressive boy, waved a hand of respect, asking for permission to speak. "Sire, you have not yet taught us how to fully Read the cuts of these totems. How are we to know what they say, and impart that knowledge to the broker who wins the bid?" Rusk, his twin, nodded.

Silent for the moment, Thess sipped more potato water and considered his boys. The twins had been birthed just three hands of cycles before. They were maturing quickly, each now taller than Thess himself, each with their own developing capabilities. So, Thess knew, Rusk would learn to Read deepest, where Rist would never know more than the basics of Reading and carving, yet would hunt and fight and love wen with the best. Thess sighed. *Too bad they don't have all of those skills in one person!* He blushed at the next thought: *Like me!* Nevertheless, he had to continue their training, for Reading was the most important skill of all for their business, and even a rudimentary knowledge of it gave a Reader many advantages over other People who couldn't. Over halfway through his expected lifespan, Thess was feeling his age, anxious to pass on his knowledge and experience to his sons.

"Come here, closer, both of you," he said. "Don't mind the dark; your fingers will do the Reading. Reading was birthed in the Dark, the Old Wen told me, many untold cycles ago when there was no light at all, even before the gods created Pursuing Dimness to light our way. Eyes are not needed to feel, to touch, to Read." He held up the totem in his left hand, and took a small blacknife from his right pocket. The top half of the totem was already crisscrossed with carvings; the bottom half was blank. "Here, always mark the top of the totem with the Cold cycle, the number of hands of dims since the cycle began, and note the weather. The rest of this relates our journey Coldward from The Tharn's Town." As he spoke, the knife in his right hand deftly made the incisions he was describing. Finally, he tossed the totem to Rist. "Now feel it with your Reading hand—feel the depths, the angles, the ridges, the curves, the patterns."

He could tell that Rist was struggling, but at last the boy said, "Two hands of hands of cycles since Tharn Manyhands was birthed. " Slowly, stumbling, the boy related the hands of dims their journey Coldward had taken. He was able to describe a few bergs they had seen floating down the New River, but not much else.

Frustrated, his brother Rusk was grimacing; he quickly snatched the totem from a hesitant Rist, grasping it lightly and stroking it with his Reading hand. He related to his Sire the amounts of grain the emus had consumed daily on the journey Coldward, how many bergs and what sizes they had encountered that were now floating Warmward in the New River. Even some subtle puns Thess had carved, comparing a young wen's bottom to the rocking motions the emus made as they waddled their ways carefully over the rock-strewn New River valley just Warmward of their present location.

Finally, Thess complimented each of the boys in his own way, then told them to pack it in for the dark; they would have to get closer to The Ice tomorrow, to try and forecast which bergs would be exiting the lake to begin their journeys Warmward. *Those will be the pay-Ice*, he mused. The bergs that got stuck in New Lake or on the land either side, they would just stay and melt and increase the size of the lake and the New River and the runoff would carve the valley even deeper in years to come. As he lay with eyes closed, awaiting sleep, he wondered if The Ice would eventually all melt away, or if it was replenished in some way. But who would ever know what happens above the Misty Sky? The gods, perhaps? Maybe he should try to find out; after all, nobody knew as much about The Ice as he. The particular knowledge of glacier calving was his primary business, his livelihood.

Strange to think that it had been his ability to Read that made the family's occupation even more profitable than it had been for his Sires before him. He gently smoothed the green trim of his sleeve cuff, the distinctive color he had earned as a Reader. As he drifted off into sleep, some early memories of Reading wafted into his mind, like the fragrant smoke from the pungent, smoldering peat fire.

CHAPTER TWO

The Old Wen towered over the hand-cycle-old Ress, as Thess was called then. She was a large wen, *old as peat*, some said, and clad always neck to calf in rabfur, with dark brown beezt-leather cap and matching boots. She smelled of peat smoke and sweat, and her hair was white as Ice. Behind her, in many, many hands of niches in the walls of her largestone house, extending into deep caves below, lay countless totems, some as thick as Thess' arms, and some as long. "Each family carves its own totems, boy," she was saying, the skin on her wrinkled face twitching in all directions, visible even if blurry, "so you'd better learn from your Sire, else your family's history could be lost. Because these totems"—her arms swung out to encompass the entirety of the dark room—"they only live when stroked by sensitive fingers, by someone who understands their language and brings them to life!"

That was when she had explained that of the senses, *Touch* was by far the best. "*Seeing*? Bah! We can see well enough in the distance, to watch for warriors and prey and velk, but close up? It is not meant for people to See the details of their arms and hands, or the faces of those close to them. That is why important People wear color trim on their furs, so others can know their rank without introduction. Touching,

Reading, these can be taught, as I am teaching you. *Seeing* can't be taught; it can't be saved from one generation to the next, and it is useless in the dark!

"*Hearing*? That is a fine sense, too, but it can't be saved, except like Seeing, only in your memory. Memory goes dim when you grow old, and wisps away to the Misty Sky when you die. No, only Touch lets us carve our knowledge permanently, makes our memories solid, to be Read by people like me, many hands of cycles later. And Read by *you*, if you pay attention."

Ress nodded, scared at the Old Wen's manner, but captivated by the mysteries that only She understood. Sensing the child's fear as well as his interest, the Old Wen smiled, producing a wrinkled visage so fearsome that it shone through the fuzziness; Thess wondered if he would have to Read it, too.

"Of course, my boy, if you are a willing Reader, I can teach you the languages of all of these totems. You may never believe what they contain, what they will say to you, the visions they will produce in your mind!"

CHAPTER THREE

*T*he next dim found Thess and the two boys attempting to approach The Ice by carefully guiding their two-legs across patches of bare land where the New Lake had not yet inundated the landscape, and where the marshweeds were not too tall.

"Pay close attention to those dark crevices in The Ice. That's where calving will begin. To either side of the lake, those cracks are of no interest. They will fall, and someday melt, and make the lake larger. My fathersfathersfather mentioned that when he first came to the Edge of the World, The Ice was a hand's dim-march further Warmward than now. Halfway toward The Tharn's Town." At his boys' grimaces of doubt, he responded. "I know, it is hard to believe that the Edge of the World is moving away, Coldward. Don't ask where it is going, or why!" He laughed. "As long as The Ice calves, it's keeping us in business!"

By mid-dim they were getting dangerously close to The Ice. Thess warned the boys, "We go no further. Some of these calves could be longer than the distance from here to The Ice." At their derisive laughter, he pointed upward and said, "Nobody knows where The Ice ends; it goes up beyond the Misty Sky. A calf shard could fall on us right now. Maybe some could fall even as far Warmward as The Tharn's Town? It never has, but it might." He laughed at his own conjecture, but Rusk looked thoughtful, as if the joke were serious.

Rusk stroked his beardless chin, looking up at the Misty Sky, then forward at The Ice, and back again. He repeated these stares several times, to the puzzlement of Thess and Rist. Finally he said, "Sire, the calf that fell last dim"—he pointed to the mountain of ice that floated on the lake, not yet beginning to melt—"it has a flat top. Wouldn't that mean The Ice ends where the flatness begins?"

Thess brought his face up abruptly; he had never considered such a thing, and here he had been coming to The Ice for many cycles now. He swallowed and said, "Rusk, that is indeed a new thought. A new *kind* of thought. But what good does it do us?" He found his mind struggling painfully to grasp what his boy had observed.

"What a *silly* thought!" Rist laughed at his twin.

But Rusk ignored him, his brow furrowed. "If we could pace off the length of the berg from here along the edge of the lake, we could know its length, the distance from its bottom to its flatness. And because its flatness rises further than we can see, above the Misty Sky, we would know that the distance to the Misty Sky is less than the length we measure!" He was beaming at his own sudden knowledge, knowledge not learned from a totem carved by others, but by his own thoughts.

From where he stood, Thess could make out the length of the fallen calf of Ice; it was enormously long, but much less than a dim's march. Could the Misty Sky indeed be just that same distance up? Closer than that? It was hard to believe. He knew that the bottommost clouds of the sky sometimes came down almost to the ground in the form of thick mist, but the Misty Sky itself? Was that even possible?

Though his brain ached at the implications of Rusk's revelation, Thess was impressed by this strange new way of thinking, and even more so by the conclusion that he might be able to know, to measure, the height of the Misty Sky. *More practically,* he surmised, *might this way of thinking about the size of a berg have some practical value?* He pondered the question, and came to a conclusion: Knowledge was always worth something, especially when no one else had it. Like an uncovered treasure trove, he would gather it first, and put a value on it later! "Boys, unpack your pace-ropes and follow me. We are going to measure the Misty Sky!"

Suddenly, Rusk called out, pointing Darkwise. "Sire! Someone is coming this way! A beezt-rider!" Thess spun around just as a velkfur-coated giant of a man, riding a great horned beezt, approached from behind a nearby outcropping of rock.

FROM HIGH UP IN HIS BEEZT SADDLE, A MAN'S LOUD VOICE BOOMED out with rough authority. "Come with me, Green-Trim. The Tharn needs a Reader. The Cold People found a god in The Ice." Sighing at this unwelcome interruption of what had promised to become a most interesting dim of berg-measuring, Thess slowly turned his head away from the recently calved ice mountain looming into the sky just a short ride away. *Business will have to wait*, he thought, *for The Tharn's Man will not!* He put away his carving knife, carefully placing the totem with its kin in his pocket pouch after inscribing it with today's information and Rusk's strange speculations about the height of the Misty Sky. Then he rubbed his bare hands together to fight the cold, finally taking green beezt-skin gloves from another pocket. The gloves matched the trim of his fur coat and sleeves: peatmoss-green—the color of a Reader.

From his high perch two man-lengths above Thess' head, the black-coated beezt-rider bent down and said again, "They found a god in The Ice." Thess grimaced. The messenger's breath was forming small clouds of condensation in the icy air, blocking his ugly fuzzy face, but not drowning out the acrid odor of distilled potato water. "The Tharn wants a Reader to investigate and deal with the stinkin' Colds." Sensing a momentary hesitation in Thess' anxious look back at the glacier, the rider said, "*Now!*"

Thess nodded vigorously. He motioned for Rist to approach, then gave the boy instructions to take the coded totem message to The Ice brokers downstream in The Tharn's Town. The highest bidder would be given the totem, along with another totem containing decryption marks. The buyer would then know the size and the estimated arrival time of bergs they had observed in the New River en route here to The Ice. The buyers would be able to board the Ice pieces upRiver without competition, and then ride them downRiver to the Warm Lands, where the tall farmers there would buy them, presumably to refrigerate their beezt-meat and other perishables. Thess knew that someday he would have to ride a berg downRiver himself, just to visit the Warm Lands and find out exactly how his Ice finds were finally put to use. But that would be much later; right now he had The Tharn's business to attend to first. *Imagine, a god from The Ice!* He shivered in anticipation at the prospect of such new knowledge.

Rist looked at his twin with a smirk, saying in a low voice, "Our Sire chose me for the important work, while you have to go see a dead god!" He took the totem and stashed it in a saddlebag. Thess watched with interest as Rist skillfully climbed up onto the back of the kneeling emu, smoothed the black and white saddle-feathers into place and removed the rabskin head covering. The bird slowly unfolded its long yellow legs and looked around, shuddering. Then Rist guided the bird Warmward before finally disappearing into the distant, ever-present ground haze.

Thess hoped that Rist's news of the floating bergs they had seen would bring good prices. His recent advancement of the family business of ice-brokering—coming to the Edge of the World to record and catalog the bergs, rather than just estimating the arrival of random Ice chunks coming down the New River—was beginning to pay off handsomely. *Thank the gods that the customers who buy The Ice never venture Coldward to see for themselves how simple this business is!* They wouldn't like the stinking marshes, he knew, or the bloodsucker bugs, and probably would not appreciate the perfumes of beezt or two-legs. He laughed. *Or my own smell!*

Then again, he knew he shouldn't worry: The Tharn did not allow strangers to venture at will throughout his domain. Several bloody wars in Thess' youth had seen to that—in one of which Thess had fought and still bore leg scars, and another before that in which his father, Thonn, had been killed—and many WarmLander skulls decorated posts outside The Tharn's Place as a reminder to all. *So,* he sighed, *even The Tharn, as brutal and unpredictable as he can be, has his uses!*

ASTRIDE THEIR EMUS, THESS AND RUSK RODE BESIDE THE PLODDING four-legged beezt, careful to avoid its three-man-span horns. The creature, foxfur in color, breathed hard, grunting woefully, a great *moo*ing, when its rider jabbed it with a pointed stick to speed up or pulled the reins to turn its massive head this way or that. *Dumb,* Thess thought, *but no more so than its driver. At least we get meat and leather from them,* he noted, *which is more than we get from The Tharn's Men.*

True to form, the beezt-rider had not identified himself. The Tharn's Men never did; to all the world they were simply *The Tharn's Men.* Uniformly large and ugly, their black velkfurs and sharptooth necklaces were advertisement enough. That, plus the ever-present double-headed bog-iron axe strapped across their backs, its length matching their height. The big man said nothing for the entire two-dim journey, not even when they stopped for food and nature's calls, nor for dark-camp. Closely observing the huge man, Thess wondered if the stories were true, that The Tharn's Men had to track and kill a velk with only bare hands and a blacknife to gain the right to skin it and wear its fur. He shivered, then leaned over, patting his emu in appreciation of its fighting abilities.

At camp that dark, as The Tharn's Man's snores drowned out those of the beezt, Thess responded to Rusk's question about the gods. "Old wens' tales, I truly believe. A race of flying giants with nonsensical names, impossible powers." He snorted. "Like the Wen of the Mist and Pursuing Dimness, they supposedly live in the Misty Sky. But if they live up there, why don't we see them moving around like we see those two glowing fuzzies? And if they are Gods with such powers"—he motioned Coldward, toward the Edge of the World—"why did one of them die in The Ice?"

Rusk nodded, but made no comment. Thess wondered what new thoughts his son would think next.

CHAPTER FOUR

$\mathcal{N}$ear the onset of the next dark, Thess, Rusk, and The Tharn's Man arrived at the site of the strange discovery, an encampment of small yurts entirely too close to The Ice. From the acrid smell of sweat and urine, Thess knew they were near a camp of the tiny Cold People even before they arrived. The little savages carved no totems, swaddled themselves in the vilest uncured vermin-fur, and were rumored to eat their own dead. Thess shivered at the thought; he noticed, too, that The Tharn's Man had taken his long axe from his back and was nervously fingering its handle. The temporary camp set up by the savages was unsafely close to the glacier, in Thess' opinion, not nearly enough paces away. He knew that this wall of thawing Ice extended endlessly left and right, interrupted only by the occasional mountain. For height, it went up through the Misty Sky; some had said it went on forever, but he now knew otherwise, thanks to Rusk's observation of two dims before. It was still high enough to fall on this camp.

Thess remained stunned by the consequences of his boy's thinking. *Imagine that you can know something you can't touch, or even see, that you can measure the distance to the Misty Sky!* The Old Wen in The Tharn's Town would have fits—she had always taught that the Misty

Sky was too far for People ever to reach, that it went on upward for manyhands of manyhands of dim-march distances, and was there to shield the fuzzy shapes of the Wen of the Mist and Pursuing Dimness from the sharp-seeing eyes of mortal People.

But now he knew better; the Misty Sky was not as far up as The Ice. Some glacier-calves came tumbling down with flat tops, he had seen that himself, but only Rusk made use of that observation to create a new thought. His head nearly hurt with the changes Rusk made his own thoughts take. Like newly fallen bergs carving new channels in the land around the New Lake, the implications were literally unthinkable. Could there be a New River of Thought following soon? Would there be thought-bergs to sell? What kind, and who would buy them? And why? He shook his head.

Thess brought his attention back to the ominous nearness of The Ice. After many cycles of observing The Ice, he was well aware that a cleft could appeared out of nowhere without warning, releasing an avalanche of ice that could crush anything to a mere smear of bloody mess. And here he was now, certainly within falling distance. Rusk, however, was only anxious to see a god, paying no attention to the potential danger. But the looming bulk of the glacier, entirely too close, caused Thess to shiver, and not from cold. He tried without success not to look upward at the threatening white mass.

Regardless of Thess' own desires, his chief, The Tharn, had wanted a Reader, so here he was, too close to The Ice and surrounded by too many savages. Several hands of the small, smelly, heavily *zure*-clad Cold People drew back as The Tharn's Man, Thess, and Rusk walked over to the spacious beezt-hide yurt where the God's body was being kept, packed in Ice. The Colds had thoughtfully made the ceiling high enough that the People did not have to bend over. The Tharn's Men, Thess knew, bowed before none save Tharn Manyhands himself. *That great axe would have quickly brought down a yurt fit only for Colds!*

Inside the yurt, a knot of the pale pink Cold People, numbering about three hands in all—*small in size and weak of mind*, Thess thought—in their drudge-brown coverings, bowed before the visitors, making room for them to approach the find. To Thess, the small people reminded him of the tiny pink vermin that burrowed in the peat fields back home, pests that ate the potatoes and other peat-crops; those were worthless, had no pelts, were not even fit to eat. Thinking of the cannibalism rumors about the Colds, his flesh crawled as the little people swarmed around.

A few of the Colds were unpacking chunks of Ice from around the god. One of them jabbered something in Peoplespeak that Thess understood to be a report about finding the god in a cleft valley somewhere in The Ice, along with other god-things to be mentioned later, and a request for food goods as a bounty. The Tharn's Man waved it all aside without comment.

The manlike creature that was the God was huge and pale, the skin of its bare hands vaguely pinkish like the disgusting Colds, but in no way was the god ugly. A hard, red bucket-like helmet covered all its head except the face, and the clothing over the whole body was nearly as green as Reader Thess' trim. The god would have been nearly three man-lengths tall, if he had been standing. But the recumbent body was laid out on its back on an uncured leather sheet, its clothed arms and legs stretched outward as if in pain. One leg appeared to be twisted sideways, dangling by the merest of skin, shattered bones showing. Thess slid the helmet off after unlocking it with a twisting motion, observing that the god's short-cut hair was the color of foxfur, reminding Thess of the fuzz of the beezt The Tharn's Man rode on. And strangely, a thick brush of that same foxfur covered the lower part of its face. Its blurred face was, well—*fat* was the word that came to Thess' mind; no protruding forehead, no tight-skinned cheeks, no overbite. *Or maybe just well-fed?* the Reader surmised. He was certain that Rusk would have an opinion.

In fact, the god's whole body appeared to be filled out, even bloated, when compared to the thin physiques of Thess and all known People. Only at The Tharn's Place could one find obese overeaters who would approach the shape of this One. And even they did not stand half so tall, and none sported facial hair. But still, for all his size and color, the god was proportionally structured, so he was some kind of man, if not just a large Person. It was the god's wrappings, its head cover, its shoes, its—not furs, but something else of a strange, close weave, incredibly smooth to the touch—that struck Thess as truly godlike.

"What kind of god d'ya think it is? Was?" Thess scowled at the sudden scintilla of intellect from The Tharn's Man. "Big one, strange clothing," the dolt continued. "Let's have the Colds strip him down, so that I can inventory the belongings, see if anything is of use to The Tharn." Within minutes the Cold had removed the clothing, some by pulling it apart, and some by dint of blacknives hacking away. Finally, the god lay naked, its now-ragged wrappings neatly stacked alongside. While The Tharn's Man commented on the god's hair—its chest, arms, legs and groin sprouted that fine foxfur—Thess was particularly interested in the bracelet, the necklace, some small, hard, hornlike plates from the pockets, and the collection of thin, leaflike layers of pliable layers bound in beezt-skin-like material. No jewels, gold or silver, not even copper, turned up anywhere. "The Tharn will not be pleased," his Man said. "These worthless trinkets will not cover the cost of sending me here, of bringing back the god to The Tharn's Town."

Meanwhile, the savage Colds were pointing at the god's groin, chittering with laughter. This reminded Thess of the disgusting sounds of rabs in their cages. Then he saw what they were pointing to and made the savages quickly cover up that part of the large body. Even a dead god deserved some dignity!

After an evening of drinking, eating, and arguing, Reader Thess finally reached an accommodation with the Cold savages and with The Tharn's Man. For their discovery, the Colds would receive peat-meat rations for two hands of hands of dims from The Tharn's farms, and the three People would take the god's body, repacked in Ice, back to The Tharn's Town for further study. For his assistance, Thess would receive the god's boots and the worthless trinkets. The Tharn would have the god's body, its necklace and bracelet, and its impossibly smooth woven clothing.

Thess knew that the god's head would soon be posted outside The Tharn's Place as a trophy, joining the similarly large skulls of those long-defeated enemies from the Warm Lands. He hoped nothing else would be taken from that giant, and that it could rest in peat forever after. During the celebratory bouts of drinking, he had wanted to ask the Colds more about their reported cleft valley in The Ice, where their leader had vaguely hinted that other gods and god-things might be retrieved from the melting glacier. But Thess had a fear of the sky-high Ice; and the effects of the potato brew, along with intense curiosity about the God in hand, eventually washed away such thoughts.

For the march Warmward, The Tharn's Man insisted on taking the long way back, going far Darkwise to make a stop at the Coldward-most outpost of The Tharn for supplies. For this longer journey, Thess opted to ride back-saddle on the beezt, behind The Tharn's Man. Rusk rode alongside, guiding Thess' shrouded emu with a pace-rope tied securely to the saddle horn. That way Thess was able to handle and study the God's clothing and other materials while riding. Besides, his bottom was sore from the long rides the dims before. Unlike the emus, the fat, wide beezt provided a lot of softer saddle space.

THE GOD'S BODY COVERINGS WERE MADE OF THE FINEST WEAVE THESS had ever encountered, giving the materials a smooth finish not found anywhere in The Tharn's Lands. He had no idea how such material could be fabricated. The god's surprisingly lightweight helmet, almost large enough for two Persons' heads, would probably become another exhibit for The Tharn's war trophies. The extremely large, peculiar footwear featured a lacing system that Thess knew would be popular; something he had never seen before—an ability to lace up the boots, to make the top of the boot smaller after the foot was already in place! He planned to meet with his bootmaker immediately upon return. *This will be useful and I will make it expensive, at least at first. Imagine having boots that fit from the knee down, without chaffing and rubbing and sore feet!* He had no concept of the origin of the spongy skins that made up the soles and other parts of the strange boots. Maybe his bootmaker could work those out, too?

Nowhere in the god's green clothing could Thess find any totem carvings that might have told him who the god was, what he had been doing when he broke his leg and The Ice found and enveloped him. Surely a god would carve daily records of his glorious adventures, for retelling around the campfires and in the public houses, to impress the wen and scare the children? But no, there were only the hard, thin plates of yet another unknown fabrication method and of an unknown material, and those two rectangular bound collections of thin, smudge-marked leaves of some unknown plant or animal origin.

While handling the hard plates casually with his right hand, Thess detected some small depressions, as if recording-marks had been carved into them. Excited, he lightly stroked the plates with his Reading hand, wondering if perhaps the depressions and reliefs might tell a story in some god language. The Old Wen had said that some People had different carving languages, but he himself, under her tutelage, had learned all of the ones of The Tharn's Town tribes. Did the gods no longer carve? Were they illiterate, already knowing everything without learning, or did they just carve in yet another way? Thess thought on these questions for half the journey, carving his own observations and ideas into daily totems for later review. He found himself trying to think like Rusk had thought about the flat-top bergs. But it was painful. *Like exploring a new landscape*, he thought, *on those dims when the Misty Sky comes down to ground level and you can only see the outlines even of your blurry hands—and not see the dangerous peat-falls right in front of you!*

Three dims later, they stopped at The Tharn's Outpost, the settlement nearest The Ice, and replenished their supplies. Peopled only by velk-coated guards, it had been from there that The Tharn's Man had been sent to fetch Thess. The next dark Warmward, near a sparsely settled village, The Tharn's Man intruded into a miserably dank and spare public-house, noisily rousting up the keeper for food, drink and wen. After many dims away from his own wen, Thess welcomed the softness and warmth of the young wen, and her other pleasures as well. *Once again*, Thess thought, *The Tharn has his uses!* Even Rusk did not sleep alone, Thess was happy to see.

For the rest of the journey, the entourage kept to the main road through vast peat field plains, long stretches of passageway worn down to the stone below, where both beezt and emus could trod easily. Thess had never come this way before; the much shorter, easier route for riding two-legs was through the New River valleys, where he had also prepared a well-stocked redoubt in a carefully hidden cavern. *A place to escape from The Tharn, if our chief ever becomes too dangerous again!* Some hand of cycles before, during a cruel purge of several coup-plotters in The Tharn's Town, Thess had become fearful that The Tharn might one day turn on him as well. To that end, during his many trips to The Ice, Thess made it a habit each time to bring along bags of coppers and velkfurs for trade, and had stored a cycle's worth of edible peat products and jerked beezt in ice pockets in the cavern. With fire-starters and adequate ventilation, Thess and his family could comfortably survive there for at least a cycle, indefinitely if they hunted rab and velks and other meat animals. Ever-present Ice ensured that water would never be a problem. On their trip up to The Ice, he had shown Rist and Rusk where the redoubt cavern was, and how to access it through an innocuous concealed passageway. *Just a precaution,* Thess thought. *I've always prepared for the best and for the worst.* He smiled, grimly. *So far, it's all been for the best!*

On this new route, Thess still recognized most of the variegated colors of peat indicating which species was edible, which was for spices, which for burning, and which medicinal. A few of the peat farmers waved their way; once or twice Thess saw large flat, standing stones with curious white streaks scratched on them. He had never seen such stones or such markings. When asked by Rusk, a peatsant farmer said that the stones were erected to signify which kind of peat was to be harvested, and the white marks on them kept track of how much.

Thess was puzzled by the comment, but figured that ignorant, illiterate peat farmers, far from the civilization of The Tharn's Town, must have their own primitive ways of handling their needs. He knew that The Tharn collected one half of the harvests from the farmers for taxes. He noted that Rusk was very observant of the strange stones and markings and of the varieties of peat, making numerous carvings as they spent the long dims returning Warmward to The Tharn's Town. Thess could not imagine what his boy was thinking, and what knowledge he was recording. He didn't ask, knowing that Rusk would tell him later. For the moment, his own head was beginning to hurt at the very thought of new thoughts!

CHAPTER FIVE

*T*wo hands of dims later, Thess, Rusk and The Tharn's Man arrived at The Tharn's Town and were met by a coterie of other armed Tharn's Men. They were escorted to the guarded entrance of The Tharn's Place, a wooden gate in a largestone wall. After a few minutes of challenges, and a few more of quieter conversation, their escorts allowed the three into the courtyard with their wagonload of cargo. The god's body and all its belongings remained on the beezt-wagon behind them, where Tharn's Men and many wen, young and old, gathered around, in obvious excitement. Stories of the god's various many attributes had raced ahead of them. After the naked body was removed from the packing ice and laid on a large stone table in the courtyard, several of the wen began pointing and giggling, but some Tharn's Men angrily slapped down a thick woolen cover over the god's exposed parts. Thess had often seen The Tharn's Men angry—their normal disposition—but never before embarrassed. *So many new things*, he thought. *So many new experiences!* He saw Rusk just suppressing a grin and shaking his head.

Tharn Manyhands, the old chief of the vast domain of Tharn's Land, was a fat, drunken, balding man, barely as tall as Reader Thess, with a gray face and rotting teeth. He staggered out of the largestone temple across the courtyard, his expensive, gold-trimmed swaddling reffox furs failing to cover his protruding stomach. The man was over a hand of cycles older than Thess, potbellied and soft. His furs, the color of an evening dim-set sky, proclaimed him to be The Tharn. "What's this big pink thing you've brought me, Tharn's Man?" Noticing Thess, he nodded. "I suppose you, Reader, have already Read the god's carvings? What was it doing in my glacier, on my land?"

Thess responded quickly, hoping to avoid any more displeasure. "Sire, this god had no carvings. And I could not determine what the clothing was made—"

"Shilence!" The Tharn shouted with a drunken lisp. "Give the clothing to my wen. They will see what it is made of. You, Tharn's Man, take off the god's head and post it outside my gate. Then immolate the body on the plaza square tomorrow at first dimness. Let my People see that even the gods hold no power over The Tharn's Land." The Tharn's eyes seemed to glow with intellect as he spoke normally, quietly, to Thess. "And you, Reader Thess, go to the Old Wen and find out what she knows about gods. See if she can Read if we can expect any more of the creatures invading my land, my Ice. Are they dangerous, even when they are dead? Are any of them alive anywhere? How would we fight them? Find out for me." He spun around and opened his arms for two of his wen, who, giggling, disappeared with him into the darkness of The Place.

Thess and Rusk bowed and scraped their way backwards out of The Tharn's Place courtyard plaza, finally reaching the street. Thess sent Rusk back to their home, with instructions to meet with Rist and find out how the berg-selling business had gone. Then, carrying the god's boots strung together over his shoulder, Thess untied and uncovered his emu and rode away, thinking *Until we saw what the Colds had dug out of The Ice, never in my life had I ever heard of any god-like creatures coming out of it. There were always old wens' tales about Ice monsters, certainly, good for scaring children—but not anything like the god we brought back. And I don't really believe that anybody would know if there are any other gods around down here, dead or alive. But I have my orders, so I will visit the Old Wen tomorrow*. But first, he had to make a stop at the bootmaker's shop. He had a new business proposal to make.

THESS AWOKE WITH A THROBBING HEADACHE. POTATO BREW HAD A kick like a wild emu! He and the bootmaker had reached a joint venture agreement the evening before, and celebrated it with a wild night at several public houses. This dim, leaving his sleeping wen and the two snoring boys without a word about The Ice or the god or the berg business, he left his largestone house, quickly cleaning up at the public bath. He walked toward the Old Wen's largestone house, hoping she would offer him a dim-breaking meal, perhaps some herb soup, anything to calm his growling, gassy stomach.

OVER A HUMBLE MEAL OF WEAK BEEZT-STEW SOUP AND PEAT-BREAD, sitting on a stone bench at a table in the darkness of the Old Wen's place, being served by an attractive redheaded, red-robed young wen he had not seen before, Thess felt once again like a small child. He marveled that the Old Wen had not seemed to age any at all, over all that time. "I was always old, little Ress"—she still called him by his child-name—"when you were here, when your Sire was here, and his."

Thess could see one difference in her now, though—dark eye-coverings across her face declared that she was blind. That explained the lack of peat-candles. The place had been dark when he was small, but the occasional candle had kept away the total blackness; now it was lit only by the dim light through the doorway and several small openings in the stone walls. The cave beyond, her "library" she had always called it, stretched far back, into darkness. He didn't ask the Old Wen about her sight; she was aging after all, in spite of her protestations. He also didn't ask about the young wen sitting at the table, whom he took to be a servant. That one sat quietly, hands folded, listening intently to the Old Wen's words. Occasionally she smiled at

Thess, in whose sight, though blurry, she was nevertheless beautiful. Familiar physical stirrings arose, unbidden.

"To answer your question about the gods," the Old Wen rasped, inhaling a smoking peat- cigar, "some are mentioned in the oldest totems, in the rooms in the caves below where I have kept them sealed for many, many hands of hands of cycles. Not much was said, just that they existed. Those totems are also the hardest to Read. Some are indecipherable, their language lost even to me."

Thess almost spit out his peat-soup. "There were totems that I didn't learn to Read?" He gasped. "I thought you had taught me everything!"

"Nobody knows *everything*, little Ress," she cackled. "You learned all the languages of the living. The dead, the lost, the forgotten—they are down there in the darkest of the dark caves." She sighed. "But if you will take this key"—she tugged at a finger-sized copper cylinder on a chain dangling from her neck—"and find the lock it opens, back there, we will try to put some dimness on the darkness."

THESS WAS STILL TREMBLING WHEN HE RETURNED HOME TO HIS WEN and boys that dark. Mell poured him some potato water, followed by peat-bread and a side of beezt-loin. When Rist and Rusk came in afterwards for their portions, Thess motioned Mell away, and spoke to the boys. "Rist, the berg business report can wait. I have other news that I need to think upon, before I report back to The Tharn." He related the Old Wen's story about the oldest totems in her caves, and what he had discovered when he tried to read them.

"Some of the totems were not even spindles," he said, shaking his head. "It is unthinkable, but some of the totems were of metal— hammered, flat *metal*." The two boys' eyes grew wide in disbelief. "Impossible to believe, because how could you carve on flatness, and into hard metal at that?" He tossed out one of the god's retrieved trinkets onto the table, the hard, hornlike material clattering on the stone surface. "But the gods did it, too, apparently, because the oldest totems, the flat ones, looked a lot like this one."

Rusk picked up the finger-length-square flat totem and held it up edgewise, stroking the depressions along its length with his Reading hand. "Sire," he said, "if the old totems were flat and had carvings in them, and you could Read them by Touch, is it not possible that this god's piece is also carved? Just with much smaller niches and curves? Too small to be Read by Touch, but by other means?"

"Gods, boy!" Thess yelled, jerking the god's piece from Rusk's hands. "*Touch* is all there is! Reading without *Touching* would be like, like, *Seeing* without eyes! Ridiculous!" His hands were trembling in anger. Anger with Rusk for the near blasphemy he was proposing, angry at himself for a dawning realization that…what? Was the boy once again measuring the Misty Sky? Thinking who knew what thoughts about those peat plains and the white scratches on flat stones?

But Rusk had pulled out a fist-sized whitestone and was making strange markings on the dark stone tabletop, much like the peatsant farmers had done in the peat fields. The streaks were each twice as long as Thess' hand and as wide as his fingers—his eyes could not sharply distinguish anything much smaller. "What if," Rusk said in a soft voice, "the gods did not Read through their fingertips as we do, but in another manner, as you yourself said, Sire—with their *eyes*!" The boy had made an assemblage of large, crooked white marks on the tabletop, corresponding, he said, to the small, unReadable indentations he was Reading in the hard plate of the god's piece. The straight and curved markings made no sense to Thess and Rist, who looked at them uncomprehending.

Thess sighed. The Tharn might have *his* head on a stake if he brought back peatsant scratches and claimed it was god-carvings. While he bemoaned his fate, a Tharn's Man stepped through the front door, yelling as usual: "Reader! The Tharn needs you to return to The Ice! The Colds have brought down more gods from The Ice, and a god-machine with them!"

Rusk brightened at the prospect of new knowledge, Rist frowned at the interruption of the berg business he was just learning, and Thess wished out loud that the gods would stay frozen and out of his life. As the three fell in behind The Tharn's Man, the wen Mell came back in, took a wash cloth, and began to wipe away the strange white markings her boy had made, atop the stone table. Shaking her head, she couldn't decide if the gods were crazy or if her own men were. As she removed them she wondered what the strange symbols meant, if anything:

CHICAGO UNA

UNA GLACIAL RECON

XAVIER RASHA, M.D.

PART TWO

FLOW

CHAPTER SIX

*R*ist's first thought was, *The sky is broken!*

The familiar Misty Sky—those thick layers of grayish-white low-lying clouds that covered Rist's whole world back home in The Tharn's Lands, stretching horizon to horizon, Dimwise to Darkwise—was *gone!* In its place overhead lay a distant, pale blue dome, centered on a shining disk so bright his eyes hurt without even staring directly at it. Only shredded remnants of home's remembered whiteness scudded across that vast expanse, just flecks and billows blowing here and there, and much higher up than he could have ever imagined.

"What happened to the sky?" he called out across the iceberg from the life-post he was barely holding onto, over the sound of rushing rapids. "Where is the Misty Sky? What happened to it?" he yelled again. His gray velkfur coat was soaking wet from the splashing river water, making it harder to clutch the life-post with both arms.

"Welcome to the Warm Lands, bird-rider!" his rough berg-companion, Cruthar, shouted back, also trying to be heard over the thunderous crashing, sharp creaks, and long groans as their shepherded small mountain of Ice slid and pounded against river stones. "Down here, the Wen of the Mist and Pursuing Dimness, they lost a sky-war to the Pale Lady and the Shining One!" Cruthar stabbed a gnarled brown finger toward the blue bowl above them. "New gods in a new sky—all blue! Pieces of the Misty Sky try to sneak over, like those"—Rist followed his direction, peering at clouds disappearing in the distant, dim horizon—"but Shining One up there"—the too bright disk—"He will burn them away to nothing."

Rist shook his head as if to awaken from a bad-dark dream. "That can't be!" he protested loudly. "How can the gods lose a war in one sky and yet live in another?" But he quickly stopped yelling, keeping all his attention on clinging to the life-post as the berg smashed first one side and then the opposite against sharp crags protruding from the river. In a less fearful part of his mind, Rist hoped that the iceberg would hold together until he and Cruthar and the rest of the berg-crew could see it safely through the River's End passage and into the hands of the final buyers in the Warm Lands. It had been a rough ride this last dim of the four-dim journey, here where the New River narrowed and flowed through bare rock canyons, a zigzagging pattern that reminded him of some of the carving styles on the cylindrical totem in his pocket.

Rist could tell that Cruthar was smiling, but that was all; the naturally blurry near vision of the People revealed only a ravaged mahogany face and ragged teeth, testament to the man's wearing years as a berg-man. Like all People in The Tharn's Lands, Cruthar wore dark furs that covered everything but his brown face and hands, the orange sleeve trim designating him as working class. "Rist, wait till you see the Wen of the Mist here"—the berg-man laughed—"she is round and white and beautiful, with sparkling colored freckles. You will be happy to see the goddess of the Warm Lands sky!"

At the moment, fearful for his life aboard an iceberg in the rushing waters of the New River, Rist was not happy about anything. Holding on to his life-post with all his strength, he watched as Cruthar, his Sire Strether, and the four other crew skillfully maneuvered the berg between massive rocks, pushing here and there with long poles, quickly moving huge air-filled beezt-bladders from one side to the other, all to keep their frozen craft upright and themselves alive.

After another terror-filled hour, the berg finally emerged into a wide, placid river. Rist gasped. The water here flowed so slowly, was so vast, that it could have been a lake. It reminded him of the black lake at the foot of The Ice at the End of the World, where the sky-filling glacier calved and dropped bergs like the one he was riding. He had been at that lake a little more than a hand of hands of dims ago, with his Sire, Reader Thess, and his own twin, Rusk. Thinking of his family brought back a memory of uncertain pleasantness: that lake was where Rusk had seen a flat-topped calf of glacier slide down from The Ice, from above the Misty Sky, then figured that The Ice must end at the flatness, so it was higher than the sky.

Reader Thess and his twin sons had been in the process of pacing off the length of that shard, so they would know how high the Misty Sky was, when a Tharn's Man had interrupted. Reader Thess then sent Rist back to The Tharn's Town to sell the bergs they had found, while the Reader and his other son, Rusk, went to see the god that the small, disgusting Cold People had retrieved from The Ice, a few dim-marches away. During his long, solitary ride back from The Ice to The Tharn's Town, Rist had taken a long time to accept Rusk's new way of thinking, of looking at things differently.

This new kind of thinking had bothered him at first, but then he began to ponder it. *What else could a man know if he just paid attention?* His twin, Rusk, had always been studious, he knew, while he himself had preferred to chase—and catch!—attractive wen and do more physically demanding activities. While Rusk spent hours poring over how to carve horn or wooden totems with the patterns of marks that Readers like their Sire could Read by Touch, Rist had spent his hours learning more about riding the tall fighting birds, the two-legs; and about making and whirling bog-iron bolos, and throwing blackstone-tipped spears. Even sailing small boats in the New River at The Tharn's Town. Yet as he had witnessed up at the black lake, Rusk's way of thinking new thoughts had brought as much praise from their Sire as had his own swift killing of the huge velk on their trip Coldward. *I may be able to do that kind of thinking myself*, he thought, *I just never had a reason before!*

While his Sire and Rusk had gone looking for a god in The Ice with that Tharn's Man, Rist had brought back his Sire's berg-record totem and its companion decoding cylinder to The Tharn's Town. There he had met Ice brokers who greedily bid for the information on the sizes and arrival times of the next big bergs, with Broker Thenuss, a gray-haired friend of Sire Thess', paying the highest price. Reader Thess, whose family had permanent and sole rights to Ice sales, granted by The Tharn (in return for an exorbitant share, of course), had created a different kind of market for Ice.

Rist never quite understood what a broker did, but he did know that in far-olden days, families had fought over newly discovered bergs floating down the New River. But like his family's ancestors had eventually done, his Sire, Thess, would travel to The Ice at the End of the World and then observe the calving, in order to predict when Ice was coming downRiver rather than awaiting random bergs floating by. And Sire Thess' advanced literacy in Reading had allowed him to record berg information on totems at The Ice itself, and then send it back via fast two-leg courier, speeding up the whole process.

The earnings from selling this berg information enabled Thess, his wen, Mell, and their twin sons to live in a largestone house, within a walled compound of emu-corrals, a warehouse, and a courtyard, rather than the common small peat-brick huts of most of the People. Rist considered his Sire's talents to be more along the lines of Rusk's than his own. However, cycles ago his Sire had single-handedly dispatched the velk that killed his own twin, earning his man-name Thess from his boy-name Ress. *Our Sire is a man of many talents*, Rist had concluded. *I hope to be like that, too!*

After taking the bag of coppers for the berg information and giving over The Tharn's nosy taxman a third of the take, Rist had questioned old Broker Thenuss about the final destination of his purchased bergs. "What do you care, boy?" snarled the grizzled merchant, whose red-trimmed furs designated his merchant's profession. "You got your coppers; in a few hands of dims I'll get back those and more from the buyers in the Warm Lands."

A sudden thought—*What's it like in the Warm Lands?*—burst in

Rist's mind. "Broker Thenuss, what if I go with your crew, along for the ride?" he asked. "I want to see where my Ice—*your* Ice—goes, and what they do with it. What would it take for me to go with your crew on the berg you just bought?"

"Ride it down for free, for all I care, boy," Thenuss answered with a sneer. "Go see the berg-chief, Strether, and tell him I said so. Just bring your own food and thatch-pad and stick your own life-pole in place!" He laughed. "And don't carry anything you don't want to leave behind!" Still laughing, leaving Rist puzzled at his comment, the broker hobbled off to the brew pub to celebrate his deal.

When his Sire Thess and twin Rusk had returned to The Tharn's Town with the body of the god from The Ice, Rist marveled with all the other People at the large, pale manlike figure, nearly three times the height of most People and over twice that of the largest Tharn's Man. To Rist, the most interesting items were the god's smoothly woven green clothing, which the Tharn had kept for himself. The Tharn had given Reader Thess the god's strange adjustable boots and some worthless trinkets in return for accompanying The Tharn's Man to retrieve the corpse from the perverted Colds. The god's red helmet went to The Tharn's trophy wall, its large head to a pointed stick outside The Tharn's Place, alongside many WarmLander trophy skulls, and its body to a pyre for public immolation.

Rist had not paid much attention to the flat metal and hornlike plates that his Sire earned from the god's possessions, and which Rusk had claimed might have writing marks that could be Read like the totem carvings, but with *Seeing* instead of *Touch*! *If the gods can See that close up, they are not at all like us People*, he thought. *We can See clearly at a distance, that which we can't Touch, and can Touch within an arm's reach, that which we can't clearly See!*

New thoughts or not, Rist had not wanted to pursue that dark, dimless pathway of thought any further, *All the way to madness*! he felt. He also did not want to go back Coldward again to The Ice with his Sire and twin to retrieve any more gods and god-stuff. Instead, he wanted to do something different, something daring—to go Warmward with one of the bergs he had sold. One would be along any day, according to the carved information he had sold Broker Thenuss. He asked his Sire about making the trip.

To his surprise, Sire Thess had agreed, and so Rist had set forth on a new adventure. At times these last few dims, riding the wild iceberg with a wilder crew, he had been afraid it would be his last one.

As the berg drifted in the slow current, Rist shielded his eyes. The blue brightness was too much to bear. And it was getting warm, very warm. Walking from post to post, carefully grabbing each to steady himself against the rocking of their ice-boat, Cruthar came over to Rist and said, "Take these eye coverings, they'll help you with Shining One." Rist took the proffered gift, which was a leather thong with two round patches, each with a slit. "Put it over your eyes, like this—" The berg-man demonstrated. "Look through the eye-slits and Shining One won't burn out your eyes. But don't look at Him directly; it will hurt." Immediately, Rist's vision improved. He felt disoriented without the close comfort of the Misty Sky overhead, with the unaccustomed brightness all around, but he would live. He was also getting hot!

Cruthar said, "And you might want to strip down to your unders, boy. The Warm Lands be called that for a reason." Within minutes, all the berg-crew were uniformly dressed—a gray, diaperlike loincloth, naked everywhere else but their feet. "Tie your furs around the post. Keep your boots on, though, Rist. Ice is still cold, even down here." Rist soon learned that heat from Shining One could cause him to sweat, even without working. *A lot to learn*, he thought. Then, feeling within his pile of furs, he found a totem cylinder in his jacket pocket. *And a lot to record!* With his blacknife in his right hand, he began carving a report about this leg of his adventurous trip down the New River to the Warm Lands. He was sure that this account would be of extreme interest to his Sire and his twin.

Each side of the river sported thick forests, almost without space between tall conifers; along the shoreline, thick brambles of flowering bushes tumbled from forest to water. Time and again, wading birds in uncountable numbers took to the sky as they neared, the wave upon wave of soft flapping a caressing river of sound, the avian bodies a swarm of twisting whiteness against the unfamiliar blue bowl of sky. The winds brought sweet-smelling fragrances that he could not identify. Rist thought it all strange and beautiful, and carved it so on his totem. He also noted the expanse of trees; back home, timber was very expensive, most of it imported from lands far Darkwise and brought in on carts. Any one of those countless numbers of trees was worth a fortune in The Tharn's Lands.

"Towers!" someone shouted. "Get out the signal mirror!" Squinting his strained eyes, Rist viewed the tallest structures he had ever seen, one on each side of the river, their heights evident even from this distance as they stood hands higher than the trees. They were bright yellow in color, but whether of stones that color or painted, Rist couldn't tell. He did see Strether feel around in his stowed furs and pull out a flat plate, two handwidths square, and then tilt it this way and that, as if to catch something invisible. Cruthar explained, "My Sire is catching the power of Shining One up there." He pointed toward the bright disk in the sky. "It shines on his mirror, and he points it over toward that tall building over yonder. Them's they call *towers*. Now you watch!"

Suddenly, from the top of the tower Darkwise—"*west*, they calls it down here," Cruthar had said, "where Shining One sets and ends every *day*"—came a small point of light, every bit as brilliant as Shining One, flashing toward the berg. Strether answered with sudden movements of his signal mirror. After several more flashes came back from the tower, the older man smiled, putting away his device. Cruthar said, "One of the tricks of our trade, bird-boy. We flashes our mirror signals to them, the towers know we're coming, and what we're doing. They flashes the message to the priests in God's Port and then the priests let us come through peaceably. Otherwise, they sends out war-man ships and kills us all." Rist gasped, at first thinking his friend was playing a joke. But the ice-man shook his head. *Seriously!*

Using a mirror for signaling struck Rist as very unusual. He had seen small mirrors back in The Tharn's Lands, but they were only expensive toys. People said your spirit was inside them, but Rist had only been able to see other People's blurred images in them. His own mirror-face was simply an indistinguishable brown patch. Mirrors had no other uses he knew of under the dimness of the Misty Sky. But here in the brightness of the Warm Lands? Well, now he had seen how to communicate over long distances if you had Shining One overhead. *Most interesting*, he carved. *What else can you do with brightness?* He carved that question onto his totem. He was sure that Rusk would think of something.

By now the signaling tower in the *west* was close enough that Rist could make out that the part of it above the trees was made of huge, finely cut stacked stones, painted bright yellow. But in the center of the side toward the river, the building was marked with a puzzling symbol, like a wheel rim painted red, yet with its spokes on the outside, sticking straight out. In Rist's homeland, the only symbols were patches of color; geometric designs of thin lines were unheard of. He asked his companion about the strange markings.

"Ye'll learn a lot real soon, Rist," Cruthar answered. "The yellow paint and red marks means that this is what the WarmLanders call 'God's Country,' their two shining gods in the sky. Them priests owns the whole place, including where we're going, namely the town of God's Port. That red wheel sign yonder means Shining One, and those spokes outward, they's the power of that god over the whole world. You, me, everybody." Rist shrugged; he never had thought of gods as having any powers over any person, much less himself. This was another new thought, more information about this new land, but the concept felt wrong to him. Nevertheless, he carved it so.

Shortly afterward, Cruthar broke out the larder and passed out drinks of potato brew and slices of cold beezt to Rist and the crew. Chewing a mouthful of meat, Cruthar went on, "These Warm Lands don't got a Tharn to protect you, or no Tharn's Men to keep no peace." Rist shook his head; it was literally unimaginable to him that there could be no one strong leader and no strong men ready to enforce justice, even if it was The Tharn's rough kind. "Here there be *priests*, boy. Priests of Shining One; priestesses of the Pale Lady. They has temples and churches, and they has some real tough Priests' Men." He shuddered.

After Rist's questions, Cruthar burped and said, "Temples and churches—that's where the priests and priestesses talk to the gods. Shining One up there"—pointing toward the brilliant disk overhead —"and the Pale Lady."

"How do the priests *do* that, the gods being so far up there? And what do the gods say?" Rist ventured. "And why would gods up in the sky care about us down here?" Having seen one god, the one from The Ice, up in The Tharn's Town, he asked, "And Shining One up there— He doesn't look at all like the god my Sire and Rusk brought down from The Ice. That one—you saw him—he was like us, only big and fat and pale-skinned and hairy and three times as tall, but still with arms and legs. Does the Pale Lady have arms and legs like us?"

Cruthar laughed and took another swig of the strong drink. "Lots of questions, little boy. First, the priests call what they do *worship*, you'll learn that real quick. And, next, the Pale Lady is exactly the same size and shape as ol' Shining One up thar. Onc't in a great while, I been told, they even gets together in the same place in the sky and makes love and then the lights go out, all over the Warm Lands!" He paused. "I ain't never thought about what you just said, 'bout arms and legs and all. Could there be more than one kind of god?" Cruthar frowned, his concern fuzzily visible to Rist. He shook his head. "Whatever, don't you mention none of that down in God's Port. The priests don't like anybody thinkin' different about their gods. You just respect 'em and nod your head when they start preachin' to you, you hear?" With that, Cruthar laid back on his insulating thatch-pad and fell asleep, exhausted by the day's strenuous work.

Rist stayed awake, thinking on this adventure and carving his observations as quickly as he could. The berg meandered slowly, past other mouths of other tributaries emptying into the main river. Small sail boats with triangular masts passed close by the berg and its crew in both directions; nobody waved at them.

CHAPTER SEVEN

*W*ithin a few hours, Rist watched as two large oar-driven boats, flying yellow flags with the same strange bright red circle-and-spokes insignia, came out to greet the iceberg crew. Though the images registered on his vision, he had trouble recognizing the intricacies of the design; the concept of an abstract symbol was still alien. As the boat crews threw anchors onto the berg, he could see that the vessels held several hands of oarsmen, and an equal number of helmeted men standing with long spears and metal chest armor. *A lot taller, almost like that god from The Ice, and with much paler skin than People have*, he thought. He hoped this would be a friendly encounter, but still felt in his boot for his blacknife. *Little good this would be against spears and armor!*

From a ledge on the forward edge of the berg, Strether talked to the big boatmen in strangely lilting, yet understandable Peoplespeak. The conversation went on for a long time, with a lot of gesturing, shouting and spear-shaking. But eventually the head man apparently reached an agreement on terms with Strether. The crews pulled back their anchors and quietly pointed downstream. Strether came back to the crew. "A good sale, boys; Broker Thenuss will be a happy investor. All we have to do is wait for the river-net to catch us. Tonight, it's cold brew and warm wen for all." He winked at Rist. "Even some for our freeloader here," he laughed. "So, boy," he said, "would you rather ride birds or bergs?" And laughed again, "Or, like us, wen?"

THE RIVER-NET WAS YET ANOTHER WONDER TO RIST. CRUTHAR explained, "The WarmLanders have stretched a real strong net all the way across this wide river." He pointed at a dark, shimmering curtain rising from the water just ahead of them, more like thin smoke than the peat-twine fishing nets Rist was used to back in The Tharn's Lands. It rose, mistlike, higher than the top of the berg. "Stay back when we hit it; it's real thin and you can barely see it, like it's made out of peat-smoke, but it is stronger than bog-iron. You get caught between it and the berg, you will look like minced beezt." With the rest of the crew, Rist made his way to the back of the berg where their safety posts had been driven into the iceberg. They all held on as the nearly invisible webbing contacted the berg, wrapping the bow of the floating ice as gently as a dry breeze, slowing it to a soft halt. Rist saw that they were still a long way from the shore on either side.

"How do we get the berg all the way over there, to the river's edge?" he asked Cruthar. The river here was slower than back home, and many hands times wider.

"Just watch, bird-rider," the crusty berg-man answered. "This is the easiest part of the trip. We don't do nothin'."

Within minutes, several hands of other pale-skinned boatmen, all still taller than even The Tharn's Men back home, but much more slender, arrived in two small boats sporting that same yellow flag of the red wheel with its mysterious marks. Coming from either side of the river to meet the webbed iceberg, the vessels appeared to be clinging to the net in some way as they moved. Each boat had a tall mast centered in a rotating vertical wooden spool, which appeared to have cog wheels that pulled the boat along the length of the river-spanning web. Rist tried to imagine how the system worked, but couldn't. *But it sure beats oars and sails!* he thought. *As long as you only want to go where the net goes.*

Climbing up the berg with pitons and twine ladders of some sort, the net-men went about their duties without a word. Rist watched these strange People with interest; maybe he could learn something about that unusual net and about what these men were doing with it. It didn't register on him until later that not only were these unhelmeted men a much lighter skin color than his own dark People, but that several of them had different colors of hair—some almost white, some yellow, a few even copper—he had been too interested in what they were doing with the mist-net.

Each net-man was dressed in a skimpy, dark blue loin cloth, wearing short black boots with spiky soles. *So that's how they move about this berg without slipping. Interesting! Better than us; they don't need safety poles.* The bulk of the men began hammering long iron poles into the surface at the front of the berg, using large hammers. The leader of the net-men, wearing what appeared to be oversized gloves of some thick material, pulled out a cutting tool that looked like the clippers that the sewing-wen of The Tharn's Town used to cut beezt-hide and other materials. But it was at least a hand times as large. *These gloves they wear, these tools they use, were obviously made for larger People,* Rist thought. *Why don't they make smaller ones, for themselves?* He carved that question on his totem, for later analysis.

At the end of a long pole, the large clippers were used to cut the mist-net apart. Rist couldn't follow exactly what happened next, but somehow one end of the cut net wound up tied to several of the iron poles. The other side of the cut—to the west—quickly flew away to the man's right, as if pulled from there. The men on that boat attached it to the tall spool on their craft. Rist guessed that it would be unwound somehow, and attached to another spool on the other side of the river. *What kind of magical material is that?* He wanted some of it; he could think of a dozen uses right away. *And Rusk will think of a dozen more!* he thought, grinning.

Within minutes, the berg began to move to the left, Dimwise

—"*East*!" Cruthar's word rang in his ear—headed for what appeared to be a town on the distant shore.

AND WHAT A TOWN IT WAS! VIEWING THE SIGHT AS THE BERG SLIPPED past two more of the same tall yellow stone towers, one on either side of the channel from the river, Rist gasped again. *This place is many hands times bigger than The Tharn's Town!* he marveled as the berg was towed into a vast harbor—*bigger than the lake at the End of the World!*—by whatever mysterious force was reeling in the smoke-net. "It's called a *city*, Rist; that means a really big town," Cruthar whispered as they approached a long pier. "Lots and lots of People live down here in the Warm Lands. Different kinds of People."

Though Rist welcomed the information, his mind and his senses of vision and smell were nearly overwhelmed by all of the newness. *More new things, more new thoughts, in this one dim*—day!—*than my whole life before! Can I understand it all?* Then, recalling his Sire Thess and his twin, Rusk—*Can I* use *it all? To earn more coppers, to make new things? To make new buildings, as big as these, back home?* Behind his eye-slit coverings, Rist grimaced in joy.

"We're at God's Port," Cruthar said as the berg posts were secured to the long wooden pier. "Be real careful, now, that you don't say anything to anybody here about the gods of The Tharn's Lands." He put a finger to his chapped lips. "They pay a lot more attention to their gods than we do ours. And I guess from the wonders of this city, their boats and their machines and their buildings, their gods pay more attention to them, too!"

Strether and all the other berg-men had to leave their weapons and furs with a tall dock attendant, who gave the crew chief a large metal pendant to reclaim it all when they departed. The big man explained to Rist, "We get all of our stuff back when we leave, but we are not allowed to carry anything back home except the clothes and hand weapons we came in with. And a big bag of coppers!" He distributed a meager allowance of coppers to each of the men for living expenses, and then left to conclude his business with the final buyers of the berg.

Rist saw that during the payoff, the lanky pier-man was dabbling with a pointed stick onto a soft, claylike material held in a flat wooden container. "He's making mud-marks," Cruthar said in explanation. "They puts that clay out in the light of Shining One, it gets hard. Keeps a permanent record." At Rist's astonished reaction, he further explained, "They reads them by Touch, some says, but others says they reads them by Seeing. Me, I don't know." Rist made a mental note to record that strange practice as well. Signaling with mirrors, writing in mud, symbols with meaning, Reading by Seeing—worth remembering, even if they were of no particular use back home, as far as he could see.

With Cruthar's facilitation, Rist was able to purchase a small bone-knife—*no good for a weapon!*—from a peddler at the end of the pier, a tool with which to record his observations and thoughts. He was carving his impressions as fast as he could, but was overwhelmed by the number of big wooden boats with colorful sails and pennants, and so many tall, strangely dressed People, both men and wen, even some with golden and reddish hair. *Like those net-men on the berg! I had no idea there were so many different kinds of People!* He could have sworn that some of them even had eyes the color of that weird blue sky. Most were as nearly as tall as the god from The Ice. There weren't many short People around like himself and Cruthar, but at least no one bothered them, hardly even seemed to notice them. After several jaw-dropping moments during which Cruthar laughed out loud at him, Rist was still astonished that wen could be so tall, and be out on their own without escorts. Many of them wore tight-fitting, wonderfully woven material strewn with colorful glass or jewels sparkling in the bright light of Shining One. *Amazing!* There was something else about some of the wen that interested him, but his attention was jerked away at every step by yet a new wonder.

One of those wonders was the machine the WarmLanders used to take cargo on and off the ships. Rist could not quite understand the way that thick rope wound around enclosed wheels—*pulleys*, Cruthar called them—worked. He knew the rope was made of thickly wound mist-net, but that was all. Back home, he had watched stonemen repair the walls around The Tharn's Town, but they used ramps of smaller stones and dragged big ones up by themselves or with large, strong, beeztlike creatures called *oxen*. *These machines look to be much easier to use*, he carved, but he had no method of recording drawings on his totem and was not certain he could describe it in words. Other strange devices of metal and more varieties of mist-net ropes abounded on the piers, but he did not see them in use and had no idea how they might work. His only comparison, the one machine he had any knowledge of, was the crude assembly of wooden cog-wheels and levers of the water-powered peat mill in The Tharn's Town, mostly invented by Sire Thess. *I can see now that I have got to get Rusk down here,* he thought. *My twin would love this!* He added that note to his totem.

Once, he jumped back in fright as a small velk approached. *Me with no two-leg, no spear, not even a blacknife!* He took a fighting stance with his useless bone-knife, but softened as he realized that the animal was not as tall as he, and on a leash being held by a tall wen! Cruthar grabbed him by his shoulder and laughed, "Rist, them's not velks here. They's tame ones, pets, little ones. Calls them *dogs*." Sure enough, the copper-haired wen sniffed down at him as she strutted past, the leashed animal padding along behind her, panting.

Rist wasn't convinced; peaceable or not, the dog came up to his shoulder. He shuddered as they walked on, then realized something. He looked back at that wen, and then others in the crowds. Unlike wen back home, these seemed to have a heaviness around the chest, covered by their smoother clothing. The sight was unsettling, but strangely attractive to him. When he asked Cruthar about the extra muscles the wen had, his companion just laughed, "Bird-boy, they ain't muscles. You sees why we likes to bring in The Ice down here, even though it be a long, long walk home. They's a lot more to these Warm Lands wen than you be used to in The Tharn's Lands. You'll find out, this dark."

Finally, leaving the docksides, the two berg-men walked through fish-smelling alleyways and pushed their way through noisy, bustling crowds of skimpily clad workers like themselves, though most of the

WarmLanders were much taller. As they went on, Rist saw other meaningless symbols everywhere—on the fronts of the buildings they passed by, on banners hanging across the narrow streets, on individual doorways—some just crude splotches of color, others intricate collections of shapes and shades, all just as nonsensical to him. His friend told him that the designs stood for shops and stores and brothels and many things you couldn't find in The Tharn's Town. "You has to learn all of them, you want to know what they mean. Reading by symbols, by Seeing." He led Rist to a nearby pub—with a plain peat-orange door, no symbols. "That color means it's for workers like us," his friend said. Inside the dark, smoke-filled room Rist's friend introduced him around to his old WarmLander acquaintances.

Any friend of big-spending Cruthar was a friend of theirs, Rist soon discovered. And he also found that most big WarmLanders looked much like his own People, even if they were paler of skin, and every one of them at least as tall as Tharn's Men back home, and many twice as. Though they made Rist feel tiny when he had to look up to talk to them, he soon became comfortable in the friendly atmosphere. And in this pub, for some reason, at least there weren't any of the fair-haired, sky-eyed strangers he'd seen near the docks. And no dogs, either, for which he was grateful. Leash or no leash, he didn't trust animals as tall as himself!

Over a few hours of drinks, amidst the wild bar tales he heard and those he shared—though he was careful not to mention the god from The Ice, or anything about the gods of The Tharn's Lands down here—he learned something of cultural differences just a few dims'—"*Days*! Rist! *Days*!"—travel downRiver from home. Their Peoplespeak was mostly understandable, even if it had some strange pronunciations. Where Rist would say "out," the locals said "oot"; where he would call something "cold," they used a word similar to "kohlod." Letting his mind slightly out of strict control, hearing the words loosely, he could let the sounds pour in and his mind would usually figure out what they were saying. As he told Cruthar, "After all, in a pub there are only so many words anybody uses."

Cruthar shook his head, not understanding. "Whatever you say, bird-man. You be a strange bird, yerself!" They both laughed and ordered more brew.

In ordinary conversations back home, the People used manyhands of words that described aspects and behaviors of the Misty Sky, but here, Rist found, the WarmLanders didn't know most of them. Cruthar explained, "Here in the Warm Lands, Rist, they's only got a few hands of words for skies and clouds. They don't have as many kinds of clouds as we does; they's lives don't depend on 'em like ours, so they don't need as many words for 'em!" Rist acknowledged that profound observation with a smile and a nod. He would carve that portentous thought.

Over a huge meal of mysterious meat—"They's called *hav*s, Rist, little animals, one fingerth the size of a beezt, pink skins, snouts, grunting critters, but they taste great!" Rist shuddered; Cruthar's description sounded a lot like that of the disgusting little Cold People the berg-man had never seen himself. But Rist knew that Colds were definitely people, though degenerates. As he enjoyed the delicious meal, he hoped that whatever animal produced the mystery meat didn't speak.

As incense smoke filled the pub and a quiet descended, Rist hoped to pull as much information as he could from his companion. "What did Broker Thenuss mean when he told me not to bring along anything I didn't want to leave behind?"

Cruthar spit out his potato brew, chortling. "Bird-boy, didn't you ever learn *nothin'* while you was growing up?" Rist listened as the berg-man related the story of ice-selling and the men who did it, and why they did it the way they did. "Ages past, manyhands of hands of cycles ago, the bergs would float through The Tharn's Town and nobody paid attention. If we ever needed any ice, we would go cut off a piece and use it. Then for a long time, many cycles, the weather got colder and no bergs came down at all. The story goes that one day a group of WarmLanders showed up and got into a fight with The Tharn of that time, saying the People were keeping The Ice bergs for themselves."

"The first Ice War," Rist commented, "I've Read about that one. Manyhands of cycles back. Far olden times."

"Yeah, well our fathersfathersfathers whipped their butts and killed them all but one. The old Tharn back then was real smart, y'know? He let that one WarmLander go home, and our people followed him, found out where he come in to The Tharn's Lands. Turns out they had carved steps in the stones of a rock cliff so's that one man at a time could scale up. It was one of them rock faces we passed through on the way down here, couple days back." Rist whistled. Some of those cliffs were hands of hands of man-lengths high. One slip and a man would fall to his death. He said as much.

"Yeah, well, they let that one survivor crawl back down to go tell his kind that we would sell them ice when it was available, and never to come back."

"What kept them from sending up more warriors again?"

"That ol' Tharn back then, as I says, he was *really* smart. He lowers stonecutters down and they chips away those steps, one at a time, till there is just a flat place left, no place to climb up. And he stations a couple of Tharn's Men there with dropping-rocks and spears to make sure they don't try carvin' no new ones." He sneezed at the thick smoke now making the pub's air almost unbreathable.

Rist shook his head, the potato brew clouding his imagination. "But how do you—*we*—get back home?"

Cruthar leaned forward. "We have a rope lift in a secret place. We put all our coppers in a bag first and tug on the rope. If The Tharn's Men like the amount and can identify us, they lower a rope seat down and pulls us up one at a time. You see, we can't take nothin' else back with us. At most, our furs and weapons."

"Where is this lift place? Same place as the WarmLanders came up to attack from?"

Cruthar lowered his voice to a raspy whisper. "No, a real secret place. We always make sure we ain't follered when we go back. Some sail-men drop us off way upRiver, near the rapids at River's End. We double back a few times and then go to our lifting place."

Sipping more brew, trying to wipe his eyes of the peat-smoke, Rist thought about his companion's comments. "Sounds like a lot of walking to me. It only took us a hand of dims to float down here. How long are you talking about to get back?"

Cruthar's short answer crushed Rist's spirit of adventure. "Almost a hand of hands of walking?" he cried. "Don't you have any emus waiting for you at the lift?"

Cruthar shook his head. "Bird-boy, first, we don't ride them birds. Just you and your uppity kind do. Second and last, The Tharn don't allow nothing that fast anywhere near the lift. Too tempting for the WarmLanders to try sumpin' again, you know?"

Rist kept trying to get Cruthar to explain why none of the strange things about the Warm Lands—the mist-net, the huge stones, the strange machines, the mirrors, the shapely wen, even the new gods and the blue sky—ever got back to the People, to The Tharn. "You can bring back stories in your head, man. You can tell other People and the Old Wen about them."

The berg-man just sighed. "Bird-boy, there's things we icers keep to ourselves. What good would it do to tell tall tales back home? First off, nobody would believe it. Second off, we can't bring back and show no kinds of them things to nobody. Then"—Rist waited while Cruthar struggled to count up to the next point—"there ain't no Shining One up in no blue sky, and there ain't no Pale Lady to show nobody." He dropped his voice low, looking around the room furtively. "And there ain't no way to make no coppers from none of that."

Rist nodded; his companion didn't understand knowledge that didn't have an immediate payoff. But he himself did. Was that something he learned from his Sire or his twin, or both? Either way, as his Sire always said, if you know something that somebody else doesn't, it is always an advantage. The knowledge of The Ice at the End of the World had made his own family prosperous. Maybe this new knowledge of the strange and possibly useful things in the Warm Lands would help Rist bring more prosperity to his Sire and himself. *I just have to keep thinking like my Sire and Rusk. And believe that it will pay off!* Under the table, out of sight of everyone, he carved that thought and others on his totem.

IN A LOW VOICE, CONSTANTLY LOOKING AROUND FOR ANY TOO interested onlookers, the berg-man went on to tell Rist about the several other Ice Wars since that first one in the dark past. Succeeding WarmLanders had cut other steps in other rock cliffs to get upRiver, and waged other wars against The Tharn's Lands. Rist nodded. His Sire, Reader Thess, had fought in the last one, and still sported leg scars from his battles. And Thess' Sire, Thonn—Rist's own fathersfather, whom he had never met—had been killed in one before that.

"Yeah, bird-boy, your family has produced some great warriors and that's why you lot have a monopoly on ice-selling. Let me tell you about that time when another ol' Tharn blocked off the New River, backed it up and then made a big flood all the way down here to God's Port. Like to have drowned them all out…" It was a long night, and they both planned to sleep at the pub's bedding rooms. But not until willing wen had bargained to escort them upstairs for other pleasures. His particular companion that dark, a very tall beauty with fiery copper hair and peat-green eyes—and a great heaviness of chest that indeed was not muscle at all—was unforgettable.

CHAPTER EIGHT

The next dim-break (*"Morning!"* Cruthar yelled) Rist found out from Strether that they would be in God's Port for several more *days*. His eyes still not adjusting to the prolonged brightness, Rist continued to wear the eye-slits to be able to navigate in Shining One's light. Meaning to make the most of his time in this strange land, and not looking forward to the long, arduous journey walking back to The Tharn's Town, he asked Cruthar to show him the sights of the city. As they wandered back to the docks, around the boats with their mist-webbing and strange lifting machines, Rist felt the sky darkening. After a while he removed the eye-slits and looked up at the blue sky. Clouds were rolling in, a familiar sight, but back home they would have been backed by layers of higher, misty clouds above them. Here, clouds were merely little islands, broken pieces of Misty Sky. Within minutes, though, the blue was totally obscured by the invading darkness and rain began to fall.

As the *day* went on and the clouds thinned, Shining One barely shone through the thin layers of high clouds. *It looks just like Pursuing Dimness, the sky-god of The Tharn's Lands!* Rist realized. He was astounded. Cruthar and passersby seemed to take no notice that

Shining One had apparently fallen to His own sky-god, and that the Misty Sky had prevailed here in the Warm Lands. *Or,* he thought, *could it be that Pursuing Dimness is just Shining One, only seen through the Misty Sky? Even worse, could the Misty Sky be just layers of clouds under the blue dome of Shining One?* He reeled at the epiphany, stumbling against the rough stone wall of the alleyway.

Cruthar caught him before he fell, and laughed. "Rist, boy, you all right? You still feeling that potato brew from last night?"

"No, my friend," he answered in a quiet voice, "I am afraid I am feeling something much worse, something that won't ever go away."

AFTER THE RAINS DWINDLED TO A MIST, CRUTHAR AND RIST continued their exploration of God's Port. "Why do they call it by this name, Cruthar? Does Shining One come here?"

Cruthar shook his head. "No, but they do have a real big temple, where they worship Shining One and His Mistress, the Pale Lady of the Night."

"What is *worship*?" Rist asked.

Cruthar shrugged. "All's I know is, they do it in the 'House of the Gods.' It ain't too far from here." He pointed to a tall building that stood above all the others in God's Port. "Over there, that's where they talks to their gods."

Rist raised his index finger. "You told me that already," he said, wrinkling his forehead as new thoughts poured in, Rusk-like, from somewhere. "But what I want to know is, do their gods talk back to them?"

The House of the Gods, the Temple of Shining One, was the tallest and most impressive structure in God's Port, according to Cruthar. Rist had to agree—the huge building stood twice as high as any other in the city, taller even than the towers along the river and at the harbor entrance—the largest man-made construction he had ever seen, by far. They approached the huge building following a paved path through high stone walls that led into a circular paved courtyard—*nearly as wide as The Tharn's Town!* Rist figured, whistling in appreciation—capable of accommodating untold hand-numbers of people. The courtyard was surrounded by a high wall made of two hands of the smooth rectangular blocks of yellowish stones they had seen in the towers. At several places along the top of that wall, evenly spaced, stood tall circular structures, each covered by a thick yellow fabric bearing that same red wheel-and-spokes symbol. Cruthar had no explanation. *Lots of mysteries here in God's Port,* his shrug said.

As they approached the wide stairway in front of the temple, Rist saw that each of the blocks of stone in the temple itself was taller than himself. Counting by finger pointing, he saw that the blocks were stacked up a hand of hands high, an unbelievable height. By comparison, The Tharn's Place, the largest stone structure in The Tharn's Town, was made of roughly finished gray stones cut from beneath the peat fields. Its uneven construction would not have reached a hand-high of these perfectly finished, smooth blocks. *And no mortar between them*, Rist saw, *just stacked!*

The largestone compound back home where Rist lived with his twin, his Sire, and his birther, Mell, had a thatched roof, like The Tharn's Place. But this place, the House of the Gods, was all smoothly finished stone, top to bottom. Through the three large rectangular doorway openings, Rist could make out gigantic cylindrical columns inside, which supported even larger blocks of horizontal rectangular stones, making a ceiling. The entire interior was painted in bright colors, with some designs and figures he could make out without understanding, and manyhands of others too small to distinguish, even at a distance.

And stretched across the entire front of the building, spanning above the three entrances, was carved that same huge red circle and its external spokes, on a bright yellow background. *The symbol on the towers, on the flags of the ships that met the berg out in the River, and on these big round structures in the courtyard*, Rist observed. Without his recent knowledge of Shining_One, he would have had no understanding at all of the meaning of this repeated drawing. Back home, all Reading was done on carved spindles, totems that you carried with you or Read at home, by Touch alone. Colors—trim on sleeves and collars, splashes over doorways—showed your status, your occupation. His Sire, Reader Thess, proudly wore the green trim of Readers, an elite few in The Tharn's Lands. Though elementary reading was fairly common, a Reader's expertise was required for research, writing, and archiving information for The Tharn's Law, for business transactions, and for family histories. By comparison, Cruthar, his Sire Strether, and the berg-crew wore on their furs the orange of the common laborer. Here, of course, Rist and the other recently arrived People wore only loin cloths and sandals with no distinguishing colors. Rist thought it strange, again, that no one here knew anyone else's status. *Do the WarmLanders have other ways of telling status? Or—* and this was heretical, he knew—*do they even* have *different statuses down here?*

Ever the practical man, Cruthar brought Rist's mind back to the temple in front of them. "The red circle is supposed to remind you of Shining One," he said, pointing to the circular pattern with three short, straight lines in each of the cardinal directions. "They believe that when their Shining One, their big god, sees these red marks, He comes to talk to them." He said that the priests periodically conducted *worship* ceremonies in the vast circular yard in front of the temple, and pointed out how three wide pathways between the high walls converged on the courtyard. "Shining One lines up at different times of the year. That pole in the middle, they use that to tell the time of day from where the shadow goes."

Rist considered all of that new information. His twin, Rusk, had interpreted the scribblings of peatsants, large white markings scratched on standing stones in their peat fields, to be some kind of writing, a kind of reading done with eyes, not by touch. Although the concept had seemed totally alien and heretical back in The Tharn's Town, Rist wondered if these designs on the House of the Gods might serve a similar purpose. According to his twin, the god his Sire and Rist had brought back from The Ice at the End of the World might also have used tiny markings on flat metal or hornlike material, to be Read by sight as well, but only by gods' eyes. But here, even an uneducated non-Reader could learn that the big red symbols meant the bright god above would come to this special place. *So the gods of these Warm Lands make their marks large and on the wall, for all to see.* It was a difficult thing to believe, but here it was. He was convinced the new gods down here did things differently than the gods back home. He quickly carved that information on his totem.

"Now, remember, bird-boy," his berg-man companion whispered as they reached the top of the many, many smoothly carved stone steps and were about to enter into the temple, "these old men take their gods seriously. They love 'em. Don't show any disrespect. The priests here run everything. This place is all the law there is. And they have big, nasty Priests' Men to make sure it stays that way." Rist nodded, wondering again why none of this fantastic information had ever been brought back to The Tharn's Lands, if only for storytelling if nothing else. He was afraid his totem would run out of room with all this new information, and wondered if the WarmLanders would sell him another.

At that moment, a short, bald, bearded elderly man in a clean white robe came limping out one of the door openings to meet them and bring them into what he called "This Holy Place." "Welcome, strangers, to the House of the Gods," the ancient priest said in thickly accented Peoplespeak, raising the sleeves of his robe and motioning the ice-men in. "Here you will discover the mysteries of Creation and your place in the world of men and gods."

Rist and his companion followed the barefooted man—"You call him 'Father,' remember that," Cruthar commented—down a long corridor fashioned from the largest, most finely finished hardstone blocks that Rist had ever seen. *How did they make it so smooth?* He wondered, *and stack them so high?* The painted ceiling had to be at least a hand of hands of man-lengths high, supported by cylindrical columns similarly painted. And the walls of this—"*Temple*," Cruthar whispered—were painted with human figures of all colors, dressed in gaudy costumes. More different kinds of colors, all in one place, than he had witnessed in his whole life before. And more things he had not conceived of before: new to the concept of two-dimensional representations of human beings, Rist immediately understood them for what they were, though he could not make out the details. "Beautiful," he finally breathed out, "the most beautiful things I have ever seen." He could tell that there were other, smaller colorful markings completely covering the walls and ceilings, but they were too blurry to make out up close, and too small to distinguish at a distance.

The narrow passageway opened into a large round room, empty but for stone benches around the perimeter and a low, circular stone firepit in front. Lit by the bright light from the sky coming through square window openings around the top, and wider than high, it was the most massive enclosed space Rist had ever seen. The whole of The Tharn's Place would have fit into this one room, he knew. And from what they had seen of the "temple" outside, this was just one room of many.

Maybe their gods do *talk to them*, Rist thought in awe, *for surely no People could ever make this building, not without a god's help!* The priest bade them sit on one of the stone benches, in front of a large fire contained in the round pit made of one layer of close-fitting notched stones. Another priest emerged from a side door, sprinkling powder from a pottery vase. At once the fire shot up explosively, sparkling throughout the room, emitting the most wonderful aroma that Rist had ever imagined possible. Even old Cruthar, the cynic, smiled.

"Outlanders," the old man said, standing on a dais beside the diminished flames of the firepit, "what we have here in the House of the Gods is Truth: how the People came to be, how the World came to be, and what role you personally have in it all."

Cruthar frowned, looking at Rist and rolling his eyes. He wasn't having any of it. But Rist, eager to learn all that he could carve and take home, was fascinated. He had never thought of such things—had even Rusk?—but he was willing to listen. He wanted to find new ways of thinking, and here was one free for the taking. He hadn't even had to ride a berg to find it! Well, actually he had, but the berg business was one thing; this temple was another.

"In the Beginning was the Darkness and the Cold," the priest intoned. To the men's surprise, other white-robed figures emerged from unseen side doors, and began to chant, echoing the priest's words: "Darkness, darkness, darkness; cold, cold, cold."

"Then Shining One smiled upon the World, and the Darkness went away for a while. But then the Darkness returned to do battle."

"Battle, battle, battle," the chorus chanted.

"After a long unending battle, Shining One agreed to rule the day, leaving the Darkness to rule half of the time. But then Shining One ejected a part of Himself to hold back the Darkness, the goddess we call Pale Lady of the Night."

"Night, night, night," the chorus of voices continued, while Cruthar kept grimacing and shaking his head. But Rist was being drawn into the whole scene—the fabulous stonework of the temple, its incredible painted decorations, the chanting of the robed priests, the soft sweetness of the incense, and the story of Creation itself. Back home, no one ever talked about Creation, and the gods were just, just—*there*. Like Ice and peat and two-legs and velks, gods were part of life and death, and stayed up above the Misty Sky, doing their mysterious godly activities. But down here in the Warm Lands, these People had a special relationship with their gods. In a strange new way, it was comforting to Rist to think of gods as protectors, not just as familiar things, like the Misty Sky or The Ice. Or threatening, like velks.

In the overwhelming environment of new and novel thoughts and spectacular surroundings, with the intoxicating odors of the sparkling fire nearby, Rist felt himself being pulled into a new understanding of the way the World worked, how it came to be. But where would he fit in? Why would gods care any more about him than they did about the rocks and the river? He hoped to find out from this strange priest.

The priest went on. "During the War in the Skies, the Darkness attacked Pale Lady, leaving unhealed scars on her face, those dark splotches that you witness every night. When Shining One found out, He gave Pale Lady a necklace of bright stars in recompense, which we still see yet today, after untold cycles of time."

"Time, time, time." Eventually the choristers departed quietly, but for another hour the old priest continued, telling secrets of the nature of the World, the gods, and individual People, and of the inevitable End of It All, when even the gods would die. After a long silence, sensing Rist's astonishment at what he was hearing, the priest asked, "Do you have any questions, my son?" Rist did, and he asked.

Frowning, the priest replied.

CHAPTER NINE

*B*ack at the pub, as evening drew close, Rist was seething. "That old *thick* told me that I had to give him one fingerth of my coppers, and then buy a *hav*—one of those tasty little meat critters we ate last night—so he could cut its throat and feed it to the flames!" He gritted his teeth so hard that Cruthar could hear it across the table. "Why would Shining One and the so-called Pale Lady want such a thing? They're way up there"—he pointed toward the ceiling —"and I'm way down here. What a load of beezt-shit!" At that, several patrons in the pub stopped drinking in mid-lift and looked his way.

"Not so loud, bird-boy," Cruthar warned in a whisper, looking around and waving off the too interested by-sitters. "I donc told you before, this be a strange place, and you better not mouth off." He sighed. "Hopefully that old priest didn't understand our talk enough to understand what you called him. But I bet he understood you didn't like what he said."

"*Wen-licker*," Rist replied, grinning, "but I doubt he knows what that is, much less ever did it." The priest had tried to explain celibacy, which to Rist was harder to believe than the weirdness about the gods wanting coppers and animal blood.

Cruthar shushed him again. "Just keep quiet, Rist, for all our sakes. We have another full day here, and we have got to stay clear of anything that looks like priests, you hear? I told you they run everything down here. They ain't got no Tharn or Tharn's Men here, I done told ya, and from what I've seen, we don't want to mess with Priests' Men. They're a lot bigger and they make The Tharn's Men look like gentle rabs!"

Rist nodded, wishing that he still had a shortspear or a blacknife to defend himself with. But the WarmLanders at the pier landing had confiscated all of their weapons. *A smart idea on their part*, he thought, *but I still don't like it!* His purchased bone-knife, used only for carving his totem, wouldn't even penetrate cloth-padding armor.

Satisfied that the pub would stay calm, Cruthar sighed. "Let me take you outside this dark—they call it 'night'—and show you something, Rist. You may respect that old priest more than you know, once you see it."

Outside, the two men walked down oil-lamp-lit, wide cobblestoned thoroughfares—both features being something unheard of, unthought of, in the dark and muddy narrow streets of The Tharn's Town—past shops redolent with unidentifiable odors, some sweet, some pungent, to the outskirts of the city, only a few hands of man-lengths distance from the guarded city gates. "We won't go outside the walls," the ice-man said. "It's a lot of trouble getting back in." He made the sign of rubbing coins with his fingers. "But here close to the wall, we can see the dark sky."

Rist looked up and saw *night* for the first time. "Gods, Cruthar, it's amazing! The Dark, but with tiny lights—firebugs?—scattered all over. And what is that—?" Gasping, he couldn't finish the question. A round, mottled, whitish disk had risen right over the city wall, which direction he couldn't tell. "Is that the, the—?"

"The Pale Lady of the Night," Cruthar answered softly, nodding, "the goddess who fights off the Darkness so that he can't ever completely defeat the light, even when Shining One sleeps half the time."

Rist had not been able to look directly into the face of Shining One, not even with his beezt-hide eye-slits, but Pale Lady he could see clearly. The brightness of Her face, the dark scars and wounds left by the battle with the Darkness, and the many strings of bright jewels, all colors, scattered across her visage. "You know, Cruthar," he said in a low voice, "if I had seen Her first, I might have believed that old priest in the temple. I would love to be able to speak with Her, and know what She thinks about me, about all the People."

Cruthar smiled. "Bird-boy, I still don't buy what the temple is selling; I don't believe that the gods need anything from us. And we don't need nothin' from them but their light and heat. But a lot of the story he tells, it does make sense, because I can damn well stand out here and see the truth of it."

Later, back in the pub, Rist carved many, many more impressions of what he had seen and heard, what he believed and didn't, and why. To his surprise, he himself was a lot more literate than he had realized. *Maybe because before I didn't have that much to say?* After all, there wasn't a lot of reason to write about every time he bedded wen or threw bolos at thicks and other vermin, or killed rabs for meat. Velks were another matter, and he was proud of the one he had helped kill along the New River, close to The Ice at the End of the World. The details of that fight, where he and his two-leg had slain the creature, he had carved on a totem that now rested with his Sire, Reader Thess. But here, here in God's Port, he had seen fantastic buildings, the temple by far the largest and most attractive, but still only just one of many, many hands of hands of structures. It hit him: *Probably more buildings here than there are* People *in The Tharn's Town!* He wished he had a way to count them all, People and buildings, but could only carve analogies and metaphors; the People had no means of counting in numbers so large.

AS RIST WAITED ALONE, CRUTHAR WENT OUT AND ROUNDED UP A PIER-man to come talk to them at their table in the pub. "Give him enough brew, bird-boy, and he will tell you his life's secrets. Maybe even his wife's!" he laughed.

Rist smiled; he hadn't known his crewmate could make a pun. Maybe there was more to the rough, uneducated icer than he had realized? But Rist had specific questions he wanted to hear and carve.

"The *biter-web* net? Ya wanna know about that there magical material?" the pier-man asked. Rist nodded. The tough, nearly invisible netting was indeed almost magical. He had seen the boatmen on his berg in some mysterious fashion untie ends of the stuff from the posts they had set in the ice, and watch it instantly spool up on man-length-diameter drums mounted on the pier. Incredible though it sounded, this net, three hands of man-lengths high, had been stretched across at least a dim-march of river. Yet it rolled up onto a spool no wider across than he himself. And most of that was the wooden spindle core around which it was wrapped.

"Them old gods made the stuff," the drunken pier-man kept on. "Down here, the Priests' Men are always digging it up in some of the mines, way down deep, where the old gods used to live. It always comes on rusted metal drums that fall apart, so they take the whole wad of stuff to their local chief. Some of his wen unravel it and cut it down and respool it on wooden spools. Them biter-webs is usually many miles long, but so thin it don't take up much space." Cruthar quickly explained to Rist that a "mile" was the local name for about one fingerth of a dim-march. "A hand of miles for a dim-march, ya know."

"How do they cut it?" Rist asked. He remembered the ice-men who had met their berg and reeled it in to the harbor.

"Each chief has one of the God's Tools. That's the on'y thang can cut it. But no problem, there's always God's Tools around where they find the biter-web. Lots of 'em, down in the mines."

"Biter-web?" Rist asked. Back home, *biters* were crawly, eight-legged black things that hid in old caves and crevasses, sometimes in a patch of peat. The size of his thumb, their bite could kill a man, or make a beezt sick. Their webs in The Tharn's Lands caught bugs, not bergs. He said as much to the pier-man.

The pier-man burped and took another long drink from his mug. "Yeah, they used to say it was made from the webs of biter-bugs, but I seen lots of biters and they don't make nothin' than you cain't cut with a blacknife." After some urging and a bit of payment, the pier-man agreed to take the two men to a warehouse where some of the "biter-web" was stored. "Don't tell nobody, you hear? They shouldn't miss nothin', they's so much stored there. But it all belongs to them priests and I don't want to wind up be'in burnt alive by them. I done seen that, and it ain't pretty!" Thinking of the old priest's demand for burning and wasting a perfectly good *hav* on the fire, Cruthar and Rist stared at each other and shuddered.

THE NEXT *MORNING* CRUTHAR AND RIST MET THE PIER-MAN AT A storage facility, another finely built stone structure with a heavy wooden door and a hasp lock. After Cruthar passed him some coppers, the man opened it and hurried away, to their surprise, leaving the place open to them. "Maybe thievery is unknown here, you think?" Cruthar said.

"Or getting burned alive is too much of a penalty for stealing?" Rist replied, and they both laughed.

The warehouse itself was a marvel. The men had never seen such large amounts of metal, of wood, of finely polished stonework. "And all the tools to make them with," Rist exclaimed. "I wish we could take a lot of it back with us. Think of building one of those temples in The Tharn's Town!" He wondered where the odors came from—rotting wood? Bad meat? Putrid oils?—because they were almost overwhelming.

Cruthar grimaced. "This building itself would be a thing of awe. The priest's story would be worthy of respect." He shuddered. "But paying your coppers for nothing, killing those *havs* without eating them, burning people alive, they can keep all of that lot." He pinched his large, pocked nose. "And these smells in here, they can keep those, too."

Nodding, Rist wrinkled his nose as well. "Yes, I agree about the smells here, and the other part, too. I just wondered how it could be that People who can do such wondrous things with stones and biter-webs, and tell such beautiful tales, could be so, so—" He didn't have the words for what he felt. "Let's just lift some biter-web and get out of here." Cruthar watched as Rist carved his thoughts onto his totem spindle. The boy replied, "I don't want to forget anything we've seen, or what we've thought here." He held up the totem with his reading hand. "In fact, if anything ever happens to me on this trip, if I don't get back, will you promise to get this to my Sire? And don't worry, nobody will take it from you. It's in my family's own language and nobody but three of us know it. Even those totems that your broker Reads, they are in our strictly mercantile language, different from what we use for family archives."

Cruthar just nodded assent. An in-depth knowledge and practice of Carving and Reading, he knew, was the key to merchant success in The Tharn's Lands. He also knew that such training had to begin within a hand of cycles of being birthed, or one would never learn the intricacies of depth, width, texture, patterns and arcs. Training had to begin with one's Sire. His own Sire, Strether, and his fathersfathers, all the way back, had been untrained. He himself had a crude, workable knowledge of the mercantile Carving and Reading language, but would never be totally literate, not able to carve details like his friend Rist.

In the poorly lit warehouse, Cruthar nearly stumbled over a large wooden spool. Cursing, he jumped back. "Hey, Rist, I think we found one, but it's different, come look!" Rist ran over and in the dim light, almost fell as well. "This is a lot littler than the one at the pier," the little man said. "Just two-fingerths of a man-length high, and a hand of handwidths in diameter. Damn, but I can carry this one by myself!" Smiling, he pointed to a large cutting tool and oversized gloves attached to the side of the wooden spool with thin wires. "We got everything we need to cut it and handle it! But can you hide it from the boatmen, lug it over dim-marches—*miles*—of stony paths, and then convince The Tharn's Men to take it up the lift?" Cruthar's tone said he was doubtful.

"If I've learned one thing from my Sire and my twin," Rist said strongly, as if trying to convince himself, "you never know what you can do unless you try it. Here, let me carry it back to the pub. Hopefully without being seen." Strangely enough, as he hefted the spool over his shoulder, he did have a plan to hide it and carry it back home.

THEIR MID-DIM MEAL—"LUNCH"—CONSISTED OF COLD *HAV* SLICES, some weird, sweet juicy fruit, and a dark liquid they called "wheat brew." "Tastes a lot like peat brew," Cruthar said, comparing it to the cheapest, nastiest drink in The Tharn's Lands.

"Or maybe beezt-piss!" Rist laughed. Today he was wearing a dark blue, long-sleeved woven shirt and matching long pants, purchased the day before from a local weaver, after they had left the warehouse. He planned to retrieve his furs from the pier-man storage when the crew began its trip back upRiver to what he now thought of as the Cold Lands, using the locals' term.

"You know, Cruthar," he said between bites of the tasty meat, "we never did see how the berg was being used. And that's the original reason I came on this trip. Before we go, let's take a look if there's any berg left to see." Later he was successful in finding the same tall, copper-haired wen for a very satisfying evening. *Now this is one Warm Lands discovery I'd really like to take back home!* he thought, *though every flat, skinny wen in The Tharn's Lands would be jealous of her hair, her height and her, her*—chest!

AT THE ARRIVAL PIER THE NEXT MORNING, THE ICE-MEN OF GOD'S Port were still busy carving away on the berg, days after Strether's crew had brought it in. Rist watched with interest as the tall

WarmLanders used extremely long metal saws, mysteriously attached to complex assemblies of jointed wooden arms, to cut off pieces of the frozen water. A part of his mind told him to pay attention to something else. It took him a full hour of watching before he realized that the top surface of the berg, though large chunks had been cut away to be floated across the harbor to other customers, still stayed the same distance above the water level as it was when he and the crew rode it downRiver. *Why was that?*

He quickly carved a note of that observation, for Rusk to evaluate later if nothing else. In his memory, he had always known that most of a berg was below the water surface, hence the value of the specialized skill and experience needed by Strether and the other icers to navigate the New River and the long, zigzag passageways of rapids at River's End. "Hit the bottom, bird-boy," their Sire had said, "you turn over in the roaring river, it's the end of you. The top that you can see is the easy part; the bottom's what kills you." Then raucous laughter. "Just like wen!"

He didn't have enough time to watch while the whole berg was cut away, but he would discuss the concept with Rusk once he got back home. Maybe there would be a way to mine a berg, to cut away more than half of it, and still deliver one to the Warm Lands for the same price as before? He wondered if The Tharn's smith could make such saws, and how long it would take these WarmLanders to catch on to the trick? He smiled. He bet that his Sire would think it worth the risk. *Rist's risk!*—he liked the concept.

Pier workers and Ice-men told him that a large part of the berg would wind up in covered, hay-lined pits, to be resold to individual houses for keeping food cold. The rest of it would be transported by other boats and even beezt-carts to outlying villages and towns. Rist understood that was a good use for Ice down here in the Warm Lands. Food storage was hardly ever a problem up in the cool Tharn's Lands; everything there was either eaten at once, or dried as jerky for keeping. Peat-grown vegetables and some edible varieties of peat itself would keep for a long time in the cold, dry atmosphere of home. Lastly, the more fragile plants were stored down at the bottom of peat pits, directly against the cold stone layer two or three man-lengths below the top surface.

———

WALKING BACK TO THE PUB TO MEET WITH STRETHER AND THE REST OF the crew, as they neared the entrance to one of the walled walkways leading to the temple, Rist and Cruthar heard a lot of crowd noise, some of it laughs, some of it shouting. They made their way through a knot of people to get to the scene of the action, whatever it was. To Rist, the jammed plaza they were in was like going through one of those forests they had seen along the river—nearly everyone else was taller and their arms and legs were so many obstacles. Fortunately, Cruthar was adept at handling such situations, and within a few minutes the two were at the front row of the churning mob. Rist gulped; they were in the wide circular courtyard in front of the Temple of Shining One. And tied to a post just a few hands of man-lengths in front of them stood the pier-man who had taken them to the biter-web warehouse! A hand of man-lengths from the post stood a copper disk with Shining One's wheel-and-spokes symbol. Rist turned quickly, warning Cruthar to do the same.

"Man's got a blindfold on, Rist," the berg-man whispered. "Can't see us for naught."

"What's going to happen to him?" Rist whispered back. Following the movements of priests around the perimeter of the courtyard, he could see that the tall circular structures atop the wall were actually polished copper disks, with a slight concavity to them—much like an eating dish back home, but at least three hands of man-lengths in diameter—which the men were uncovering, one by one. As he had observed on their first visit to the temple, each yellow fabric cover bore that same red-wheel-and-spokes symbol that Rist was now used to seeing here in God's Port. *What are those for?* he wondered, scanning the horizon in both directions. It was afternoon, and Shining One was about halfway down from the top of His sky-dome.

Rist looked at the angle of that bright disk, to the large

uncovered copper mirrors, and then at the pier-man's post. And where the shadows stood. With horror, he realized what the configuration meant, and gulped again. "Cruthar, they are going to use those big disks like mirrors, and—" He hushed as the crowd began to murmur. The reflections from the bevy of copper dishes were all being focused on the one copper shield in front of the pier-man. Its paint began to smolder and smoke; Rist could feel the heat increasing.

Suddenly, a robed priest appeared on a raised platform before the crowd, said something loud and gruff in a WarmLander language. Somebody nearby whispered, "He is talking about the power of Shining One, and what happens when His protection is withdrawn. The wretch stole some of the Priests' godscloth, if you can imagine."

At a nod, another priest pulled a rope on the nearly incandescent copper shield and it fell over to the pavement with a loud *clang!* Instantly, the pier-man was at the focus of the concentrated One-light. He began to cry, then scream, as Shining One's mighty power, now directed onto him, brought his thin clothing to a smoldering state. Even the blindfold began to burn.

Rist couldn't believe it—*They are cooking a man alive! And for what?* He refused to think it could have been his own theft of the biter-web. A man in the crowd had mentioned *godscloth*; was that its name? If so, he was in as much trouble as the burning man in front of him. Though he didn't like to think on it, he and Cruthar stood out from the largely WarmLander crowd, or rather, stood further down and darker. He wished he could leave, but that would draw attention. He didn't want to watch any more, or smell anymore; he had roasted rabs over fire and they had the same aroma, but they were already dead. He closed his eyes; behind his slit-goggles, few people would be able to tell.

The execution post itself quickly burst into flame, as all the while the pier-man screamed and writhed against the tight ropes holding him in place for his torture and execution. Hair ignited; skin swelled, blackened and burst. Within a minute, the man was thankfully silent, but a bevy of priests kept the giant mirrors focused on him, moving some wooden machinery to keep the overlapping images of the shining disk constantly on the smoking ruins of the victim.

Cruthar put a hand on Rist's shoulder. "I done told you, boy," he said in a low voice, "they is serious about the power of their gods. You see now what they can do with it." As they turned away to leave with the hushed crowd, the berg-man said, "I am just glad ol' cooked-meat there never saw us here. It could be us smelling like roast *hav* now, 'stead of just him." He shuddered.

CHAPTER TEN

*a*s Strether brought the crew together that evening before departing, they made one last visit to the pub. Rist had wanted to carry back some of the *hav* meat, or maybe even a breeding pair of the animals themselves, but Cruthar said that was impossible. "Boy, we have tried to steal all kinds of things here and take them back home, but they search you on the boat when you leave, and The Tharn's Men at the lift won't allow anything up but you and your coppers, anyhow. And your coppers first!" He stared at the boy. "I reckon they'll let you bring that pretty blue shirt back, though. Don't weigh much. Don't know, though, about them gloves and scissors."

Rist was nervous. Still upset by the burning of the pier-man that afternoon, he had other reasons to feel guilty. Under his shirt, around his chest, was the entire spool of biter-web netting that he and Cruthar had stolen the day before. Using the God's Tools, he had cut and folded the wispy material, trying first this way and then that, until he found a size and configuration that allowed him to wrap all of the webbing around himself. To his amazement, the dim-marches of material length weighed almost nothing. Against his skin, it was neither warm nor cold. The God's Tools themselves, well, if he couldn't bring them along he would just never be able to cut the stuff, so they were strapped tightly under the godscloth. But then, why would he want to? In his mind, he could see stringing it across the New River, capturing a berg, and slicing it away, making two bergs out of one. Would there be profit in all that? *If you never try, you'll never know!* But the fate of the poor cooked pier-man hung over him like a cloud, bothering him, scaring him. Cruthar had said, "The fellow knew what he was doing! We didn't force him to do nothin'!" Rist finally accepted that, but dreaded getting caught and suffering the same horrible fate. If he had seen the execution first, he might not have stolen the biter-web. *Too many ifs*, he thought wryly. *But if I make it back home with this net, I will make us rich!* That was an *if* he could accept!

As Rist waited for the last decent meal for gods knew how long, a white-robed priest walked into the pub, followed by a hand of large Priests' Men resplendent in their yellow chest armor bearing the red symbols of Shining One. Several of the men had much larger vicious-looking dogs, big black animals straining against their leashes, snarling, growling. To Rist, they were just smaller versions of the velks back home, though those were almost as tall as the birds he rode. Some of the armored men had those pale skins and sported the variety of hair coloring that Rist had seen on others in God's Port—white, cream-colored, foxfur, copper-red. It could have been a most interesting scene if Rist were not afraid for his life. Pointing at Rist, the priest shouted out something threatening, in a totally unknown language.

Rist quickly slipped under the table and behind the wooden bar-slab. Pulling out his totem and holding it up, he made eye contact with Cruthar. The berg-man nodded and sighed. Rist left the spindle on the bar-slab, then crawled out the back entrance, toward the piss-ditch to his right in the alleyway. Behind him the pub had erupted in screaming and crashes, barking and growls, the sound of metal against metal, the crunch of metal against bone, a cacophony of screams and curses. Making an instant life-or-death decision, looking back to the pub's back door and then at the pit of urine and feces, he held his breath and slid in under the wooden shitting bench.

Ages passed while Rist waited for his life to end, caressed by the warm, tickling movements of masses of maggots. Luckily, he was able to brace himself against the cistern's stone walls, lest he drown in the disgusting filth. Every few minutes, he would surface enough to catch a breath of vile air before descending again into the pit. Once, upon letting his face rise out of the gooey mess, he saw one of the armored Priests' Men standing above him, the huge head of the dog-velk visible through the shit-hole. In panic, he burbled down into the safety of his slimy prison. Eyes closed against the shit, he smiled. The sound he heard, the warm stream of liquid drenching his head, told him that the big man was just taking a piss.

HOURS PASSED, AS DID MANY PUB PATRONS, EACH ADDING TO THE putrid layers of protection above Rist. After a long period of coming for air and encountering only silence, he popped his entire head above the shit surface and saw that Dark had again descended. Hearing no noises from inside the pub, he worked his way up, finally grabbing the shit-bench and hoisting himself up. Then he heaved out his guts, the stench of piss and shit and the maggots being too much for him to bear. He saw some wriggling white things in his puke, and puked again, even more than he thought possible. He knew he had to get away, but where?

At the harbor, by the welcome light of the risen Pale Lady, Rist found an area under a pier and took off his clothes to wash them as well as he could in the water of the harbor. The woven shirt would never be the same, he frowned to see, but most of the stinking mess on it was gone. His pants and loin cloth, the same. He was surprised to see that where he had swathed the biter-web netting around his chest, the god's cutter and gloves still attached, there was no clinging crap, no maggots, no nothing. *Amazing! Maybe it is magical?* But in his mind, he threw that notion off. Amongst his People, "magic" was used solely to connote something done by gods that People could not do—bring the Dim, the Dark, the Cold, the Warm, the rain. That sort of thing.

To think of a *thing*, a tool or material, as magical, took away some of the mystery and awe. And whatever the biter-web was made of, it still took a man and a large cutter—admittedly, a strange God's Tool, but still a man-operated tool—and the big gloves—to trim and handle the stuff. So it was made by some kind of even larger People, somewhere. Some *when?* But—dug up out of mines, "where the old gods lived." Were those old gods the same as the one his Sire and Rusk had brought back from The Ice? Rist sensed a pattern emerging, but like one of the wooden-peg touch puzzles he had played with as a child back home in The Tharn's Lands, he couldn't fill in the blanks without the pieces he knew were missing.

He had seen true gods, for a fact—Shining One and Pale Lady, probably the same gods as Pursuing Dimness and the Wen of the Mist, just seen through the cloud layers of the Misty Sky at home, but in a clear blue sky here in the Warm Lands. But they looked nothing at all like the god from The Ice. At home, it was said that gods lived above the Misty Sky, which protected them from the prying eyes of the People. At least that much of his former belief was true. But those disks in the sky, the blue sky and the night sky, they had no hands, no feet. It was true that Pale Lady did have what looked like eyes, dark patches, and did wear sparkling jewels, but Rist was a practical boy-man: *No hands, no feet—can't cut biter-web nets or put on these gloves!* It was truly a puzzle; he wished Rusk were there with him to think on it. Actually, he wished he were home, thinking it over with Rusk *there.*

As the gentle wavelets of the harbor of God's Port lapped over him, Rist pondered the questions of gods and of his own existence until welcome sleep overtook him.

AT DAYBREAK, SHINING ONE ROSE DIMWARD ("EAST"), ROUSING RIST from a deep sleep and strange dreams. The tempting odors of cooking meat caressed his nose, and he could tell they were coming from a small fishing vessel beached nearby. A fisherman was frying his catch, it seemed to him. The low-lying boat, only about two hands of man-lengths long, with a single mast and reefed sail, had apparently been too small to tie up to a high pier, so had been beached, being anchored merely with a rope and a head-sized stone, resting onto the gravelly shore.

Rist approached, hoping to beg for food, but finding no one aboard. Maybe the owner had been called ashore before his meal was finished cooking? Rist calculated that no matter what crime he committed now, he could not be punished any worse than being burnt alive in front of that temple, so he would steal the boat. *For a while,* he thought. *The owner can get it back; I won't destroy it.* Heaving the anchor stone aboard, he shoved the craft out into shallow water and pulled himself aboard. Using the two oars, he moved outward for some time, all the while afraid that an alarm would be raised. But all was silent. Clear of the piers and the big incoming cargo sailboats, Rist raised the triangular sail and tried to catch a wind. His total experience on water, apart from the iceberg ride downRiver, had been in small one-sail boats in the New River next to The Tharn's Town. Even then, he and the others had depended on the flowing river to take them safely downstream, the sail only providing final guidance to a waiting friend onshore. He wished he had been more attentive to his sailing instructor, but who would have ever thought he would be in such a situation as this, sailing for his life?

The morning clouds that Rist had seen each day before were with him now, bringing a welcome, fresh-smelling wind out of the East, pushing him toward the entrance to the harbor. He smiled, tying the lines in place before he went over to the grill to eat the frying fish. That odor, added to his growing hunger, almost caused him to faint. The boat's owner had thoughtfully left a blacknife on his table, which Rist used to fillet the fish. He gobbled it down too quickly, having to pause to chew and spit out bones. A loaf of not-too-stale bread—*not peat, but wheat*, Cruthar had said, whatever *that* was—completed his meal and filled his stomach.

The slight rocking of the boat was causing something to roll around on the table next to his eating plate. A cylinder of wood? He felt it with his reading hand. Carvings? Writing? Who? What? Gulping, with trepidation, Rist dared to Read the strange message. It was carved in crudely hashed markings, straight lines, no arcs, in a dialect similar to his family's merchant-writing. *Bird boy*, it said. *I got your totem. This boat for you. Priest look for you. Can't take you from here. Come to harbor door. Use flasher. 3 flashes. Wait. 3 flashes. They let you out. Turn up river. Not down—world ends that way. Try to find us. Two-masted boat. Red color. Cruthar. Take bath when you can, stinky.*

"Cruthar, you old liar. You can Carve and Read!" Rist laughed aloud, scanning the horizon for a harbor "door." Did he mean harbor *entrance*? *Opening*? But though he tried, Rist could not see a red boat or a red sail anywhere. Meanwhile, the strong storm wind was blowing him out through the harbor, which was roughly shaped like a snake's mouth, toward the entrance. A tall stonework tower stood on each spit of land, guardians of God's Port. In the middle of the entrance, his boat was still very far from both. Rist wasn't worried; no spears could possibly make it this far! But he took the flat, silvery plate and angled it to flash the tower on the upRiver side. Three times. Wait. Three more times. No answering flash from the tower. Disappointed, he wondered what was wrong.

A huge splash not a hand of man-lengths from his boat told him what was wrong. "What the—?" Looking up, he saw a dark object coming out of the sky from the other side of the boat, apparently from the other tower, rapidly growing in size. Rist didn't know what it was, but somehow they were throwing man-sized stones at him. He had been blithely sailing in one direction, but was an easy target only if you had a giant's spear-thrower of some kind. He immediately tied the sail at an angle, and slammed the rudder handle in the opposite direction; the boat handled well, beginning to turn in a wide circle. He didn't know how long he could keep doing it, but he would try to stay out of range from the one tower until it shot, and then move in closer while the other one shot. And if they both shot at the same time? In fear, he shrugged. "You never know till you try!" he shouted in the wind.

The barrage of stones finally stopped, so Rist moved the boom back and let the storm winds carry him past the entrance to the harbor, out into the wide river. *And now what?* he thought. *I never learned to tack upwind*—he'd missed those lessons while learning others from a number of willing wen—*and I don't know what's on the other shore if I go straight across. Probably Priests' Men and their nasty dogs. My only hope is to go downRiver farther, no matter what Cruthar wrote, then go ashore somewhere, and walk my way back toward home.* Behind him, he saw large ships, sails blooming and oars in full swing, coming his way. The sails bore the red circle and spokes of Shining One. *That damned priest!*

DARK FELL, AND RIST WAS STILL SAILING DOWNRIVER. HIS PURSUERS had apparently given up the chase, or decided to wait until Day (not *dim*!) to come after him. Or, did they know something about the River that he didn't? Something Cruthar had warned him about? *The world ends that way; what could he mean by that?*

When Day came again, Rist was alone on the River and hungry, but at least out in the middle, where he preferred. He didn't want to come across any more stone-throwers like those at the harbor mouth at God's Port. On the lookout for more towers, possibly with other unknown weapons—*maybe those burning mirrors?*—he was otherwise enjoying the scenery along both sides of the River, sights that were wholly new to him. Trees, for one—downRiver this far, the trees were giant, towering, majestic, each of them with more wood in it than in all of The Tharn's Town. Back home there, the only wood available was from scraggly, stunted varieties barely a hand of man-lengths high, with no clear lengths available for making lumber for boats or houses. Fine, long wood, he knew, was very expensive and only occasionally brought in by beezt-cart from some distant lands out Darkwise (*west*, he corrected himself). Here along the River, though, stood uncountable tall, straight trees, probably where the WarmLanders got the lumber to build those big ships that had chased him before giving up. And those strange lifting machines and assemblies on the docks.

The little boat took Rist by distant shores of colorful flowers, beautiful blossoms in (again!) countless numbers, of countless varieties, some so odorful that he could smell their wafted perfumes out in the middle of the wide River. And Dark—"Night"—was beautiful. "The lights in the skies are stars," the old priest had said. "And if you serve Shining One through obedience and sacrifice, then when you die, you will become one of them. Ever fighting the Darkness, helping Pale Lady hold off the Darkness that swallowed all Peoples in the dark past." That one inducement had almost been enough for Rist to fully accept what the old man was saying. "Religion" is what Cruthar said they called their relationship with their gods. "These guys think they know everything. But if they really talk to their real gods, how come they don't give 'em Ice of their own? Why they buyin' it from us?"

As usual, his berg-mate had a simplified answer to almost everything, but in this case, he had had a simple enough question, a question that was valid and needed an answer.

THE NEXT NIGHT, AS THE STARS CAME OUT AGAIN, HIS HUNGER satisfied by a hard-shelled swimmer of some kind he had caught with a fisherman's net left aboard the boat, Rist lay on his back and studied the lights in the sky. Away from the firelight of God's Port, he could see in the deep darkness uncountable pinpoints of lights of varying colors, most of them fixed in place. The several hands of bright lights that moved rapidly across the sky (*west to east, north to south*, he recalled the new names of the cardinal directions), the priest had said were lesser gods that watched People more closely. Ordinary humans who performed the sacrifices of blood and money, *they* were the manyhands of faint, distant lights. "You can be a brighter light, the more you give to our temple," the old man had said. Rist wondered if that were true. And if it was, how did the gods take you and make you a tiny light in a big black dome of sky? *Can't do anything with no hands, no feet!*

CHAPTER ELEVEN

The next morning, Rist awoke suddenly to a roaring louder than when the glacier had calved at The Ice at the End of the World. The boat was traveling faster now, which he knew meant that the River was speeding up, becoming either shallower or narrower. The width looked to be about the same, so shallower it must be. Looking downRiver, he saw not far ahead only a sharp, close horizon, stretching all the way eastward, with no river beyond it. Recalling Cruthar's warning about the End of the World down this way, he quickly swung the boom and grabbed the tied-off rudder, desperately seeking to get to the shore. Not knowing if he would make it before the boat was swept over whatever threatened ahead, he untied the anchor knot and tied the rope around his waist. With the shore only a few man-lengths away, he lifted and swung the anchor stone as hard as he could, bolo-like, watching as the rope snagged in thick bushes overhanging the water's edge. He jumped.

Pulling himself toward the bushes, Rist glanced over at the boat; in the near distance, it disappeared, sail and all, over the edge. He shuddered and shivered, hoping to get out of the River alive. The bushes didn't offer a lot of support, and the anchor stone was already pulling the rope back down into the River's moving surface. As he grabbed some stronger limbs, he untied himself and let the anchor go. The rope slithered into the water and was gone; Rist clung to the thickest branches he could get to, all the while fighting to keep breathing in the water's spray. One thick limb appeared to be able to hold his weight, and he grabbed it with one wet hand. It held!

Slowly, Rist made his way up the limb, every second afraid that it would break under him, but he finally got his whole body out of the water and up past the brushy fringe of vegetation of the River's edge. Once on solid ground, he lay on his back, thankful to be alive. *Thankful?* The thought hit him. *To whom? Or what?* Across the River, Shining One was just rising over the trees ("daybreak" the WarmLanders called this moment). *All right then,* Rist nodded east, *if You saved me, then thank You!*

HIS LIFE NOW NOT IN ANY IMMEDIATE DANGER—*UNLESS THE PRIESTS' Men and their dogs come this far downRiver,* he mused—curiosity overwhelmed Rist. He had to see what this End of the World looked like. After all, he had seen The Ice at the End of the World in the other direction, as Coldward as the world went. Now, the Warmward End was very close, too. Had any other People ever seen both ends of the world? He thought not; somebody would have Written about it. *Sire will be happy to know that the world has two ends, both seen by his son, the risky Rist. And Rusk? He will be trying to figure out what the length of the world is!*

The Warmward End was close, and loud. The intensity of the waterfall noise hurt his ears, but he pressed forward, careful that he not fall off by mistake. And there it was! Over a ridge of large boulders that he climbed, Rist was standing on a sheer cliff face that dropped off so far down that, he thought, *It must be like standing on The Ice at the other End, and looking down at The Tharn's Lands!*

Downward, the scene was unbelievable. Mist from the seemingly endless waterfall to his left, *east*, filled the sky, drifting in his direction with a strong wind. The thunderous waterfall, mind-numbing in its size, seemed to fall down forever, disappearing in the shadow-darkness below. Rist knew it didn't just vanish because he could see the occasional flash of Shining One's light on the water spray. *Just like at The Ice, there is a lake down there, so far down!* Looking straight out, the mist was less. Away from the shadow of the cliff, the distant landscape was being lit by Shining One, that shadow moving ever closer to his location. A silvery ribbon of river meandered across the land, disappearing in the distance. The rolling hills down there were mottled green and gray—*trees and rocks*, he concluded—but they also sported an occasional rectangular patchwork of colors. It reminded him of looking at the peat fields back home, upon coming down from the high valley of the New River. Were those *farms* down there in the distance? Could there be People down there, past this End of the World, looking up his way, as he and his Sire and twin had looked up at The Ice going through the Misty Sky? Did the other people down there have another sky, other gods, too?

But looking upward at the lightening sky, Rist saw clouds scuttling from his position straight out across the Bottom Lands, as he was beginning to think of them. No, the same clouds meant the same sky, the same Shining One and probably the same Pale Lady of the Night. As if to provide final truth of his observation, several squawking flocks of white birds flew overhead, descending at last into that same darkness. It had to be the same world as the Warm Lands, as The Tharn's Lands, just farther down. He wondered if the world even *had* an end in this direction? And when he thought about it, did The Ice at the other end, Coldward, itself extend forever, or did it have an end somewhere, too? It was too much to consider without the thinking support of his Sire and Rusk. He carved his speculations on the wooden cylinder that Cruthar had left him, fortunately having stuffed it in his pants pocket during the long ride downRiver from God's Port. Briefly, he hoped that Cruthar did indeed take back that other totem of his to his Sire and Rusk. There was simply too much unbelievable information on it to be lost!

And then Rist saw it—the dark shadow that had swallowed up a fingerth of the Bottom Lands was shrinking, receding toward him, toward the cliff! But how—? Rist glanced at his own shadow, formed by Shining One. Although shadows had been very rare occurrences in the ever-misty, cloud-covered Tharn's Lands, they were literally a daily feature of life in the bright Warm Lands, where nobody paid them any attention. In fact, Cruthar had pointed out to him a standing pole in a public square in God's Port where People could look at its shadow and estimate the time of Day by where the shadow pointed. Recalling the execution by concentrated light that occurred in that same place, Rist had ignored the one more strange foreign custom of time-telling by shadows, being impossible in the ever-cloudy dimness of The Tharn's Lands and thus unworthy of remembering.

But now that his own long shadow, cast where his body intercepted the light from Shining One, was shrinking as that god rose higher, Rist could see that the shadow of the cliff down in the Bottom Lands was shrinking the same way. He knew that shadows were just the absence of the light of Shining One. He wondered briefly: *Is it possible to concentrate shadows, like those priests did with the light when they cooked that pier-man? Would that make things colder, reducing the need for Ice?* He quickly carved those disturbing speculations and promptly forgot them. Survival was at stake here, becoming more immediate and urgent. He was trying to ignore the hunger pangs that returned after his narrow escape from the waterfall.

Rist tried to recall the strange way of thinking that his twin, Rusk, had used when they were at the foot of The Ice at the End of the World. "If the shard from the glacier has a flat top," Rist had said, "then that's where The Ice ends. And if that shard is above the Misty Sky, then if we measure the length of that shard when it is on its side, we will know that the Misty Sky is lower than that shard is long!" Almost without thinking, he took out the signal mirror from his pocket and flashed its light from Shining One down into the darkness below: three flashes—wait—three more flashes. His signaling hadn't worked when he was leaving God's Port, but it was the only flash-language that he knew. The mirror did not light up anything that he could see from his high vantage point, but maybe somebody down there would see it? If there were People down below to see it, would they recognize what he hoped were friendly flashes?

From the edge of the darkness below came answering flashes: *three —wait—three!* But they weren't whitish flashes from Shining One; they were small beams of red light, almost like rods as they shone through the dense mist of the waterfall, striking his chest directly as small dots! As he stood in shock, the red beam again flashed through the mist, again touching his chest, but now drawing figures on it, swirling, dancing figures! His near vision couldn't distinguish what the symbols were, but they were definitely not random! *Yet another way to Write, to Read? With tiny beams of light, from way far away?* In one corner of his mind, Rist anguished over the realization that there was just too much that he didn't know. Another part was scared, yet another part just intrigued. And hungry, too.

His conscious mind reacted immediately. *Somebody is down there! And they know this signal! But how did they signal back with a red beam of light? With dots and figures and swirling lights on my chest? How could they see up here, so far? And how far down are they?* Desperately he tried to act as though Rusk were with him to make that calculation: *I am standing on the top of The Ice—here, this high cliff— and my shadow shortens at the same time the shadow of the cliff shortens, so—?* He couldn't draw any conclusions, not having any experience in that sort of thing. *But, I do know that the Bottom Lands are probably not any further down than the top of that Ice shard was.* And another thought crept in. *How wide was the New River when the biter-web caught our berg and pulled it all the long way into the harbor at God's Port?* He looked again over the cliff face, into the mist and the receding shadow. *Miles long,* the pier-man had said, *dim-marches long! Could my roll of biter-web be long enough to reach down to the Bottom Lands? If it hasn't been trimmed, then according to that pier-man, it is many dim-marches long.*

Driven by an intense curiosity that he couldn't explain, he wondered who down there in the dark had flashed a message back with that strange red light. At least they had recognized the signal, so they should not be enemies. And being so far away, they probably didn't know of his troubles with the Priests' Men in God's Port. He considered his plight: knowing that his return home would be manyhands of hands of walking, a lot of it through hostile territory of the unfriendly Priests' Men and their snarling dogs, finding enough to eat along the way, and then trying to find an unknown site across the River where he would have to find a secret cliff site, there to plead for a lift upward by Tharn's Men who would ignore any plea of poverty.

With those dangers facing him immediately if he tried to return Coldward, Rist decided to trust to his newfound faith in Shining One. *Hands or no hands, at least He gives me light and warmth! And shadows to help me find my way. Maybe He will help me out with what I am about to do, here!* He had long since put away thoughts of how the same shining disk had fried the unfortunate pier-man. *Those priests set up those mirrors with their hands;* they *did it, not Him up in the sky Who has no hands*! He still wondered why anyone could be so cruel; Rist himself took extra care even when killing rabs or thicks, so that their pain of death would be swift and not lingering. Maybe in these new worlds, somebody somewhere could explain such things? *And maybe they have some food down there?*

One of the huge trees was just a short distance away. Rist took off his shirt and tied it around his waist. Then, wearing the god's gloves, he carefully unwound enough biter-web to wrap around the tree trunk, tying its whole width into a knot that almost disappeared as he drew it tight. As he walked away toward the cliff face, he allowed the biter-web to unspool over his head, like a sheath. When he tugged with the giant gloves, the material held tight. When he relaxed his grip, he could control the friction. *Not magic, but certainly very useful!* He hoped that Rusk would be able to think out how such a thing could be made to act so strangely.

When Rist had unwound and rewrapped the long length of biter-web several dims—*days!*—before, he had been thinking of somehow utilizing it at the lift, to be pulled up with it by The Tharn's Men there, and to take it home that way. But here he was, preparing to lower himself down to the Bottom Lands, hoping to find better prospects there. At least there was no long list of known dangers like he assuredly faced upRiver. Already he was missing his Sire, Reader Thess, and his twin, Rusk. *And even ol' Cruthar*, he grimaced. *Not to mention food, shelter, wen, and a way to stay away from the Priests' Men and their vicious dogs and killing mirrors!*

Climbing over a large boulder that protruded from the top of the cliff edge, noticing that the light of Shining One was nearly overhead by now, with both his own shadow and the shadow of the cliff face almost disappearing, Rist carefully let the biter-web begin to unspool over his head, and with the friction of the god's gloves controlling his descent, slowly lowered himself over the edge, into the misty distance below.

PART THREE

FALL

CHAPTER TWELVE

"*ShadowFall!*" the princess said aloud, startling her handmaidens. Loving the sound of her own voice, Princess Perneptheranam said it again, louder—"*ShadowFall* is today!" As her excited exclamations echoed throughout the cavernous polished pink marble halls of the palace, Perneptheranam, Lordess of the Sisterdom of *ShadowFall*—"Pernie," as she called herself—shivered with delight at the festival to come, right below her balcony, in the vast public plaza just outside the portico. Pushing aside her maids, ignoring their pleas to wear the royal sandals, she strode through a massive marble archway out onto the semicircular balcony, enjoying the damp coolness of the smooth stone floor against her bare feet. A tingling breeze wafted through translucent shimmering swaths of the rainbow-colored *godscloth* covering her from head to toe, further stimulating other senses with a light pair of twin tickles up *here* and a frivolous friction down *there*. That same soft wind also brought its gift of mixed delicious aromas—meats and sauces, spices and fruits—all rising up from the boiling pots and cooking pits, fifteen meters below.

Pernie was further stimulated by the vistas from this balcony, her domain: out in front, across the bustling crowds below, over past the river, lay her wonderful fields—grain, maize, cane—soft rectangular patterns of pastel shades that stretched to the far hazy horizon. To her right lay her grazing fields for vast herds of cattle and emus, appearing to her as colorful blanketlike masses, slowly moving, just like the hundreds of acres of wind-blown crops. To her left, twenty kilometers away, lay the northernmost boundary of her lands, marked by the Dark Uplands, a massive, unscalable uplift of Earth, craggy rock cliffs stretching all the way from east to west, unbroken save for the massive waterfall, many kilometers wide, that poured down the water into Mother's Lake at RiverHead.

She often wondered why her Sisterdom was not called *WaterFall* instead of *ShadowFall*, but she never dared ask the Lordess Mother or her own priest, the dark and mysterious Wakan Kech. Sighing, she thought, *Tradition is* always *their reason, but they never explain* why! But she knew she was only mentally joking with herself. *ShadowFall is where the Shadow Falls!* As everyone would witness today when the sun was highest. *A few hours from now.* Pernie glanced longingly at the fishermen working at the distant river's edge, casting their huge nets, smoothly and expertly gathering in the bounty of flashing fish and sparkling eels. Even from this distance she could see exquisite muscles moving under their broad bare backs, working for the people, working for her.

Pernie leaned over the balcony and waved at the bustling throngs of her subjects gathered below. Seeing her, they broke out into shouts of happiness, of respect, even of love, for their "Princess Pernie," although they knew it would be worth their tongues if they were ever caught saying that familiar version of The Royal Name to her face. But in the spirit of the moment, she shouted back "Pernie loves you, too!" and waved to them, bringing on even more cheers, which echoed through the palace behind her. She smiled and turned back to her handmaids, summoning them to bring the sandals and the morning's hot *chai. Yes, I love them,* she thought, *my people, my property. My slaves.*

As Pernie reclined into her down-stuffed leanback, a handmaiden delivered a tray of *chai* cups. Taking one, savoring the taste and the immediate lift of the hot beverage, she mused about her Sisterdom and its people. *They love me,* she thought, *and I do love them, too, as I love my pet animals. And we all love these festivities, when everyone can be happy. Yes,* she thought, *our namesake festival happens this morning, but…* Mixed with her anticipation were warm but poignant memories of the previous night's activities with the Chosen Man—the sumptuous dinner, the sweet wine, the sensuous music and intimate dancing, and everything else that followed. He had been so handsome, so charming, so sweet, so attentive, everything any woman, even a princess, could ever dream of.

What a shame that he would have to be beheaded today.

CHAPTER THIRTEEN

*A*t the base of the sheer cliffs of the Dark Highlands, Rist was in danger. Hanging upside down, he could see, through the slits in his beezt-hide eye coverings, that the entire length of his godscloth lifeline was tangled all around him in the top limbs of a huge tree, spreading from there across the forest like a gigantic biter-web of translucent, nearly invisible bluish material. *Tangled up, like me!* he thought, in near panic. A calmer part of his mind noted that all of the surrounding trees were of several species unknown back home in The Tharn's Lands. *I'm alive and unhurt as long as I stay up here in this tree,* he thought, *but how long will that be?*

Not far away in the forest, a pack of loud, crazed, slavering dogs, their sharp teeth bared, bayed as they ran toward the tree where he was caught *Like a bug in a* biter-web! Rist thought. And running behind the crazed animals, a hand or more of very large men—*"Low Landers,"* *would they be?*—were pointing toward him, one of them stopping to shine a thin beam of red light that danced around his body. *Was he the one signaling me at the top of the cliff?* he wondered. *Is that some kind of sun weapon, like the Priests' Men's mirrors, but smaller?* If so, he would be dead even before the dogs got him. He only had a few minutes to do something, anything!

Taking a deep breath, rapidly trying to suss out some solution to his predicament, he recounted how he had arrived in such a perilous state. His descent was quick and easy at first. The huge gloves allowed him to let the sheath of godscloth slide through and unwind upward without damaging his hands, and he had known (had *hoped!*) that it was long enough for him to reach the bottom safely. But when he was almost down, high winds suddenly swept upward along the cliff face, catching the long sheath of godscloth, sail-like, buffeting him against the sheer rock face.

In desperation he had used the big scissorlike cutters to detach himself from the sheathing, to fall the last few man-lengths of distance into vegetation below. But by some strange property of the nearly weightless material, the entire length that he had unwound above him, many hands of hands of man-lengths (*miles?*), detached itself from its tie-off point above, and fell with him. Then, the same winds that caused his problem rescued him, by blowing him and his huge bundle of godscloth like wind-borne seeds, finally softening his fall, draping itself across hands of trees, himself dangling like a loose tree limb. *The Warm Lands gods must have looked out for me*, he thought. *Until the dogs showed up!* As if in mockery, the disk of the main Warm Lands god, Shining One, stood high in the sky, almost directly overhead. It was too brilliant for Rist's sensitive eyes, even with the slitted eye patches he wore.

And with the vicious creatures at the base of his tree now howling for his blood, and half a dozen very large Low Landers close behind them, Rist wondered if he had gone from the boiling pot into the burning beezt-dung fire!

AT THE PALACE, PRINCESS PERNIE MUSED ABOUT THE UPCOMING sacrifice of her newest lover. In memory, she recalled when her High Priest, the wiseman Wakan Kech, had first explained it all to her five years ago during her first ShadowFall ceremony, after her first night with a Chosen Man—*With* any *man,* she thought—back when she was barely thirteen years old yet already experiencing her menses. "Dearest Princess," the tall, dark Wakan had intoned, softly but sternly, "as thousands of years of tradition dictate, the handsome head of the Chosen Man, lovingly preserved, will decorate the topmost segment of the Arch of ShadowFall for the entire year to come. That will be his spirit's way of welcoming the warming sun and the gentle rains, of keeping away the crop chewers and all the other pests." He had smiled. "And so he will keep the fields fruitful to feed all of ShadowFall, your vast Sisterdom." Then he whispered conspiratorially, "And to profitably feed several other realms of your Sisters as well. Don't forget their debts to you."

Wakan's time-worn visage had been solemn back then, his black eyes and deep resonant voice, his long, braided black hair and his hooded scarlet robe presenting a striking visage that intimidated the young princess into silence. Back then, her first time, Pernie had wished her lover's sacrifice weren't necessary; she wished it weren't so now, either, because she desired this Chosen Man's affections, his physical attention, again, *indeed, at this very moment!* But hearing the continuous clamor by her people down below for another appearance at the balcony, and over that the onset of the staccato priestly drumming, punctuated by a dozen brassy horns announcing the beginning of the rituals, she knew it was not to be. *So I, Princess Perneptheranam, Lordess of the Sisterdom of ShadowFall, am as much a prisoner of tradition as the young man who will be slaughtered soon. He was the best lover I've had in many years!* She sighed, then mused, *Why wait another year? I might just have Wakan take a look at some of those muscular fisherman.*

DRESSED IN RESPLENDENT DEEP RED GODSCLOTH ROBES, WAKAN KECH, High Priest, and Advisor to the Princess of ShadowFall, stood on a wide, three-meter-high stone platform at the base of the Arch of ShadowFall, looking up to admire its simplicity, its beauty. Carved in high relief in the living stone of an outcropping of rock half as large as the Princess's Palace, the arch itself reached up twice Wakan's height and stretched twice *that* in width, a recumbent relief sculpture in the shape of a rainbow, with a hollowed-out center below the bottommost arc. To an unschooled onlooker (*Like most of the peasants here*, he thought, *and many of the noble guests!*) the recessed stone rainbow might have been simply melted into the surrounding stone by the branding iron of a god. But Wakan knew it had been chipped out, one tiny flake at a time, by ancient stone carvers working to the master plan of an unknown and forgotten genius. A keystone-shaped wedge defined the top of the Arch, with three successive tilted wedges arranged down each side, their different slopes giving rise to radial triangular shadows where they met. A smooth, curved vertical wall ran straight down from the bottom arc of the rainbow to the horizontal floor, giving the appearance of a hollow "bowl" under the Arch itself.

In all, the carving was a beautiful sculpture, even to the ignorant who did not know its true astronomical functions. *But for those schooled in its use, like me,* Wakan thought, *the arch lets us observe how the sun creates shadows, so we can forecast events in the heavens. Such as today, ShadowFall, the longest day of the year.* For this day, the changing of the seasons, the ancients had provided a signal that all could see, princess, priest and peasant alike: a sudden horizontal shaft of light, framed by shadows of intricately positioned stone, would appear: the Arrow of the Sun, its sharp end stabbing a wedge on the north side, indicating the death of Season Blossom. And the birth of Season Warm.

Wakan Kech admired the ancients who had designed and carved this incredible holy site. He had first seen it five years before, when he accompanied the Princess's palace retinue and thousands of her transferred slaves to ShadowFall when she assumed authority over her new Sisterdom. The Lordess Mother, ruler of all Motherland, had gifted him to the young Princess Pernie at the royal girl's request, and Wakan had been allowed to bring with him several of his Kech countrymen, who like himself were slave prisoners. Wakan relished the opportunity to leave the oppressive atmosphere of Mother's City, far to the south, and to help establish a new Sisterdom here at the very northern boundary of Motherland, next to the mysterious Dark Highlands twenty kilometers away.

Upon arriving at the abandoned city, emptied centuries before by some forgotten disaster, *Probably plague or war or drought,* Wakan thought, but did not know. He and his fellow Kech had been very happy to find the palace's ancient library of surviving bound books, tightly wound animal skin scrolls, and even some (unfortunately, dead and unusable) ancient reading machines. *And many crystal godspheres, which sometimes may speak to us briefly even though we cannot understand them,* he regretted. Among those written languages that they could already read, Kech had found information that taught how the arch operated. How the shadows told the hours and indicated the seasons, and how the Arrow of Sunlight stabbed a particular point at the moment of midday on the day of ShadowFall.

And so I reinstituted the ancient rite of ShadowFall, complete with its grisly ritual human sacrifice. He often wondered that if the Arch was supposed to bring good fortune to this region of Motherland, why had the previous population disappeared? *Maybe this time, we will do better!*

For many reasons, he had thought at the time, recounting them to justify his own participation. First, the sacrifice was a yearly demonstration of the Princess's power of life and death over all of the people in her Sisterdom, a power theoretically absolute and arbitrary. In actuality, Pernie had seldom condemned any of her subjects, and never for any trivial offense, unlike her dozen savage Sisters. The Chosen Man tradition also allowed every peasant and lesser noble to feel relief that they themselves had not been selected, while they still understood at a gut level that Princess Pernie always held their very lives in her hands.

Secondly, the mounted head of the Chosen Man at the Arch, the most public site in the city, would be a constant reminder of the Princess's power every day. Because all control in Motherland depended on the acquiescence of its slave-subjects, and because most of the population increase came from Motherless slaves brought back by Her armies raiding the Western Highlands, such nonverbal signs of dominion were necessary. *It keeps down rebellions, and minimizes the killing.* By such reasoning, an acknowledged self-deception, Wakan Kech was able to pardon himself. He hated killing of any kind; in his own homeland up in the High Antis, even food animals were given a painless death, complete with rituals asking forgiveness.

To Wakan's relief, all preparations for ShadowFall had gone as planned. The townspeople and the farmers had brought their goods into the plaza, set up their tents and booths and banners and pots and gambling games, lending a rainbow of colors, friendly commotion, delicious odors, and an air of excitement to the holiday. On an adjacent raised stone platform, he saw representative delegations from several neighboring Sisterdoms—Four Peaks, Stone Pyramid, High Tables, RidgeBack, Ancient Towers—complete with small complements of armed warriors in full black leather regalia, carrying their usual bannered spears with pennants now flapping in a sudden breeze from the North. *Those weapons are not just for pageantry*, he knew. In preparation for today's influx of outsiders, Wakan had cautioned his own palace guardsmen to keep a close watch on these foreign men. Unfortunately, assassinations were not unknown occurrences amongst the Sisters. With some satisfaction, he saw several dozen of his guards, clothed like peasants and concealing their shortswords, jostling around the base of that platform, ready to ascend the steps if necessary. In the shadows, unseen but alert, a dozen other armsmen with springbows watched over the peasants and nobles alike. Wakan smiled.

On this perfect day, though, Wakan could not be as fully absorbed in the festivities as usually happened. He had one niggling concern: just before he had left his chambers, a border guard captain at RiverHead, using one of the few red-beamed *godslights* that still worked, signaled the capture of a small, dark, manlike creature, of a kind never seen before. Incredibly, the message said that the thing was not a monkey because it wore clothing. The being was caught in a tall tree, wrapped up in a massive tangled web of what looked like godscloth, a huge amount of that material, thousands of square meters of it, draped over the forest. *Worth a fortune, if true,* Wakan mused. And more, the guard speculated, the little beast and the godscloth had apparently fallen down from the Dark Highlands! Wakan shook his head in disbelief; if that story were not completely accurate in every unbelievable detail, he would have to severely discipline that guard. He always stressed that reports to him should contain only facts, not speculation. But even so, he was intrigued at the alleged discovery.

He set that thought aside; important rituals and festivities would be starting soon, culminating in the sacrifice of the Chosen Man at the appointed hour. Smiling grimly as he waved to silence the priests' drumming, he nodded to the waiting black-hooded axeman who would do the deed, who nodded in return. *What a waste of a young man's life,* Wakan thought, *but better that ignorant, uneducated lad than someone skilled. And better his head serving as a reminder, than me having to have the guards kill hundreds more in another uprising, as happened four years back. At least, this "tradition" requires that I make the selection, and I always choose for the best physique but the least intellect. And Pernie has never complained!*

As the crowds quietened, gathering around the high stone platform underneath the sculptured Arch of ShadowFall, Wakan Kech cast another concerned glance northward, toward the stark range of sheer cliffs in the distance that marked the Dark Highlands, wondering what the new discovery might bring. But at that moment the Princess emerged from the palace, walking down a wide arc of glistening pink marble steps, with her godscloth robes setting off her long beautiful red hair, a veritable rainbow in motion, graciously nodding in acceptance of the cheers of her excited subjects. With her came four springbow men dressed all in black, head to foot, only their eyes showing. These were the palace guards, protectors of the royal person, who would kill instantly upon her command, or even before, if they sensed a threat. All the audience understood this and grew hushed.

Wakan welcomed the Princess to a massive stone throne, framed in the background by the ominous Arch of ShadowFall. At last, the crowd cheered. Wakan made note of the contingents from the other Sisters, who among them cheered and who didn't. His perfect memory could recreate the scene at any time. To his right, the Chosen Man, in full naked glory, strutted out to more cheers, flexing his impressive muscles and bowing to the crowd. Wakan himself had prepared the potion that mercifully dulled the youngster's mind to his imminent fate. He noted the progress of shadows across the Arch and the Bowl; in just a few minutes, the shadows would form the Arrow of the Sun to indicate the moment of midday. *And the end of this young man's short life,* cringing at the thought. As the final moment approached, the crowd's cheers grew louder, finally silenced only by the swift *swish* of the axeman's instrument of death. The sweet smell of gushing blood quickly overcame the exquisite aroma of the Princess's perfumes. *The odor of power*, he mused, his stomach churning.

Picking up the severed head of the Chosen Man by its bloody hair, Wakan sighed and waved it to the hushed crowd, beginning the long ritual of fertility prayers.

CHAPTER FOURTEEN

"*H*ere is the creature, Priest Kech," the captain of border guards said, jerking on the chain attached to the iron neck bank around Rist's neck, nearly pulling him off his feet. "I suppose it *is* some kind of man, because it had a loincloth and a shirt, and these big gloves"—he handed those objects to Wakan Kech, who noticed that they were larger than his own big hands—"and these huge scissors."

Likewise, Wakan tried those out. "This equipment is larger than my hands can handle," he said. "Was this—*monkey man*—was *he* using them? With those little hands?" The captain nodded. "Sire, he cut himself out of the godscloth and let himself down from a tall tree, after we pulled the dogs back. That's the only way we could get him." The big man then related how he and his guards had spent the remainder of yesterday gathering up the thousands of meters of godscloth draped like curtains over dozens of trees. "Sire, it was a real mess. But watching our monkey-man here, we found out we could cut it with those big scissors." The captain stopped, then whispered, "Sire, I didn't know that stuff *could* be cut."

Wakan motioned for the man to be silent. This was one secret he did not want the other Sisters to know about, not yet. He could envision a whole new industry, of custom-cut godscloth, useful for hundreds of items, at any price he decided on. In all of the history of Motherland, even in his own High Antis, nobody had ever been able to cut so much as one fiber of the material. And handling it could sometimes be dangerous—when wrapped up tight, if you caught the edge, it was sharper than any blade, being the cause of many severed fingers and hands. And even severed necks, in several of the Sisterdoms. It was a rare find that ever uncovered a length of godscloth that could be made into clothing—*For royalty only*, Wakan noted—or for nets, curtains, or anything else. "A meter of godscloth" was a common remark meaning "priceless" or "impossible." Over the centuries many square kilometers of the stuff had been found in ancient ruins, in underground mines, sometimes just lying across vast regions of land, strewn across the landscape like worthless nets and ribbons. Apparently the gods—*or ancient people*, the scholars back in Wakan's land had surmised; he himself did not choose to share aloud that heretical theory here in the superstitious Motherland—had manufactured the material by some unknown process, for their own gods-only-knew uses. *And when they departed, they left their trash behind*, Wakan concluded. *The most valuable trash in the whole round world!*

Wakan thanked the guards for their service, then let them know with his full authority that any leaked word of the discovery of the little man, the godscloth, the glove or the cutting tool, would result in painful, lingering death for all of them together. Their stoic looks showed him that they had expected nothing less. *Fine!* Wakan hoped this was true; the young Chosen Man's end had come quickly, but the penalty for a violation of his direct orders often took several excruciating weeks of excruciatingly painful torture by death-herb, and he had to observe for himself every last detail of the dreadful plant's effects, a solemn obligation that always sickened him.

Wakan told his female aide, Rumi Similla, to give the captain a sizeable sum of silver for doing his sworn duty efficiently and quickly, and to make sure that most of the money was fairly distributed to the entire contingent. *Those guards at the Dark Highlands cliffs seldom have* any *duties to perform. Mostly they look for anything interesting that comes over the waterfall from the highlands above.* He snorted. *And probably keep the most valuable items for themselves!* Wakan turned his attention back to the little creature. *Man, monkey, midget, elf, dwarf—what?* He was thankful for the intriguing distraction; the whole ShadowFall ceremony always left him in a mildly depressed fugue state. At least it was over for another year, though that handsome severed head on the spike would remind him of it every day…

Standing in front of Wakan, the small being barely reached his knees, but was apparently human in all respects, just in miniature. *Stunted features, big head, very muscular*, he thought. *Rather large in his chest, like some of the mountain dwellers in the High Antis, back home.* In addition to the confining chain around its neck and hands, it was clad only in a dirty loincloth (the guards had removed a tiny blue shirt, somewhat shredded, from around its waist, along with some kind of slitted eyepatches and the thong strap that held them). The creature was the color of mahogany, with dark eyes and pitch black hair; its skin was smooth and almost hairless otherwise. Its shoes—*Animals don't wear shoes!*—were an interesting leatherlike hybrid of boots and sandals. Wakan concluded that his captive was just yet another variety of human being, specially created for the cold environment of the far north, with large lungs able to breathe the thinner air there, dark skin to absorb life-giving light from the sun, and a small size because of limited food and the need to hide from predators. Being from the lower reaches of the High Antis, Wakan himself was normal in all respects, the proper height and proportions. *Or so I tell myself!*

Coming from a well-educated highland civilization, Wakan had always known, as indeed the ancient writings claimed, that other kinds of people lived in other lands, and that their features were shaped for the conditions in those lands. And according to the information in the palace library, in the years before his own arrival at ShadowFall, human bodies of various kinds, small and large, had come over the waterfall into Mother's Lake. Wakan had deciphered very old reports saying that some primitive watercraft, even a number of carved wooden spindles of no identifiable use, had been retrieved as well. All of those artifacts were still stored in the vast network of tunnels and dungeons under the palace, but not all were categorized yet. His assistant priests would have to search their domains for such artifacts and more information. But according to the same texts, most of the bodies and all of the boats were smashed beyond recognition. *They had to fall over six hundred meters,* he knew. *And in all of these centuries of Motherdom, nobody has yet scaled up those perilous heights to see where the strange people came from. So how did this little creature come down without injury?*

Wakan spoke to the little man. "Who are you, my uninvited visitor? Where do you come from, and what do you want here in ShadowFall?" To his surprise, the dark dwarf began to jabber in a language that was almost familiar. Not the meaning, but the cadence of speech, some familiar sounds amidst the gibberish of snorts and tongue-twisting grunts. Where had he heard those sounds before? As an educated scholar-priest, Wakan knew many languages, having been taught by elder priests in his homeland, those with access to the godspheres from the beginning of time.

Wakan himself had been captured twenty years before by armies of the Lordess Mother during an invasion campaign into the Dry Lands of the Nawat, south of Motherland and far to the north of Wakan's homeland. By an unfortunate circumstance, Wakan and a contingent of other High Antis wisemen had been on a lengthy field expedition to that thinly populated Dry Lands region of *Chi'a,* there to study an ancient pyramid complex covered by a huge God's Dome. The gods —*or somebody in the ancient past,* Wakan believed—had created huge hemispherical domes of the same impenetrable clear crystal as the numerous kickball-sized godspheres found in the High Antis, utilizing those domes for some unknown reason to cover over large tracts of land that contained time-worn buildings. The local *Chi'a* natives, the Nawat, only knew legends about the domes, the usual "The gods did it" superstitions.

With only a small protection force accompanying their expedition,

Wakan's small group was easy prey when Mother's Army had arrived for plunder and slaves. After a brief battle in which Wakan's own armed guards were slaughtered, he and the other wisemen and their guides were taken as prisoners, destined to become slaves to Mother. But because Wakan was able to talk in a kind of pidgin Motherspeak to the enemy captain, and then prove his further worth by translating the captain's commands to the huge collection of Nawat prisoners, he was kept alive along with the others.

Exhibiting the same language skills at Mother's Court, Wakan had quickly earned Her favor, obtaining similar privileges for his Kech compatriots. The others were then sent to various of the Sisterdoms, to serve as advisors to the princesses who owned them. From reports he heard, only a few of his countrymen had since been killed by their princesses.

For the next fifteen years Wakan had been kept as a translator slave and minor advisor at Mother's Court, until She had given him to Princess Pernie prior to the young girl's assumption of the new Sisterdom of ShadowFall. Wakan often thought of his years at Mother's Court, far to the southwest of ShadowFall, next to the Deep Blue Salt Sea. The Lordess Mother, while absolutely ruthless and frequently cruel, nonetheless loved and collected all kinds of knowledge, establishing libraries and museums of captured documents and small artifacts, especially those related to the adjacent Motherless highlands. She tasked Wakan and his compatriots and others to study those peoples, their languages, customs, and natural resources. *Especially their resources*, Wakan thought. *Because in Mother's hands, knowledge means only* power—*the power to spy, to plan, to invade, to pillage, plunder and enslave.*

After his capture, Wakan had feared for his own homeland, but through a long series of believable stratagems, he had been able to divert Mother's interest and attentions to other surrounding highlands, other successful invasions, all the while leaving his own people untouched. For all his fears of Her lust for empire, Wakan retained mixed feelings for his sovereign Mother, some of hate, some of affection. After all, even though he had been Her captive, without any rights whatsoever. She had left him physically whole, had made love to him, had fed and kept him and provided him with libraries and museums. *So we few, we fortunate Kech, were not painfully relieved of our manhood, as was the fate of so many highland men brought back as slaves to work the mines and farms of Motherland.*

And so this little man before him, like Wakan himself now a personal possession belonging to Princess Pernie—who thankfully did not practice such mutilation in her Sisterdom—would be safe in that most important masculine respect!

CHAPTER FIFTEEN

*T*he day after ShadowFall, after Pernie had bid farewell to the delegations from other Sisters (*And hopefully, all of the spies they undoubtedly brought with them,* she thought), she called for Wakan. "Have my priest bring that new little creature for me to see," she told her handmaiden. "I always love to learn about new things." Pernie spoke the truth. Unlike her envious dozen sister princesses in Motherland, Pernie alone, the youngest, had not spawned children every year of her maturity. *At seventeen, I could have had half a dozen of the little power-seeking vipers by now!* Wakan Kech's knowledge of herbs and chemicals had allowed her to stay childless as long as she wanted, while enjoying Chosen Men and others as often as she wished. *My Sisters breed like rabbits,* she thought, *and have so many offspring, each of whom will someday fight to seize their own mother's Sisterdom, as soon as they are able. No wonder they have so many wars down south, so many crops ruined, towns burned, lives wasted!*

But Wakan, through his foreign knowledge, had helped her avoid all of that unproductive activity, so she and her priest could spend their time and energies to maintain her Sisterdom, its fields, its irrigation, its roads, the health of its people. Though unheard of anywhere else in Motherland, with Wakan's help Pernie was also quietly experimenting with having all of the children in her domain learn their letters, and those who could the numbers, and a select few, even the *geoms. That way, as Wakan says, they can carry out my written orders to the far reaches of the realm, without the inaccuracies of oral commands. And the number of land surveyors and map readers and crop weighers and basket counters can increase along with the population. And so can the numbers of my well-trained and well-fed royal guards. And the more of* them, *the more they will be able to hold back the raiders and rustlers and vagabonds, and see that my Sisters don't attack us anymore.* And since those guardsmen were all uniformly strong and clean, she occasionally welcomed the most heroic to her private chambers. She said another silent prayer of thanks for Wakan Kech and his potions.

While waiting, Pernie's thoughts drifted back to the first year that she and Wakan had occupied ShadowFall. Just six months after their arrival, two adjacent Sisterdoms—RidgeBack and Four Peaks—had joined forces to annex the coveted ShadowFall realm with its fertile fields, fine fishing, and majestic abandoned city and palace complex, which included the legendary site of the Arch. Her Sisters had planned on a merciless onslaught of their civil-war-tested troops, anticipating a quick victory over the small, green force of Pernie's new palace guards. At best, had they prevailed Pernie would have spent the rest of a miserable life shut up in a palace room. At worst—well, burning at the stake was a typical fate of the losers in Sisterdom wars. She shuddered at the memory, how badly things could have turned out when she was but thirteen years old.

But her treacherous Sisters had not known about Wakan's hidden military talents and secret knowledge, none of which he had trumpeted during his years at Mother's Court. Keeping his own counsel until an opportune time arose, Wakan had read ancient writings on warfare and strategies, experimented with new weapons, and waited. And most importantly, he had brought along prototypes of the godspring-powered crossbows, devices that propelled sharp arrows of god-iron over long distances. Over the years he had commandeered long-ignored warehouse caves full of that supposedly unusable metal, in both coiled form and short uncuttable rods, from all over Motherland. Once settled into ShadowFall, Pernie's smiths had turned out many thousands of the weapons in short order, top priority.

Unlike the other Sisterdoms who kept their slaves totally disarmed, in Pernie's realm every adult had been trained in springbow use, and in the first battle their unexpected numbers quite overwhelmed the attackers. As she remembered it, Pernie sniffed; in all, that early attack had been a fortunate war for her. As a result of her smashing victory, ShadowFall had gained several hundred field hands and salt-mine slaves, all previously emasculated and now docile, and permanently overawed at her power—and Wakan's. Along with good chunks of the lands of those Sisterdoms, conquests approved by the Lordess Mother, ruler of all. Pernie knew that her Mother approved of such innovative planning and deception; she had sent Pernie congratulations along with Her approval of the legal annexations of the prize territories.

With the recently conquered lands serving as a buffer, providing advanced warning of any unwise invasions from other Sisterdoms, ShadowFall enjoyed as peaceful a prospect as any realm in Motherland. And Pernie herself would much prefer to learn everything that was in the books and scrolls—and the dead reading machines and godspheres, if ever possible!—in her library. To know the meaning of the strange devices and pictures in her museum. And over the years that he remained alive, Wakan would teach her everything that he knew. That kind of knowledge would expand her mind. And she couldn't do any of that if she was worried about wars and assassinations and uprisings. Not to mention overseeing the overseers of her crops and herds. *I may live another fifty years. I have to protect my subjects, my people.* In her deepest meditations, she wondered if she could find another to replace Wakan, when the inevitable occurred. No, ShadowFall was enough for her. More than enough, and protected by a weapon that so far had not been replicated.

Pernie and Wakan had determined to keep the secrets of their unique and deadly armament closely held as long as possible. With that godspring-powered crossbow—*springbow*—in hand, Mother could rule the whole round world, if she lived long enough. Despite continuing gentle suggestions from Mother, Wakan never got around to writing down the source of the godspring material itself, never described the ancient process by which it could be formed into bows of incredible springiness. Even back in the High Antis, knowledge of that secretly formed, yet remarkably resilient material was tightly held among only a few scholars, and its power used primarily for construction, such as shaping large stones for construction blocks and for making paving tiles. Its use in spring-powered weaponry was strictly forbidden by the peaceful customs of the High Antis, though Wakan occasionally rued that his own guards on the Nawat expedition had not carried some such weapons as those he had concocted for Pernie. Then again, if he had not been captured, he would never have had such power as he now did. *But power only for good*, he thought, *not for myself, not for empire!* He prayed that he would always only use it so.

———

"IS HE ABLE TO TALK, WAKAN?" PRINCESS PERNIE ASKED. THE PRIEST, standing in front of the Throne of ShadowFall, motioned at Rist, who stood beside him, still chained. Perneptheranam sat still, waiting for a reply. Her gaze fell on the little man, a stubby, squat, dark creature, now dressed in a white robe, his normal-sized bare feet seeming of almost comical proportion. Beside him stood Wakan Kech and a squad of six young guards. The princess wondered, *All of these* big *men to protect me from that* little *one?*

"Your Highness, he does talk. But I have not deciphered what he is saying," Wakan Kech answered with a slight bow. "Though its speech —*his* speech—sounds familiar, I have not been able to understand its significance. However, it—he—does answer to the name 'Wrist,'" Wakan said, touching one wrist with another, "and he knows that I am called—" He pointed to his chest and tapped it.

"*Wakken*," the little man said, smiling.

At that, the princess said, "Very good, Wakan. And hello to you, too, Rist." At the sound of his name, the little one smiled and bowed low. "That is a good start," she said, smiling. "I am sure you will do well with this little challenge." Behind her, her handmaids tittered, whispering. "Yes, my dears," the princess said, turning back to Wakan. "My girls would like to see if this little man, squat and stubby though he may be, is manlike in, his, his—*other* parts."

Wakan sighed, motioning to a guard to remove Rist's robe. Once that was done, it was obvious to all that the presence of the scantily clad young handmaids had caused the same physical effect on the little man as it had on the stone-faced young guards present. Those men dared not show the smiles—or other physical reactions—they felt. "Goodness," the princess said with a drawn breath. "Dress him at once. Obviously, his stature is small only when he is clothed." The handmaids were grinning, whispering. Wakan heard the one called Anklya say quietly, "A three-legged man? Is that possible?" Wakan shook his head. Although he himself frequently enjoyed the intimate company and pleasures of favorite females, he kept that part of his life as private as possible. Though being the acknowledged second-in-command of a powerful realm had its privileges, he had seen in Mother's Court what sort of troubles, sometimes fatal ones, could come from unbridled passions of any kind. So his own personal life he kept out of the common gossip as much as possible. On the other hand, he was now happy for little Rist, who certainly would be finding favor in Princess Pernie's court, not the least of which would be from the royal handmaids. *I will need to mix up quite a bit more of that baby preventative potion!* he thought.

But the Princess had already shifted her attention from Rist's physical assets to the financial windfall he had brought to ShadowFall. "You say that Rist fell down from the Dark Highlands, and brought with him kilometers of godscloth?" The little man stiffened, looking first at the princess and then at Wakan.

"*Godscloth*," Rist said slowly. "You call it the same name that the People do?"

Wakan shook his head; only the one word *godscloth* was recognizable, the rest of it mere gobbling sounds. But that was a beginning. Wakan said the word again, enunciating it carefully: "Gods. Cloth." Rist smiled and nodded his head, repeating it over and over.

"Gods. Cloth. Gods. Cloth." *Finally,* Rist thought, *these tall people are starting to make sense. Maybe they* can *talk!* He had been wondering if he had fallen into a land of mental defectives, since almost nothing of the sounds they uttered made any sense. But now, now there was hope.

Wakan motioned for a guard to give him a silver godslight tube, turning it on with a touch. At the sight of the thin red light shining on him, Rist jumped. "Gods. Light," Wakan said. "The light of the gods." But Rist only comprehended the word *gods*. "*Gods*," he said, "*gods*."

Turning to the princess again, Wakan shook his head. "Princess, we now have two words in common at least, and that is a place of beginning. If you allow me the time, I will learn how this one speaks, and teach him our language."

"Continue, Wakan," Pernie replied, "And have your men take an inventory of the godscloth. You mentioned that he had an implement with which to cut it. I don't have to tell you what it means to the economy of Motherland if ShadowFall can process this material to fit, for nets, for clothing, and who knows what else. But it has to be kept as ShadowFall's secret." She stood and stretched. "For now, also do an inventory all of the godscloth we have in storage, and arrange for this this—windfall!—to be made secure." Wakan bowed, as did Rist, and the men started to leave the court. "One moment, Wakan," the princess said in a soft voice. "You can leave little Rist in those chains, but I think I will talk to him some more." At Wakan's surprised look, she continued. "My handmaids will escort him from here." Wakan saw one of the young guards from the corner of his eye, blowing a silent breath of relief—or was it frustration?—as they departed.

RIST WAS RETURNED TO WAKAN KECH TWO DAYS LATER. "NOT THE worse for wear, I hope, little Rist," the priest said as the smiling blonde handmaid Anklya gave Wakan the end of the chain. "Or at least, not that I can see." Fairly reeking of Anklya's royally restricted selection of perfume, Rist looked at him with a smile, not understanding his words but knowing full well what Wakan's sentiments were. *Not really a bad smell,* Wakan thought, reminded of the lush tropical flowers from whence the scent originated, in the far southern Sisterdom of Three Rivers, *but certainly a lot of it!*

"So let's get to work, Rist," Wakan Kech said. "The Princess means well, but she does possess the impatience of a teenage girl, and it will go badly for you if you can't show some—*other*—skills in addition to the one you so obviously already demonstrated." Taking the neck iron off, he left Rist's legs in shackles. "Not that you would have anywhere to run to, here in ShadowFall or elsewhere in Motherland, being as different as you are. But it would be one devil of a time if you got loose and just hid." He laughed, thinking of the handmaids over the last two days. "But I bet I know where you'd go!"

Wakan led Rist down through dark torchlit stone-block tunnels under the palace, finally stopping at a large wooden door half again as tall as the priest. Producing an iron key of prodigious size, Wakan unlocked a massive metal lock and swung open the door, revealing a vast hallway beyond. A musty odor, the smell of dead centuries, permeated the whole space. Wakan rubbed his eyes, while Rist coughed a few times. Once inside the ancient room, Wakan lit a series of gas-burning lamps high on the walls, revealing hundreds of cubbyhole shelves brimming over with scrolls, bound books, loose piles of sheet papers, stacks of metal plates, and display cases. "Thousands of documents, maps, drawings and pictures here, little Rist," Wakan said, waving his arms. "Let us see if we can discover any knowledge that applies to you."

Rist stared in wonder at the overwhelming assemblage of objects in the vast room. This one room was larger than Sire Thess' largestone house back in The Tharn's Lands, and had nearly the volume of the priest's fireplace room in the Temple of the Gods in God's Port. And full of—*what?* He knew the pieces were human-made, but what were they? He was still staring when the large man brought over a stack of thin sheets of unknown material, stuck together at one side and covered with beezt-hide. When Wakan opened the "book," as he called it, all Rist could see inside were blurry smudges on a yellowed background.

"Can you *read*, Rist?" the big man asked, pointing at the letters.

Rist didn't understand, except that the man must have thought he could make some kind of sense out of the dark areas. He shrugged, another common gesture easily understood. Wakan's posture showed that the tall man was discouraged, Rist thought, though his own lack of sharp near vision prevented him from discerning any details of the priest's face. Rist wanted to help his newfound benefactor, but didn't know how. Then he recalled that his twin, Rusk, had been excited to touch some thin bone and metal plates retrieved from the god that they had recovered from The Ice at the End of the World and brought back to The Tharn's Town. His twin, he remembered, had used his sense of touch to feel the minute carvings in those objects, and had wondered aloud if the gods used a different form of Reading and Writing, namely indenting shapes on flat surfaces instead of the spindles, the totems, that People used for Writing and Reading.

But maybe somewhere, in this huge collection of things obviously meant to contain information, he could find a carved spindle, a totem, something he could use his Reading hand to interpret?

While Wakan focused his attention on yet another volume of thin leafy sheets, Rist wandered through the musty room, his leg chains kicking up dust as he shuffled through corridors formed by stacks of those unknown volumes. Dusty wooden crates with undisclosed contents stood stacked in the corners, an odor of age permeating the still air. In the distance Rist saw that one set of shelves held many hands—"*Dozens!*" he could hear Cruthar yell—of dark glassy spheres about twice the size of his head. He had no idea what use such things could be, and kept exploring elsewhere in the strange new environment.

And suddenly, there they were—totems! A shelf full of them! From across the vast room, against a far wall, Rist could clearly see the familiar writing and reading media. As he grew closer, the totems became blurry, as he knew they would. He tried to pick one up, but his hand was stopped by a transparent solid. Having never seen clear glass before, Rist nevertheless soon discovered how to slide one pane back behind another, gaining access to the precious totems on the shelves. The first one he selected was of velk bone, but a bone that had been broken, half of a longer bone. Using his Reading hand, the left, he gently stroked the extremely worn, somewhat rough surface, picking out a phrase, a meaning, here and there. This one was old, carved by one of the People during a long-ago battle with the WarmLanders. *Today, the Warmies attacked from Warmward, along the river,* the carver had written. *I was gravely wounded by one of their spears. I write this in hopes that the finder will tell...* But there the totem-bone was broken, the rest of the message lost.

Rist tried to remember what Sire Thess had said about WarmLander wars. The last one had been when Sire Thess was young, long cycles before his twins, Rist and Rusk, had been birthed by Mell, Sire Thess' wen. *This poor man's message was never delivered,* Rist mourned his unknown countryman. *If I ever get back home, I'll —what?* He didn't even know the name of the carver. But if he took the totem with him, maybe the Old Wen would recognize the style? Over the next hour, Rist tried reading all of the hands of totems, but could make sense only of three or four, and only sketchily at that. *How melancholy,* he thought. *Love letters, traders' receipts, even a plan of attack. All washed downriver and over the Edge of the World, to end up in these sad, lonely shelves!* And if he had interpreted the dates correctly, accounting for the Tharns of previous ages, all of the writers were long since dead, their messages also dead and now lost in a strange land.

A sudden wave of homesickness swept over him. He missed arguing with his twin Rusk, and listening to his Sire Thess' stories of the olden days; missed even having his birther, Mell, smile at him and hug him warmly when Sire Thess wasn't looking. Not that he hadn't thoroughly enjoyed the, the, *attention*, lavished on him by those chesty young women in their sheer godscloth gowns, but now the import of his exile from The Tharn's Lands, thinking of an impossible return journey scaling those high cliffs, sailing up that swift river, and making his way through a hostile land, which would be the only way back home, began to impact him. Away from all danger (as far as he knew), safe and secure in the palace of a girl who must be important ("Pernie," he thought he heard one of the other girls call her), with the attention of the tall Wakan (surely a priest of some kind, but hopefully not like those evil ones in God's Port), Rist should have been completely satisfied. *But nothing here is familiar, just these dead messages from dead people.* Like all other People in The Tharn's Lands, Rist was not physically capable of shedding tears, but a primitive drive in his DNA caused his eyes to squint and swell.

CHAPTER SIXTEEN

"*R*ist," Wakan called as he came across the room around the stacks of books, "there you are, my lad! What are you doing back here? I thought you had tried to escape, shackles and all." He saw the spindles, totems, that Rist had left lying around on the floor where was sitting. "What are those, Rist? Some kind of gods?" At the one common phrase they both used, Rist jerked his eyes up at the priest. He stood, holding one of the spindles in his Reading hand, pointing at it with his right forefinger. He was unable to focus on the details with his eyes, but could feel by touch every nuance that the writer had carved, all those years ago. Wakan didn't understand, so Rist held up the totem close to his own eyes, as blurry as ever, and kept pointing to the carvings on it. He mimed carving on it, with an invisible knife.

Eyes wide, Wakan finally understood. "My god, Rist, you *read*—and I suppose you also *write*—on these, these, spindles, spools?" Taking the totem from Rist, he pretended to read it by sight. "God. Cloth. God. Rist. Wakan," he said slowly, looking at Rist's reaction. Rist beamed; the man understood. But that's not what the totem said, not the trader's report on ice profits. He pondered a moment. *Wakan must be pretending to read, but doesn't know our language. But at least it's a start!*

Wakan smiled, too. *At least it's a start!*

IT TOOK THE TWO OF THEM SEVERAL DAYS OF INTENSIVE, FULL-TIME daily effort to work out a useful vocabulary of common words, though Rist's tongue had difficulty forming some sounds: "Pin-chess," "Pree-stuh," "Shadoo-Fowl," "Dawk Hie-lanz." Pernie was pleased with the spoken progress, but Rist would never learn to pronounce her full name, so "Pin-chess" she would remain. She thought it most endearing. (Wakan had already warned him, in strict confidence, never to call her "Phe-nee!)

They both found that verbs were best learned by demonstrating the actions they represented. "Sit," "stand," "run," "bow," "wave," "read," (though neither thoroughly understood what the other meant by that), "burn," "eat," "drink," and so on. Nouns were easier, and to their surprise, some were common in both languages: "water," "spit," "bug," "flies," "fish," though with slightly different intonations. Wakan was convinced that once there had been some one common language that had changed in different lands over the ages, keeping only a few of its original sounds. He knew he would never have the time to investigate that hypothesis further, but would keep making mental notes and someday write it down for others to pursue.

After a week, Rist could converse in a pidgin Lowland tongue, even though Wakan told him that there were a dozen languages in everyday use throughout the adjacent Highland nations. "Even more than that, counting all the sub-tribes."

During these language lessons, Rist was kept in leg chains and in the lower regions of the palace, so that he could not see the outside, not know where he was, or be able to plan an escape even if he could somehow get out of his iron shackles. He wanted to go out at night, and see if the goddess Pale Lady rose into the sky here in the Lowlands as She had in the Warm Lands, and whether the daytime god, Shining One, remained a bright disk in the sky, too brilliant to view. Of course back home under the Misty Sky, the goddess was called the Wen of the Mist—never revealing her true face through the everlasting cloud cover, a beautiful face dark-scarred, as the god's priest had told him, by the Dark One in an ancient war, and now festooned with the sparkling colored jewels given her by her shining god-mate. Rist had discovered that the male god of The Tharn's Lands, Pursuing Dimness, was simply the same god Shining One, only as seen behind clouds, a discovery that nobody in The Tharn's Lands had ever spoken of.

Rist felt as if yet other discoveries were to be made, new ideas that his creative twin, Rusk, would love to know about. What use they would be in his daily life, he had no idea, but a curiosity kept building. *Why do all these outlanders know some much more than we People do, back in The Tharn's Lands?* he wondered. *And why has no one ever found out these things before me?* The robed priest, Wakan, seemed to know almost everything. Once that man learned to speak better, Rist concluded, he might be able to explain.

DAYS LATER, ONE MORNING AFTER FIRSTMEAL, RIST ASKED WAKAN A question that had been bothering him since the day he was captured. "Wakan. What is red godslight? How it shine? How guard see me on top of Dawk Hielanz?"

"Hold on, Rist," Wakan replied. "I will answer your questions in order. The red godslight is attached to the far-seer. It is just one of the mysterious objects that the gods left for us when they departed, back at the beginning of time, after they made the world and all that's in it." Rist didn't understand half of that statement, and the priest couldn't answer follow-on questions about who the gods were, where they had gone, and why some were being found by The Tharn's People in The Ice back home. Wakan wasn't certain what Rist had even meant by that. Ice was a rare commodity in the Lowlands, and only found on mountaintops in High Antis, or in frozen ponds during Season Cold.

The little man seemed to think there was a lot of it in his homeland, permanently there. "High like Dawk Hielanz, Wakan. For true."

Accepting Rist's story as merely another tall tale, Wakan explained that many of the devices the gods had left behind no longer worked, as if they had died, and in long-ago times, people back in the High Antis had buried them, with full honors and reverence. "The far-seer lets your eyes observe things far away. The red beam of light is an aiming device attached to it. A spot of light touches things that the far-seer sees, so you know where it is pointing. So when the guard captain saw your mirror flashes at the top of the cliffs, he looked through his far-seer and the beam of light showed him exactly where it was pointed. The natural tremors of his hand were enough, so far away, to make the jiggling patterns you saw." A few more minutes of explanation and Rist was mostly satisfied. But not entirely. Something had not registered in the little man's mind.

"But how could he *see* me, so far up there?"

"The far-seer device that the gods left behind," Wakan explained, "it lets you see far away as if were up close." Wakan's answer, half of which Rist understood, stunned the little man.

"You make eyes see better, far away, with far-seer?" Wakan nodded, glad that his captive understood so quickly. Then Rist took a deep breath, trying to think as his twin Rusk would, as his Sire would, *in a different way.* "Can far-seer—make *Rist* eyes"—he pointed to them—"see what—*Wakan* eyes see? Close?" Rist moved his forefinger from his eyes to his extended fingertips, repeating the motion until the taller man dropped his jaw.

Wakan was astonished. A few minutes of conversation revealed to him why Rist was taking so long to learn from books, was not able to interpret symbols on paper: *He can't see them! His eyesight is blurred close up.* Eventually Wakan understood that Rist's people could not see clearly anything within about three arm's lengths from them—faces, books (if they had any). Not even, *especially* even, the marked surfaces of their reading materials. The written language of The Tharn's Lands was apparently entirely composed of the myriad of symbols carved into those spindles, "totems" they were called. No wonder no scholar in Motherland had ever deciphered those markings! Wakan had never heard of such a thing, though a faint memory of some elderly blind tradespeople in Mother's City came through, of an old man making marks on the posts of his fruit vendor's stand. "To know how much produce I have left on the table," the old one had replied, when asked. The priest promised Rist that he would have the glass smith see what he might be able to do for the little man's near vision. He was amazed. What other surprises might little Rist have?

———

A DAY LATER, FROM THE SHELVES FARTHER BACK IN THE MUSEUM, RIST brought Wakan one of the dark crystal balls, a godsphere. But now it was lit from within, now it was making sounds. "Rist touch it, and it talks," he said. "What this ball, Wakan?" he asked. "How talk?"

Shocked, Wakan only gaped. "Your *touch* made it talk? None of *us* —" He dropped the subject. Somehow the little man's presence had unlocked a mystery that Wakan and his assistants could not. They had only ever had minimal response from years of handling these ShadowFall spheres, nothing that ever lasted or displayed anything significant, at best only short meaningless gibberish or weird patterns. The priest shook his head. In the High Antis, there were priests who could touch the godspheres and get them to talk, to teach, before they faded to darkness and grew quiet. Were the godspheres in Motherland meant to be touched by Rist and his people? How would such a thing be, and why would the gods—or ancients—do it?

Wakan was aware of what the godsphere was displaying while Rist held it. "I am not sure why it talks, but I know some of what it is showing us. See these colored areas?" Rist looked, but could only make out blurred blotches of color. "They represent areas of this round world." At Rist's quizzical look, the priest explained, "Back in my homeland, scholars have studied some of these godspheres that were uncovered from ancient ruins for which we have no record. The scholars could eventually translate some of the spoken languages, from which our nation benefitted greatly. They think that some of the globes represent our world, all of it." Rist listened intently, but only sketchily understood any of it. Wakan repeated, "Our whole round world. Motherland, the Dry Lands and your Highlands, your river, they are all part of a round world, like this globe."

Rist laughed at the idea. "No, Wakan, world flat, not ball. Look outside and see." Eventually the concept became clearer, but only after Wakan explained—repeating himself several times—that the Wen of the Mist, called "Moon" in Motherland, was a round world itself, and that what the WarmLanders had called Shining One (here, "Sun") was a burning round world the same size. "We know this, Rist, because when our world comes between them at certain times, a circular shadow is cast on the Moon. That proves our world is round, too. Otherwise, such a shadow could not be cast." Rist believed that the big man believed his own story, but reserved judgment until he found some other proof. *A round world? I cannot think this new thought!* As so many times before, he wished his twin, Rusk, were here to listen to these strange stories. Without a totem to carve this information onto, Rist knew that he himself would probably not believe the conversation later.

Later he asked Wakan again what the voice in the illuminated globe was saying. Wakan shrugged his shoulders and frowned. "We can read some of the writing, Rist, we believe, but have no idea of what the voice is telling us. Listen for yourself; can you help translate?" When Rist touched the globe again, its light came on from within, and its voice began an unintelligible speech:

"Twenty-third-century Earth political map. Touch any continent to hear and see its history."

Neither man understood the language, though Rist thought that *"rrth"* sounded similar to the name of the peat fields back home, *"mirr."* And some of the other sounds were partly familiar to ones that Wakan knew in several Lowland and Highland tongues. But nothing made any real sense.

Rist was fascinated with the eerie light coming from inside the globe, as the colors on its surface appeared to rotate. On a hunch, he stroked it with his reading hand to feel if it had any writing carved into its smooth surface. To his surprise, the images stopped their rotation and the sphere lit up brighter, with small but very realistic moving pictures appearing on its surface. Wakan could see them in detail, but all Rist could make out were more moving blurs of color.

The voice suddenly changed in tone, becoming louder and more authoritative, though the men still could not understand it:

"Your precise coordinates at this time are not available," it pronounced, *"because of a lack of geosat contact and resultant absence of metadata. However, available networks of scattered geographic quantum sensors indicate that your location, within a two-kilometer circle of probability, is approximately two hundred kilometers southeast of Newer Orleans, in the Gulf of Mexico. Your altitude data show that you are on the seabed, over six hundred meters below mean sea level. If—"*

The voice ended in a crackling noise, and the inner light faded away. Despite repeated touching by the two men, the globe did not respond. "I am afraid it died, little Rist," Wakan said sadly. "This often happens when we somehow bring ancient god-things to life. Their life forces flare for a few minutes, then vanish." Without saying it aloud, the priest figured that somehow the globes and the far-seer tubes were related. He wondered why the godslights attached to the far-seer tubes kept functioning, being that they were probably as old as the spheres. When he thought about how they were used, outside all day with the guards or atop his observation tower, the idea hit him: *Maybe it is because they are out in the sunlight, not locked up in a dark museum?* What a strange thought! Was it possible they drew energy from sunlight? He filed that strange supposition in memory, for later retrieval.

"Ball talked to *us*," Rist said. "How it know us?" Wakan shook his head. Though he had given it passing interest years before, remembering how some priests in his homeland had occasionally accessed godspheres, he had not known about this mysterious response feature, how mere touch might bring them to life. But he had heard the term *"Mess-koh"* from a hidden booming voice at the crystal dome up in the savage Nawat highlands of *Chi'a*, shortly before his capture. He had always believed that most of the godspheres had died, and that they represented this world, the vast lands around him and others far, far away, and not just some other domain of the ancient gods.

Where had Rist touched? How had he brought the globe to life? The flickering images had shown a vast sea, floating vessels of huge dimensions, and flying machines of some kind. Did the ancient gods, *people,* have such devices? Did they not take them all when they left? Wakan sat back, trying to absorb the information that little Rist had uncovered, trying to accommodate new knowledge with what he believed to be Truth. *With a stroke of his hand*, the priest thought. *Just by a mere touch, the globe recognized him as a qualified recipient of knowledge. How could that be?* Wakan had never believed in magic, but what he had witnessed was beginning to make him wonder.

The priest knew that little Rist was quite a genius in his own way, or maybe just very lucky. Or both. He wondered if all of the little man's people, so far north, were equally bright. If so, he for one would welcome the immigration of many more such intelligent—or lucky— little people to Motherland, to ShadowFall.

EVER CONCERNED ABOUT POSSIBLE THREATS TO THE MOTHERLAND, Wakan pumped Rist continuously for information about the lands and peoples upRiver above the Dark Highlands cliffs. He learned that the populous Warm Lands city in the kingdom three days upRiver, which its inhabitants impudently called "God's Port," possessed huge stone buildings, large concave mirrors for both signaling and burning— concepts Wakan had never imagined but which he could see would prove immediately useful in the Motherlands—and enormous quantities of godscloth. Wakan was certain of that last claim, as evidenced by the thousands and thousands of square meters that had fallen off the cliff with Rist. But he was not as sure of Rist's claims of how those people used it.

Pulleys? Ropes? Nets? Having never had access to godscloth cutting tools, Wakan did his best to visualize such common uses of a material that in Motherland was worth more per square meter than a pound of rare metals. He frowned. *Weapons?* But according to Rist, the highly developed civilization of sun-worshippers did not possess springbows, as far as he had seen. Furthermore, their city of God's Port being days upRiver from the waterfall, the sun-worshippers were no immediate threat, either. *Unless they decide to come down on godscloth ropes, like Rist did?*

PART FOUR

FEAR

CHAPTER SEVENTEEN

*P*rincess Perneptheranam was perplexed, upset, bothered. Early that morning, just a week after ShadowFall, after her handmaids had had their almost daily fun with little Rist, one of them, Anklya, announced a visitor, all the way from Mother's City. *The first messenger from Mother since Her congratulations on my winning the war against Four Peaks and RidgeBack, four years ago. That is never good news,* the princess thought. *Where Mother is concerned, just being left alone is always the best thing!* She hoped that there were no new wars, for which ShadowFall would have to supply troops, or even worse, to send food and weapons. She knew that Mother still wanted the secrets of ShadowFall's springbows. *If that's it, maybe we could sell it or provide her a few weapons, instead of sending our people? Without Wakan Kech's knowledge, nobody will be able to make any more of them, anyway.* That secret process was known only to him, a legacy from his distant homeland, far away through hostile tribes and unclimbable mountains, far beyond Mother's reach.

Lord Sechenal, a Mothersman, was impressive, Pernie thought. A dark-bearded fellow standing well over two meters, a giant among Motherlanders (but not much taller than Wakan Kech, she noted), he appeared in formal court attire, dressed in a kilt of extremely rare opaque tartan godscloth, a pullover to match, and a dark leather vest with straps for the swords and knives he had (graciously, but involuntarily) surrendered to the palace guards. Black boots and spurs indicated his high station, showing that he was one of fewer than a hundred horse-riders in all Motherland. Pernie often wished that her own realm had been naturally inhabited by such beautiful creatures— she owned but six—but Mother possessed the only large herd outside the surrounding highlands, and allowed only the most trusted Courtsmen to ride them. Mother's own Mothersmen palace guards retained equine rights, as did the most favored Courtsmen like Lord Sechenal. But because of the expense, Mother maintained only a limited number of horses and riders. It had never dawned on Mother or anyone else to use such rare and noble animals for plowing and other farm chores, not with oxen, cattle, and slaves so plentiful.

Keeping his deep blue eyes firmly fixed on Princess Pernepetheranam, Lord Sechenal bowed deeply, and spoke. "Your Highness, I come from your Mother, bearing Her words. An invitation and a command." Taking a small scroll from within his leather vest, he read, "Dear Daughter Princess Perneptheranam, Lordess of ShadowFall. You have held your domain for five years now, and I congratulate you on your successes. Your recent victories over your neighboring Sisters were innovative and prudent, yet not vengeful. Your crops yield enough to feed your own people and through trading, those of four other Sisterdoms. Your fishermen produce wonderful catches that we enjoy, even here in Mother's City. You are well loved, and appropriately feared, by your subjects, which is something I wish your Sisters would learn.

"However, because it has now been five years, it is incumbent upon you to send contestants to the Motherland Game, which will occur on next EqualDay. Upon that day each Sisterdom will field four champions. The outcome of The Game will determine which Sisterdom may provide ten advisors and counselors of its own choice to Mother's Court, there to serve your Mother for the next five years."

Then Lord Sechenal rolled up the scroll, handing it to Pernie's handmaid Anklya, who brought it over to the princess for confirmation.

Pernie sighed. She dictated a reply to her court recorder to give to the handsome messenger, who insisted on returning that very evening. She would have liked Lord Sechenal to remain so that she could elicit from him any court gossip that might affect ShadowFall, and perhaps even be entertained in other ways overnight. Victory in the Motherland Game was important, not only for helping direct the nation in vital policy matters, but also in the struggle of the daughters for succession rights when their Mother eventually passed. Though Pernie wanted no part of that particular battle, she could not avoid being prepared for whomever the next Mother might be. She desperately prayed that it would be her Sister Messinex of Three Rivers, the only one to whom she felt affection and respect. Previous wars of succession in past millennia had destroyed so much, killed so many, that The Game was eventually established by common consent among the Sisters as a palliative alternative to total civil war.

Pernie wanted Messinex to succeed as Mother for several reasons. Messinex was the one Sister who annually sent Pernie tribute and gifts (tropical fruits and vegetables that didn't grow in ShadowFall, and varieties of seeds for experimental planting) as well as friendly advice on surviving among their vicious enemy siblings. Being ignored—at best!—by the other eleven princesses, Pernie felt warmth only toward Messinex. There had been no other such comfort in her childhood, especially not from the Lordess Mother. The common Mother of all thirteen Sisters, their Mother had been impregnated by thirteen different fathers, men whose names would never be known to anyone else. Men who were executed and disposed of quickly, after the successful births of their baby girls. Nobody ever knew the fates of her baby boys.

And now our heartless Mother calls for the horrible Game again. More brutality, more death. *Wakan and I always talk about more civilized ways to run Motherland, but this ancient ritual is a grim reality I must face. I will think it over but I must discuss this with him; he continually advises me that I must often make life and death decisions for the good of the many, sometimes even unjust ones, and so I shall. But who among my ShadowFallers do I send out to die?*

CHAPTER EIGHTEEN

*A*s the sun rose on the day that Lord Sechenal arrived, Wakan was allowing Rist to accompany him outside, unshackled, up to the observation tower on the roof of the palace, the little man wearing his slitted eye patches for sun protection. Wakan figured that Rist would enjoy seeing the extent of the Sisterdom, and even those dark cliffs from which he had descended. The glass smith had not yet perfected any lenses that would help Rist's severe farsightedness, but Wakan knew that up here atop the palace, the unimpeded views in all directions would allow the little man to appreciate from whence he had come.

Wakan felt a sense of satisfaction in sharing knowledge with Rist, something he would not have done with any man from the other surrounding highlands or for that matter, any man in Motherland, either. For Rist could not ever be a threat to ShadowFall or any of Motherland; Wakan had come to understand from the little man's tales, that his homeland of The Tharn's Lands was located in the far distant north, upRiver. After some conversation, he was able to explain to Rist that a *kilometer* was roughly the equivalent of three-fingerths of a dimmarch. "Smaller than *mile*," Rist said with a smile; Wakan did not recognize that reference; Motherland's system of measurements was as ancient as Time immemorial. But by calculating an estimated speed of river current, Wakan figured that Rist's home lay hundreds of kilometers north, maybe a few thousand or more. *Far enough not to worry*, he concluded.

Though he did not believe Rist's story about kilometers-high mountains of ice "at the end of the world," Wakan realized that Tharnslanders would never come south in large numbers, and in fact, estimated that ShadowFall itself probably had as many thousands of inhabitants as Rist's entire homeland. Wakan did not understand the tales of the "Misty Sky," thinking it impossible that human life could exist without ever seeing the sun and the moon except through mist and clouds. *But somewhere in all those wild stories,* Wakan concluded, *there is some element of truth. And that truth, whatever it is, is not a threat to us.*

"This is the far-seer, Rist," the High Priest said, putting Rist's eye to the smaller end of a tapered, meter-long metal tube. "I have pointed it at the Dark Highlands, at the point where you came down. Take a look."

Rist squinted, unfamiliar with the process of looking into a small opening. Removing his slitted eyepatches, at first he could make out nothing, then as Wakan adjusted something on the far-seer tube, an image formed. He could see trees, the same kind of trees he had fallen into! Jerking away from the eyepiece, Rist tried to find those same trees without the help of the tube, but saw only tiny dark green patches where Wakan was pointing. He moved back to the eyepiece and let out a gasp. The far-seer did exactly that, what its name said it did! Rist breathed deeply and said, "I never saw such things. How it works?"

Wakan laughed and said that it was something the gods had done with light and glass, that ShadowFall only had five of the devices—the one the guard had used to find and signal him, three other small ones good for both eyes, and another one like this one, too big to bring up the stairs to the open tower here. *Strangely*, he thought, *many tubes that look like far-seers don't seem to have any lenses in them, just shiny flat areas at both ends. Even though their godslights still function.* But a working godslight under a dead far-seer was awkward to use, though many of them were stacked in the museum below.

"Now, Rist, look at all the rest of ShadowFall—fields, the river, the herds." Rist strained to see, but Wakan laughed. "No, little friend, look at them through the far-seer." Rist did that, amazed to watch field hands from this distance, looking like tiny insects. He wished his twin, Rusk, could look through this amazing far-seer. *How would he react; what would he do?* At that moment, as he swung the vision machine a little to the south, hoping to see more tiny workers scurrying around like bugs, something came into Rist's view that stunned him. Gasping, he turned and looked up to Wakan. "Wakan," he stumbled out the word, "You have *birds*? *Two-legs*?"

Wakan heard his name, of course, and then the word "emu." Shocked that Rist knew the word, he said it himself. "Emu? Emu?"

Rist heard Wakan saying, in Peoplespeak, "two-legs, two-legs." He nodded his head, enthusiastically. "*Two-legs! Wakan, emus!*" Rist fairly shouted.

Wakan replied, "All right, Rist, we both know that word. But why are you so excited?" Thinking for a moment, it struck him—Rist must have emus back in Tharnsland. He asked him that.

"Yes, yes, Wakan," the little man answered, "in The Tharn's Lands we have two-legs, emus, but not so many. You have, have"— remembering Cruthar's numbers lessons weeks ago in God's Port —"manyhands, I mean, *hundreds,* of two-legs. ShadowFall is so rich!"

After a while, Rist was able to make Wakan understand that in his homeland, emus—two-legs—were rare and expensive. And that they were ridden, mostly by higher-caste men for hunting velks and game animals, for occasional fast transport, and for war. But Wakan could not conceive of Rist sitting atop an emu, and laughed aloud at the ridiculous image it brought to mind.

Suddenly, down below in front of the palace, Rist heard a snorting sound, and looking over the edge of the tower, saw a large dark figure of a man riding toward the Palace on a strange animal. "What is that, that, four-leg, Wakan? It looks like a skinny beezt, but made different."

"*Horse*, Rist. It is called a *horse*. People ride them." Below them at that moment, Lord Sechenal, Mother's messenger, was handing the reins to a stablehand. Having recognized the visitor, Wakan gloomily concluded that The Mother must have sent a summons for The Game. *It's been five years,* he thought. *But I was hoping we could delay our participation for another five.* Groaning inwardly at the trouble that man was bringing, Wakan calmly explained to Rist how the saddle, stirrups and reins were used to control the animal. Rist watched closely as the big LowLander swung from his saddle on the 'horse'. "Same thing me, Wakan, I sit on two-leg, *emu,* with saddle and reins. I ride him and I fight *velks* on him."

Finally comprehending Rist's explanation, Wakan's eyes grew wide. "How do you fight on your emu, Rist? What weapons do you use?" Rist mimed thrusting a spear and swinging a sword, which didn't surprise the priest. "And bolos, Wakan, swinging iron bolos," he said swinging his right arm in circles above his head, finally letting go of the imaginary projectiles. "With bolos I kill velks, Wakan, bigger than you." As Rist kept recreating his battle stance, Wakan took all of the action in, smiling. A surprising thought came to mind: *I hope you can truly fight well on your big bird, little Rist, because I think I may have an important battle coming up for you!* He had a plan that would prove the little man a liar—or a hero!

WHEN HE ANSWERED PERNIE'S SUMMONS LATER THAT MORNING, Wakan Kech winced at her official confirmation of the news of the Motherland Game, which he had suspected from observing Lord Sechenal's unscheduled visit. Wakan had witnessed several Games in the years he was in Mother's Court. Vicious affairs, each Sister trying to gain advantage over the others, usually by introducing some new kind of fighter. Wakan remembered a blond giant of a man, over two and a half meters tall—from WaterEdge, was it?—in a Game fifteen years before, carrying a sword his own length, who cut down swathes of other combatants, though grievously wounded himself. In the end, his princess's Sisterdom had won the contest, though he himself died shortly after. *Some kind of victory!* Wakan remembered with disgust. Because only one team—usually just one champion—would be left standing at the end, the fighters almost always fought for themselves individually, rather than as partners as a team, making the contests rely on brute force and endurance rather than planning and skill. *No wonder Motherland continues to roil in savagery!* Wakan thought. *That is no way to choose royal advisors!* Though a devoted student of the long history of Motherland, he was not certain that The Game was much of an improvement over the internecine warfare of the olden days.

Though Mother, and therefore the Courtsmen, all claimed that The Game produced new tactics, tested new weapons, and strengthened the warriors, Wakan never saw that happen. In his experience the slaughter of at least forty-seven men out of the forty-eight, and sometimes even that last man, had never accomplished anything other than a cycling through court of a new set of ambitious thieves who suddenly had five years in which to do their best to steal everything they could for their Princess's Sisterdom and for themselves. It did work, roughly, to some extent, if only by preventing all power from concentrating in very few hands for many years, since the new advisors themselves were later exiled from court for the rest of their lives.

How inefficient a process, Wakan thought, *when peaceful negotiations could do the same thing without bloodshed!* But he knew that Mother, the other Sisters, and the court all enjoyed watching the brutal hours-long spectacle of death by combat, and the anticipation of their spoils should their own Sisterdom prevail.

"Princess," Wakan said to Pernie, "Our guardsmen are the strongest and best prepared of any men here in ShadowFall. Though as loyal as they are to each other, I would not like to see any one of them have to kill his fellow man. They must fight as an integrated team."

Pernie nodded. "I agree, Wakan, as radical as that idea is. It will come as a shock to the other Sisters. Because it will take us several weeks to travel to Mother's City, we now only have a little over two months to prepare. So as to find the very best fighters, people that my Sisters might not expect to encounter in the arena, I want you to quietly survey the field hands—and the fishermen," she added, "and try to find the strongest and quickest among them. Even a woman, if you think one qualifies. Find a few dozen, let the guardsmen train them in individual combat for two weeks, and then select the best from among those. And do another weeding out two weeks later, and then one more time just before we leave for Mother's City. Let my guards compete with that last group. That should give us at least enough good men from which to choose our four champions."

Wakan quickly made mental notes. He was proud of his charge's maturity, her willingness to think things through, to understand alternatives, even unpleasant ones, and to prepare for all eventualities. *Even though she is the youngest of the thirteen Sisters, I believe that Pernie is the wisest already. How wonderful it would be if she could become the next Mother!* A treasonous thought, that, which he quickly set aside. But the appeal of such a situation was there, and the possible glory for a new Motherland culture, one much more civilized and benign, was a vision that once considered could never be swept away. But first he wanted to evaluate little Rist's wild claims about bird-riding and fighting. Could ShadowFall possibly have a secret weapon?

EARLY THE NEXT MORNING WAKAN TOOK AN UNSHACKLED RIST OUT on a walking tour of the nearer fields and the pastures of ShadowFall. As they passed through the city, looking back, Rist noted that the palace of the Princess stood at least three times as tall as any other building, its polished pink marble towers glistening in the moist dew. Unlike the larger city of God's Port, up in the Dark Highlands, ShadowFall had no temple and other large buildings than the palace. But apart from the severed head mounted on a spike at the Arch of ShadowFall, Rist had seen no evidence that Princess Perneptheranam was anywhere nearly as brutal as those priests upRiver. Remembering the execution of the thief for allowing Cruthar and himself into the godscloth warehouse, Rist shuddered. Execution by focused sunlight was very cruel.

Wakan and Rist crossed a wooden bridge that spanned the river.

Rist marveled at the idea; he had never even considered that a passageway could be built over a river. Of course, in The Tharn's Lands, the river was very wide and swift, with many rapids downstream, especially when traveling to the Warm Lands. But still, Rist knew that his twin, Rusk, would not accept the idea of a bridge as it was, but would immediately start planning ways to improve on it. With that in mind, Rist determined to come up with his own concepts, based on his travels to date, for ShadowFall. Like The Tharn back home, and the priests of God's Port, one's prosperity, if not his life as well, depended on being valuable to the ruler. *I hope I can be valuable to Pernie,* he thought. *I just hope I can. Maybe something with the birds, the two-legs?*

After a midmeal of strange-smelling meats, spicy vegetables and sweet wine at a vendor's tree-shaded courtyard café, Wakan and Rist continued on the tour. Rist was not familiar with the "crops," tall plants standing in countless straight rows, vegetation three times his height, with yellow threads above them and thick long leaves, wrapped in bundles. "Corn," Wakan said, peeling off green leaves and revealing a bumpy yellow tapered cylinder underneath. "It feeds us, and feeds our cattle." The "cattle" Wakan referred to resided in their hundreds in a mud-filled lot behind a fence of twisted thornlike wire, emanating an overpowering stench. Similar to the beezt of his own home realm, these "cows" were larger, with less hair and smaller horns. The "horses" they passed by were much more interesting to him, but Wakan pointed out that the Princess had only a small herd, half a dozen. "Horses do not breed well anywhere in Motherland, Rist," the priest said, "Many of them die at birth. So they are very rare and very expensive." He did not tell the small man that his guards were secretly training between five to ten men to ride each of those horses, and to carry spears and springbows with them. *More surprise weapons,* he thought, *for when the next Sister comes looking for plunder.*

An hour later, after traveling over several kilometers of irrigated flatlands, they arrived at a fenced-off field. Rist grew excited, running up to the tall thorn-wired enclosure. "Emus, Wakan. Many, many emus!"

Wakan smiled. Now he would see if Rist was telling tales, or if he indeed could ride one of these big birds. "Can you ride one, little Rist?" he asked, calling on an accompanying foreman to give the little man anything he asked for.

"A rope with a loose noose on it?" the foreman asked, handing it to Rist. "You asked for it, here it is, but what—?" He broke off in mid-question as Rist walked briskly through an opened gate, swinging the rope over his head in an ever-widening circle. The foreman and Wakan were both surprised; they had never seen anything like it, as Rist approached a gaggle of emus that just stood looking at the small dark creature now walking toward them with something in his hands.

Rist carefully approached a group of five emus who just stared at him. "They do not recognize me or the rope," he whispered to himself. "Now, all I have to do is—" He roped a two-leg over its head with the first throw, quickly tightening the loop. The bird, surprised, stood there as Rist went up and stroked its legs in the manner he had been taught cycles ago by his Sire. Responding to the same instinct as had its relatives in Rist's homeland, the bird kneeled. Rist pulled out the soft cattle-skin square hood material he had requested, and placed it over the emu's head.

"Good," Rist said in a calming voice, "now don't get upset when I —" At that, he jumped across the bird's back, quickly grasping its body between his legs. "I should have asked for a saddle while I was at it," he said regretfully. "But the reins I put under the beak here should help." To his surprise, the emu accepted his presence as a rider. He had been worried about severe pecks from that beak, and was wearing his eyepatches just in case.

From the other side of the fence, the two Motherlanders were astonished. "I never would have guessed, Sire," the foreman said in amazement, "that a little man could ride a bird like that. Amazing!" Wakan agreed, but kept looking closely at Rist's actions. *If this one Tharnslander can ride and fight on that bird, then I need to recruit many more of his countrymen. A bird-riding cavalry of our own!*

As Rist removed the bird's head covering, the emu just turned and looked at its rider somewhat quizzically, shaking itself, stepping right to left in a parody of dancing. After a few minutes during which the little man made soothing sounds and stroked his new steed, the bird settled down. "Go!" Rist shouted, loud enough to be heard behind the fence. "Go, two-leg!"—this latter in Wakan's own language. The man-ridden bird swiftly ran off into the distance, and for a moment Wakan wondered if he had made a mistake to let Rist loose like this, free to run away. He cursed softly, but soon the bird and man returned, Rist grinning from ear to ear. "Give me saddle and proper reins, Wakan, and I will have a better steed than back home!"

On the return walk to the palace, Wakan asked Rist if he thought he might be able to ride to battle on an emu. "Against *men*?" Wakan nodded, solemnly explaining the importance of the Motherland Game to the Princess and her Sisterdom. Surprised and initially appalled at the suggestion, Risk considered his options—remain as a strange pet for the palace handmaidens *Until they tire of me!*—or use his velk-hunting skills against the enemies of the Princess. After a minute of silence, he said, "If no other way, Wakan, if ShadowFall need me, I fight. For her, for you."

As Wakan shook his hand, Rist sighed, but knew that at last there was something here in Motherland that only *he* could do, something he could contribute and not just feel like a plaything for those palace girls. At *that* thought, he envisioned the maid, Anklya, his favorite, but put that memory away. *Until tonight!* he thought with a grin.

———

"WAKAN, I WON'T HAVE IT, DO YOU HEAR!" PRINCESS PERNIE SELDOM shouted, and never at Wakan Kech, but now she was extremely upset. The priest wondered at first if she was in her menses, but caught himself. His herbs most often counteracted the worst effects of that period, and even so, she was still absolute ruler, commanding respect even in his own thoughts! "You will not expose our little Rist to the dangers of the Motherland Game! What if he—he—*dies*?"

Wakan had expected some resistance to the idea of Rist riding a war-emu as a surprise entry in The Game, an event that would upset and unbalance many of the other Sisterdom's champions. *They all expect smash-and-slash brute-force attacks,* Wakan mused, *not an assault by a tiny man on a big bird. Not attacks with spiked iron bolos and spears from the rider, and from the huge clubbed feet of the bird!* And Rist was going to try out needle-spiked anklet spurs for the birds, so that they could kill more efficiently, even without a rider. Wakan was impressed with Rist's creativity, though a bit disappointed that he was taking to killing so easily. In preparation for further field tests, Wakan and a guard trainer had provided Rist with a saddle, reins, stirrups, a cinchable belly strap—and Rist's requested spiked iron bolo balls. The little man had performed admirably against the dummy opponents. *The springbow comes last,* Wakan thought. A small one, scaled down just for Rist's own size. Another deadly surprise for the other Sisters' fighters!

To the Princess, who now looked at him with anger, Wakan bowed and smiled. "My Princess, had I not seen our little Rist in the last few days in practice combat against our well-padded guards and simulated straw targets, I would not have dared make such a suggestion." He breathed in deeply. "And that is just with the iron throwing bolos and small spears we have made for him. With his own springbow, he will be invincible." *I hope*, he added silently.

Princess Pernie sniffed. Wakan could tell she was thinking of Rist's talents and possible fighting skills, weighing the risks against advantages. "You have always been correct, Wakan, and I know you have only the best interests of ShadowFall in mind. But do you truly think we should risk the life of our guest at The Game?" Shaking her head, she motioned for Wakan to come closer to her chair; in the throne room a court recorder would be taking notes on everything, for eventual reporting to Mother. But here in Pernie's private chambers, she and Wakan often had wide-ranging discussion not for the record or anyone else's ears. "My maids never tire of him, especially Anklya," she told the priest. "He is the most energetic man they have ever encountered," she concluded, smiling. "I myself have wondered, but think it not wise. Who knows what kinds of maladies he may carry?"

She smiled again. "However, in a few more weeks, if my maids stay well, who knows?"

Wakan laughed. "My Princess, The Game is on EqualDay. By that time, Rist will have learned the springbow, and will have studied what the guards and I can teach him of the uncivilized combat tactics of the other Sisterdoms." As Pernie considered this, and the possible success of her own people at The Game, Wakan said, "And you will still have time before The Game, should you still desire, to…to introduce Rist to your own Game." As the Princess chuckled, Wakan knew that he had succeeded. Rist would fight; he would earn the privileged status afforded him by the beneficence of ShadowFall. *Or die trying.*

CHAPTER NINETEEN

*L*ordess Mother awoke in pain, joints aching excruciatingly, severe tight cramps in her legs. Turning her head on her satin pillow, she snorted as she saw her sleeping bedmate, one of those big blond muscular slaves captured from the highlands of the far northeastern edge of Motherland—*Her* Motherland! One kept whole and not emasculated, per her orders. *Thank the gods I did that!* she thought, smiling at the night's memories.

Rousing herself in the nude with the aid of her ever-present four chambermaids, she stood as those darlings washed, wiped, douched and perfumed her, clothing her in iridescent, multicolored godscloth. As Mother raised her feet one at a time for slippers to be fitted, she motioned to the tall, dark Mothersman standing watch by the chamber door in his black leather armor with a long broadsword, ever ready to do her bidding. With a finger motion across her throat, she nodded her head toward the sleeping lover. *With any luck*, she thought, *I won't have any of that one's seed take hold. I've been lucky for nigh onto sixteen years now.* A smile briefly crossed her face, thoughts of little Pernie, her lastborn. *Now there is one princess I do love*, she thought. *But the only one!* Thinking of Pernie's father, she smiled. *I'm glad I let that one live. But back then I was young and in love. Not since! Never again!*

As she entered the toilet room, a brief scream echoed from her boudoir, followed by a choking gurgle. Mother smiled. It would be a great day!

After firstmeal, a lively concoction of tart fruits from the southern Three Rivers Sisterdom of Princess Messinex, mixed with lightly buttered, soft-smelling whitefish from WaterEdge on the eastern coast, Mother and her retinue of maids walked through cavernous hallways to the enormous open space under the dome of Mother's Palace, now empty save for the ever-present contingent of leather-armored Mothersmen guards. Still feeling the effects of the previous night's strenuous lovemaking, she continued walking shakily toward the pyramidal Crystal Throne dais. *This place is always cold and damp in the morning*, she complained to herself. *Miran Kech tells me that the dome here generates its own weather because of its volume of air, and because sunlight bathes the outside of the stones in warmth.* She liked and respected the wisdom of her Kech priest, as she had done with his predecessor, Wakan, but hoped that an even wiser man existed somewhere in her domain. *I do wish some smarter priest could figure out a way to keep this place more comfortable!*

At the foot of the staircase, the maids stopped and remained behind. From this point on, tradition demanded that only Mother could continue, climbing up the too-high, changing-color steps leading up to the large, transparent crystal chair. Though she had performed this ritual daily for over thirty-five years, Mother still feared the Crystal Throne—sitting on it, the loss of control, the surrendering to the mysterious crystal. Though not much larger than a high-backed chair in the dining hall, the throne was the one visible conduit through which Mother supposedly communicated with the Goddess. While sitting on it she would hear voicelike sounds but never could understand them, see images and visions that had no meaning to her, feel sensations that made no sense at all. During her reign, after having secretly suffocated her predecessor, the old woman who had been her own birth mother, Mother had suffered continuing self-doubts about what the goddess or gods were trying to say. But she could never let on; the Crystal Throne was the sole basis of her power over the multitudes of Motherland.

Raising her godscloth covering, Mother turned and slowly sat her bare skin on the nearly transparent stone-slab seat, and waited for the Message to arrive. An instant of cold, followed by a flash of stinging and sharp tingling that caused her an intake of breath. Then suddenly she felt as though her flesh itself was gone, replaced by a warmth that suffused upward through her body, cleansing it, placing her mind at ease. *Is this love?* she wondered. *But why does the Ancient Mother never show Herself? And why do I never remember what happens?* Still hating to submit, she nevertheless felt her own will vanishing into a now-familiar kaleidoscope of patterned, multidimensional arrays of symbols and sounds, images and voices, unknown colors and ethereal musical tones. Information of some kind, she supposed, but none of which she understood. "Quantum integration initiated?" a faint whisper seemed to ask in some unknown language. "Protocols established. No local lunar operator present to q-comm." *More meaningless noises!* As had happened almost every day for all these years, Mother's last conscious thought before slipping away was, *This must be the lyrical language of the gods. But I don't know the words! And I can never remember anything of it!* As she slipped into unconsciousness, she made her repeated effort to understand what was happening, but she never remembered anything other than a swirl of unbelievable colors and a descent into *nothingness*.

After a seeming eternity, Mother regained her senses, shaking her head so hard that her long red pigtails snaked around her shoulders. She stood and smoothed her colorful godscloth robe, then raised her arms and loudly blessed her maids, her Mothersmen, and all the citizens of Motherland. She always did this, because it was always expected. *They think I receive divine wisdom from this throne*, she mused. *And maybe I do. But I'll be damned if I recall any of it!*

Feeling the fruitless decades of unfulfilled frustration, she frowned, feeling an uncontrollable rage mounting, a roaring rising in her ears, yellow sparks flashing through her vision, a fire in her brain, the all-consuming headache that followed every session on the throne. *When*

Mother's not happy, she thought with sudden fury, *no one is going to be happy!* As she carefully walked down the high stairs, ignoring the rainbow of colors that followed her descending steps, she mentally began choosing victims, the more innocent the better. *More people are going to die today!* Recognizing the sudden shift in Mother's visage, the handmaidens took shallow breaths, lowered their heads, and averted Her eyes, praying that She would not vent Her wrath upon them.

CHAPTER TWENTY

*F*ar to the northeast of Mother's City, in the Sisterdom of ShadowFall, the High Priest Wakan Kech and his liege, Princess Perneptheranam, were going through intense discussions about the possible outcome of the upcoming Motherland Game. In her private chamber, with nothing being written down by the usually ever-present recorder, Pernie enjoyed sniffing at some burning incense fragrances while she spoke with her senior advisor and mentor. Wakan found the scent almost intoxicating, but he was too wise to become too enamored with the Princess herself. *Though she is the most attractive female presence in Motherland,* he thought. *Of course, I was present at her birth, and…*

"If the last man standing is my subject," the princess said, "I will be allowed to provide ten chosen advisors to Mother's Court, replacing those from Six Points, who will be sent home for good. Getting rid of those men, those who agitated for my Sisters to attack us, will be very important. And each Sister will be required to give me failure tribute, any one thing I ask for. Even more so, it will be my chance to exert some pressure, choose some direction, for a better Motherland." She frowned. "But I remain fearful for my little Rist. I am very fond of our bird-rider." Wakan knew that the princess had indeed grown very close to the little brown man. For the same reasons, Rist had become the favorite of palace handmaidens as well, spending most nights with Anklya, a tall blonde beauty. *A surprising young man*, he acknowledged, *for one who is barely taller than my knees!*

Outwardly, Wakan just nodded. A lot would be riding, literally, with their miniscule warrior; in his opinion, winning The Game was all-important for ShadowFall and for Motherland itself. With his subtle arguments in favor of education and freedom for all Motherland's peoples to enjoy, as did the citizens of his homeland in the High Antis, Wakan and Pernie both had hoped for years to be able to convince Mother's Court that Her subjects—in reality, her *slaves*, as were all people in Motherland—should be educated, given a consistent treatment for offenses, hardly ever death, and tortured only when necessary, not on mere whim. But any given part of that liberalization was a revolutionary concept, and except for Sister Messinex, far to the south, not one other Sister would hear any of it.

Millennia of slavery and noble privilege argued against any change in the administration of power, and Mother usually went with the majority opinion of her daughters. Eleven of the thirteen Sisters ruled as absolute despots, causing Wakan Kech much grief to contemplate. His own homeland had no tyrants, no slaves, and all its citizens were educated to some degree. Had he not been captured by Mothersmen all those years ago, he would still be enjoying a peaceful, honorable life in that mountain nation. *At least, until Mother's armies found the High Antis!* He sighed at the thought. One of his goals all these years had been to keep Motherland's attention away from his own homeland. So far, it had worked; the immediate surrounding Highlands offered all manner of tribes and nations for conquest and slaves and resources. His High Antis was thousands of kilometers beyond any of those. He shook off the disturbing thought. *There's too much I need to attend to, here and now!*

The ancient and honorable tradition of "last man standing" in The Game bothered the Princess and the priest the most. "If possible, I would have all of my people coming home," she said softly, "especially little Rist." Wakan agreed, but pointed out that in all the centuries of history for which records existed, no full team of four had ever survived the melee, and that the chances of any Sisterdom's champion surviving to the end now were no better than one in fifty-two. "If that, Your Highness. I recall that one time, years ago, when you were very young, the last man standing, a blond giant, was mortally wounded and died later the same day. But he did win the contest for WaterEdge."

Pernie was deep in thought for several minutes, until the standing priest grew uncomfortable. Finally she spoke, slowly, in her official voice: "Wakan Kech, as your Princess and sovereign, I order you to devise a manner in which ShadowFall champions will survive the contest and return home. At the very least, you must promise me Rist will live. Whole." With that, she left the chair and exited through a false door, leaving Wakan alone. He gulped. He had been given an impossible assignment, one that even he might not be able to pull off. *Will she hold me to that order?* he wondered. *Will she relent if little Rist is killed?*

For all of her years they had been close, almost like father and daughter. And for last five years he had been her chief priest and advisor after her succession to the Sisterdom of ShadowFall. But even so, she still held absolute life-and-death power over him, no less than the peasants in the fields and the mines, no less than the draft animals and meat birds; she could have him imprisoned, tortured, mutilated or killed without any kind of recourse. Would she, if he failed? Though he loved her, respected her, he did not want to discover.

RIST TOOK TO THE CHALLENGE OF THE GAME WITH ENTHUSIASM. Reviewing the performances of the emus, he found that the one bird he had picked the first day was not the one he would need in a fight to the death. He had been lucky, he thought, to have chosen the most docile of the flock as his first demonstration ride. But after a few days of trying other birds, he found that the most aggressive creatures proved to be the better "war-birds," as he now called them—in both languages.

After a week's worth of experimenting, he chose three birds of equal attitude and aptitude. "Wakan," he said, speaking his mentor's name correctly now, "these three wanted to peck my face off at first, and kick me in the groin. That kind of spirit is what my emus back home had. They had to be fearless to stand up to a velk, and kick its eyes out."

Wakan nodded; several times Rist had told him the story of his velk kill en route to the so-called Ice at the End of the World with his father and brother. By now, Wakan was beginning to believe all of the little man's stories; he also believed that Rist was incapable of telling lies. *I don't think our Motherland could survive without falsehoods,* he concluded. *I wonder how Rist's people can ever give orders, or transact business deals, or keep the family peaceful at home, up there in those icy lands, without the benefit of lying?*

After a week of observation, Wakan had few doubts about the abilities of Rist or his new emu steeds. Hour after hour, Rist practiced with bolos, throwing them against strawman targets, usually with great force and equal accuracy. It had taken some experimentation until Rist finally proclaimed that the fabrication of the bolos was satisfactory. "There is a proper length," he told Wakan and his guard trainer in ever-increasingly nearly perfect Motherspeak, "and a proper weight, which together let me control exactly where it will land, how it will encircle the prey. Er, the opponent, in this case." Satisfied that the little man was at home again in his bird-saddle, used to the bolos once more, he decided to bring out a scaled-down springbow that he hoped could be also used with such expertise.

Rist took the arm-length weapon from the guard trainer, hefting it from one hand to the next. He appeared to be ambidextrous, Wakan noted, unlike most of Motherland's people, who generally favored their left hands. Wakan attributed the difference to Rist's people's way of writing and reading by carving and touch. The priest continued to be unhappy with Rist's lack of progress in trying to read written print; despite the best efforts of the glass smith, there was still no combination of lenses that could produce a "near-seer." Wakan wondered if he should assign an assistant to comb the ancient texts, or better yet, set up some kind of research procedure to help the smith proceed down a productive path. But that thought never quite led to action, as the urgency of the approaching Motherland Game took priority.

In addition to instructing the little man in Rist-sized versions of Motherland weaponry, the priest and the guard trainer had also been selecting the best fighters according to the elimination protocols that Pernie had ordered: start with a large number of selected fighters, train them all, finally pitting them against each other in mock combat for another competition. Two more rounds of such attrition would produce at least ten candidates. Those would contend with ten men from the palace guards, from which the three most promising fighters would be chosen. Three, plus Rist on his bird.

For convenience, Wakan had a special pen erected outside of and adjacent to the palace, a fenced area where Rist could access his emu and then ride out to the practice fields, saving long walks. For the first few days, the little man's morning ride from the palace, over the river and out to the fields, was a spectacle of intense interest for all of ShadowFall, with onlookers stopping their tasks, jaws agape, staring at the strange sight. Rist enjoyed the notoriety, and often would swing his bolos above his head to the delight of the crowds of watchers. But as the days went on, interest waned (partly because Wakan put out subtle warnings for people not to take too much time off from assigned chores to watch). Eventually, Rist would only get a smile and a nod from most people as he rode out or back, though small children still liked to run alongside the bird-warrior, chanting "Bird-man! Bird-man!"

Wakan worried that word of the strange little warrior might seep out to other Sisterdoms, but then, what could they do against this new kind of weapon? In a little over a month, Rist and his birds and the integrated ShadowFall team would be out there in battle for all Motherland to see.

CHAPTER TWENTY-ONE

"*P*riest! Priest!" the shouts came, along with the sounds of men pounding on his door. "We have spies! Assassins!" With a grunt, Wakan Kech rolled out of the arms of his favorite woman, landing on his feet at the edge of his bed. Within seconds he had donned fighting pants, an armored pull-shirt, and boots. Opening his massive security door, he saw two of his large guards, panting, sweating, covered with blood. "What is it, men? What's happening?"

"Sire," the larger man gasped, "we caught half a dozen spies who climbed the palace walls, sneaking toward the Princess's chambers. We killed some of them—" Bending over, he spat blood, unable to talk. The other guard took over: "Sire, four of them we killed, but two escaped. One is atop the palace, near the far-seer site; the other ran out toward the bridge."

Wakan pulled one cord that rang small bells in the Princess's chambers, signaling that she should slide into her secure safe-room shelter; the same cord also rang bells to bring other guards to reinforce the Princess's security. Another pulled cord summoned physicians to his own door. "The healers will be here soon, men," he said, "to bind up your wounds. Rest easy inside here." A glance back at his bed showed that his night's companion had already departed through his private door, to her own rooms. Her perfume, mixed with other scents, still lingered. *Why tonight?* Wakan grinned ruefully. *But I am glad it was not ten minutes sooner!*

He pulled yet a third cord, to waken Rist. In less than three minutes, the little man arrived in vest armor, panting, tiny springbow at the ready. "Wakan," Rist said, "you said to be ready to fight if you rang that bell. Here I am." Wakan gave his small ally very specific orders about finding, intercepting, and, if necessary, killing the escaping would-be assassin. Rist nodded and ran down the hallway toward a door that only he could unlock.

Those chores assigned, Wakan himself picked a springbow from its wall mount and headed for the far-seer tower, other guards now following him. He felt that Rist would prove himself this night. *Or we will have lost a much-needed champion!*

Outside, Rist saddled and mounted the emu that he had kept hobbled for his daily ride out to practice for The Game. This war-bird wore the needle-spiked anklets that Rist had wanted to experiment with, for use against the strawman targets. *Well, maybe tonight, real flesh and blood targets?* In the light of the slim crescent, Pale Lady of the Night, Rist goaded his steed toward the bridge, where Wakan had said the intruder had landed. Though his thoughts were racing with the prospects of the fighting to come, he did note that this was the first time he had seen the Pale Lady goddess at night here in the Lowlands. Except for a small sliver of light, Her scarred face was not visible, Wakan had said, because her spherical roundness kept it in shadow, a concept Rist still found hard to believe. But Her necklace of colored jewels still sparkled across the darkness from the bright edge. To Rist, it was a good omen.

By the time Rist arrived at the near end of the bridge, he could just make out a group of dark figures of men who were getting into a boat at the river's edge. Following the priest's directions, Rist made no challenge calls, offered no quarter. Anyone outside on or near the river at this time of night was a suspect and Rist was to injure or kill them. One of the men got off the boat and yelled out to his companions, "It's just a damn big bird running this way, boys. No cause for alarm. Let me take off its head!"

As Rist sat silent on his steed, the one man approached him, holding an axe, apparently thinking he was going to finish off a bird, in the dim light of Pale Lady not seeing Rist astraddle its back. Without a sound, Rist gave the knee-squeeze command—*kick!* In an instant the silhouetted figure went *whoof!* and fell backward, gurgling, split from crotch to breast. The other men, pushing the boat out into the river and hearing no sound, took no notice. Rist almost retched from the stench of the eviscerated intestines splayed on the ground in front of him. *One down, more to go!* his murderous thoughts raged. *These men tried to kill Pernie!*

Rist quickly ran the bird up to the rise in the middle of the bridge, cranking his springbow back to maximum power. As the bird thumped the wooden boards, another one of the men yelled out, apparently unaware of his first comrade's fate, "It's just a damn emu, boys, like Ilgen said! Don't worry about a friggin' *bird!*" He sat down and took an oar. "Let's go downriver a bit and find another place to get ashore. We can try again to kill the little redheaded bitch and—*ulp!*" Rist's iron arrow caught that one in the mouth, tearing out the back of his head, throwing him backwards into the river.

As the dead man splashed, the others yelled, one pulling out a long knife as if to throw it toward Rist. Rist's second bolt caught him in the chest, knocking him into the river without a further sound. The other two men apparently decided that they couldn't fight a bird that shot arrows, and began rowing downstream as fast as they could. But Rist rode down off the bridge, alongside the river, easily outdistancing their boat. "Stop!" he yelled in Motherspeak, "Or I will kill you both!" Hearing no response, he stopped his emu, took aim and fired at the boat. A gurgling scream told him that his aim was still good. "Thank you, Pale Lady," he whispered, "for Your light this night." *But if I were going to assassinate somebody,* he thought, *I think I'd wait for a darker night!* Rist would not be aware until later that his night vision was much better than any Motherlander's; to them, the crescent Pale Lady offered very little illumination. To them, this *had* been a dark night.

The lone survivor in the boat waved and yelled "Surrender!" but then quickly reached down and pulled up something that Rist could not make out at first. A bow, already strung with an arrow and ready to let loose! Rist's sudden involuntary jerk on the reins caused his emu to cant sideways, and just in time, as an arrow sped by close enough for Rist to feel its passage in the air. The archer was very good, Rist observed icily; shooting in low light from a rocking boat.

Shreeek! Screaming, Rist's steed fell backward, victim of a second arrow from that same bowman. Thrown, Rist slammed hard into the packed earth roadway adjacent to the river, losing his springbow. *And I have broken something, too, it feels like!* Numbness made his right arm useless, as he struggled to his feet, looking for his lost weapon. In the river, the enemy archer, apparently thinking he had dispatched the attacker, was rowing furiously downstream. Rist concluded that the would-be assassin didn't realize his error. Finding the springbow intact, Rist ignored the thrashing emu, using his good left arm to load a bolt from his quiver, then padded down the road to locate a good ambush spot.

Hiding behind a tree as the boat grew closer, Rist stepped out into the open and fired without warning, planning to wound his opponent without killing him. He was sure that Wakan would want a live captive for interrogation. The bolt whizzed, and a scream from his target told him that he had succeeded. Smiling, Rist tied the open end of the next bolt with a coil of thin rope and shot it into the side of the boat, then securing his end to the tree beside him.

As the river current pushed the tethered boat to the water's edge, the archer held both arms up in surrender, his left one sporting a bolt from Rist's springbow. As the groaning man crawled painfully onto the shore, Rist shot him in his right thigh. Over the man's screams and curses he said, "I'm taking no chances, you killer. Now be quiet or I'll put one in your other leg. Or your crotch. Understand? Do you speak my language?" Muffled grunts of pain told him that the writhing man understood.

Palace guards, running and panting, ready to battle the attackers, finally caught up to Rist but stopped in astonishment to admire the bird-man's campaign against the enemy. As they roughly took the wounded archer into custody, ignoring his shouts, the numbness in Rist's right arm departed suddenly, leaving only a nexus of horrendous pain, the worst he had ever experienced. Swaying, Rist slowly succumbed to darkness and fell.

HOURS LATER, A BLOOD-SPATTERED WAKAN KECH MET A BANDAGED and moaning Rist at a washing fountain outside the doorway to the dungeon. At the little man's horror-stricken face, he said, "No, Rist, this is not your blood. I was able to reset your shoulder without surgery." Rist managed a weary thanks, trying not to grimace at the throbbing pain in his shoulder. "It will take a week or more to heal properly, but much of the pain should subside in a few days. But no springbows, my friend, and no bolos and no bird-riding, not any time soon." Rist was sorry to hear that his wounded emu had been put down. "That fellow's arrow took the bird in the gut," Wakan said, "and there was naught to be done."

Then the priest wiped some of the blood from his sleeve. "No, all of this blood's from your captive, a stubborn one, Rist," Wakan said. "Simple threats and fire did not break him, not even cutting off his—" He stopped; Rist shuddered, imagining the thankfully unsaid details. "But ultimately nobody can withstand the horrors of the death-herb." Shaking his head, Wakan went on: "The first hour of it is the worst, when you realize that you have days of shrieking whole-body pain ahead. Unless a merciful enemy will kill you first."

Wakan washed off the dripping blade of his iron knife, saying, "After I had wrenched all the information I could, I did give the poor fellow surcease." Rist shuddered again; he didn't mind killing velks —*or even bad people, like tonight*—in a stand-up fight, but had no stomach for torture of the helpless. That in itself was a concept he had only first come across with the God's Priests in the Warm Lands above the waterfall. Back home in The Tharn's Lands, death usually came swiftly; no one had thought of prolonging pain unnecessarily. Rist wondered why the people of these downRiver lands would think of such things, people who built such wonderful stone structures and marvelous machines. But as he thought on it, he could see where torture might be useful in quickly obtaining information. He wished he had a totem to carve that thought. *But maybe it is better forgotten?* he thought. *Strange foreign lands, strange foreign ideas!* Rist shuddered again, for the first time in his life concerned for his own morality.

Wakan went on: "Our poor prisoner here told me that he was part of a group hired by a warrior guildmaster from Four Peaks." Recognizing the name of the other Sisterdom, Rist frowned.

"Yes, I know, Rist; Four Peaks have never forgotten their defeat four years ago, when we whipped them and RidgeBack soundly and seized some of their lands and slaves. Their assassins had trekked unseen far upriver, on the other side of our fields, carrying their boat with them. Then they came down tonight, in near pitch dark, from that unexpected direction. With orders to kill the Princess if they could, and to discover what strange preparations ShadowFall was making for the Motherland Game, what we were doing with monkeys on emus." Rist asked him what a "monkey" was, and bristled as Wakan described the creatures. Unsmiling, Wakan stared at Rist. "Somehow they must have heard about you." A long pause. "I suppose we were lucky that they went for the Princess first; I did not think to provide such security for you, but that will change after tonight." *Along with more guards on the other side of the fields, too,* he noted mentally. *More defensive expenses, wasted manpower, less productivity. What a shame!*

With a soft mist of royal perfume clinging to her, the tall blonde handmaiden, Anklya, came and said that the Princess was calling for Wakan and Rist. After they washed themselves, redressed in robes, and became presentable, they went to the throne room for an audience. Wakan noted with satisfaction that the guards there were doubled per his orders, with shortswords and springbows at the ready. He and Rist had both worried that yet other boatloads of assassins would show up later, when the immediate threat was over and the guards more relaxed. That was what they would have done, had they been planning such an attack. But Wakan spoke to the warriors to ensure that they stayed alert. There wouldn't be any further disturbances tonight.

Dismissed after telling their stories and receiving the princess's heartfelt thanks, Wakan left by himself, Rist staying behind by command. Wakan knew that the little man would be receiving Pernie's gratitude in another fashion this night, shoulder pain or not. *That should help with his healing*, he thought. As Wakan returned to what he hoped would be his own similar rewards that night, he smiled; Rist was now as accepted in ShadowFall as he could possibly be!

CHAPTER TWENTY-TWO

"Our little man is an expert springbowman, Sire, the best I have ever seen," the husky guard trainer told Wakan, as Rist, riding a bird in the distance, kept shooting iron arrow after arrow into a long line of head-sized targets atop posts. "I do believe he could place an arrow in a square the size of a man's hand, from a distance of a hundred meters." The trainer had heard of Rist's night-time battle with the would-be assassins, when he had killed three and captured another, using a springbow in the dark, shooting at a moving boat. The little man was equally impressive today.

"I hope so, guardsman," the priest replied, "because he is going to need it." Every five years, the venue for The Game was changed. Last time, it had been in a wide-open field, where individuals could run a kilometer to get away from pursuers, or to tire an enemy. That had not provided good enough viewing for the Mother's Court nobles or the mass of bloodthirsty citizens, so Mother had decreed a different arrangement this time. Wakan's spies in Mother's City reported on the construction of a massive arena where The Game would be held—an oval field two hundred meters long and a hundred wide, with surrounding bleachers above an unscalable wall fifteen meters high to keep the combatants in. *No escape this time*, Wakan thought. Thirteen gates, spaced equidistantly around the perimeter of the field, would provide entrances for the Sisterdom champions. Gates that would be nailed shut after the fighters entered the field for the final, deadly competition.

ShadowFall did not have the resources to duplicate the expensive stadium of Mother's City, but Wakan did have men lay out a lime pattern of the same size on a flat field. "Stay inside this line at all times," he told the competitors as he and the guard trainer herded the men onto the field. "In Mother's City there will be a fifteen-meter-high wall here, with archers looking down to ensure you don't try to escape." The ragged group of men laughed aloud, jeering "Me, run?" "Them others, they better not try escapin', they's dead meat!", and quite a bit of other self-aggrandizing chatter. *All nervous*, Wakan saw, *as I would be. As I* am! Looking over the mob, Wakan quietly noted four men who appeared calm, men whose eyes were also looking over their competition. *Good; those are the men who will most likely survive mock combat. And real combat!* Sighing, he stood by as the guard trainer shouted out instructions. It was going to be a long couple of weeks!

MEANWHILE, RIST KEPT BUSY WITH HIS OWN REGIMEN, INSIDE ANOTHER lime-rimmed oval out of sight of the normal-sized men fighting in the competition. Wakan and the trainer had said that he and the other champions of ShadowFall were going to try and kill as many other men as possible, as quickly as they could, acting as a coordinated team. "You, Rist, because you are mobile, you will ride your bird around all of the other teams and try to shoot an arrow through whomever you perceive their leaders to be." Wakan made it sound easy, but Rist knew he would be putting himself at risk right away, becoming a target for the slings and arrows of forty-eight violent men. Pretending that his lime-lined oval was already full of those assassins, Rist practiced zigzagging his emu across one side to the other, then backtracking, sometimes even running backward, all in a planned effort to keep his opponents off balance.

Meanwhile, the other ShadowFall fighters would be moving together, using their new springbows, to clean up after his first shots. "A leaderless pack is often ripe for the kill," the guard trainer said. "In the first few minutes, seeing such a small man on such a big bird, might keep them confused enough. When their leader goes, our guys can finish the job." Rist tried to imagine what was going to happen afterwards. He couldn't. This warfare would not be like a velk hunt. He tried to think of velks with spears and swords, but couldn't visualize that effect. Now, if he had a lot of emus, he could... He held that thought and rode straight over to Wakan, where the other men were training.

"You might have a good idea there, Rist," the priest conceded after hearing the little man's plan. "I have not heard of any rule that says we can't bring more birds and other animals along with the champions. I was told 'four men and their weapons'. Who is to say that the weapons have to be iron?" He grinned maliciously. "How many birds can you train? How many birds can three other men control?"

"Not control, Wakan," Rist said with delight. "Not control, only prod and let loose."

ONE MONTH BEFORE THE MOTHERLAND GAME, WAKAN AND THE GUARD trainer met with Rist and the three selected champions: Thrak, Eddor, and Een. Thrak, a big redhead, was a fisherman, born in a rough neighborhood of Mother's City and released from a death sentence in prison to immigrate northward when Wakan and Pernie had taken possession of ShadowFall five years before. The smiling blond Eddor, a renowned wrestler in his home Sisterdom, hailed from Three Rivers, Sister Messinex's domain; he had been his princess's gift to Pernie upon her accession, a man whose job in ShadowFall was training citizen-soldiers for their reserve duties. Grim-faced Een, a palace guard, one with a record of bravery, had killed one of the would-be assassins last month. Wakan recalled that these three had been among his first choices. Three big men, all killers, they were tall, muscled and darkly tanned from their time in the training field, and now dressed in kilts and pullover shirts, in ShadowFall's lavender colors.

At first, when Rist arrived on his emu, they all laughed. "A brown midget on a bird? Are you jesting with us, Priest?" Thrak chuckled. "We expected another fighter, but *this*?"

Wakan held up an arm and the men snapped to attention. "Watch this little man, this Rist, go through his paces with his emu. Watch closely, and try to learn. All of your lives depend on it." The men laughed again, derisively, but did as they were told.

Rist pulled his springbow from a packet behind him, goaded his emu to top speed, and then began to pierce a long line of air-filled cow bladders atop posts, all head-high. One after another, iron arrows deflated their targets, until within a few minutes Rist had punctured them all, over fifty. The other fighters gasped. "Damn all, Priest," Thrak shouted, mouth agape, "if that runt can do that on the field of combat, he could kill every Motherless son by himself!" The other fighters agreed, their sudden respect showing as Rist pulled up his bird in front of them.

"Where you from, Mister Rist?" Thrak said. "How'd you learn to do that?" from Eddor.

"Got any birds big enough for *us* to ride?" Een asked.

Wakan was pleased. These men respected ability, and Rist certainly had enough of *that*!

PART FIVE

FIND

CHAPTER TWENTY-THREE

"This one's still alive, Sire!" Rusk called out. "Come and see!" Clad in his gray velkfur coat and matching head covering to resist the glacier's cold, Rusk was standing in the cleft of a void in The Ice at the End of the World, where rivulets of water from the melting glacier had cut an opening big enough for the teenager to climb into, all the way from a distant edge to the stony ground beneath. His Sire, Reader Thess, grunted as he squeezed his own hefty blackfur-clad body through that narrow passageway.

"*What's* alive, Rusk? Gods? Ice animals? Worms?" As he stood up in the confined space and brushed frost from his face, Thess saw what his son had discovered: in the subdued light which filtered through the permanently overcast Misty Sky, lighting up their crevasse, Thess saw a strange large green made-thing, a machine, a part of which extended from the glacier wall. The exposed curved portion appeared to be a cylindrical shape, a hand of man-lengths in diameter, with a crumpled front. How far back into The Ice it extended, he couldn't tell. A large black bubble of some sort took up close to half the diameter of the right side of that protruding surface.

The dull finish of the object did not appear to be from any kind of metal, and using his lodestone, Thess confirmed that suspicion. *It's hard, like horn, but not iron.* Thess grimaced at that, because back home in The Tharn's Town such a mass of finished metal would fetch a lot of coppers. But at the moment his primary attention was focused on that bubble. *Something behind it is moving!*

"Sire, see what I mean?" Rusk said. "Something's alive behind this hard bubble!" Thess held up his gloved hand and told his boy to calm down. He himself was shaking, too, but he told himself it was from excitement and not from overwhelming fear. How could anything be alive at the bottom of a glacier that extended all the way up into the Misty Sky? Something that had probably been iced over since The Beginning of All Things? Maybe, he rationalized, the dim light from overhead had just melted something inside the big green cylinder, loosened it up, so that it was falling around inside the black bubble?

Thess said, "Rusk, step back and let me examine your find more closely." His son did so, and Thess dropped to his knees, putting his face against the weird curved surface. As he did, an intense light suddenly filled the void behind the window, illuminating—*what?*—before again becoming deep black, as black as a Dark with no Wen of the Mist shining above the Misty Sky. In shock, Thess fell backward onto the stone surface. Inside the black bubble was a *face*! A white face with big black eyes and an open mouth. But it was not a *human* face! Thess was thankful for the sudden blackness that now hid it from him. A troubling thought occurred: *Did that deep blackness also hide* me *from* it? Again, his shivering was not caused by The Ice around him.

AFTER RECEIVING ORDERS FROM THE THARN TO GO BACK TO THE ICE to retrieve yet more gods and a large god-machine, Thess and Rusk had first gone to send Rist off on his berg-ride Warmward to see how their final customers downRiver in the Warm Lands used the icebergs they had sold to the Ice brokers in The Tharn's Town. They expected him back within a hand of hands of dims.

Preparing for bringing back what a Tharn's Man had called "a large god-machine" with no further description, Thess arranged for The

Tharn to provide a six-wheel articulated wagon, comprising a two-seater up front over two wheels and a four-wheel cargo bed in back, pulled by a four-beezt team. Two of the large and silent Tharn's Men, their chief's personal bodyguards, would act as teamsters, setting off Coldward on a slow journey of at least three hands of dims, across rocky roads and rough peat-farm pathways.

Thess and Rusk saddled and rode their two-leg birds, their emus, up the quicker dimward route in the New River valley. Thess took an extra dim to check a well-hidden cave in a rocky cleft where, over years of traveling to The Ice, he had stored a cache of dried foods, spears and blacknives, and a good supply of coppers. *Just in case,* he told himself. *The Tharn is mostly reasonable, but his occasional drunkenness and old age might create problems for my family someday, and I always plan for contingencies. So, a hideout as far away from The Tharn's Town as I can get!*

After traveling back to The Ice and cataloguing prospective bergs that would eventually be moving downRiver toward The Tharn's Town, they tracked down the Colds and the newfound "gods" and the god-machine allegedly discovered by them. At a smelly collection of the Cold People's filthy yurts, they met up with The Tharn's Men and their big wagon. Thess hoped it would be large enough to bring back the god-machine, whatever it was.

By the time they were inspecting the Colds' new discoveries, Thess and Rusk were growing concerned that Rusk's twin had not yet returned home. Rist had started downRiver a hand of dims before they left Coldward. Though the berg-crews usually took a long time to return from the Warm Lands, they were still hoping at any minute to see Rist astride his emu, to hear his boasts about traveling so far Warmward.

But at the moment, concerned about Rist though they were, both men were busily assaying their momentous find. They agreed not to mention any possibility of a possible living thing inside it to anyone else. The Colds themselves had said nothing about it; maybe they hadn't seen that *face*? Thess knew that The Tharn did not like the very concept of gods, of any beings with more power than himself, so that he would be especially displeased if they brought him back a living one. Fortunately, the Colds had already wrapped up the two discovered god-bodies in beezt-skin shrouds before Thess and Rusk arrived. *At least those two "gods" are definitely dead!* Thess thought.

Composing himself while running his hands over the machine's smooth green surface, Thess said, "The front of this, this—*god-machine*—is made of hornlike material, not metal. And it is crumpled, as if something hit it." He was having difficulty describing the made-thing, because he had never seen a cylinder so large. The only other similar shapes in The Tharn's Lands were the small spindle totems he and his sons carried for carving information, or large pottery vases shaped on a potter's wheel, or maybe fence posts. Cylinders of any other kind were not common anywhere in The Tharn's Lands, and extremely large ones like this were nonexistent, to Thess' knowledge.

Thess pounded on the god-machine but heard no noise other than his own thuds, detecting no hollows, feeling no yielding. It was very hard. Seeing the obviously smashed end, he could not imagine anything large enough to do so much damage to such a big, solid thing. Looking up the crevasse ceiling far above, he asked, "Or, did it fall a long distance, and hit this solid rocky ground below our feet? We need to study it." Thess had no idea how they might go about analyzing the thing, but it would be an interesting challenge, once they got it home. Doing *that* appeared to be the main challenge at the moment.

He sighed and said, "Let's get it out of this crevice. I will talk to the Colds, get them to hack it out." Negotiating that loathsome tribe's effort took the remainder of the day; the Cold People—short, filthy, the pink color of peat-grubs—were nevertheless stubborn dealers. Their chief had the upper hand and knew it. Finally, Thess made an overly generous payment of coppers and of future obligations of food crops, just to get this task done quickly for The Tharn. He hoped The Tharn would understand the expense!

As dimness turned to Dark, the two men rode their emus to their camp nearby, where the large Tharn's Men were lounging, picking their teeth with blacknives after a beezt-rib meal, the remains of which were still simmering on a spit over the campfire, an enticing odor. "We will have the god-machine safely out of The Ice by next dim," Thess told the men as he and Rusk climbed down from their steeds. Rusk, he noticed, was busy carving the day's findings into his wooden totem spindle. *Good! The boy keeps excellent records. They will be useful when I have to explain to The Tharn why it cost so much to retrieve this, this* god-thing. *This* machine*!*

As the next morning dimness arrived, Thess and Rusk were examining the excavated green machine, which revealed itself to be a truncated cylinder, nearly flat on the bottom, with the black bubble now on top. Rolled over onto its flat side by the Colds, they saw that the object, crushed nearly flat at one end, was hemispherical at the other, but with no apparent doors.

A tool of some kind? Rusk mused. *Or a storage bin?* Using measuring cords, he paced off the dimensions. "I measure its length to be three hands of man-length cords," he said to his Sire, using the measurement terminology of The Tharn's Lands. "Though it may have been shortened a man-length or more on the end where it was crushed. And its width, its diameter, is a hand of man-lengths." Using his carving knife, he whittled the information on the totem in his left hand.

"And its weight, Rusk? Can our big wagon can handle it?" Thess asked. He had seen that it took a swarm of Colds, many hands of them, to chop the machine out of the glacier with their axes and picks, then to nudge it just a short distance after they'd removed it from The Ice. Then the creatures had used shaped logs underneath the machine to support it over the marshy surface, with several beezt towing it. He didn't relish the thought of dragging such a huge load over the long distance across muddy roads, mist-saturated peat fields, and stone-riddled bare ground, all the way back to The Tharn's Town.

Thess argued loudly with the Cold leader, getting the crew to load the machine onto the articulated wagon. After hours of pulling and pushing over a ramp of logs, the cylinder was eventually lodged on the floor of the wagon, its damaged end still dangling precipitously over the rear of the wagon bed. Thess didn't like the look of the overburdened wagon, and insisted on a test run, to pull the load over a few hands of man-lengths of road and see the results. As he had feared, it was a disaster. The weight of the god-machine pushed the wagon axle-deep into the dirt, even on this firm ground. Thess cursed, "Damn! This wagon, these beezt, will never make the trip back to The Tharn's Town! It will take forever!" The Tharn's Men remained passive; they would receive their coppers no matter how much the bird-riding Reader yelled and complained. But even they did not want to have to lever and lift their wagon out of a long succession of mudholes all the way back home.

Rusk walked around the god-thing, thinking about his Sire's frustration. At that moment, in the distance a small iceberg calved from the glacier, loudly crashing into the black lake at its foot. As the berg began moving, starting a journey across the lake that might eventually lead downRiver, Rusk asked with a smile, "Sire, do you think it might *float?*"

"SIRE," RUSK SAID, OUTLINING HIS PLAN, "I WILL HIRE THE COLDS to slide the cylinder over to an open space in the black lake here. If it floats in a deep enough spot, I will direct them in making a log-raft around it, tie it in place, and fashion a rudder for guidance. We can take apart the wagon for the planks." He pointed to the two large Tharn's Men, who were now lounging around, doing nothing. "I could use their help on the trip downRiver."

Thess took note. "I will tell them The Tharn wants them to help. They are big and strong and can use long poles to push off and to stop."

Rusk was thinking about his impending trip. "Sire, do you know how long it takes for a berg to travel that distance?"

Thess nodded again, saying from memory, "About four dims, on average, for the trip."

Rusk said, "Sire, I estimate two to three dims to build this raft, a few more to get over to the River mouth, then four dims traveling downRiver like the bergs do. Two hands of dims, no later, and I shall meet you in The Tharn's Town."

Thess agreed to return to The Tharn's Town by two-leg, guiding Rusk's own emu by a rope behind his own steed. "Rusk, I figure I will need eight dims return journey, running the birds fast, not stopping too often to rest and eat. But wait another dim or two to make sure. Then I will be at the dock, awaiting you."

After Thess departed, Rusk went about the business of having the Colds move the god-machine to the lake and observing whether it would float or sink. Standing on protruding rocks above the lake's surface, two groups of Colds used their long ropes to drag the god-machine into the water. To Rusk's delight and surprise, the cylinder floated, black bubble on top, with less than half its diameter submerged; if it had been top heavy, or if the crumpled end had leaked, it didn't show. Maybe it *was* hollow?

He instructed the Cold leader how to disassemble the articulated wagon, and how to use the planks and logs to build a raft around the floating god-machine, cinching it up with ropes and careful to keep it upright, with the bubble on top and the rounded end forward. It seemed to be weighted closer to the bottom, so stayed stable. The next dim he was happy to see the machine still afloat; the damage at the one end apparently did not affect its ability to float. Strangely, it appeared as if the damaged end was even buckling back out.

Rusk used long planks from the wagon, mounted on a wheel-axle, to fabricate a rudder. With a water-worthy craft, he was ready to begin the journey down the New River to take his strange green cargo to The Tharn's Town.

CHAPTER TWENTY-FOUR

*T*wo hands of dims later, Rusk and the two glowering, sweating Tharn's Men, aboard the makeshift log-raft that surrounded the floating god-machine, were on the New River, approaching the main dock at The Tharn's Town. Successfully maneuvering the raft into position, the two large men used long poles to slow their final approach. At the rear of the assemblage, Rusk quickly turned his large flat rudder to guide the makeshift raft-craft to safety. Already waiting for them at the dock, Thess was directing a crew of orange-trimmed rowdies to pull the raft in and tie it down, in preparation for pulling out the green cylinder cargo. He was surprised that the crushed end was now almost hemispherical, as if it had popped back into shape, like an inflated beezt bladder.

Rusk waved at Thess. "Sire, I am happy to see that you were able to arrive ahead of us. Did you have a good ride?" Thess nodded, ignoring his sore bottom from all the time in the saddle. He motioned to a group of men who pulled up a long, low-slung, four-wheeled cart. "That will get us to The Tharn's Place."

One of the largest crowds ever gathered in The Tharn's Town lined the muddy streets as Thess' and Rusk's strange procession departed the docks and headed toward The Tharn's Place in the center of the city.

Four beezt, harnessed to the large wagon, strained as the wheels sank ever deeper in the mud. Thess called out for planks to be placed in front of each wheel, after which the wagon lurched forward, a process that was repeated many times over the distance, to the bellowing dismay of the beezts and the curses of the rowdies.

The Tharn's Place looked just as it had hands of dims ago when Thess and his twins had brought back the first large god from The Ice, but this time the right-hand side of the palisade gate was decorated with that first god's rotting, vermin-eaten head on a pike—a public declaration that The Tharn was more powerful than any god.

The Tharn, now clothed in the finest black velkskin that covered even his prodigious belly, was in rare form—sober, clean-shaven and in good spirits, demonstrably excited to see Thess' treasure. He strode out of his palace, pushing aside the several attractive wen who always clung to him, down the stone steps, and stepped onto stone pavement. Around the plaza, many hands of citizens stood as well, trying to get a closer look at the dead gods and their large machine.

"Two dead gods and a god-machine? Well done, Reader Thess, well done!" At The Tharn's command, two of his men sliced open the beezt-skin shroud around one of the gods' bodies. At that, Thess, Rusk, and all the onlookers, The Tharn included, gasped aloud. One of the bodies, clad neck to feet in a tight, nearly luminous golden covering, was a yellow-haired god—obviously from its long, fine golden hair and smooth, beardless face, and its delicate features, a *wen*—but with a pronounced chest that gave her an unusual, yet attractive, contoured shape. Rusk heard behind him a rough voice whispering, "Yeah, now The Tharn gets to see what we been seein', down in the Warm Lands." Several other People laughed knowingly. Another voice countered, "Quiet, berg-man. Don't let *our* wen know about that! We'll catch it if they do."

Rusk turned and glowered at the two, whom he recognized as mere orange-trimmed rowdies. One stared back at him sympathetically, as if to say something, but apparently thought better, shrugging and moving farther back in the crowd. Ignoring him, Rusk turned his attention back to his Sire and The Tharn and the dead gods.

The Tharn hesitated for a few seconds and quickly told his men to open the other shroud. The next dead god was encased in a shimmering blue covering, complete with matching helmet. *Like the first god we brought back*, Thess thought. *I wonder why the golden-haired wen didn't have a helmet, too?* One guard was struggling to remove the god's helmet, without success. Rusk volunteered to help; he'd seen how the other god's head covering had fit, dims before, and it took him only a little time to do the same lift-and-twist action here, too.

Holding the helmet, Rusk stood back in semi-shock. This dead god, unlike the previous one and the wen beside him, was even darker-skinned than himself and all People. A common reaction arose from everyone: *Gods come in different colors?* Excitedly, The Tharn shouted for everyone to leave the plaza, but motioned for Thess and Rusk to remain while the guards closed and barred the palisade gate.

"What's this, Reader Thess? All gods are supposed to be pale, like The Ice. How can there be a dark one?"

Thess shrugged, trying to construct a worthy answer. "Tharn, Sire, the gods are...mysterious. Maybe this one was...from *elsewhere*?" He judged The Tharn's facial reactions. His ruler was not unintelligent, just strictly bound by rigid tradition and ritual, as were most all of his subjects. Most of the time The Tharn was relatively rational in his judgments, but his final word was always...final. He had once been a good warrior, and was now a somewhat decent administrator, Thess thought, but not as educated in history or commerce as the leader of the nation should be. A fair but firm man, yes, but occasionally subject to irrational outbursts. You didn't want to be the target of that wrath. Thess had to choose his words carefully.

"Sire, could this one have been...even a *warrior*, perhaps? Maybe a conflict among the gods brought them down from the Misty Sky, dropped them all onto the Earth, and let The Ice envelop them, back at The Beginning of All Things?" Thess was hopeful that he had threaded that philosophical needle satisfactorily, mixing accepted legend and rational conjecture.

Apparently he had. The Tharn said, "We may never know, Reader Thess. However, thank you for your usual logical reasoning." Walking around the wen-god, poking her curves with a finger, he said, "I am going to have my house-wen strip this one and examine the body for what we may learn from it. And the dark one, too. You may have the helmet for study."

Thess bowed in thanks, hoping for yet more reward from The Tharn. His ruler then asked about the god-machine and Thess told him everything they had found out, omitting only any mention of the movement inside the black bubble or *that face*!

Seemingly satisfied with the explanation, The Tharn said quietly, "You may submit your expenses and your reimbursement request totem to my treasurer"—Thess bowed again, happy at that—"but your continuing task will be to take that big thing"—he pointed at the machine—"and see what use you can find for it. If it is hollow, maybe we can cut it open and use it as a water tank, if nothing else. So see if you can open it, or cut it, or burn through it." The Tharn patted up at the curved surface, five times his height, laughing, "The gods might be dead now, but they weren't foolish! I need to know if this big thing is a threat or a treasure. Find out what you can." Turning on his heel and summoning his waiting harem of wen, he motioned for the guards to bring in the gods' bodies.

Thess turned to Rusk with a grimace. "How can we get this wagonload of god-machine over the muddy streets to our compound?" he asked. Rusk sighed; it was to be bellowing beezt and planks-on-mud all the way across town. Someday, the streets of The Tharn's Town had to be stone-paved!

CHAPTER TWENTY-FIVE

*A*ppropriate to his wealth and status, Thess' largestone home compound was one of the finest in The Tharn's Town, featuring the many-roomed two-story house itself, a high, stone-walled courtyard out back, and a lofty warehouse with several emu corrals adjacent. He often used the private open area to conceal projects that were too large for their warehouse, and now for that reason, the god-machine sat there, hidden by stone walls from public view. Thess and Rusk wanted to try to perform their impossible task of analyzing the god-machine without more prying eyes than The Tharn's occasional spies, whose nosiness couldn't be helped.

Over the years, on the graveled surface of their courtyard, Thess and his twins had trained their emus in the open air for riding and fighting, and once had fabricated large wooden gearing systems for waterwheel mechanisms, the only large machines ever seen before in The Tharn's Town. As part of Thess' numerous activities, the family also fabricated small and large wheels for cartage, threw pottery on potter's wheels, and worked on various other projects. Such ideas and fabrications had made and kept the family well-to-do, and more importantly, maintained them in The Tharn's good graces. The berg-brokerage business, a Tharn-bestowed monopoly, though currently the most profitable, was only one of Thess' and his twins' industrious endeavors.

Over the next few dims, using the wooden parts from the raft and wagon, Rusk carpentered a system of low-level scaffolding and ramps around the machine to enable himself and his Sire to access, to touch, and hopefully to Read, every part of it. Unable to see any details close up—the universal condition among the genetically farsighted People— by sensitive touch alone they were able to discern a pattern of very subtle depressions in several places around the machine's smooth green surface. Rusk then reproduced those sensed patterns with a pointed piece of chalk at a reduced scale on the smooth top of a flat stone worktable there in the courtyard.

The white lines were large enough for Rusk and Thess to distinguish, although nothing in their arrangements provided any context for them. The collection of long white lines, some intersecting, some parallel, some perpendicular, and several connected curves, all seemed random. Thess said, "Rusk, do you think it is a form of god-writing? That it can be Read as we do a carved totem?"

Rusk was not certain of anything. "Sire, maybe we can't truly Read it by Touch, but maybe these scaled-down visual patterns will show us things we can't Touch all at once." Now smoothing his sensitive Reading hand over the large black bubble atop the machine, Rusk had no luck: no more depressions or protrusions, and the deep blackness behind the bubble surface still remained. Between themselves, Rusk and Thess were glad that the blackness held. What kind of fearful creature had moved behind that surface before, they could only imagine. They hoped that the thing was not inside the cylinder, hungrily waiting for them to enter.

At lastmeal that evening, Rusk asked, "What could that bright light in the black bubble have been, Sire? Some kind of fire inside the machine? And what did we both see moving?" Thess' wen—Rusk's birther—Mell, sat with jaw agape as the conversation revealed what her men had seen at The Ice. By rigid convention, she kept silent until called upon by Thess, but seeing her curiosity aroused, he told her in detail what he and Rusk had experienced at The Ice. "So you see, Mell, this has to remain a family secret. No one is to know, else The Tharn might seize the machine and we would lose whatever treasures it yet holds for us." Mell smiled and nodded. Thess was correct, as always. She loved him, and her boys. She just wished that Rist were there to enjoy the good fortune. And the mystery!

EARLY NEXT DIM, RUSK FOUND A SINGLE DEPRESSION THAT UNLOCKED the glass bubble. "Sire!" he shouted, "there is a small dimple next to the bubble! Come quickly! See!" Thess scrambled up the steps of the wooden scaffold, his gaze turning to Rusk's finger tapping at a dark spot at a level even with his shoulders. "It was not there yesterdim, but I hear noises; something must be happening!"

As they stood there, the black bubble lit up brilliantly, turned transparent, swinging open as if hinged from the back. Inside was the *face*! Thess and Rusk both jumped back, nearly falling from the raised decking. Holding onto each other in abject fear, they nevertheless continued staring at the occupant seated in a cavity in the machine. Not human, but human-sized and appearing to have humanlike features, from a large, smooth, white hairless head on armless shoulders, down to a wide waist area that ended on a solid platform, the being —*creature*—whatever it was, turned a featureless head toward them. The face was as white as The Ice, with black-pit eyes and a lipless mouth.

To the horrified men, it made meaningless noises: "UUUUU... NNNNNN...AAAA...GEEEE...ESSSSS..."

"Sire," Rusk whispered, "the thing there, it's speaking to us. Should we answer?" Thess had not been so terrified since his last battle with a huge canine velk. And *that* enemy, he had at least understood. *But this one? An enemy? A god? Something else?* Gulping, he nodded to his son, trying to hide his fear. He couldn't find words to speak.

Shaking, Rusk moved closer to the cylinder. "Who are you? *What* are you?"

The white-thing turned toward him. If it had been a human visage it would have been looking him directly face-to-face. It began producing intermittent sounds, almost as if it were trying to talk from its motionless round mouth. Among the gibberish, it said, "Where?"

That word was familiar to Rusk, and he smiled broadly, answering, "*Where*? *Where*? In The Tharn's Town! Welcome to The Tharn's Town!"

The white-thing became silent, as if in thought, but had no facial expression. Rusk motioned for Thess to approach. "Sire, it's trying to speak, for sure. I even understood the word 'where'!" Overcoming much of his trepidation, Thess came over to more closely inspect the strange speaking-machine. Standing on his toes, he looked inside the cavity where it sat. Had it been a man, the white-thing would be missing everything from its waist on down. And no arms! It seemed to be attached to a small platform at its waist, but able to rotate in all directions. What was it? Surely a made-thing, a machine, but with the power of speech? How could that be?

Thess had always told his twins not to trust anything outside of their own direct experience. But at this moment, observing the moving —*living?*—white-thing sitting in the cavity in the big green cylinder, he was having a difficult time taking his own advice. Literally, he was not believing his own experience!

Finally, trying to exude a confidence he didn't feel, he spoke forcefully to the white-thing-machine, "Who are you? What are you? Why are you here?" The thing turned toward him, its mouth moving but not as if speaking words. The sounds came out, mostly gibberish. *"Who? Where? Pilot. You-En-Aa-Gee-Rrr-Ess. Sur-vey. Where is... this? Gee-Pee-Ess erratic. No sig...nal. Pow...er...ing dow...enn..."* The thing stopped moving and the luminous glow inside its small chamber went black. The black bubble *whooshed* and slowly rotated back into its original position, closing tightly, leaving not even a detectable seam where it contacted the green cylinder surface.

Blowing out a long breath, Thess said, "Rusk, what we must have here is a made-thing, a machine. Maybe the 'gods' even knew how to construct such talking things as this white-thing." He remembered the guffaws he himself had encountered when building the first waterwheel mechanism for The Tharn, all those cycles ago. And how disbelieving eyes had lit up when he demonstrated how to grind peat-grain faster and finer than by hand with *mano* and *matate* stones. A revolution in agriculture—and his first fortune!

Swallowing hard, Thess said softly, "Rusk, I believe these so-called 'gods' we brought back are—*were*—just bigger men. And if another *man* can build this speaking white-thing and this big green cylinder, then maybe *we* can learn to do it, too." His waterwheels and gears had been grinding peat and providing motion for wood lathes and saws and grinding wheels for many cycles now. *A machine is just a machine!* He was anxious to see if he could ever match a god's technology.

Rusk had been listening intently. "Sire, I agree. Let us see what we can learn from the white-thing, if it will open up again. And perhaps with its help we can gain entry into this green cylinder, if it is hollow. Since it floats, it must be. I think that at least a hand of these god-giants could fit into it, if that's what it was used for." He beamed. "Maybe the dead gods were traveling in it, as if it were a wagon of some kind? One that lost its pulling beezt and its wheels, maybe up on top of The Ice? And ran into a crevasse way up on The Ice? And fell and crashed?"

CHAPTER TWENTY-SIX

*M*ore dims passed while Rusk continued his examination of the strange "god-wagon," as they now called it. Though still anxious to hear news about his twin Rist, Rusk was at the moment absorbed in the challenge of the green cylinder. His first concern was about the apparent self-repairing of the formerly crushed end. *What kind of machine fixes itself?* he wondered. *Or is it like a peat-brick, which I can compress in a vise, yet expands back into its original shape?* His sensitive Reading hand kept finding yet other slight impressions, seams so subtle that he had missed them on earlier investigations because he hadn't been used to such shallow, unfamiliar markings. He suspected that some of the smaller figures were a form of writing, and others were known only to the gods. What he wanted to find was a door opening! After carving his failures on his totem he climbed back up on the scaffold for another session of touching.

Finally, after another hour of fruitless searching, in frustration he slammed his palm hard against one cross-hatched set of dimpled impressions halfway up the side of the cylinder. To his shock, a curved door sprang open, apparently hinged at the very top of the cylinder and extending downward almost to its flat bottom. Opening with force from the bottom upwards, the curved door knocked over the wooden scaffold platform with a loud *crash!*, throwing him to the ground. A dense smoke-like gas curled up from inside, quickly dissipating in the air overhead.

With a sudden splitting headache and a bruised leg, Rusk lay for a moment to recuperate from his fall, looking up into the open doorway. The interior of the god-wagon was now dimly lit, from its very walls, it seemed. *Curious, that! Are there fires inside Ice-clear walls to light them up so?* Though he could not make out the details, he could tell that the inside surface of the open door had rectilinear markings on it, reminiscent of the marks on the small hard chips they had found in the clothing of the first god they'd retrieved from The Ice—but too blurry to make out their exact shapes.

Lifting himself up from the ground and shaking his head, Rusk poked his head inside the god-wagon. It had a floor even with the bottom of the door, waist-height to him, from which four large chair-like frames rose in the back. *Seating arrangements for god-giants*, he figured. Along with rectangular frames on the walls and other unrecognizable features overhead. With curiosity overwhelming him, he was finally able to overcome his fears and climb up onto the floor of the cylinder.

The *smell*! Odors Rusk had never encountered assaulted his nose, irritating his lungs, and in panic he jumped back out into the courtyard. Strangely enough, the smells were not of decay and death, but reminded him more of the smoke from the poor-quality peat-coal that farmers sometimes used to drive out biters, grubs, and other pests from their fields and shrubs. *Fumigating,* they called it. Coughing out the nauseous fumes as best he could, he sat back on the ground, pulled out his totem, and recorded his impressions of this short but memorable incident—the opening of the god-wagon. *Surely, Sire Thess will be pleased.*

By then Thess was running into the courtyard. "Rusk," he said excitedly, "I heard the noise! I see you found a way in! You have opened up the machine! What have you discovered about our treasure 'wagon'?" His son summarized the findings, and they both climbed up into the open door of the cylinder to investigate further. Though severely farsighted, inside the well-lit interior Thess could make out a small angled platform, a shiny tilted metal surface that was attached to the flat forward wall of the enclosure. He walked over, stood on his toes, and touched the top of the plate, hoping to find something carved into it that he could Read.

"I can feel a set of depressions on this flat little table here, Rusk," Thess said. "Since you opened this 'wagon' by touching a raised set of figures, maybe more touching here will reveal other information about it?" He thought for a moment, then said, "I will touch each of these depressions, one at a time. You carve the results on your totem, in case we learn something." Rusk nodded, blacknife ready to begin documenting.

"First, I will touch the one on the upper leftmost part." Thess did so and immediately the front wall of the enclosure lit up with colorful displays, moving patterns, blurry to their sight. Thess jumped back. "Whoa! What do we have here?" At the same time, Rusk had fallen backward against one of the giant "chairs," its dark covering crumbling into dust under him. The stuff smelled like the nauseous fumes had when he first opened the door. Something had rotted away and he had stirred it up, like that fumigating smell. Climbing up, Rusk found himself sitting on a kind of flexible webbing, not unlike a biter-web but much stronger, his legs not touching the floor. *These were big gods!*

Thess continued, ignoring the odors and the meaningless, chaotically moving colored figures on the lit-wall in front of him. The moving shapes, though amazing, were less impressive than the white-thing that had spoken to them under the opened black bubble outside. "Now, the depression to its right." Nothing changed. "Rusk, now the second one to the right." Sounds filled the enclosure; from the broken cadence it was not just noise, but speech like the white-thing's, and almost totally meaningless to both men, seemingly emanating from a humanlike figure that appeared on the lit-wall: *"Power intermittent. Degradation of sensors. Survey crew absent. No biosensor data. Many qomps not responding. Global qomp access sporadic, incomplete. Loss of memory. Situation abnormal. Request solar recharge as soon as possible. Citizens Rasha, X'ohna, Jennings, please report.*

Repeating..." The garbled, unintelligible noises sounded out again, faded, then stopped. The lit-wall went dark at the same time.

Rusk said, "Sire, these sounds must be speech, but of a kind I do not comprehend. A few words seem to make sense, though. '*Low,*' '*loss,*' are our words. Could the message mean that the gods were lost? Laid low?"

Thess shook his head. "Let me press a few other depressions; maybe we can learn more." But after a hand of more pushes, nothing changed, no more sounds were forthcoming.

"Damn!" Thess sputtered. "These gods built this, this, 'wagon,' and I want it to work again. Think of what all we could do with it!" His imagination was in full swing—possessing a shrine to the gods in his own courtyard! *Talking* gods at that! Now, if The Tharn could be persuaded to let Thess keep it at home for further research...

The front wall lit up again, speaking again, but this time in the language of People, in a deep, emotionless voice, coming from the out-of-focus, humanlike figure. *"Damn. These. Gods. Built. This."* Thess and Rusk stood, mouths open. The wall continued, the image talking in perfect Peoplespeak, but in words without context. *"Qomp scans of cortical matter of two present mammalian individuals of unknown variety indicate human-level sentience. Surveillance and analysis of spoken language indicates polyglot creole—English grammar construction, some Russian words, Finnish phrases, Pan-Arabic tenses."*

The men understood that they were being addressed, but the sounds were without meaning. Finally, the lit front wall presented the three-dimensional figure of a human man, light-skinned with red hair, dressed in tight-fitting white clothing—as near as they could focus on him, it looked like the first god they had retrieved, many dims ago, whose rotting skull now decorated a spike at The Tharn's Place gate! Standing in front of a white background, he was apparently speaking directly to them. "Who are you?" the figure asked, in People language. The accent was a bit peculiar, but completely understandable.

Trembling, Thess answered with as much dignity as he could muster, feeling very strange in talking to a lifelike figure on a lit wall.

"I am Reader Thess, Ice Trader and Entrepreneur, of The Tharn's Town, capital city of The Tharn's Lands." Turning to Rusk (and hoping that the figure could follow his hand): "And this is one of my twins, name of Rusk."

The lit-figure remained unmoving but replied. "There is no record of your faces. And your features, your weights and your DNA scans do not correlate with any available data. Residual qomps have scanned and analyzed your brain structure, your thoughts and your speech." Roaring sounds, like the small waterfalls found Coldward, interrupted the speech, then: "Qomps show current location to be in central Wisconsin, Union of North America, seven hundred meters above mean sea level." A rasping, screeching noise erupted, hurting the men's ears. "Global access...incomplete...decay......-ty thousand years elapsed..." Then the figure faded and the front panel turned totally black, followed by dead silence, as the interior lighting began fading to nothing.

Reacting to the dimming of the light and afraid of being shut inside the strange god-machine, Thess motioned for Rusk to follow, and they both jumped down from the cylinder. As they exited, the curved door slowly rotated downward, once again seeming to meld into the cylinder's surface.

Rusk whispered, "Sire, I think this was indeed a wagon, a transport, of a kind. And I think it is dying. Just like the white-thing did." Eyes shut tight, shuddering, Thess nodded agreement. It was just too much to absorb!

SHORTLY AFTER LASTMEAL THAT DIM, A POORLY DRESSED MAN knocked on the massive wooden door of Thess' house, asking for Sire Thess. Mell admitted him, bringing him to the dining room where Thess and Rusk were sitting, having a peat-beer and discussing their findings and what to do next about the god-wagon. Rising, Thess motioned for the visitor to speak. "What is on your mind, sir?" he asked, noting the visitor's frayed furs, its faded orange trim denoting his status as a common worker, its worn condition indicating that he was poor as well.

"Sire Thess, I be a berg-man," the ragged man said meekly, "one who was with your son Rist, down to the Warm Lands, some hands of dims ago. We has news of him, if'n you want to come down to the dock pub and meet Sire Strether and the crew."

Full-throated, Thess yelled out his relief and joy, Rusk adding his shouts to the din. Mell held onto Thess and cried. The berg-man smiled at the reaction, hoping it meant he would receive some coppers of gratitude for his message. He did; Reader Thess could be very generous on occasion.

"READER THESS, RUSK," STRETHER SAID, IGNORING THE NOISY denizens in the smoke-filled riverfront pub where he was sitting at a table, "this is my son, Cruthar. He has a message for you. We jist got back a hand of dims or so ago from the Warm Lands. I knowed you would want the news 'bout Rist, so here you are."

"Pardon me, Sire," Cruthar began, lowering his head toward Thess. "Sire, I was prob'ly the last man to see little Rist, down in God's Port, in the Warm Lands. I set him up to sail away in a little boat. He couldn't leave with us because they were on the lookout for him, and questioned us hard when we left. We did wait upRiver from God's Port for a couple of days—dims—but he never showed up." Surprised, Thess shook the man's hand, grabbing him. Strether motioned for a serving-wen to pour more peat-wine. Knowing it was going to be a long story, Rusk sighed, pulling out chairs from the table for himself and Thess. Whereas Rusk himself was typically very concise in his own speech, to the point of being accused of brusqueness at times, he was well aware most People in The Tharn's Town could take forever to make a point!

After a long swig, Cruthar related a very detailed story of their berg-trip downRiver to God's Port, commenting on Rist's astonishment at the awesome city of the huge buildings; of how Rist had insulted one the Solar Priests; how he, Cruthar, helped Rist steal a spool of biter web-like material called *godscloth*; and how they witnessed the solar-incineration of their unfortunate accomplice. Thess was appalled at the behavior of the priests, though approving of Rist's initiative in absconding with the miraculous godscloth material. And dismayed at the realization that Rist had probably disappeared farther down the New River, rather than returning to The Tharn's Lands.

"And Sire," Cruthar continued, pulling out a spindle from his jacket, "Rist gave me this totem for you right when the fight was breakin' out in the pub. I tole him I'd get it to you, so here it is." Thess' heart jumped, and he motioned for Rusk to take it and Read it aloud.

Nervously, Rusk took the totem in his Reading hand and began relating Rist's account: "At first, I thought the sky was broken."

CHAPTER TWENTY-SEVEN

$\mathcal{E}$arly the next dim, Rusk walked around the green god-wagon once more, all the while re-Reading the rest of his twin's totem reports. He had hoped that Rist might shed light on the strange god-wagon, but so far to no avail. In frustration Rusk cried aloud, "Rist, my brother, did you see *anything* like this cylinder, down in the Warm Lands?"

But Rist's carved messages only spoke of impossibly tall buildings, of the near-magical godscloth, of unusual configurations of ropes and wheels, of strange-colored symbols and markings on walls and banners. "And—believe it or not, down here the sky overhead is clear and blue. Pursuing Dimness is a shining disk in the sky, too bright to look at; they call it Shining One. And the Wen of the Mist is a dimmer disk with jewels strewn across Her face, a face ravaged by dark splotches of wounds. Here, She is called Pale Lady of the Night."

Rusk laughed aloud at Rist's ridiculous comments; surely somewhere in the carvings was a joke of some kind. Or maybe the Warm Lands actually did have a different sky and different gods? Now, that was an interesting speculation: *Can different lands have different skies? That is possible,* he surmised, but it begged a question: *What is a sky anyhow? Something up high that divides Men from gods? What might be on the other side of sky? Pursuing Dimness and Wen of the Mist, most certainly. And anything else?*

Rusk's brain almost ached at a chain of thought he had never considered before, mainly because it had not impacted his daily life until now. Even Sire Thess had not speculated that far out. But a nagging problem kept arising: How *did* those two shining but dim gods move above the Misty Sky? And what exactly *were* they? The dead gods Rusk had seen didn't look like that—*they* weren't round, didn't shine, had no internal fire that lit them up. That's why Sire Thess thought they were just people—*big* people!

In unsatisfied puzzlement, Rusk finally set aside those incomprehensible thoughts, and went on to Read more of Rist's carved details of the properties of the miraculous godscloth, a mystery yet, but surely comprehensible. *That* stuff his twin had actually handled, had seen used by WarmLanders, and its possible applications in The Tharn's Lands were limitless. Rusk could imagine nets across the river, like down in the Warm Lands, to catch and hold bergs, to wait until prices went up, and better harnesses for emus and beezts, and strung up as fences on beezt ranches. *Maybe as traps for velks?* But the problem to be solved was, what could such a material be made of? Could more be made? And he wondered why no berg-man had ever brought back such tales, or any of the godscloth itself.

In Reading further, he found where Rist had asked the same questions, along with berg-man Cruthar's explanations. Rusk thought, *So, my family is not the only one that keeps valuable information secret!* And Rist's comments about the physiology of the WarmLander wen was intriguing, but probably exaggerated, he figured. *Of course, our wen have functional milk glands that swell slightly upon lactation, like all females of any animal species, but they are never very prominent. Or permanent.* Then again, Rist's description sounded a lot like the strangely attractive blonde god-wen body that The Tharn had kept.

Unfortunately, Rist's carvings shed no light upon the mystery of the god-wagon that stood above Rusk in the courtyard. He would have to solve this enigma himself, because Sire Thess had been so overwhelmed by the strangeness of the white-thing, of the lit-wall figure speaking to him, that he was no longer as rational and perceptive as usual. Rusk sighed; his Sire had always been the most imaginative, creative man of all the People, which is why he and his family were wealthy. But Rusk recognized that his overwhelmed Sire couldn't be counted on right now.

Taking the pieces of the door-destroyed scaffold and stairs as raw material, Rusk hammered together a low step-platform that enabled him to walk up to the curved doorway, carefully avoiding the location of the door itself. Placing a scaffold with steps on top of that platform, he could reach the glass bubble on top, where the white-thing resided. "White-thing," he murmured, "talk to me." With hope, he tapped on the tiny dimple again, hoping for the bubble to swing open as it had yesterdim. Noiselessly, it did, exposing the white-thing inside, some pungent fumes escaping into the air as it opened. Rusk wafted those away with his hand. "Speak to me," he commanded, sounding more confident than he felt. The white-thing responded immediately, turning its flat face to him.

"Who...are...you?" the voice was emotionless, without tone. "Where...are...crew?"

Rusk gulped. He had asked for speech and here it was; understandable, in his own language, a perfect Tharn's Town accent of the People. "I am Rusk, son of Sire Thess. Who are you? I don't know what 'crew' means."

The white-thing hesitated, and Rusk worried that it might die again. But it continued: "There is no *you*. This voice emanates from Pilot, an onboard qomp with Developing Intelligence protocols." Again, hesitation. Then: "*Crew* are three human persons on inspection survey of glacier. United North American Glacial Reconnaissance team. Stationed out of Midwest District, Missouri Prefecture, United North America."

Hearing the words, not all of them understandable, Rusk was dumbfounded. This—*machine*?—was not a Person, but spoke like one? Like the realistic imagine on the lit-wall inside the god-machine, the one that spoke to them yesterdim? The "gods"—*large people?*—

who had traveled inside it were surveying a glacier? The Ice at the End of the World? His Sire had to come out here!

At Rusk's urging, Thess reluctantly returned to the god-wagon, went up to the open bubble, and spoke to the white-thing. "How long were you in The Ice?"

The white-thing hesitated. In its monotone voice it said, "Sire Thess, There is no 'you' here. You are speaking to the craft's pilot, a Developing Intelligence qomp that is integrated in this craft. In answer to your question, the duration of time since this craft descended for an emergency pickup is precisely twenty-nine thousand, seven hundred and sixty-two years, seven months, six days." Thess had the sinking feeling that this number, incomprehensible as it was, represented a long, long time. An unimaginable time. He asked for clarification.

"Based on the analysis of your speech, Sire Thess, a standard 'year' is equal to your 'cycle.' The elapsed time, in your nonstandard numbering scheme, would be called 'close to two times a hand of hands of hands of hands of hands of hands.'"

Thess reeled; no such number had ever been contemplated in any calculation, even in any philosophical supposition, on any record in The Tharn's Lands. And with no context, he couldn't believe it. Having no way to count, or even imagine, numbers so large, he rejected them out of hand, shaking his head. Almost paralyzed by fear, he sat down on the scaffold, eyes closed. This was another blow to his sensibilities; he could not endure yet another.

But Rusk, standing behind Thess and listening to the exchange, knew that, though they were unimaginably large, the numbers were just numbers—and that the god-wagon and its "crew" were much, much older than anyone could conceive. Yet here it was. He moved beside Thess and asked, "White-thing? First, do you have a name?"

"Sire Rusk, the designation of this craft is Transport Craft UNA-201."

"I shall call you *Una*; is that acceptable?" He pronounced it *Oo-nah.*

"Sire Rusk, yes, but be aware that Una is not a 'you' or an 'I.'"

"Understood." He didn't fully, but decided to appear to have.

Hearing Rusk, Thess opened his eyes and looked up at his son with admiration. *Rusk is still thinking thoughts differently? Or thinking different thoughts? No matter; he is able to deal with this, this,* Una, *and I can't!* He felt like he was running out of brains.

Rusk asked, "Una, will you open the door again for us and let us in?"

In silent response, the door cantilevered open again, slowly this time, and lifted without pushing against the repositioned wooden platform. "Thank you, Una." The dark bubble rotated shut. Rusk and Thess climbed down from the scaffold and then up through the opening, lifting themselves up into the overly large gods-chairs. "Now, Una,' Rusk continued, "Please light up the front wall and talk to us from there." Una did so, the wall screen now filling with a three-dimensional image of a wen, one who looked like the big blonde wen-god, the dead one that The Tharn had kept. Rusk still found her unusual shape attractive.

"Is this satisfactory, Sire Rusk?" the blond-wen image asked, in the same flat Una-voice. Rusk and Thess smiled at each other. She was not in proper focus, so apparently the gods didn't know *everything*! But Rusk was determined to discover as much as he could, as fast as he could, before the god-machine "died" again.

With Thess' approval, Rusk began asking questions of this captive god-image, penetrating questions that resulted in shocking answers. The session went on for an interminable time, until the interior lights began to fade once again. They left, retiring for midmeal. Mell had prepared a wonderful beezt-roast and peat-vegetables, and they stuffed themselves.

"Rusk, my son," Thess said, between bites, breathing heavily. "Do you believe what this Una-thing has told us? Who the gods were—that they really were just large people from long ago? When The Ice was made? How we People came to be? What the whole wide world was once like?" On the verge of tears, he hefted yet another peat-beer. "If true, it means we People are very, very ignorant, and very, very poor. And very small, too. What wonders the ancient world had, and how pitiful we People are now."

After a long swig, he spoke to a puzzled Mell. "The Ice covered the ancient world of the gods all around this area of The Tharn's Lands very quickly, leaving only the ancestors of us People, protected in a scab-land of peat and caverns, living underground in a marvelous city made by the gods. But our own god-machines, the ones that saved us back then, are now long rotted away to rust and dust and forgotten. And because of lack of nutrition over countless ages, we People shrank in size." He blew out a breath. "I don't think any of our People will accept this story. I am not certain that I do myself." Mell shook her head. That strange tale *was* hard to believe!

Thess shook his head; he and The Tharn and many other men had fought the WarmLanders before, and they were large people, too. But no warrior ever spoke of them as giants or gods. "We will not instill fear in our people!" The Tharn had said back then, and no one had. Large skulls on spikes outside The Tharn's Place had quelled most curiosity.

Rusk said quietly, "Sire, I truly don't care so much what happened in those ancient times. They have gone by, but this Una was *not* able to tell us about the condition of the rest of the whole wide world *today*. Probably because it has been covered by The Ice for an unimaginable time. As far as we know, we People now may be as well off as anyone remaining in the whole destroyed world." He knew better, having read about the wonders of God's Port that Rist reported, but didn't think it wise to say so at the moment, not when his Sire was so depressed.

The next dim-rise, Thess and Rusk returned to investigate Una more thoroughly. This time their focus was on the craft itself, how it worked, what all it was capable of. They were becoming afraid that The Tharn might grow impatient and come seize it before they knew the details. Upon gaining entry and getting seated, Rusk immediately asked, "Una, how many beezt did this wagon require to move it?"

Una answered. "Sire Rusk, this craft is not pulled by animals—it moves under its own power. A small q-fusion generator at the rear provides propulsive power for all modes of transport. Please look at the forward screen."

Rusk and his Sire didn't understand *power* or some of Una's other words, but knew it was a kind of substitute for *beezt*. And the "screen" was just too close for his eyes to focus on. "Una, can you make the image clearer, please? It is not in proper focus, being too close."

Una hesitated, then answered. "Sire Rusk, Sire Thess, both of you, please open both your eyes wide. Then look at the red spot on the front screen and do not blink." Rusk did as he was told, and Thess did likewise. There was a slight flash of light, making them blink. "There," Una said, "your visual impairments—acute farsightedness—have been analyzed and corrective measures have been taken to give you perfect vision. Now, please observe the image."

The image on the screen was perfectly clear now. Surprised, Rusk looked down at his own hands—they looked as clear as if they were distant! "What did you do, Una? This is wonderful!"

Holding both palms up, Thess was likewise stunned at the sight. They were both clear! "Rusk!" he yelled, "what has Una done to my eyes? You...you are as clear as a distant emu!" He reached out and stroked his son's face. "Is that really you?" A quick stroke revealed the memorized similarity, confirming that the detailed face in front of him was indeed Rusk's own, no longer a smooth, blurred visage but one of remembered textures, now corresponding to visual features he had never experienced.

Una spoke. "Sire Rusk, Sire Thess, this craft is outfitted for minor and corrective surgery. Lasers and microbots handle all but the most critical medical exigencies. Is your vision better now?" Rusk didn't answer, being too busy looking at fascinating details within the cabin —the lettering, the screens, the pushbutton depressions.

"It's true, Sire," he told Thess, observing the older man's distinctive face, creases and crevices, like a ravaged landscape seen from afar, as wrinkled as a furrowed peat field, darker lines against a dark face, but somehow projecting strength and determination. "It's what we truly look like. Our eyes must have been partially blinded, since The Beginning of All Things. But now we can see what has been hidden from us. We can now *see* what we can *touch*." He wondered, even though he didn't believe in magic, *Maybe it is magic of a sort? Whatever it is, it is wonderful!*

Una interrupted his reverie. "To your original question, Sire Rusk, please look at the forward screen." That plate showed a small three-dimensional model of the green god-machine called Una, as seen from three different directions—front, side, and top. Rusk had never seen such a presentation before, but understood it at once as a novel and clever way of showing a lot of information at one time, on a small scale. He would remember—and carve—this trick! As Una spoke of a feature, the details of the particular referenced image would expand on the screen, as if a person were looking at it up close. *Very, very clever!*

Una continued. "Sire Rusk, this craft is capable of using wheels"—the three-dimensional model sprouted numerous black wheels below its cylindrical shape—"or treads"—strangely shaped, beezt-skin-like material, stretched over wheels, emerged from the bottom—"articulated limbs "—eight huge, biter-like legs with big pads for feet—"or short-term aerial propulsion"—holes appeared on the sides and bottom, meaning nothing to Rusk. But the image was shown rising from the ground, into the air—surrounded by shimmering haloes of changing colors, primarily a greenish tinge—and apparently traveling at enormous speed. Rusk could not believe that the huge green cylinder, the one he was sitting in, could actually float in air, and move in the sky like a gull-bird!

"Sire Rusk, the craft also operates as well on top of water and under it." The lit-wall screen showed the small model Una speeding across a vase expanse of water, then diving deep into it. *Like a beezt, like a bird, like a fish, too!* Rusk noted. *Is there anything Una can't do?*

"Una"—he gulped—"how do I use these, these, *propulsions*?" The word felt strange on his tongue. *Are these words similar to a spell, like some superstitious People believe, like some old wen out in the peat fields who can supposedly use words to drive out vermin? Do these new words themselves have some kind of force, or do they open up a spell of some kind?* Even for Rusk's different ways of thinking, such concepts were hard to grasp.

"Sire Rusk, only a verbal command as to mode and destination is required." Rusk asked for more detailed information on the flying aspects, but understood nothing of the explanation: "MHD fields draw in outside air, ionize it, eject it through micronozzle arrays on the entire exterior surface. Combined with magnetic field manipulation and antimagnetic borophene screens, this enables lift, attitude control, and directional velocity vectoring."

Without knowing what most of those words signified, Rusk was trying to think things through. "Uh, Una, if you 'die' while we are in the air, do we fall?"

"Sire Rusk, there is no 'you' here, only a DI simulation that cannot terminate. Power from the fusion pack has been randomly interrupted because some non-quantum distribution components have aged out, corroded, or outgassed during the thirty millennia of non-activity. After sufficient incident sunlight rebooted the exterior shell complexes, and after you awakened the internal system several *days* ago, onboard nanobots have been effecting repairs to most damage. Una does not anticipate any such failures again, though operations may be somewhat erratic or limited in scope. Mean Time to Failure is now estimated as approximately five years."

"So we won't fall if we fly?"

The Una-image nodded assent. "Yes, Sire Rusk. And even if something unexpected occurred, the craft would land safely using stored auxiliary power."

Rusk didn't ask if the dead god-crew had been killed in the crash from one of those heights. He was not totally certain what all Una's explanations meant, either, but with his curiosity aroused he was assured enough to attempt something that no Person had done in—"*In thirty thousand cycles!*" He looked at Thess, who was still in a near state of shock from Una's continuing revelations and from his newfound near vision. *My Sire is uncertain right now*, Rusk thought. I *must make the decisions he would, were he himself!*

With a nod toward his Sire, Rusk said, "Una, fly us up a few man-lengths and then stop!"

Rusk and Thess felt a slight *lurch* as the god-machine moved upward from the courtyard. Instantly, the side walls of the cylinder turned transparent; whether they were "screens" or actually transparent walls, Rusk couldn't tell. He was glad, though, that the floor of the flying cylinder remained opaque. *Or is that solidity just a "screen" too?* He didn't dare question Una on that. The view outside was partially obscured by a pulsating green glow below their craft, extending out some few man-lengths, but what he could see was literally awe-inspiring.

Trying to absorb the reality that he was now floating five man-lengths above the courtyard, Rusk eagerly looked to see over the stone wall surrounding the courtyard; in the dimming light of Pursuing Dimness, he made out neighboring thatched-roof houses. His eyes were now wide in amazement, his mouth open in awe; he was speechless. Below and to their right he and Thess saw the emu corrals; in the far distance, the New River. To the left, in the distance, the shadow of The Tharn's Place loomed over the low rooftops of The Tharn's Town. Directly below them was the shimmering green halo, apparently what was giving Una the *power* to fly.

"Rusk," Thess whispered, almost pleading. "How is this possible? Only peat-birds and gull-birds and river-birds can fly. Nothing this large can! *We* can't!"

With a big smile, Rusk replied, waving his arms wide. "Sire, Una *is* flying. And so are *we*! Look out these clear walls—we are in the air, above our courtyard. All around us, below us, is The Tharn's Town. We've always been told that the gods could fly. This must be how they did it!"

But Thess squeezed his eyes tight, shutting out the unbelievable panorama spread out around him. "Please, Rusk, take us back down. I cannot absorb all of this now." Shaking his head and grimacing, a disappointed Rusk so ordered.

CHAPTER TWENTY-EIGHT

*a*fter a few peat-beers, Thess was calming down; Mell, at his side, continued to wipe sweat from his feverish forehead.

"Rusk," Thess said, "I know in my mind that this, this, Una-thing can fly. That we flew up in it. But in my heart, I still can't believe it, any of it. That the gods were only people, that they built Una, that they knew so much more than we ever will." Head in hands, he bent over the dining table. "I know all of this is real, but I can't begin to fully accept it all."

Rusk was barely paying attention, just enjoying his newfound near vision. Seeing his birther, Mell, up close for the first time had been a heartwarming moment. In her face were similar lines as in his Sire's, not as deep, but angling upward from her mouth as if relaxed, caring. Though he had little previous experience with detailed facial features, he instinctively recognized the significance of his birther's closed lips turning up at the ends—the first smile he had ever seen. He'd had no idea that near vision could bring such joy to his heart and peacefulness to his mind. *What have our People been missing all these cycles, all these years! What will other People think if we can have Una repair their eyes?*

Finally listening to what Thess was saying, Rusk objected. "Sire, you have always taught us to only accept as fact our own direct experiences, not mere gossip or worse, unfounded superstitions. Yet out in our courtyard is the greatest discovery in the history of The Tharn's Lands, maybe the most wonderful made-thing, machine, ever, anywhere. You *have* to believe it!" He was about to have a breakdown in discipline himself, at his Sire's obstinate refusals.

Birther Mell came to Rusk, hugging him as she had when he was a small child. "Rusk, Sire Thess," she said quietly, thoughtfully, while stroking his hair, "if that big green thing *can* fly, and it *can* travel as high and as fast as any bird, may you not use it and fly to the Warm Lands and find our Rist? Please?"

Her men stared at her. Their Mell seldom spoke except in the most innocuous terms, never demanding anything, never suggesting new ideas. Yet in the one simple question she had skillfully addressed both the reality of the Una craft and the best possible use for its amazing capabilities.

"We don't know how far it can travel, Mell," Thess sputtered, unused to his wen's outburst. "We don't know if it is safe. And we don't even know where Rist is!"

Rusk answered his birther's inquiry. "Birther Mell, Sire, why don't we experiment with Una, see how high it can fly, how fast. And if it shows us it won't fall from the sky, why *don't* we go downRiver and find Rist?"

"STEP UP, MELL," THESS SAID, AS HIS WEN STOOD IN FRONT OF UNA'S open door. "You won't believe what you will see." He grinned at Rusk, who smiled back. Within two minutes, her near vision repaired, Mell began sobbing, stroking her men's faces. "Sire, Rusk, is this how you really look? You are both so, so, *beautiful*!" A look of anger and determination flashed in her face. "Why was this beauty kept from us all our lives? *Why?* Can we fix everybody's sight?"

Thess held her closely, stroking her hair. He was wondering the same thing, just now appreciating the fine texture of his wen's long black hair, its fine detail as appealing visually as it always had been by Touch.

"It's a long story, Birther Mell," Rusk said. "Una tried to explain it to me, but it happened when People were very new, many hands of cycles ago." He asked Una to light up the screen to let Mell see what wonders could be found inside the Una craft, what all it could do.

After a short time, Mell asked, "And so we can fly, Una? How high can you fly? And how far?" Finding Rist was topmost in her mind.

"Birther Mell, I can fly anywhere in the earth's atmosphere, and any distance."

Mell was speechless, but by now nothing surprised Rusk, even though he had no idea of what Una's answer signified. He had a sudden inspiration. "Una, how high is the Misty Sky?"

"Sire Rusk, the lower level of what you call the 'Misty Sky' is an average of three thousand meters at this moment of twilight." That number sounded large but Rusk had nothing by way of comparison— except that The Ice had gone up even higher, into the Misty Sky. Then another unbidden vision, an astonishing question, arose.

"Una, does the Misty Sky go on forever?" Irritated at himself for thinking of such a stupid question out of nowhere, Rusk's own mind answered it: *Of course it does! What* else *could be up there?*

But Una answered, "Sire Rusk. The present cloud cover averages some two thousand meters thick at this moment of twilight." The concept that the Misty Sky was of finite thickness was a shock, one that Rusk would have to see proof of, himself.

"Una," he asked sarcastically, "Can you take us *above* the Misty Sky?"

THESS STARTED TO OBJECT, BUT SAT DOWN WITH HIS ARMS AROUND HIS wen, fearful of what might be coming. Una moved for several minutes, its passengers aware only of swiftly moving breaks in the surrounding mist as seen through the transparent walls, as if they were moving upwards at great speed. Then Una stopped gradually, so that they felt only a slight weight-lessening sensation when the god-wagon's motion ceased.

For several minutes, none of the People could speak as they tried to take in the vast panorama spread out around them in all directions. Visible through the transparent walls lay the Misty Sky—but *below* them!—an awe-inspiring, turbulent expanse of milky clouds, dark in one direction.

"Sire, it's, it's beautiful, beautiful," Mell mewed. Thess and Rusk nodded agreement, themselves unable to speak.

Rusk was trying to absorb the enormity of their situation, the new environment, the possible dangers. He knew from Una's answers that the gods of olden times used to fly over and through the Misty Sky as easily as his own People sailed on the New River. But he also knew that Una had crashed once before.

"Una, are we safe here?" he asked. "Do we still have 'power'?" He wasn't sure what "power" was, but apparently it propelled Una and kept it afloat.

"Sire Rusk," Una answered, "yes, you are safe. And warm; the environmental controls show you are experiencing temperature, humidity, oxygen, air pressure, all within normal ranges. Do you wish to change anything?"

All three People kept surveying the awe-inspiring sights from their vantage point above the Misty Sky, which was a vast sea of spreading clouds, defining the horizon in all directions. Above them, another strange sky spread out like a dome, some scattered clouds strewn across a darkening background. Apparently the dark portion to their right was Dimwise, and to their left, Darkwise, on the far horizon. But something else floated above that horizon, a strange red disk, almost too bright to view. Mell was shaking her head, pointing at it, close to sobbing.

Suddenly, embarrassed, Rusk asked, "Una! What is that red disk over Darkwise, close to the horizon?" With a sinking feeling, he felt the answer before it came.

"Sire Rusk, that glowing object is the setting sun. What you call Pursuing Dimness." Rusk was overwhelmed at the sight, but more so at the realization that the accepted cosmology of his culture, of his idea of his own place in the Universe, was completely false—his twin Rist had not been joking. *There is only one sky! And we People have never seen above it. Until now. And our shining god is not fuzzy, but sharp-edged! And a disk!* At Mell's tug on his arm, he turned to see on the opposite horizon that a much dimmer disk of the same size as—*the Sun?*—but yellowish and marred with gray spots, with strings of colored beads across its face, was just rising above the turbulent panorama of white mist.

"Sire Rusk," Una continued, "now rising over the clouds Dimwise —to the East—you may observe Earth's primary satellite, the Moon. Known to you as the Wen of the Mist."

Rusk stumbled backwards and held onto the giant rotted seat, staring at the strange yellow disk with the dark splotches and colorful pinpoints of lights. He felt sick, not knowing what to do next. As he had been in childhood, when frightened by dark-night feardreams, he needed the strength and comfort of his Sire and his birther, right away. But they, too, were quivering in fear.

Gathering his courage, Rusk spoke in a raspy whisper, "Una, please take us back down."

———

As Una descended toward the courtyard, the craft suddenly stopped. "Una, what's wrong?" Rusk yelled out in surprise; they were at least two hands of man-lengths above the ground. "Take us on down!"

"Sire Thess, there is a possible hostile threat below. Please observe. Awaiting further orders."

Rusk and Thess rushed to look over the shimmering green glow beneath them in their courtyard. There they saw two hands or more of Tharn's Men, holding torches and spears, staring up at them, awestruck at the craft and at the People they could see inside it through the green haze and transparent walls. Thess blurted out, "What are they doing, Rusk? Can you tell?"

"Sire, I don't think they are friendly, not with so many of them, not with torches and spears. Why would The Tharn be threatening us?"

"I don't know." Thess turned toward the lit-wall screen. "Una, can they hear me, below?"

"Sire Thess, I have enabled a loud-speaker. Your voice will be amplified for the men below to hear you." Rusk was taken aback by Una's latest surprise, but Thess appeared to accept it without further thought. Rusk thought his Sire was finally adapting to the new world that Una had brought them. *Even if Una is really from an Old World, a much, much older world!*

"Below there," Thess bellowed. "What do you want?" His booming voice cowed the warriors below, but their leader stood his ground, if uneasily.

That Tharn's Man yelled back, "Sire Thess, The Tharn wants you to report to him immediately! His spies have seen his 'flying bird thing' going up into the Misty Sky. The Tharn demands that you bring his flying god-machine to him right this minute!"

Breathing hard, Thess turned to Rusk. "We can't let Una take us down. We can't let The Tharn have Una. Quickly, what do you think we should do?" He paused, thinking out loud. "The Tharn might be drunk. Or scared. No matter; I am not going to give away our own future to that ignorant man!"

Before Rusk could respond, Thess made a decision and told Una to *loud-speak* his voice: "Tharn's Men. Tell The Tharn that we will be flying away for a while. When we return, we will discuss what is to be done with this—flying machine!"

"Come down now from that...that...green bird!" The foremost Tharn's Man wasn't waiting; he threw his stone-tipped weapon directly at Thess.

Thess ducked to the floor of the god-wagon. The spear struck —*midair!*—and bounced off of—*nothing!*—as if glancing from a large stone. The other Tharn's Men, mouths open, hesitated. "Kill him! Kill him!" their furious leader cried. More and more spears bounced off the invisible barrier, and by this time other Tharn's Men, were swinging large swords at Una, even though the craft was floating in the air far higher than those weapons would reach.

But Rusk yelled, "Una, take us up higher, quickly! Three hands of man-lengths! Now! Sire! Birther! Hold on!"

A weight seemed to pull them all down against the floor of the god-wagon. They were aware only of an acceleration and a quick stop, which threw them up against the ceiling of their craft, followed by a slam down against the floor.

"Sire, Birther! Are you hurt?" Rusk asked.

"We're fine," Thess answered, picking Mell up. "Both of us." But Mell was cowering, holding onto Thess and whimpering.

Rusk rushed to look down at their attackers. He saw The Tharn's Men, now appearing the size of little dolls, shaking their spears impotently. Growling, the Tharn's Man leader once again hurled his spear toward Una, quickly followed by all of those of his men. Within seconds, the spears once more stopped in midair, again falling back to earth before the unbelieving eyes of the warriors. Rusk could read the shock in their eyes: *A strong magic!*

After their spears repeatedly bounced off of—the *air?*—and the god-machine had unbelievably risen even farther out of range, the guards realized they had exhausted all their inventory of violent means. At the command of their furious leader, the frustrated warriors gleefully set fire to Thess' compound. The family looked down, helplessly and with horror as their home, warehouse, and emu corrals —the emus themselves!—were torched before their very eyes. *They even burned our two-legs!* Rusk thought in fury. From their vantage point, even though Una's magic shield had protected them, the family was distraught at the needless destruction of all their belongings and especially of their birds.

Thess tried to comfort his wen and his son. "I have more coppers stashed away," he said sadly, "and a place for us to go, with food and drink for all of us for at least a whole cycle." But he had no idea as to what the rest of their lives would be like. The Tharn was not a forgiving man, and The Tharn's Lands were not all that large. Thess had always planned ahead, but this situation was outside any expectation whatsoever. He had a thought. *The Warm Lands, maybe? Some other place?*

Below them, the fire from their estate had spread, glowing clouds of flying sparks igniting other thatched roofs. Thess felt sympathy for those innocent townspeople, now rushing to get water to fight the fires. He knew The Tharn was sure to blame him for the damages and deaths. Sighing, he ordered Una to return to above the Misty Sky, far from The Tharn's wrath.

After the immolation was complete, more upset by their failure than by the invincible and impossible flying machine, The Tharn's Men contingent departed, cursing, to return to their chief and report on the magical disappearance of his subjects—and his flying machine— up into the Misty Sky.

ONCE MORE RISING ABOVE THE MISTY SKY, THESS WAS THINKING furiously about what to do next, where to go. But Mell, surprisingly adaptable, was trying to appreciate the reality of the whole wide world she saw around her. Overhead, the Wen of the Mist glowed brightly against the darkest sky any of the People had ever seen, a sky sparkled with tiny white lights and a wispy cloudlike shape that bisected the overhead horizon-to-horizon black dome. "And what are those lights, that milky path, Sire?" she asked. But Thess could barely speak above a whisper, as Mell continued to gaze in wonder. "And all that blackness behind it?"

Rusk asked the question of Una, and a human image—the dark-skinned god this time—appeared on the front wall of the cabin. "Sire Rusk, the lights in the sky are *stars*. They are similar to what you call 'Pursuing Dimness,' but which most humans call 'the Sun.' They are extremely far away, and so appear tiny to you. They are not. The cloud of stars you call the 'Milky Path' is known as the 'Milky Way' to most human cultures. It is an edge view of our galaxy, a group of stars which comprises untold numbers of disks like the Sun.

"And the blackness beyond it all is called the Universe."

Thess sat quietly for several minutes, mind racing, his pulse quickening; he was nearly ill of stomach. *So much newness, so many new facts!* After calming himself down, his mind went back to more familiar thoughts, purposely forgetting for the moment the danger of ever returning to The Tharn's Town or indeed, to anywhere in The Tharn's Lands: *This new information must be of value—no People have seen any of this, not even in legend or myth. If this god-wagon, this Una, can move in any direction as fast as it did* up, *it alone would revolutionize transport! Imagine, bringing crops directly to The Tharn's Town without beezt and carts! Imagine watching The Ice calve and returning with that news in minutes instead of taking dims of travel by emu...* The possibilities overwhelmed him; Thess' mind could not handle the shock, and he slumped back in his giant chair, shaking his head, as Mell comforted him silently.

"Sire, are you ill?" Rusk asked, interrupting his Sire's feverish thoughts. Having experienced the new and upsetting knowledge himself, he deduced his Sire's condition. "Sire, all of this, this, new *information* is so hard to accept, but as you have always demanded—out there beyond these clear walls is the evidence. The Misty Sky is below us"—he pointed down at the turbulent moonlit sea of clouds below them—"And the Wen of the Mist—the *Moon*, Una calls it—is truly a glowing disk. As was Pursuing Dimness—the *Sun*—before it sank into the Dark over there.

"The whole world is not as we have known it to be," Rusk continued, his own mind racing, "And we have the chance to make use of this experience. What shall we do with it, Sire? And Una tells me that this god-wagon—*aircraft* it is called—is able to travel many dim-marches in mere minutes. Shall we ask Una to take us somewhere?"

Mell spoke first: "To find Rist?"

PART SIX

FLIGHT

CHAPTER TWENTY-NINE

*T*he Misty Sky—*Cloud cover!* Thess thought—below Una stretched out as far as the horizon in all directions, wavelets of cloud-tops moving like grass in a field. In the early-morning light of the *Sun* (as Una's passengers now called it), that shining object was indeed too bright to look at directly. The vast blue sky overhead surrounding it in all directions, like an enormous curved ceiling in the distance, was, to Thess, as awesome as the brilliant disk itself.

"Sire, everything is just as Rist wrote," Rusk said, still impressed by the sight of being above what he—and all People, for unimaginable cycles—had thought was the infinite sky. "And the *Wen*, er, the Moon, has disappeared into the Dark. Rist said that in the Warm Lands the Sun and the Moon are still considered gods, but called by other names."

Thess had a disturbing thought. The voice and the image this time were of the blonde wen-god. Thess liked her bodily curves, though he didn't exactly know why. Fearing any answer, he asked, "Una, are the, the 'Sun' and the 'Moon' some kind of gods? If not, what are they?"

Rusk dropped his jaw at his Sire's unexpected question. *If they aren't gods, what else could they be? Then again, the big dead gods are just humans on a larger scale, and* they *are not big and round.*

"Sire Thess, they are large inanimate objects that many human cultures have worshipped as 'gods.' But they are not living creatures of any kind. The Sun is a glowing ball of fusion fire a million times larger than Earth—what you have called 'the whole wide world.'" Una paused, as if to give its listeners time to absorb the concepts being presented. Una's Developing Intelligence was learning more about its small passengers than they were of it.

"The Moon is a rocky satellite of Earth. It is much smaller than the Sun but much closer to Earth, so they appear to be the same size. The Moon orbits the Earth, and together they both orbit the Sun."

Thess gulped, shutting his eyes. He didn't know what "million" meant, or "orbit," or "satellite," but understood that his former gods were not alive; they were very large *objects,* very far away, doing very unimaginable things.

DESPITE MELL'S PROTESTS—WHICH AT ONE TIME WOULD HAVE BEEN quite shocking, for any wen in The Tharn's Lands—Thess ordered Una to find his hidden redoubt: "Along the river, somewhere about halfway up from The Tharn's Town to The Ice at the End of the World. A small canyon with an entrance high up from the path, a narrow cleft that I covered with scrub brush."

Ignoring Rusk's misgivings about dropping below the Misty Sky —"*Cloud cover!*" Thess insisted they call it from now on—and being reported by peatsants, Thess had Una descend and began his search. "Things look so different from so high up, Rusk. I don't know if I can tell where that cave is."

"Una," Rusk asked, "from Sire Thess' description, can you locate his canyon and the cave?" Una responded on-screen with several possibilities, zooming in closely. After Thess dismissed all but two possible sites, Rusk asked Una to drop down into each location to check them out. The final one was it.

"I can see my canyon from up here," Thess said. "We will have to go to the ground. Can you do that, Una?"

Una answered, and the craft settled down into a narrow cleft in the rock-strewn hillside. Thess took Mell and Rusk inside his concealed cave for a tour, showing off his labor of hands of cycles past. "Stacks of beezt-jerky here"—he pointed to sealed-up stone niches—"away from vermin, kept at cool temperatures the year around." Another niche ended in an ice wall. "And here is beezt-cheese and -milk, and imperishable peat-bread." A beezt-sized stone vat contained "the best peat-beer I ever made." Thess went on to say that he and his twin, Rees, had often camped at this place, many cycles ago when they were young. "It was always a refuge of last resort," he said. "Never really thought I'd need it, but here it is." He slid a heavy stone slab on the floor, revealing a pile of shiny coins. "And a good amount of coppers, just in case."

On the firepit spit, Mell cooked them a lastmeal of marinated beezt-jerky, spiced by a selection of herbs that Thess had thoughtfully provided over many cycles. After eating, she implored Thess once again to go searching for Rist, down in the Warm Lands.

"No, Mell, I will not," he insisted. "I am too confused right now, with all of the revelations that Una has made, what it represents. I don't know how safe that 'craft' actually is, or if it will fall from the 'cloud cover' as it must have when The Ice began." Rusk could tell that his Sire was struggling to maintain his composure. "I don't even know who our People are, who *we* are. I cannot begin to think coherently, and will not risk all our lives on a possibly fatal expedition Warmward."

That Dark, Thess' cool cave was toasty warm, the hearth-fire smoke venting up through natural cracks. "Smoke dissipates throughout the rubble far above," Thess explained. "It will never be noticed." Rusk appreciated his Sire's well-thought-out amenities, but spent most of the night awake on a straw mat on the floor of Una. Thinking.

THE NEXT DIM-RISE, RUSK TOLD HIS SIRE AND BIRTHER THAT HE WAS confident that he and Una could find Rist. "Rusk, my son," Mell begged, "don't go alone. Losing one of you is terrible enough. Losing both…" She didn't finish, but just put her head on Thess' shoulder.

But Thess had been thinking, too. "All Dark long I wrestled with our plight, and I have to agree with you, Rusk," his Sire said. "You are able to think new thoughts, and think thoughts differently, so you are the one who should work with Una. Your birther and I will remain hidden here. We are well concealed, even if The Tharn comes looking for us. We are well provisioned, and we have a library of totems to Read." Rusk noticed that Sire Thess did not mention his armory of spears, knives, and shortswords. *For all the good they would do against The Tharn's Men!* Rusk thought.

The decision being final, Mell sighed. After firstmeal, Thess oversaw the provisioning of Una—meat, water, cheese, peat-beer. "And a sword and a hand of spears," Thess said, out of Mell's hearing. "In case any WarmLanders may be hostile."

After brief handshakes, hugs, and tears, Rusk gave the command, "Una. Rise above the—*cloud cover* and head directly Warmward."

TAKING FOR GRANTED THE FORMERLY OUTRAGEOUS IDEA OF FLYING above the Misty Sky, and now with Mell and Sire Thess safely ensconced beyond The Tharn's reach, Rusk was feeling comfortable in his newfound environment. He was wondering when it would be possible to see the New River from above; in that way he could follow Rist's route, hopefully down to God's Port, see its huge buildings—and maybe obtain some of its magical godscloth. He was determined to have some of that biter-web-like material, by any means necessary. Out loud he said to himself, "If Rist went downRiver and saw a 'broken sky' with only scattered clouds and a blue sky above him, then eventually the cloud cover below me should go away and I can see downward to the New River as he saw upward from it."

Rocky peaks rose above the clouds on each side ahead of Una, the turbulence seemingly channeled between the upthrust rocky mountains, speeding up as it flowed Warmward (*south*ward!). Then suddenly, down below—a dim-march down, Una said—Rusk could make out a narrow, shimmering, ribbon-like surface winding its way out of the rapids, the moving water slowing into a long, wide lake. *It's the River! But a long way down there*, he thought. "Una, please take me down closer to the River."

"As you wish, Sire Rusk. Una will remain ten man-lengths above the water surface. In standard scientific terminology, that is equivalent to approximately eight meters." Rusk could not translate that unit. He knew right then that he would have to learn Una's units, its numbering systems. Already Una was having difficulty in explaining huge numbers in terms of 'hands.' Hopefully, the ancient counting system, based instead on "two hands" as Una had said, would not be too hard to learn. He was looking forward to it. When he had time.

Rusk was again in awe as Una lowered him above the wide, slow-flowing New River, a placid body of water winding its way through vast fields of towering vegetation, all under a peaceful blue sky. Somewhere down this river, he knew, he would find Rist!

As UNA CRUISED SLOWLY DOWN THE NEW RIVER, SOME TEN *METERS* above the water, matching the pace of the water flow, Rusk was enjoying the scenery. Tall trees, each worth a fortune back home, lined each bank as far as the eye could perceive. He marveled at the unclaimed timber. *Enough wood to rebuild The Tharn's Town manyhands over!* Birds of unknown species, colorful and loud, rose in flocks to escape Una's predatory mien; apparently anything large and flying was perceived as a threat by them.

From Rist's report, Rusk expected soon to see the welcoming towers of God's Land. So he was delighted to spot the tall yellow cylindrical buildings, the ones Rist had reported, with the strange red-painted symbols on them, a figure similar to a spoked wheel but with horizontal and vertical lines pointing in the four directions. He thought,

Just like Rist wrote, here are the buildings that mark the boundary of God's Land.

Rusk could see the impressive constructions, manyhands times taller than The Tharn's Place. But hadn't Cruthar mentioned that some towers like these were protected by big rock-throwing machines? He decided against flying between them to find out. He said, "Una, fly higher and directly overland, to the big city of God's Port, to the tallest building there." *Rist said that the priests there were educated men, even if cruel in their punishments. I myself haven't offended them, so surely they will help me locate him.* Rist had identified the priest's temple as being the tallest structure in the city. As an afterthought he said, "Just keep out of range of those sun-burning reflectors, if you will."

Approaching the vast city far inland and from due north, avoiding the other pair of twin towers that guarded the harbor, Rusk saw laid out before him a sight of awe and wonder—God's Port—a beautiful pattern of rectangular stone buildings on wide streets radiating like spokes from a central hub. A hub with the tallest building in the city. "Una, that tall structure there at the center of the city! That must be the priests' temple, the one Rist wrote about."

In astonishment at the massive stoneworks, the numerous stone buildings, and the colorful banners spread across the broad avenues, Rusk found it hard to believe that such magnificence could be produced by evil people who burnt others alive. He also realized now that by comparison The Tharn's Town was…small, ugly, and very dirty.

Una dropped down to twenty-five meters, still far out of the range of any potential spears, and slowly flew over the city, from the harbor docks—"Where Rist left from!" Rusk pointed, excitedly—drawing crowds of awestruck lookers who pointed toward them, some shouting. At Rusk's command, Una reached the courtyard of the large temple and descended a bit, remaining ten meters above the central plaza. "Una, keep a watch on those large covered disks," Rist said. "Those are the killing machines that concentrate the Sun's rays. If they are uncovered, we are being attacked." He had Una drop further, down to a hand of man-lengths—"Four meters," Una said—high enough for him to see out over the crowd, yet low enough to make out individuals. He was becoming very appreciative of his newfound near vision.

By now, manyhands of hands (*hundreds*, Una would say) of people were gathering. *All of them tall,* Rusk noted. *And of many different colors of skin and of hair.* Below him, the crowd pulled back as two hands of big, burly guards with polished chest armor, helmets, and long spears appeared, clearing a pathway down which a tall, thin, pale bearded man in a pristine white robe walked confidently toward them. "Here comes a priest now, I'll bet," Rusk whispered. The man sported that same red symbol emblazoned across his vest.

All those spears concerned Rusk. Thinking of Una's "magic" way of stopping The Tharn's Men's spears in the air, he asked, "Una, can the shield protect me from the spears and swords outside, the way it stopped those in my Sire's courtyard?"

"Sire Rusk, yes. The protective magnetic borophene shield can be as wide as ten meters in all directions above the ground."

Rusk smiled. "Then do it, and set us down on the ground here."

CHAPTER THIRTY

$\mathcal{A}$s Una landed, Rusk opened the curved door and stepped out. It was *hot*! He removed his thick velk coat, tossed it and his footwear back into the aircraft, and stood on the courtyard pavement in a loincloth and thin undershirt, spreading his arms wide to show he had no weapons, and smiled broadly. The crowd drew back, as did the guards themselves. Rusk could imagine their fear; if this had happened in The Tharn's Lands, prior to all of Una's explanations and demonstrations, he would have been fearful, too.

The priest, however, walked up toward the craft, stopping ten meters out, pressing his hands against the air, as if a wall prevented his further passage. The bearded, robed man shouted out something that Rusk couldn't understand at first. But upon the priest's repeated shouting, Rusk finally realized that the man was speaking in a thickly accented Peoplespeak.

Rusk spoke. "Hello, I am Rusk, of The Tharn's Lands. Far to the—the—*north*, upRiver. I am come searching for my twin, Rist. He was here, in your temple, some, some, *weeks* ago." He was hoping that the unfamiliar terms of time were making sense to the priest.

The man roared in response. "What is this big green thing? A god?

You, black dwarf, are you a messenger from a god? How can you fly?" Rusk realized the man had his own agenda, and wasn't interested in Rist's. He repeated his message.

Rusk replied, "I am not a god. I am a man. This green thing is a god-wagon, one that I own. It flies me wherever I want. I repeat, I am looking for my twin, Rist. He looks just like me!"

Around Una, the crowd was closing in, touching the invisible shield. The guards, emboldened by their priest's defiant voice, were appearing to become agitated. The priest spoke more softly now. "How can you fly? How can you make the air into a wall to keep me away? Tell me, are you not a god?"

Rusk shook his head. "No, I am a man. Please hear me. This flying thing is a machine; no more a living thing than are your pulleys and stone-working tools."

The priest continued staring in disbelief, when suddenly a look of recognition flashed across his face. His demeanor changed from supplication to aggression, and he yelled out for all the crowd to hear: "Little dark man, are *you* the godscloth thief whom we tried to catch weeks ago? The other criminal that we burnt here in this plaza"—he waved his arm around dramatically—"he told us he had accomplices, dwarves like yourself. You all look alike to me, but—are you *that* thief?"

Reluctantly, Rusk backed up and stepped back in the aircraft, while Una closed the curved door. But the priest, now preaching to an angry mob, shouted, "People of God's Port! This criminal stole our godscloth! He insulted me, a priest of the gods! And now he has stolen a flying machine from the gods! He must be stopped! And punished!"

"Una," Rusk asked, hopefully, "is it possible to protect me from these People, while I try to talk sense into that priest?"

"Sire Thess, yes. The motion-resistant field can be maintained indefinitely."

Desperate for a solution to finding where Rist might be, not wanting to miss this opportunity, Thess was thinking desperately. "I just want to speak to the priest without him seeing me. Can you do that? With that *loud-speaker* you used at our home?"

"Sire Rusk, yes. The transparent walls will be opaqued from outside. Your voice will be transmitted through an external speaker so that you may converse with people outside. But the shield field will have to be reduced to very close to the exterior surface of the aircraft. Is that acceptable? If so, you may speak now."

"This is Rusk, son of Reader Thess," he began as the clear walls became solid to the crowd outside, his voice booming loudly from the surface of Una. The God's Port people backed up at the godlike booming voice. But the priest and his guards stood their ground, Rusk noticed. "I come from far north of you, from The Tharn's Lands. Many of you have bought and used the icebergs that we send down the River." He paused, hoping that practical fact would establish his credentials and create a bit of trust among the crowds outside the aircraft. "I have taken control of this ancient flying machine—an 'aircraft.' It won't harm you, and I mean you no harm, either. I am searching for my twin Rist, who was here in God's Port some weeks ago. If someone can help me find him, I will reward you with a large bag of coppers. Again, I mean no harm. I only need your help."

What Rusk saw then was the priest waving his arms, occasionally shouting, at other times speaking quietly to a number of guards, who came and went. Thess waited patiently, hoping that this meant that the authorities—the priests or whomever—were coming to terms with reality and would speak rationally to him. At the first sign of any real danger, he would have Una quickly whisk him up and far away from the temple, and from the city, if necessary. But he wanted to stay close to these people, some who may have seen Rist—presumably when he had left on a sailboat, if Cruthar's assumptions had been correct.

A few bolder of the crowd pressed forward, attempting to touch Una's surface, the shield now only a handwidth from the hull. The guards allowed this, which Rusk thought strange. *Maybe it is good to let them get close to Una*, he thought. *They can see that it is a solid machine, not anything living or godlike.*

After several hours of nonresponse to his repeated pleas for assistance, Rusk decided that he should just leave and go searching out of the harbor and down the River. But a loud *thump!* shook the craft.

Outside, he could see that the mob of people had drawn back several man-lengths—*meters!*—from Una. "What are they doing?" he yelled aloud. Another *thump!* And another! "Una, what are they doing out there?" he demanded.

"Sire Thess, it appears as if they have positioned a net of some kind over this aircraft fuselage. Around the perimeter of the net, they have positioned large stones to hold it down."

"Well, get me out of here!" Rusk yelled, panicking at the vision of being captured and roasted by insane priests. "Take us up ten—*meters* —now!" He braced himself for the sudden acceleration, but Una did not move.

"Una, now! Up! Quickly!" he ordered again. Still no motion.

"Sire Rusk, this aircraft is programmed not to attempt to penetrate the borophene complex mesh that now surrounds it, the material you refer to as 'godscloth.' Such action is prohibited for crew-safety reasons. Even with your direct command, the qomps in the mesh net retain override authority and will prevent liftoff. The mesh net must be physically removed before that."

Rusk fell back in astonishment. He was trapped here, like a fish in a net, like a bird in a trap? The fine, wispy material that he could see outside Una was strong enough to hold down this huge machine? *More like a bug in a biter-web?* He shuddered. Surely Una had some means of escape!

"Una, can those people outside us get inside here?"

"Sire Rusk, they cannot. Unless they have access to largescale borophene disassemblers. The primitive tools observed hereabouts would not be useful to them."

"Then, Una, if we are safe and cannot move, why don't I try to rest a bit? I have food and drink for over a hand of dims, a *week.* Maybe the people outside will eventually come to their senses, see they have nothing to gain by keeping me here. And then let me leave, at worst, or help me at best?" He thought out loud, "Maybe I can even offer them a cycle's worth of free Ice?"

Then he shook his head, trying to think of something beyond mere

Ice commerce that would help get him out of God's Port. Meanwhile outside, the guards had driven away the crowd. As darkness fell, a cadre of armed guards built bonfires and stood watch. Worried, Rusk asked Una whether a bonfire would harm himself or the aircraft. Assured that he was safe from such fires, he finally fell asleep.

CHAPTER THIRTY-ONE

*A*s planned by Wakan, the arduous southern trip from ShadowFall to Mother's City over largely unpaved gravel roads barely scraped out from the flatlands, would take about three weeks for the slow caravan of wagons. When the Princess, Wakan, Rist, and the long entourage of ShadowFall wagons all departed at sunrise, Wakan's senior assistant, Rumi Similla, waved them goodbye. For the duration of the Princess's absence, Rumi was vested as Assistant Administrator of ShadowFall, with all of Pernie's governing powers save penalties of torture and death,.

As the caravan of wagons and horses vanished in the misty distance, Rumi stationed her guards near the palace entrances and commanded that all border crossings be reported to her immediately. She found she enjoyed giving orders, and was wary of possible incursions by neighboring Sisterdoms while her Princess was away. All the other princesses were supposed to be going to Mother's City too, she knew, but the duplicity and ambition of Pernie's Sisters knew few bounds. She sighed and walked back toward the palace, with a glance at the Arch of ShadowFall; indicative morning shadows showed her that another ceremony would be due tomorrow. *Tomorrow*, she thought, *tomorrow, I have to witness and document the beginning of Season Harvest. The things a ruler must do!*

PROTECTED BY A BRACE OF GUARDS AFOOT, PRINCESS Pern`eptheranam sat inside a blue godscloth-curtained coach pulled slowly by four white horses. She had not wanted to make a showing of her most expensive animals, but Wakan insisted. "You have a reputation to maintain, Princess," he said. "Your realm already produces more food than any other of the Sisterdoms; you are the most beloved by your subjects, the youngest Sister by several years, and word has already spread of your newest subject, little Rist. You must present a spectacle for the subjects and the Courtsmen in Mother's City." He didn't mention that the enormous amount of fitted godscloth covering all of the fifteen wagons in her caravan could be valued as the total worth of several lesser Sisterdoms. Pernie had eventually acquiesced, with reservations. Luckily, the miraculous godscloth covering kept the interior or her coach cool and dust-free; riding in open air, her companions outside were not so fortunate,

Eyes burning from the red dust of the roadway, Rist himself rode atop a tall blue-curtained wagon containing several emus hidden from sight by layers of the opaque material. Pernie's other champions likewise drove similar wagons pulled by oxen—a particularly muscular breed of beezt-like cattle—each vehicle carrying several birds also hidden by godscloth curtains. In fact, the entire caravan of wagons, carrying handmaids, supplies, armed guards and the men who herded many hands of cattle to Mother's Court for feasting, flaunted the same opulent curtains of godscloth, a demonstration of nearly unimaginable wealth. That same material served a more practical purpose, too: at each night's encampment, Wakan had the caravan wagons circle together closely, with the Princess's in the center for her security and with guards posted all around the circumference. Then layered swathes of godscloth, as wide as the height of the top of a wagon, were unrolled all around the circle of wagons, essentially providing an opaque and impenetrable wall.

"This innovation of yours, Rist," Wakan said, "protects our secret from other Sisters' spies." As Rist watched his warrior team letting their dozen emus out for their evening exercise and fighting practice within the circle of wagons, the little man agreed. "Wakan, and I think our godscloth will have many important impacts on how things are done in Motherland." Then he thought, *I just wonder how it will affect The Tharn's Lands, when I return home with it. If I ever do!*

Wakan had insisted on that unique godscloth wall, too. "Princess, our caravan of wagons will show the Motherland that we have the secret of cutting godscloth, and that we have the material in abundance. Our nightly campsite shroud only adds to that demonstration. New customers for us, and free advertising." Before their trip, Wakan had hoped that Rist could show them how to change its color as well, from the near-luminescent light blue at least to ShadowFall's lavender or some more appropriate shades. But Rist had no idea of how to do that. "I was just lucky to find the big gloves and scissors," he'd said.

As the days passed Rist was fascinated by the variety of vegetation and animals the caravan encountered while they traveled southward—trees of more sizes, shapes, and colors than he had ever seen, some with huge snakes dangling like vines; herds of tall, graceful, long-necked, four-legged beasts; vast swathes of humped, horned beezt-like cattle; river creatures like big green logs with mouthfuls of sharp teeth. He had never imagined such variety; back home in The Tharn's Lands, he recalled, there were very few species of large animals and even fewer of smaller ones. He wondered how these warm climes could produce so many more kinds; he'd have to ask the wise man, Wakan, about that.

But most intriguing of all were the numerous towns and temples along the way. Each princess, it seemed, lived in a massive fortified stone building in the center of her domain, and each Sisterdom typically required all passersby to be stopped and searched before entering its borders, and a passage fee assessed as well. As a Sister-led caravan heading to The Game, Pernie insisted on exemption to these rules, and that was always eventually granted, but never without a noisy confrontation by local border guards first. It helped that all of the other Sisters had already left for The Game and weren't there to contest the situation. Defying a princess could mean quick death or long-lingering torture, so Pernie's entourage usually proceeded without much delay.

As they drew closer to Mother's City, Rist grew more and more concerned about the idea of fighting and killing strangers, just for Princess Pernie. *But I'll be fighting for Wakan, too, and for his dreams of a better Motherland.* He observed his teammates Thrak and Eddor and Een, each driving a wagonload of emus, big brown men sweating in the heat. *I am sure they are thinking similar thoughts. And when the time for The Game comes, I will be fighting for them, as well.* In the back of his mind, he was worried that one of the other Sisters' teams might have their own surprises.

CHAPTER THIRTY-TWO

The next dim, in God's Port, Rusk's situation had not changed; he and Una were still trapped under a godscloth net in the temple plaza. A frustrating routine began whereby every hour one or more priests would come to Una, proclaim their faith in Shining One and the Pale Lady, then demand that Rusk—"and any other criminals illegally occupying the stolen property of the gods"— immediately disembark and stand trial for the theft of godscloth and other belongings of the city and the gods, and for the assured punishment for insulting the priest. Rusk kept the walls opaque to the outsiders, wondering why the number of guards was increasing daily. Una told them that additional layers of godscloth netting were being overlaid, and tried to explain the inability to escape the seemingly flimsy, almost vaporous, material.

"Sire Rusk. The borophene complex is embedded at each nanotube intersection with numerous *qomps*—quantum computers—that interact with the onboard qomps on what you call 'Una,' to prevent collision. The net comprises a multifunctional webbing that was originally suspended far above ground level, hundreds of thousands of meters high, at the edge of the atmosphere. Collision prevention is integrally programmed into the net qomps so that if the net does not iris-open, the aerial vehicles must decelerate and stop before contact."

Rusk knew that he did not understand much of what Una was explaining. But he tried to summarize, visualizing a flying insect and a biter-web. "Una, these nets—the godscloth—were once suspended far up in the sky? And it somehow knows how to prevent you from running into it? Like a flying bloodsucker bug trapped in a biter-web?" The image was frightening.

"Sire Rusk, that is an apt analogy, although you lack the detailed knowledge of the physics of how that objective is accomplished."

Rusk pondered his situation. Surely, with all of Una's advanced capabilities, something as simple as a net, no matter its construction, could not keep it stationary. Thinking about how Una had "inflated" the crumpled end of its cabin, a different thought occurred. "Una, the air-wall shield, can it be extended out a ways, some meters, away from the 'fuselage'?"

"Sire Rusk, that can be done, but only very slowly. It will depend upon the programmed response of the borophene net for this geographical location." *Damn!* Rusk thought. *The godscloth acts differently depending on where in the whole wide world it is located? Will we* ever *learn everything that the ancients were capable of?*

"Then do it if, Una, and push it as far out as possible, the whole ten meters if possible. And let me watch it all." From what he could see from inside, it appeared as if fine mists swirled all around Una's surface, catching sunlight this way and that, a chaotic mixture of faint colors, wispy and ephemeral. Rusk saw that the anchoring stones were all moving inward, as would tent stakes if a tent were being lifted up from inside. The mists seemed to coalesce about ten meters out in all directions, the large stones still remaining as anchors, hanging down, touching the ground. He was still trapped, but at least the restraining godscloth was farther away.

Rusk asked, "Una, do those 'qomps' in the godscloth nets talk? Can I ask them anything?"

"Sire Rusk, communication is only one way, and it is only of a limited sort. The qomps override this craft's control circuits to prevent motion toward them. There is no way to interrogate them."

A flurry of activity beyond the new limits of the godscloth net drew Rusk's attention. Who knew what the locals were trying to do? After a while, it looked like the entire exterior around Una's shield was being boarded up. And within an hour, Una was indeed in darkness, everything Rusk could see having been covered with slabs of wood, stone, thatch—blocking off all sunlight. Una assured Rusk that nothing could bypass the shield. But he said, "Una, keep a lookout for any other activities that may harm us. Just let me think."

Hours passed, while Shining One climbed to its apex in the blue dome of sky, unseen by Rusk. He kicked around ideas out loud, submitting them to Una when appropriate, but even then he could not figure out a way around—or through—the impenetrable godscloth net. By now he was feeling more and more as if it really were a biter-web, with himself and Una the snagged insect waiting to be eaten alive by —*what?*

Remembering earlier moving pictures that Una had shown to him right before his first flight, Rusk said, "Una, show me all your *propulsion* capabilities again, the ones you presented that first day." Instantly the front wall screen lit up and began illustrating the available modes of transportation: wheels, tracked wheels, extended legs for walking, flight, floating, submerging. Rusk started to say something when a wailing alarm sound filled the cabin.

"Sire! You are under attack!" Outside, the solid material covering the air-wall was burning. As charred material fell away, Rusk saw why —the large mirrors around the courtyard were focused on them!

He yelled, "Una, can those mirrors burn you? Can they burn me?"

"Sire Thess, the concentrated sunlight can burn away the organic materials that have been piled around the air-shield. The air-shield will not stop the sunlight. Depending upon the number of concentrators focused hereupon, the outer surface of the fuselage may sustain thermal degradation. It is impossible to calculate until direct measurements are made." Una paused as if thinking.

Surely, a machine does not think! Rusk mused. *But who knows what the ancients could do?* The cabin temperature began to rise and the walls were getting warm to the touch.

"Sire, the concentration of solar energy is such that the exterior of the fuselage is beginning to ablate..." Rusk didn't know that term, but he didn't want to wait around and be roasted in this machine. *There has to be a way...* "*Una! Una!* Can you sprout those legs and *walk* us out of here?"

"Sire Rusk, yes, that is possible." Rusk sighed, angrily. *Why didn't Una suggest this before? Can't a machine think ahead?* A pause, clanking noises below him and a swaying motion inside the cabin told him that Una was readying itself to walk. Through the wall he could see biter-like extensions protruding, feeling the aircraft jerkily rising on long legs. "Now, it is done. Where do you want to go?"

Rusk yelled in response, "Anywhere, Una! Just get us out of here!" He paused and said, "To the harbor, please!" Through the walls he saw robed people on top of the plaza walls desperately trying to move the large reflectors to refocus their beams on the moving Una, without success. Una walked like a giant biter, its eight long articulated legs coordinating in a smooth motion, with the overlaid nets of godscloth maintaining their distance like a shimmering cocoon. Eight large pads slammed down loudly onto the pavement, one after the other, each time cracking the flat stones.

Piles of stones and burning planks fell off as the air-shield pulled the nets away, the large anchor stones dragging along, tearing up more pavement. In front of Rusk, obscured from direct view, crowds of God's Port people stood in awe, some angry, some fearful, as the monstrous creature plodded its way toward them.

Worried that somebody up in front might try to barricade the street or bring in rock-throwers, Rusk asked Una to pop open the black window on top and let people see the white-thing inside. "Una, can I speak like I did yesterday through your skin, but use its own voice instead of mine? And make it loud, loud enough to hear over the whole city?"

"Sire Rusk, yes to both. You may begin." Outside, Rusk saw a mob of people, some hesitant, some defiant. He asked Una to slow down and not hurt anyone unnecessarily, but he did want to keep moving. "Out to the harbor," was his order. He didn't know how long that would take. He hoped Una would know the way. From ground level, he had no idea which direction to go.

Rusk spoke loudly, his amplified voice sounding like Una's, but deep and threatening: "People of God's Port. Your priests have offended my messenger and me. They must pay for their disrespect or I will visit destruction upon you all."

Shocked people drew back from the spectacle of a walking, talking Una and the trailing net-dragged anchor stones—a giant green biter, pulling its web behind it! Then, panic as those closest tried to escape down side streets, away from the loud monster. As Una strode past, some few reached out to touch the godscloth draped over the borophene shield, as if in respect or supplication. Those left behind in Una's path turned to look toward the open plaza where the Priests' Men had turned their mirrors upon the messenger of their god. A murmur grew, a fever rose, and an angry mob rushed into the plaza and toward the temple. Rusk was glad that the people were out of the way. That they were rushing into the plaza was interesting, but he was focused only on what he could see in front of him, on getting out of the city.

Only a few dozen denizens of God's Port dared follow Una as it walked high on multiple legs, its body and footpads dragging the godscloth nets and their man-sized anchor rocks down the narrow streets, adding debris as the nets now entangled with street vendor kiosks, stalls, and canopies. Colorful street banners, dragged down from overhead, festooned the strange junkyard arrangement, which appeared to most shocked inhabitants to be a monstrously large green insect lumbering across God's Port toward the dock district, carrying with it a host of entangled biter-web victims.

Upon arriving at the harbor, Rusk had Una locate a long pier, one where no boats were docked. "Una, tell me again," Rusk said, "You —we—can float, once we get off this pier and into the harbor here, right? And we can submerge safely, too?"

"Sire Rusk, yes to both questions. You will experience a brief jolt as you fall four meters to the surface. Please prepare." Two minutes later, Una was floating and Rusk was picking himself up from the cabin floor. "Una," Rusk groaned, "I need to acquire some padding, a mattress or two, otherwise I will be pounded to mush like so much rab-meat before I find Rist!"

Rusk saw that the water level around Una was about halfway up the side of the craft. He said, "Una, listen carefully. I want to go to a deep part of this harbor, floating on top, and move around until the nets are clear of the fuselage. The anchor stones and the other junk will be holding the edges down. Understood?"

"Sire Rusk, yes."

"Then please drop down quickly to the bottom of the harbor, and move out of the way before the nets fall over us again. Understood?"

"Sire Rusk, yes."

"Una, will we be able to gather up the nets from the bottom of the harbor, maybe using two of the extension legs, like arms, and hold onto them?" He tried to envision any possible problems. "Is there a way to untie the anchor stones?"

"Sire Rusk, yes. This craft does contain extensible 'arms' that can gather up and fold the borophene nets. Once so folded, the qomps will not be configured to prevent interaction. The extensibles also contain borophene disassemblers, so the nets may be cut to release the anchor stones. All of the material may then be folded to a very small size and placed in storage in an exterior panel."

Rusk's jaw dropped. Una's capabilities bordered on magic! But he didn't ask why Una had not volunteered to cut the nets away in the first place. He thought, *So this machine does not create, cannot imagine!* But another consideration immediately crossed his mind: Cruthar had warned Rist about the towers at the harbor entrance.

"Una," Rusk asked, "Is it possible to keep us deep underwater and swim out of the harbor, into the New River, and downRiver a ways?"

"Sire Rusk, it will be done."

DENSE FORESTS COVERED BOTH SIDES OF THE RIVER, WITH THE riverbanks sporting a variety of flowered plants. And birds! More birds flew overhead in one day down here than in a hand of weeks in The Tharn's Lands, and of so many different kinds and colors it was a wonder. Rusk tried to calculate the worth of using Una to bring some of the strange birds and flowery plants, and even a few trees, back to The Tharn's Town for sale. *Any price,* he thought. *But then, what would I buy with all those coppers? And in all probability I can never return to The Tharn's Lands, anyhow.* That prospect saddened him, giving up the only home he'd ever known, the only culture. But he was beginning to realize the backwardness of his homeland, the superstition, the tyrannical rule. *The one man who burned Sire Thess' home, and killed our emus!* As his anger rose over that memory, he figured that there had to be a better place to live, and with Una's capabilities, he was determined to find it. Right after he found Rist.

He looked at the new sights along the River, up at the clear blue sky. He recalled the wonders of being above the Misty Sky, of being underwater at God's Port, of all the wonders that Una kept surprising him with. *With Una's abilities, there is a whole new wide world out here, to explore, to see, new things to learn and to do.* This *is the kind of wealth I want!* This *is how I want to live!*

Hoping to see some sign that Rist had passed this way, Rusk watched one riverbank, then the other, going no faster than the River flowed, so as not to miss any evidence. Two full days passed, but he saw nothing that would indicate Rist's passage. He would not think about any possibility that Rist might have gone back north or even inland, into unexplored territory where who know what dangers lurked. So downRiver he continued.

Searching for lost Rist.

UNA'S SHRILL VOICE WOKE RUSK FROM TROUBLED SLEEP: "SIRE RUSK! Alarm! A waterfall is dead ahead! Your orders?"

Rubbing his eyes, Rusk asked, "Ahead of us?" A quick glimpse of the forward screen answered his silly question. Not two hundred meters ahead, the world ended. In both directions, left and right, a sharp line demarcated what looked like the end of the world. To the left, stretching into the misty distance, an infinite waterfall. To the right, a sharp cliff, the end of the land. Directly in front of him, an approaching abyss; in the distance beyond and below, a patchwork of colored fields.

"*Fly*, Una, *fly!*" Rusk said. Una's path took them over the edge of the world, but surprisingly, without losing altitude. Gasping, he looked down through transparent walls and the ever-present green shimmer into an unbelievable waterfall, the entire New River pouring over a fantastically high cliff, many hundreds of meters down, into a huge misty lake at the bottom.

He hoped that Rist had survived this place. He said calmly, "Una take me down to the lowlands below." As they descended, Rusk could make out buildings in the far distance. "Look, Una!" he cried. "A city! People!"

CHAPTER THIRTY-THREE

That boy's skull is misaligned, Rumi Similla thought, *and its shadow is interfering with my observations*. Standing in front of the massive rainbow-shaped curvature of the Arch of ShadowFall, the perpetual solar calendar carved into the massive limestone outcropping adjacent to Princess Pernie's palace, Rumi was patiently waiting for the sun to reach its zenith. At that time the internal shadows of the calendar would indicate the day of the year. Today would be Announcement Day, she knew, and the farmers needed to know the date certain for planning how to attend the Princess's crops during harvest, four weeks hence.

But that damned skull! "Hold me up so I can adjust it," she ordered the tall guard beside her, who immediately lifted her up her own height, taking care not to look at her bare legs under the loose red robe. Grimacing, she took both hands and reset the rotted, nearly skinless skull back onto its vertical spike at the apex of the Arch. *Now it won't interfere with the rays from the Sun.*

"Let me down," she ordered. The guard did so, again turning his head to avoid any unapproved views of her legs and other sights. He didn't want his own head on that spike, or any other!

Rumi rubbed her hands with ointment from a jar in her pocket to clean them, brushed back her long black hair, smoothed her robes, and nodded for the guard to leave her to her duties. Taking a seat in another ancient carved-limestone sculpture, this one a weather-worn stone chair six meters in front of the Arch, she began to notate in writing the conditions of the day: *Clear, cloudless, blue sky,* she inked on the parchment page, *the disk of the Sun nearly overhead. Shadows aligning with stepped markers. Image of the Sun streaming through its aligned passageway hole at any moment...* Now!

The bright disk appeared through its appointed passage hole, touching the inside edge of the designated stone step; the vertical shadows were once again perfectly aligned, as they had been doing for untold millennia. *Forever, if Wakan Kech is correct.* With a slight yelp and a sigh, she finished documenting the occurrence for the royal archives. Rising, she turned to the waiting crowd below. "The Arch of ShadowFall once again tells us that *Harvest Time* begins *now*. Plan accordingly." It would be another four weeks until the actual crop-gathering began, the precise day depending on the weather. *We'll have another shadow-telling about that time,* she mused, *to keep the farmers happy, even though I could just count the days until then.* But she knew that the Sisterdom's citizens wanted to see a physical demonstration of the Arch's shadows and the Sun in action. As ever, she marveled at the ancient astronomers who had carved this precise, ever-repeating instrument into the large limestone outcropping so near the palace. *But, I suppose, in reality they built the palace to be next to the Arch.*

As the cheering died down, Rumi left the stone stage and, accompanied by the ever-present royal guard, made her way a hundred paces to the palace. Thinking of the skull on the spike, she mused, *Wakan Kech reinstituted this "tradition" when we all moved to ShadowFall five years ago, saying it was written in the ancient documents found in the catacombs under the palace that the annual sacrifice of a young healthy male would protect the Princess, her crops, and all of us. But it seems barbaric, like something the primitive Highlanders would do, not us civilized folk here in Motherland.* Shivering, she remembered that gruesome ceremony, just over two months back, when the handsome youth was beheaded and Wakan Kech spiked the dripping skull above the solar calendar sculpture.

Back in the palace, Rumi felt safe but anxious, her outside guards remaining at the doorways to prevent any more attacks from other Sisterdoms like those earlier in the year. With Princess Perneptheranam and her High Priest Wakan Kech having left to travel to Mother's City for the Motherland Game, the administrative duties of ShadowFall fell to her, Wakan's chief assistant. *But just for a short time, and then I'll be relieved of all this*, she sighed.

In the meantime, in the throne room, she took her seat in a red velvet padded chair behind a wide wooden desk, woefully eyeing the long line of waiting petitioners. A palace guard with an unsheathed sword stood at ease at her left, a symbol of authority. *And an enforcer of my will*, she reflected, enjoying the role for all her reservations. *I know that our Princess inherited this role, this power, these lands, these slaves—even me!—because she is a true daughter of the Lordess Mother, but I find these mundane duties below my abilities. If I had such power as the Princess, I could do so much more. If only...* But she kept her ambitious thoughts to herself. To do otherwise would invite torture and the headsman's axe.

Rumi kept her back to the open portico of the balcony, with the light of the sun behind her, presenting a silhouette to those approaching. *Wakan taught me this*, she mused. *"Let them think they are always in your shadow, that you mediate between the gods and mere men."* She smiled, motioning to the guard.

"First citizen, please come forward," the guard announced. As an unkempt and odiferous farmer stepped up to Rumi's desk, she sighed again at the hundred or more people still jostling and complaining behind him in the hallway beyond, wrinkling her nose at the man's bodily odor. *Peasants don't bathe very often, do they?*

CHAPTER THIRTY-FOUR

From his viewpoint a hundred meters above the River, Rusk was amazed at the sight unfolding before him: a vast, mist-covered lake at the bottom of the huge waterfall he had just descended from, and the continuing New River beyond that, wider than ever, placidly flowing through what appeared to be a vast expanse of colorful checkered croplands to his left (*east,* he had learned from Una) and to his right (*west*) in the far distance, a small city. "More stone buildings, hundreds of them," he whispered, almost in awe. *First God's Port, now this one. How did they find, and cut, and stack all of these big stones?* He had already flown over forests at the base of the huge waterfall, and wondered why the timber in those trees hadn't been used as lumber for the structures. He would have to ask Una about all of that at his first opportunity but at the moment he was more concerned with finding a place to land. *And to look for Rist!*

During the initial descent from the tremendously high waterfall and cliff, while flying over those trees, Una reported some strange red lights tracing patterns on its fuselage but informed Rusk they were not weapons and therefore not dangerous. Rusk ignored them, focusing instead on what he hoped was a peaceful civilization ahead. *And maybe Rist!*

This city itself was a lot like a smaller version of God's Port, he concluded, but the architecture of the tallest building, obviously a palace of some kind, seemed somehow to be *friendlier* than the huge temple of the Solar Priests, the plaza of which he had escaped from a few days before. *It's not so intimidating,* he thought, *and seems more welcoming, more open.* The lack of a defensive wall around the city or the large palace itself testified to its relative sense of security, an aura of openness, of trust. *Surely a peaceable people.*

He hoped.

"Una, take me down to, oh, five meters above the ground, and let's fly over in front of that palace." As the aircraft neared the city, descending, through Una's transparent walls Rusk could see gathering crowds looking up, pointing, some running to keep up. Within minutes Una was stationary, hovering outside a balcony of sorts, suspended above a faint shimmering mist of green. Below him, big guards were yelling, their long spears probing the air above them, unable to touch Una's surface. *None of those rock-throwing weapons,* Rusk noted with relief. *And no big burning mirrors, either!* But he could see that other armed men were assembling in the open plaza below, carrying strangely shaped, curved metal implements of some kind.

INSIDE THE PALACE, RUMI SIMILLA HEARD THE SHOUTS FROM OUTSIDE. Putting down her quill pen and waving away the whining supplicant at the desk, she strode to the balcony to see what was happening, her guard bringing up the rear. Outside, she saw—"*Guard! What* is *that floating thing?*" she screamed. She saw a huge green cylinder floating high over the plaza, a strangely transparent black bubble in its middle section. And some dark little person inside it!

"Rumi Similla," the astonished guard blurted out, "I-I-I don't know. Some kind of bird? A big bug?" He pulled Rumi back into the presumed safety of the room, shielding her from the horrific threat. Behind them, the unruly mob of petitioners pressed forward to see the strange sight, the guard finally wielding his sword to keep them back.

Below them, in the plaza, a cadre of armored guards was rapidly assembling in a circle under the flying thing. Rumi was somewhat pleased with their quick reaction time, but was still too confused to think of what to do next.

Aboard Una, Rusk said, "Una, let me use your loud-speaking."

"Sire Rusk, it is ready. The shield is contracted to so allow. But be aware that this craft is unable to descend any farther. Qomps in the borophene weapons below will override."

Rusk hesitated, but not seeing any threat himself, spoke anyhow. He thought Una worried too much at times. *If a godscraft can worry.* "People, my name is Rusk," his amplified voice echoed through the open balcony doorway. "I come from the far north, in search of my twin, Rist."

Inside, watching, Rumi heard the strange loud voice but could not understand the language. She did make out the word "Rist," and the little man inside the flying thing *did* resemble the dark dwarf that Wakan Kech had found, the one who rode a bird, fought off the assassins, and who Wakan had taken to the Motherland Game. *Rist? That Rist?* She tried to recall what little she had learned of Rist's speech. If this *flying thing* belonged to *that* little Rist or to *this* one, it was probably no threat, and she wanted to be friendly, but—how can it *fly*? Trying to convince herself to believe her own eyes, she thought, *It has to be a machine of some kind; Wakan Kech taught us that there is no magic!* Struggling free of her objecting guard, she strode to the balcony railing and addressed the flying man in her loudest voice. "I know Rist. He is a friend. Can you understand my speech?"

Rusk heard only "Rist" but that was enough. Thinking back on Una's facility with Peoplespeak, he asked, "Una, can we translate that woman's speech?" It was quickly done, and Rusk continued via loudspeaker. "Yes, wen, I understand you. Is Rist here?"

Shocked at the stranger's voice spoken in her own language, Rumi tried to regain her composure, replying. "Rist was here but has gone. Can you please come down, inside, to talk?" She wanted to hear more from this small man, but was equally intrigued by his flying device.

What that would thing mean for ShadowFall! she thought. Then: *What would that mean for* me?

"Una, take me down to the ground," Rusk said, assuming that a peaceful welcome was assured. At first, Una did not move, but then the guards backed off, presumably to a safe distance. As Una descended, the suspicious guards loaded their springbows. When it touched the ground and the side door began opening, the guardsmen, thinking Rusk meant to attack, opened fire and a dozen springbow darts pincushioned Una's surface around Rusk's apparent position.

"Sire Rusk! This craft's systems are compromised! Overriding qomps in the borophene rods have…" Crackling, roars, then silence as Una's voice died. The interior lights flickered and failed, the transparent walls opaqued, and the side door started to rise, stopping halfway up. With a leaden *thump!* Una fell a final few dozen centimeters, throwing Rusk to the floor of the cabin. Afraid of what might be happening, he crawled toward the half-opened door, which as he exited slowly closed seamlessly into the fuselage. As he attempted to stand, a large guard slammed him in the head with the butt of a spear.

Rusk collapsed into darkness.

RUSK AWOKE WITH A SPLITTING HEADACHE, SHAKING OFF A WARM, WET cloth from his face. "Where am I? Who did this?" His vision was doubled, blurry; he couldn't make out any definite shapes, just what appeared to be tall, pale people. And he was tied to his bed!

As he tried to get loose, a wen's voice spoke, softly. "I am Rumi Similla," it said, tenderly but with forcefulness, "and I welcome you to the palace of Princess Perneptheranam, in the Sisterdom of ShadowFall." Rusk did not comprehend her language at all, but it sounded friendly enough. But his head was pounding with pain!

The wen figure reached out and wiped Rusk's forehead with that warm, damp cloth again. "I am sorry for your mistreatment but my guards—*we*—have never seen a flying *machine* before, and they thought you a threat. You will be released." Other hands untied Rusk's binds and helped him to sit upright. He noticed that the bedclothes were the finest, softest he had ever encountered, and *perfumed*! *What kind of luxury is this*?

Rumi continued talking, walking as she did around the brightly polished marble room where Rusk was now able to focus his vision. The speaker was a tall, pale-skinned wen and with that shapely chest he'd first seen on the dead god at The Ice and then amongst the wen in the puzzled crowds in the temple plaza of God's Port. She had long, flowing black hair that ended at her waist, a waist corded by a golden rope, holding a thick red robe tightly above her hips. Rusk felt a surge of desire; it had been several weeks since he'd visited the upstairs of the river pubs in The Tharn's Town. But he put away that feeling and that thought. *Am I in danger here?* he wondered. *And what did they do with Rist?*

The wen kept speaking, but Rusk understood nothing. *Damn! If we could get back out to Una, everything could be translated.* He then remembered Una's last words and that final fall. *If Una is even alive!* Making motions that he needed to get back to his aircraft, Rusk tried vainly to leave his comfortable captivity, but the tall wen—obviously the chief over the armed guards, as ridiculous as that sounded to Rusk —refused.

After being escorted to use the strange "necessary" and to wash up, he was dressed in a soft golden robe by two very attractive young wen. Then, followed an exotic meal of—Birds? Fish? Vermin? he couldn't tell—and a wonderful black, flavorful beer—much better than peat-beer! The tall wen chief sat across a table from him, speaking in a very measured cadence. *As if I can understand her better if she speaks slowly!* Rusk thought.

Rumi was growing impatient. *Surely this, this*—dwarf!—*spoke our language at first, and now pretends he can't?* A sudden concept presented itself: *Does he have to be inside that big machine to speak as loud as he did? Does that machine control his speech?* Ordering the guards to bring along the dwarf—"Rusk," she did understand at last that that was its name—she walked downstairs and outside to the big cylinder he had arrived in. Now, its surface was not transparent but a uniform green, the color of newly grown wheat, and it rested on a flattened bottom, surrounded by the Princess's guards. That was a wonder in itself. She frowned at the many springbow arrows stuck in its body. *Was it alive?* she wondered. *Did they kill it? A living machine? How could that be?* Trying to deal with such alien, mind-altering concepts disturbed her more than the flying machine itself.

As Rusk walked around the 'Una,' as he was apparently calling it, Rumi saw him making hand motions, waving toward the sky. In all the gibberish he was spouting, she heard the distinct word *patitsa—bird!* "Rusk, your word for 'bird' is the same as mine." Repeating herself, she pointed at Rusk, then at Una. "Rusk's bird?"

Rusk laughed. *Finally, this wen is showing some intelligence! We may be able to talk without Una's translation after all.* Smiling at Rusk's reaction, Rumi was thinking the same thing.

CHAPTER THIRTY-FIVE

*H*alfway to Mother's City, Rist saw a huge pyramidal temple off to the east, and during the rest stop, asked Wakan Kech about it. "That pyramid dates back to the time of the gods, Rist," the priest said. "It was constructed over a godsdisk, one of hundreds scattered about Motherland." Wakan described the disk as a round metal plate some seven meters in diameter, over half a meter thick, with a one-third-meter-diameter hole at its center and many tubular appurtenances sticking up. "Pipes of a kind, they look like, but the metal can't even be scratched by any of our tools. As a scholar, I am more interested in studying the script of the ancients, so I sent over an artist today to draw up what she could see within the sacred chambers of that pyramid, the godsdisk itself." Holding a large sheet of paper, he stepped back several meters so that Rist's genetic farsightedness would allow him to make out the shapes of the strange symbols:

TATA INDUSTRIES SEAFLOOR WELLHEAD #1602
CON LICENSIA DE REPUBLICA QUINTANA ROO
NOVIÉMBRE 2138 CE

"And what do those markings mean, Wakan?" Rist asked. He had first encountered similar ones as tiny unreadable engravings on objects taken from a god found in The Ice at the End of the World, back in his homeland. Since then, he had learned that inhabitants of the strange Warm Lands downRiver also made their writing that way. These block symbols looked similar to those many others displayed on buildings and shops in the Warm Lands and on ancient tapestries on the walls of the dank libraries below Pernie's palace in ShadowFall. Back in The Tharn's Land, under the dim Misty Sky, all writing was done by carving your meaning onto wooden or bone spindles, and reading meant touching those cut-marks and interpreting them.

Wakan sighed, placing the paper into a leather file pouch. "Some say that they are a prayer to the gods, and are holy writings, and that is why that hundred-and-fifty-meter-high stone pyramid was built over it, thousands of years ago. But there are many, many similar disks of the same uncuttable metal, each with its own less massive temple. From what I can tell, the markings use a common set of characters, but that's all. I believe they say something that was important to the ancients. I just don't know what."

Rist shook his head. *So many mysteries!* Ever since touching the godsphere, he had been wanting to ask Wakan about what it meant about the "whole round world"; and he wanted to know more about the Old Days in Motherland, what the priest called *history*, but Wakan always seemed to be busy conferring with the Princess or attending to the needs of the caravan to give him any private time.

CHAPTER THIRTY-SIX

*O*ver a hand of dims passed (*A* week, *Una would say!* he thought), and Rusk realized that he was as much captive as guest; in his small, featureless, windowless room he was both bored and frustrated. Bored by not being allowed access to Una outside, frustrated that he could not continue his search for Rist. The wen, Rumi, was absent much of the time, apparently with other duties. With nobody attempting to talk to him, without anything to do, and with Rist's fate still unknown, he was becoming desperate. Finally, through gestures and sounds to the guards outside his door, Rusk was allowed to see Rumi, pleading to let him have her guards pull their arrows out of Una's body. But it soon became clear that no one guard could remove his arrow by brute strength and hands alone, so Rusk suggested through mime motions that the local beezt-like *oxen* be harnessed to provide pulling power.

After several humorous but frustrating attempts, Rusk was allowed to work with a blacksmith and some farmers to fashion an iron yoke framework to be pulled by four beezt. He then attached it by rope to the protruding end of an arrow, and very slowly was able to pull the projectile from Una's outer skin by animal power. As the arrow dropped to the ground and the hole miraculously filled in by itself, Rusk was disappointed that Una did not come to life right then. *Is Una truly dead?* he wondered. *If it is broken, how can I ever find Rist?* Rumi had indicated through sign language that Rist had departed just a few days before his arrival, to travel a long way south, apparently to fight. *Rist, fight?* That part he couldn't accept, perhaps he was misunderstanding her? He resolved to learn the language of this strange place on his own, if Una would not be there to help.

Frustratingly, Rusk was not allowed to pull any more arrows from Una; apparently the guards themselves would be doing that. Dragged back inside the Palace, he fumed at the delay. Would he ever find Rist?

That evening, guards escorted Rusk to a larger room, one obviously outfitted for a guest rather than a prisoner. Though still windowless, the apartment was well appointed, with colorful hanging draperies on the walls, a table and chair, a washbasin, and a chamber pot. "A great improvement," he said aloud, knowing that the wen running the palace was bound to have spies watching and listening to him, though he couldn't find the spyholes. Rummaging in the desk drawer, he was astonished to find a familiar object: a totem!

This is so strange, he thought, *to see the markings on a totem.* Without thinking, his Reading hand began its motions on the wooden spindle, seeking out the curves, the depths, the finished edges that would speak to him. To his surprise, its first words were: *I, Rist.* This was his twin's carving! Rist must have stayed in this very room, must have left this totem for himself or someone else from home to Read. He searched the rest of the desk and the niches, but there were no more totems. Eagerly he continued Reading:

I, Rist, carve this report after leaving The Tharn's Town to the Warm Lands. My previous record ended when I left the pub in God's Port in the Dark Highlands before coming here to ShadowFall.

Rusk eagerly fondled his twin's carved report of his adventures and findings in ShadowFall—the beautiful Princess Pernie and her handmaids, especially the tall and shapely Anklya; the strange priest Wakan Kech; the springbow, an incredible new weapon for shooting bolts long distances; the stables of two-legs and his training in fighting from them; and his upcoming trip to Mother's City to fight for the Princess and ShadowFall. But irritatingly, no mention of what The Game entailed or his part in it; not even what it was for! The record ended frustratingly short, but only a short time before Rusk had arrived in Una. *Before I crashed in Una!* He wished he could have arrived before Rist left, but it had not meant to be.

THE NEXT DAY, RUMI ASSIGNED A YOUNG WEN, ANKLYA, TO HELP Rusk with learning to speak the local language. As the tall blonde wen announced herself with a knock at his door, he thought, *Rist was right about this one! She is beautiful, with those large green eyes. And that pleasant shape of the Warm Lands wen I saw in God's Port.* He soon confirmed that the fair-haired beauty had been with Rist soon after he arrived, teaching him the local language when the priest Wakan Kech was otherwise occupied. She had also spent some very personal time with him. And it only took the one night for Anklya to find that Rusk was indeed a twin to Rist. Rusk thought, *There are some important lessons you can learn without knowing the language!* He was certainly going to enjoy his time in Rumi's land, however long it took.

A quick learner like his twin Rist, Rusk was speaking pidgin Motherland within a week.

HOLDING A TORCH ALOFT, ANKLYA ESCORTED RUSK DOWN INTO DARK chambers below the palace, within a labyrinth of damp, moldy stone walls that appeared to Rusk to be even more ancient than the library caves of the Old Wen back home. At a massive wooden door, Anklya used a large key to open it, brushing away dust and old, dry, drooping biter-webs. Beyond the opening, Rusk could see a dark room that seemed to go on forever, shelves along the sides and tables stacked with thick rectangular shapes.

Anklya said, "This place is where Wakan Kech, our High Priest, brought your twin, Rist." She touched her torch to a gaslight sconce along the wall, and Rusk was amazed to see other gas lamps light up the wall, one by one, until the entire front part of the vast room was illuminated. In the dark distance the room seemed to go on forever. Anklya affixed her torch to a standing fixture, then picked up one of the rectangular shapes, a bound beezt-hide-covered object. Opening it to reveal numerous thin sheets of material, she said, "Rusk—*book, pages.*" Rusk took the strange object, noting that the thin, leaf-like *pages* were marked with black symbols. He shrugged. "Rusk, Rist said that he couldn't read the writing, and I guess you can't either?" With his improved eyesight Rusk could make out the rows of tiny inked figures clearly, knowing that they were a kind of writing, but he was not literate in their meaning. Like with the markings on some of Una's screens, a kind of god-writing, he was still lost. But then Anklya went over to a row of wooden shelves and returned with a totem, from the look of it, an ancient one. Rusk immediately Read it—a report on an Ice delivery, long ago.

"This be Ice information," he said slowly, "long time ago. No good anymore."

Anklya smiled and hugged him. "I had expected that you could Read carvings, Rusk, just like Rist did. Now we can make better progress." She walked him farther into the *library*, past manyhands (*hundreds!*) of ancient shelves of books, a few of other totems, until they came to a shelf full of globes about the size of Anklya's head. "Touch this, Rusk, and let's see if you can do what Rist did."

Rusk took the ball from her. It was cool to the touch, and heavy, but with both hands he could hold it without dropping. He didn't know what he was supposed to do with it, but apparently Rist had impressed her with something.

The globe began to feel warm, as if alive. Within moments, moving color images began to appear inside it, shocking Rusk so much that he almost dropped it. "What—?" The globe appeared to show visions of a miniature world, with tiny people walking around, unusual machines of several kinds doing incomprehensible things—even one that looked like a miniscule version of Una! And speech: *"Hello, your DNA enables you to access this Information Sphere. This message will repeat in all extant languages."* Rusk shrugged, as did Anklya; they both knew that the globe was speaking, but out of the gibberish only the occasional word meant anything.

After a few minutes of speech the globe dimmed and turned to black. Rusk wished that Una were still alive; he was certain that it could understand this round thing. After touching more of the spheres without any response, Rusk indicated frustration and they both left for upstairs, Rusk taking some of the ancient totems with him for further Reading.

The next morning, excited, Rusk was able to gain an audience with Rumi Similla, who listened for just a few minutes to his tales of godspheres and magic pictures. After hearing nothing new about the flying machine from Rist, she dismissed him. *If only my people could make that thing fly,* she thought. *Meanwhile, this little one is getting on my nerves with his wild tales about talking globe-stones. If Wakan Kech couldn't bring those spheres to life, there is no way a brown dwarf from the Dark Highlands could! But before the Princess and Wakan Kech come back I'll have to do something else with this Rusk if I want to increase my status here, my power. But what? I have just got to learn more about that flying Una thing!*

AN OPPORTUNITY FOR RUMI TO DO JUST THAT AROSE A DAY LATER. "Rumi," Rusk asked in the formal tone that Anklya had taught him, "may I try to repair Una, my flying machine?" Except for arranging to pull that first springbow arrow from Una, and for several visits into the catacomb libraries below the palace, for all the rest of the days that Rusk had been a guest—or a captive?—he had not been allowed out of his room, much less back into the plaza to see his flying machine.

Rumi, still worrying about the capabilities of that 'Una,' had instructed her aides and assistants to investigate it, to determine how it worked, and why it had crashed. But no one had been able even to open the door again. They had studied it externally without pause, repeating Rusk's oxen-pulling method to remove all of the remaining arrows. The arrow holes once more seemed magically to repair themselves, as if the thing were alive, but it did not respond to any touches or voices or anything else. Metal tools would not scratch it, nor hammers dent it. And other springbow arrows shot at it would not penetrate it again. Rumi's researchers could not find anything to make it come back alive, much less fly.

And she wanted that to happen before Pernie and Wakan returned. *With that machine, if I take it to Mother, I can earn my own Sisterdom —just fly it directly to Mother and demand lands of my own!* Having long chafed under her status as a mere assistant to a foreigner—as she considered Wakan and all his fellow Kech—and watching the Princess discharge duties and decisions that she herself could perform equally well—*if not better!*—her imagination fired up with possibilities. *My daydreams could come true if I had that flying machine! But probably only little Rusk here can get it working again. He must have some special knowledge.* She would let him work his magic, learn it herself, then seize the Una. After that, the dwarf was expendable as far as she was concerned.

"Very well, Rusk," she said with a knowing smile, "you may attend your machine, but do not fly away." She motioned for two guards and Anklya to accompany Rusk. "If he can open that flying thing, he is not to be allowed to go inside it alone." And she added, unnecessarily, "You all know the penalty for disobedience."

In the plaza Una lay inert, surrounded by a dozen guards with springbows and spears at the ready. Making his way through the ring of big men, Rusk asked one of the guards to lift him up toward the black bubble on Una's top surface. The guard did so.

"White-thing, can you hear me?" Rusk asked as his fingers found the slight depression that had previously triggered the canopy opening. *It worked!* The bubble turned clear and began to hinge open from the back, revealing the white-thing (*pilot!*) seated in its recessed compartment. Rusk jerked backwards and the guard who had hoisted him up dropped him, but Rusk was ready and landed safely on his feet. The springbow guards all stepped back, afraid of the strange white creature that was turning toward the dark dwarf. But they remained alert, Rusk saw. He didn't know whether those arrows might kill the white-thing as easily as they had disabled Una.

"White-thing! Is Una dead? Are you all right? What happened?"

The voice was weak but still forceful, and fortunately in Peoplespeak, not understandable by the ShadowFall guards. "Sire Rusk, there is no 'I.' Una is not dead, a Developing Intelligence does not perish. The attacking borophene bolts contained remnant qomps that overrode this craft's defenses in a manner never experienced or anticipated, causing all systems to cease operation. In the hostile environment thus encountered, Una's programming will function only for you and your Sire, Thess. The other entities nearby are considered possible adversaries. What are your wishes?"

Rusk thought furiously. He desperately wanted to continue searching for Rist, but did not want to risk Rumi's large guards taking Una away from him, or holing him up in the Palace any more. Rist's totem carvings had told him that these Sisterdom people could be friendly, but had also given warning that the local princess, one "Pernie," had absolute power of life and death over every single person in her Sisterdom, even the gruesome practice of human sacrifice. In a strange side comment Rist had also mentioned that he himself was training emus—two-legs—for fighting by themselves, but did not elaborate further.

Around Rusk the guards were growing more restless, demanding that Anklya tell them what the mysterious and scary white-thing was saying. Rusk whispered, "Anklya, tell them that you will take me inside this machine, where I will have the white-thing explain in your tongue what is happening." She agreed, and they both crawled through the opening door. The quivering guards were not anxious to follow; after all, Rumi Similla's orders were that the dwarf not go in alone, and Anklya was with him.

Once inside, Rusk made his move. "Una, if I am being heard, shut the door and take us up a hundred meters immediately!" The door slammed shut quickly and quietly, and Una shot up rapidly, slamming the unprepared Anklya to the floor.

"Rusk, what is happening?" she screamed.

But Rusk just smiled and said, "Just watch! Una, transparent walls please."

Anklya could hardly believe her eyes: she could see clearly through the walls of the flying machine, down to the earth below, where frightened guardsmen were shaking their spears and springbowmen were launching arrows at them. Rusk laughed as those bolts fell far short of their target. "Those arrows won't reach us, I'll bet. But even if they do—Una, put up your shield."

Anklya stood, amazed, at the green shimmering mist below them and at the vast panorama of terrain around them in all directions. "It is so beautiful up here, Rusk. I had no idea that I could ever fly. Oh look, the guards are like little bugs, the palace like a dollhouse!"

Even in his latest triumph—*escape?*—Rusk remained pragmatic. "Anklya, can you stay with me?" She nodded briskly, smiling. "And is there any place we can descend to and get some food and water? I am already hungry and thirsty." She soon solved that problem; they landed far south of the palace city in the plaza of a small village, a clean settlement of painted stone houses, surrounded by fields of colorful crops.

"I was born in this place, the village of Sahl," she said, "and there is a wonderful marketplace, a *sook*, where we can buy anything you want to eat." But the town was empty of people; only an occasional dog or cat wandered by on the dirt streets. Apparently the locals had all left, probably scared off by the big flying machine coming down out of the sky. The colorful marketplace, all crowded stalls and canopies, was completely abandoned, but the stalls were bulging with types of fruits and vegetables that Rusk didn't recognize but which Anklya said were safe and tasty. She located a basket stall, took one under each arm and proceeded to select items from the bushels of produce. Rusk walked behind her, shortsword in hand, just in case. He was surprised at the unfamiliar yet pleasant odors of cooking meat and sliced vegetables and fruits, a spectrum of smells all new to him.

After loading several baskets full of food and carrying jugs of water and wine back to Una, Rusk placed appropriate amounts of coppers in payment at each stall. He also located some stalls with local weavings and stuffed sewn pillows, and paid for those. "We're going to need something better to lie on Una's floor. And I'm glad you know the prices, Anklya. I wouldn't want these people to think a little dark man would cheat them!" They both laughed.

Back inside Una and flying south a hundred meters up, Rusk asked, "Anklya, you said you wanted to go with me, but is there any reason you need to return to the palace? Do you *have* to for your job?"

She frowned, shivering. "Rusk, for me to leave ShadowFall without permission is already a death sentence. So I would prefer to stay with you. I can't go back."

"A *death sentence?*" he said, startled. "Who dares do such a thing? In The Tharn's Lands we don't have such great buildings and weapons as your city does, but we would not tolerate such actions!" But then he recalled the wanton destruction of his Sire's home and all the family's belongings, and his suppressed rage arose. *Our emus!* Killing the birds was a crime he could never forgive. He swore that he would take some kind of revenge for that. Then he calmed down, not showing any external anger to the already nervous Anklya, but knowing that it would stir inside him until it one day boiled over.

But first, I have to find Rist. Together we will go home and take revenge upon The Tharn! Rusk was surprised at his own treasonous thought; such actions had never occurred to him before. But Sire Thess must have had some inkling of such a possibility, to have taken such expensive and extensive precautions with the well-supplied cave in the cleft. *My twin, my Sire, and I—we will have our revenge. And with such a machine as Una, The Tharn can't stop us!* But as always, finding Rist had to be his first priority.

Interrupting his chain of thought, Anklya sighed. "Rusk, the Princess *owns* every citizen; we are her personal property, do you not understand? Truly, we are no more than pets, or just brute cattle that talk. And *your* land is not that way? How does your land even function?"

Rusk sputtered and said they would discuss all of that later. Right now his focus had to be on finding Rist before his twin did something typically rash or stupid. "How far south is this Mother's City? And why is Rist going there? And training emus to fight?" He was not happy with the possibility that his twin might be heading into danger.

Anklya explained the tradition and practice of the Motherland Game, and of Wakan Kech's idea of springing Rist and his war-birds as a lethal surprise upon the competing teams from the other Sisterdoms. "The Game, the melee, always occurs on EqualDay of the fifth year, which is just three days from now. The Sisterdom that wins The Game provides our Mother with personal advisors for the next five years, and receives failure tribute from the other dozen princesses.

"That is why our princess and her chief advisor Wakan Kech and so many other high officials of ShadowFall were not there to greet you, Rusk. Your twin Rist made quite an impression on all of them, and Wakan Kech even wants more of your People to come live in our lands."

Rusk was happy to hear that last comment. He thought that many, many People back home would like to emigrate from the Cold Lands down to the warmer climate. He wanted to carve that information for later review, but realized that he had not been recording his thoughts since he began flying with Una, because Una could play back everything he had ever said in its presence. *I am depending on a machine instead of my own Carving hand*, he thought with disgust. *But at least Una remembers everything, and without error. And that is very convenient!*

Rusk asked Anklya about the strange talking globe they had experienced down in the library vaults under the palace. "Wakan Kech said that Rist had been the only person in ShadowFall who was able to make one talk consistently. Apparently back in his native Kech land, their 'godspheres' speak to many more of his people, and reveal what the whole wide world was like before the gods left us." Rusk had marveled that he and Rist were the only people who could make those globes light up and talk. *But this Wakan Kech's people can, too? More mysteries!* He decided not to tell Anklya about his own recent discoveries about the true nature of the 'gods.' *When she's more ready*, he thought. *Best not to overwhelm her with too many new thoughts. A flying Una and I are probably enough newness for now!*

Below them, the terrain rolled out like a multicolored carpet, flat croplands eventually fading to flat grasslands, then to channel-scarred scrublands, finally succumbing to barren, hilly desert. The main road, a rutted dirt surface only lightly scraped out of the ground, veered off westward from the river. From their altitude Rusk could make out high, flat-topped mountains gray and blue on the horizon.

Anklya confirmed that the whole of Motherland was primarily a vast basin, surrounded in the north by the Dark Highlands from whence the giant waterfall fell into the lake, and by other highlands in the West and South. "In those southern mountains is where Mother's armies raided and captured many men, Wakan Kech among them, twenty years ago. When Wakan was teaching us youngsters about geography, he said that even higher lands are to the south, on the other side of a wide, deep saltwater lake. But with cliffs too high ever to climb, and swarming hostile tribes armed with terrible poisoned weapons, Mother's armies would not survive any battles."

Rusk wanted to ask Una so many things about not only Motherland but the whole wide world, what cities there were and where, what kinds of people lived where. And what kinds of weapons they might possess. He did not want Una damaged—*hurt?*—by any 'phene arrows or anything else. But he was too busy for idle talk; Rist was probably in danger down in Mother's City, with his strange ideas. *Fighting other men from an emu? Ridiculous! Killing velks is one thing, but* people?

EqualDay was two days away. Rusk said, "Una flies quickly, so I can plan to arrive at least a whole day before that murderous Game, giving me time to find Rist and get him away from there."

Anklya nodded. "This year, I was told by Wakan Kech, The Game will take place in a big stadium built for that purpose. It should be easy to find from high up like this."

With a plan in place, Rusk was having Una fly slowly, only a bit faster than the speed of walking, so that he could encompass the landscape and understand their environment, in case that knowledge were needed. He prayed that Una would not crash or stop; having to walk these vast distances in dangerous country would be a disaster. The terrain now mostly remained flat and uninteresting, save for an occasional hillock or copse of trees surrounding a small pond of water —"Oases," Anklya called them—most often with a small village of mud-brick huts nearby.

Once, off in the distance to the east, appeared a high pyramid, even taller than the temple in God's Port, its polished white surface a brilliant jewel in the afternoon illumination of the sun. "According to what Wakan Kech taught us, there are many such stone structures in Motherland," Anklya explained. "Sacred sites covered by monumental constructions. Nobody really knows what they are, or who made them, or why. They are very ancient." Rusk asked Una to remember the location of the pyramid site; he wanted to return at a less stressful time and investigate that magnificent isolated structure. Meanwhile he assessed the terrain, hoping not to have to walk it.

An hour passed. While Anklya had gone to sleep on one of the reclining cabin seats, Rusk took the opportunity to think about how he might find—*rescue?*—Rist. First off, his twin would not know what Una was and would fear it, just like every other person who had never seen or maybe even conceived of a flying machine. But if he could somehow recognize Rist from high above, maybe he could use Una's loud-speaking to tell him of his, Rusk's, approach. He didn't know if Una might be stopped again, by more of those 'phene arrows. He'd have to have the shield screen up in that case, and then drop it if Rist wanted to come inside and fly away.

But what if Rist wanted to stay with his newfound friends and his princess, not come back to The Tharn's Lands? Thinking on it, Rusk would not blame his twin; after all, their family probably could never safely return to The Tharn's Town anyhow, not with The Tharn's wild fury against them. *And our home and emus burnt!* ShadowFall itself seemed like a nice place, notwithstanding his own fugitive status, and maybe being wanted for kidnapping, too? *Or maybe if Anklya is truly property, I'm only a thief? I wonder if Mother's City will be any safer... Hopefully Rist will have some answers. Then we can go home and rescue Sire Thess and birther Mell, then take some kind of action against The Tharn—and then what? Stay at home, or come back down here?* In his thoughts, he had no answers. But Anklya had said that Wakan Kech wanted more people like Rist to immigrate to ShadowFall; Rusk thought that Sire Thess could convince any number of People to come down to these warmer, safer lands. Maybe *all* of them?

PART SEVEN

FIGHT

CHAPTER THIRTY-SEVEN

*A*s the caravan approached the capital, Rist observed a large contingent of big Mothersmen, armed with long spears, directing them into a maze of low-trimmed hedges no higher than Rist himself. Within the patterned greenery the other Sisterdom caravans were already assembling, and their parade positions were being assigned. At Wakan's loud and commanding insistence, ShadowFall's entourage had been directed to lead the procession. An hour later, Rist and the other wagoneers lashed their oxen to go forward from the maze into the city proper. Mother's City was abuzz with activity, its citizens crowding every streetside and balcony, open window and towertop, watching intently as the Thirteen Sisters and their long trains of wagons and animals arrived for the Motherland Game, parading down the main processional boulevard.

Atop his high-perched seat on a wagon with a concealed cargo of emus, Rist was in awe of yet another fabulous city, this one surpassing any wonders he had yet seen: tall buildings of smooth colored stones, all with red tile roofs, many of them taller than the temple in God's Port, with wide colorful cloth rectangles strung above the streets, exhibiting shapes and symbols that Rist took to be Motherland writing. The parade of hundreds of vehicles, marching troops, cattle herds, and camp-followers wended its way past countless structures of all shapes and sizes—squared, bulbous, domed with spires, even small pyramidal buildings—each with their own banners blossoming, their various symbol-laden flags fluttering, *A festive atmosphere for a game of killing*, Rist thought, reminding him of reports of the festival at ShadowFall, which had ended with a young man's severed head embedded on a spike. Having seen the deteriorating skull over the Arch every day since his arrival, he thought, *I'm glad I got there* after *that ceremony.*

Rist himself was a center of attention, being mysteriously small and dark, even if he held the high honor of driving the wagon directly behind the Princess's godscloth-festooned vehicle. But the initial hoots and jeers of "Monkey man!" and "Midget!" gave way to gasps of shock, then loud applause as Rist stood and bowed to the onlookers, waving his shortsword. The sudden appearance below him of the spears and shields of the large ShadowFall guardsmen accompanying the procession on both sides of the boulevard served as forceful persuaders. Wakan Kech had seen to that.

Oblivious to the mobs in Mother's City, Rist took in the fragrances of a multitude of multicolored flowers and the elegance of strangely shaped trees that filled the median strip dividing the wide street for two-way traffic. And traffic there was! Side streets full of four-wheeled wagons, and two-wheeled carts that he had never seen—some pulled by *humans*! From vendor booths along the way came aromas of cooking meats, boiling stew pots, sweet tangs of sugar candies, spices old and new, and others that he did not recognize, but which made his mouth water. He was going to enjoy Mother's City. If he lived long enough.

Rist did notice the swarms of the "honey-sweepers" who darted in and out of the procession, quickly removing the inevitable horse dung and oxen droppings, ever washing and mopping the stone streets as they dodged marchers and riders and teams and wagons. He could have sworn that some wen were even tossing out flower blossoms onto the street. *To welcome us?* he wondered. *Or just to cover the smell of animal shit?*

The smooth, stone-paved thoroughfare the caravans were traveling on converged in the distance at an enormous hub, the tallest building in the city, the white dome-roofed Mother's Palace. The awe-inspiring size of the palace was complemented by concentric rings of encircling high walls. In the outermost wall, thirteen gates opened simultaneously around the perimeter, and the caravans went their separate ways, each finding a designated private area for a campground and smaller buildings to accommodate the nobles. The Princess and Wakan Kech and a dozen lower-level ShadowFall nobles—financial, agricultural and defense advisors—took up residence in the large white smooth-stone houses, while Rist and the other champions made their ways to a walled oval in a grassy camping field. Inside the courtyard, a white stone wall some ten meters high surrounded them, providing a welcome privacy.

Rist and the other drivers brought their wagons into their specified area, thankful that the high stone walls kept away all the other Sisters' subjects and Mother's City residents. Once inside, they pulled the wagons into a tight circle and together unrolled a godscloth canopy over the whole oval area. "This overhead covering should keep us safe from prying eyes," Rist told his teammates as they set up tent poles. "Nobody else has this much material, and they couldn't cut it even if they did. So let them wonder what surprises we have for them in the arena." The other men nodded; they had long since learned to listen to their little leader, and respected his demonstrated abilities with war-bird and springbow. So they obeyed out of deference. And because Wakan had ordered them to.

Rist and the other fighters let their birds out for exercise and feeding, the curious emus strutting around the wagon perimeter, always looking for a way out. The Game would begin in two days. *Enough time*, Rist thought, *to outfit these birds and get them ready for the fight of their lives. And ours!*

CHAPTER THIRTY-EIGHT

*O*ver a tasty meal quickly prepared in a near-magical oven within Una's tiny kitchen area, Rusk asked Anklya how far they had to go to find Rist. He had wanted to see more of Motherland, to scout out escape routes, but had to rescue Rist first, if *rescue* was the proper term.

Anklya answered, "Rusk, our Princess's procession left ShadowFall three weeks before you came. They should have arrived at Mother's City by now. I do not know how long they will have to ready themselves for The Game. EqualDay, The Game day, is the day after tomorrow."

Rusk replied, "I have to find Rist before he fights. He can't get hurt." Silent for a moment, he said, "Una can take us down there in minutes, any time I so command." He waved a hand at the vast expanse of Motherland all around them. "I had wanted to understand the surrounding countryside we will be in, in case Una fails again at any time, so we can walk out if we have to. Are there mountains we can run to? Rivers we can sail?" Turning to the front of the cabin, where the wall screen displayed the blonde god-wen, he asked, "Una, tell me how soon we can fly into Mother's City, rescue Rist, and leave safely."

Una answered through the god-wen's image, "Sire Rusk. To answer the first question, you must identify where Rist is. Only then is it possible to extrapolate a rescue operation."

"Can you first identify if there are any weapons within range that can damage or hurt you?"

"Sire Rusk, there is no 'you' or 'I' present. But yes, Una will perform a long-range borophene and qomp scan of the city prior to our arrival."

"How soon can we get to Mother's City, Una?"

"Sire Rusk, Mother's City is not a recognized landmark in the database. The distance to the nearest large city, apparently some three hundred thousand in population, is estimated from remaining geo-qomps as about four hundred kilometers away. Una is capable of arriving there within half an hour."

"Your Una is quite a magical machine, Rusk," Anklya said with a chuckle. "It's like an ancient legend come true, a wondrous carpet that can talk, and fly anywhere in the whole wide world in seconds, and become invisible like a ghost."

Rusk dropped his mouth open. He hadn't considered…"Una, can we become totally invisible?" He was trying to drop the "you" pronoun to avoid Una's tiresome explanations.

The machine voice seemed to sigh, if that were possible. "Sire Rusk, yes. The borophene shield possesses the appropriate refractive properties to enable stealthy operations for visible and all other wavelengths." Rusk laughed; a simple "yes" would have sufficed, since he did not know what Una's technical explanation meant, almost none of the words. But why hadn't Una said something before? He answered his own question in a low voice: "Because I didn't ask!" He wondered if he would ever comprehend how a machine thought!

"Then make it so," he grumbled, "but let us continue to see outside."

TRUE TO ITS PREDICTION, UNA ARRIVED OVER MOTHER'S CITY WITHIN half an hour. Looking out over the metropolitan area as the craft slowly flew at an altitude of a hundred meters, Rusk was astonished at the size of the city; many times larger than God's Port, with untold numbers of red-roofed stone buildings of many pastel colors. At the very center of the city stood an immense palace, its huge white dome extending higher than the Solar Priests' temple, with hundreds of adjoining structures, parklands, and small lakes spread out over an area many times larger than all of The Tharn's Town. Wide roadways radiated in the cardinal directions from the enormous palace complex, giving it the appearance of a spoked wheel. *Or a giant white biter-web*, Rusk thought.

Anklya whispered in awe, "That must be Mother's Palace. Pernie's own palace would fit inside one of its small buildings."

Rusk nodded. "I think the whole city of ShadowFall would fit into one small corner of it." He had no words for the numbers of buildings stretching from horizon to horizon in all directions, much less the number of people who lived there. He sighed. "How do we ever find Rist in all of this?"

"Sire Rusk, it is possible to perform a DNA scan on all visible persons. Any DNA close to yours will be identified and located."

Surprised that Una had responded not to a direct question, but to his rhetorical musing, Rusk concluded that the machine must have some reasoning capabilities after all. "Then proceed, Una. Find my twin!"

The search was not done quickly. Una insisted on flying very slowly over the city, apparently using its instruments to search in a rectangular grid pattern from one edge of the walled city to the other. As they flew, Rusk saw pennants and flag of all colors draped between buildings on the main thoroughfares, as if a celebration were going on, but few people were on the streets. Was the population somewhere else? Where? Would Rist be there, too? Surely, Rist was *somewhere* in this city... Rusk expressed his dissatisfaction to Una.

"Sire Rusk, the scanners only detect persons in a direct line of sight, not inside buildings or underground."

At what he considered to be an insubordinate reply, Rusk fumed, but sat quietly. *Maybe Una has some sense of pride, after all?*

After more long minutes of tedious waiting without results, Rusk said, "Una, just go search around that large domed palace. Surely if Rist is with the Princess, she will be somewhere around that building and not in these empty neighborhoods."

Anklya smiled at Rusk's frustration. "Your Una does not use the same reasoning that a person would, does it? If *I* were looking for an unusual person in such a big city, even with just my own eyes, I would be searching for something that makes him stand out."

"Such as?" Rusk asked, irritated. "Being short, like me? And dark-skinned? Not too many of our kind in this big city of big people, do you think?"

"Or maybe look for big birds? Emus?" she replied with a sniff. "Not too many of those roaming around down here, either, do *you* think?" Rusk added those avians to Una's DNA search, whatever "Dee Enn Aee" was.

After more minutes of scanning around the palace complex, Una announced, "Sire Rusk, large avians have been identified." Una stopped; thirty meters below them was spread out over a wide grassy field populated by thirteen oval-shaped courtyards of sorts, each surrounded by high walls. Stretched across the top of the one directly below them was a light blue tent-like material that obscured whatever was beneath it. A dozen other such courtyards surrounded it, but they were all open to the sky, populated by men practicing with swords and spears; surprisingly, four horses were running around in one.

Finding it remarkable that any fabric could be stretched over an open area at least fifty meters across, with no center pole holding it up, Rusk asked, "Una, what kind of cloth is that tent made of?"

"Sire Rusk, the tent material comprises a multilayered qomp-embedded borophene complex, which you call *godscloth*."

"Anklya, you said that godscloth was rare and expensive, but that Rist had brought a huge amount when he came down from the Dark Highlands?"

"Yes, Rusk. Now ShadowFall has an enormous amount of it." She blushed. "But it is supposed to be a secret from the other princesses."

"So to use godscloth to cover an arena like the one below must mean that ShadowFall is under it." He turned to the front screen. "Una, are the emus, the big birds, down below that tent?"

"Sire Rusk, yes. Infrared scanners detect a number of large avians moving under that tent."

"Emus and godscloth!" Rusk shouted with joy. "Rist must be down there!" He told Una to drop down closer but to stay undetected.

"Sire Rusk, any closer than ten meters and the shield may interact with the tent material."

"All right, ten meters it is. Do you see Rist anywhere, Una?"

"Sire Rusk, the sensors do not detect any person of Sire Rist's stature, only large humans tending to the birds. And—and—" Rusk was shocked at Una's hesitation. "What *is* it, Una?"

"Sire Rusk, there is a stockpile of the springbow weapons under the tent. Some with borophene bolts. The tent must have shielded them from the initial distant scan. You could be in danger!"

Groaning, Rusk directed Una to return to a hundred meters. Springbows and 'phene arrows again! Surely Rist wouldn't shoot them at Una, would he? Then again, Rist wouldn't be expecting his twin to be flying inside a big green bug, either. And there were other big men with him; how would *they* react? He couldn't take the chance.

"Una, can we remain floating for a while? You are not going to fall again, are you?"

"Sire Rusk, there is no 'you' here, but your message is understood. Under present conditions, this craft is capable of staying aloft for five years."

Relieved, Rusk conferred with Anklya about next steps. "We can't land nearby and just walk up to that walled compound. We don't know what their reaction would be to me." He paused. "Or even to you, a large wen."

"I am a *woman*, Rusk, not one of your *wen*," Anklya replied curtly, then smiled. "But if I were to enter Mother's Palace by myself and announce that I have come from ShadowFall with a message from

Rumi Similla, to be delivered only to Princess Perneptheranam, then perhaps I could get Rist outside where he could be rescued."

"No death sentence?"

"Not if she believes I came with an urgent message."

"How did you get here? She will ask."

Anklya curtsied as if in court. "'My Princess, if you will bring little Rist out into an open courtyard, I will show you. And I will introduce you to Rist's twin, too.'" Rusk admitted that her plan was the only way forward he could imagine. He had Una land, invisibly and quietly, in the middle of a large green parklike field about half a kilometer from Mother's Palace, adjacent to the wide promenade entrance.

ANKLYA WALKED OUT OF THE ENCLOSED BACK CABIN OF THE UNA, where she had freshened up. "Look at me, Rusk," she said twirling around in the aisle next to the cabin's seats. "Do I look presentable?" A fragrance she had obtained from somewhere heightened Rusk's appreciation of her attractiveness.

Rusk only snorted and nodded. "Yes, Anklya, in your translucent white godscloth gown, you're like a princess yourself. Now, do you think you can get to Rist, and have him come out this far so we can all go away?" He thought for a moment. "Or if you can get under that godscloth tent and have him pull it back, put those weapons away, I can land Una there. Which might work."

"I can only try," she replied, with a bow to the small man. "Wish me luck." And with that she asked Rusk to open the side door, finally descending as though she really were a princess. Rusk quickly had Una shut the door, hoping nobody saw Anklya appearing as if from thin air in the midst of an open field. He then ordered Una to hover, unseen, ten meters immediately above Anklya as she walked toward the palace. He would swoop down and rescue her if she appeared to be in danger. If there was a delay for any reason, he would return Una to the godscloth-covered courtyard and wait there above it.

As Anklya stepped out of Una, the first thing she felt was heat and humidity. *This is oppressive,* she thought. *But the sweet smell of these bushes and their flowers around this field, this park, balance it out.* She hoped her court perfumes would counteract the instant sweating she felt, but the toilette in the Una had not had anything but water with which to clean up. Shrugging off such concerns, she walked briskly toward the long, marble-paved roadway that led to the formidable entrance of Mother's Palace.

Remaining above and behind her, Rusk marveled at the beauty of the approach to the palace: a polished white marble promenade five hundred meters long and a hundred meters wide, framed by alabaster walls at least two meters high, its gradual upward slope and slight gutters obviously designed to handle significant rainfall. At the end, a hundred marble steps led up to a pair of massive polished black metal doors set back into a carved stone portico sporting four huge white fluted columns. He marveled at the doors—at least ten meters high, the portico itself a hundred meters in both directions! He wondered how many man-years it had taken to construct such a magnificent building. *All of The Tharn's Town would fit inside this palace!*

On each side of Anklya's long, lone path—where *were* all the people of Mother's City?—stood dozens of armed guards, their long spears and broadswords shining, obviously intended for more than decoration. Una did not detect any 'phene weaponry among them, so Rusk felt safe. At least for a while.

Gathering up as much courage as she wished she actually possessed, Anklya walked up the wide white steps, past closer formations of those intimidating armored men, and approached what appeared to be the head guard, a tall, unarmed man dressed in black leather and wearing a matching helmet, standing in the center of the portico, arms crossed.

That guard, tall even for a Mothersman, glared down at her through a slit in his helmet. Anklya gulped, holding her head up to stare into that slit. "Sir, I am Anklya, of the court of Princess Perneptheranam of the Sisterdom of ShadowFall." She held up the medallion on the chain around her neck bearing the ShadowFall sigil.

The guard reached down to handle the medallion, saying nothing.

Anklya persisted, "I have an urgent message to deliver to the Princess, from Rumi Similla, whom she left in charge while attending the Motherland Game."

The guard made some kind of hand signal, and two of the door guards came down steps, each tightly grabbing one of Anklya's arms. The head guard said something in an unknown language and Anklya was swiftly escorted through a side door and thrust into a tiny dark room. The door was slammed shut behind her. With no light, Anklya felt her way around the cold stone walls. *Barely two meters square! Like an animal cage! Am I now trapped, imprisoned?*

She stood for what seemed like hours, finally tiring enough to sit on the cold stone floor. Now thirsty and beginning to feel hunger pangs, she felt the first inclination to panic. *But surely the Princess's status means something! That guard must have recognized the sigil, and Princess Pernie says ShadowFall is one of Mother's favorite Sisterdoms!*

After a while she hesitatingly tapped on the door. "Can anyone hear me, please?" To her surprise, the door opened and a familiar figure stood there in silhouette. Wakan Kech! "Dear Wakan!" she cried. "I was so afraid." The priest did not smile as she attempted to hug him.

More in puzzlement than in anger, Wakan said, "What are you doing here, young maid? More importantly, how did you get here? The trip from ShadowFall requires weeks, with armed escorts, and I didn't see any of our soldiers here." Wakan escorted Anklya into an antechamber through a smaller entrance next to those massive metal doors, motioning for her to sit on a bare wooden chair, while he reclined on a plush leanback. She could tell from his demeanor that Wakan was not pleased, but also that he was truly concerned.

"Wakan Kech," she began after taking a long draught of cold water from a slave-provided glass and pitcher, "you will find this hard to believe, I know, but our little man Rist has a twin, an identical, name of Rusk." She trembled and took another sip.

"I have heard Rist tell of this Rusk," the priest said. "How would I not believe that?"

"And this Rusk, he has—he has—a"—she gulped again—"a flying *machine*. We *flew* from ShadowFall to Mother's City!"

Wakan Kech sat up straight and stared at Anklya, his thoughts churning, his mind caught between wanting to call the guards to throw this maid into one of Mother's dungeons, yet hoping that such a miracle might actually be true. After all, such machines were legendarily possible, and when little Rist had touched one of the godspheres in the catacombs under Pernie's palace, one of the moving images it portrayed seemed to be a flying mechanism of some kind.

Gathering control of himself, he said, "Anklya, if this is true, then where is this Rusk, and where is this machine?" Sobbing, Anklya broke down and told Wakan the entire story, of Rusk's arrival in the big green machine that Rusk called "Una," how the palace guards had shot it down, how it had repaired itself. "And I escaped with him, Wakan Kech," she said, finally restoring her own determination to be a free person. "I wanted to fly, to see the whole wide world. And Rusk offered that to me." Biting her lip, recognizing that her life now lay in the hands of the priest, she pleaded, "Please don't let the Princess kill me; I just *had* to fly in that Una, to help Rusk find his twin, Rist."

Wakan Kech swallowed hard. Within himself he felt that her story, fantastic as it seemed, was reality, at least to her. Maybe it was at least partially true? From her perfume and clean dress, she certainly didn't appear to have endured a three-week trek from ShadowFall. And she knew about Rist's twin. And nobody in ShadowFall had ever discussed flying machines; he hadn't shared the details of Rist's godsphere revelations with anyone, not even Pernie.

No, he wasn't going to allow this young woman to be put to death, not when she had been brave enough to walk right up to Mother's Palace, and to—to *fly!*—and as far as he knew, was only the second person to experience such a miracle. No, he would have her take him to this Rusk. But where? Having such a machine seen in Mother's City would certainly risk its seizure by Mothersmen and a grievous loss to ShadowFall. Such a device could make ShadowFall and Pernie powerful beyond all belief. *Maybe even a competitor to Mother*

Herself? He quickly discarded such treasonous thoughts. *One thing at a time. But what a thing!*

But then there was The Game, the day after tomorrow. Could he risk upsetting that millennia-old tradition with the sudden news of a flying dwarf? The announcement itself might set off civil wars as the other Sisterdoms tried to acquire such power at ShadowFall's expense. And ShadowFall needed to win The Game to provide new advisors to Mother. If Rist and his team were to lose, and Pernie was known to have possession of that machine, she would have to give it up to the winning Sister; that would be disaster for Pernie and himself. But if Rist were to be killed, Pernie had made it clear that Wakan himself would not live. And what would this flying Rusk do if his twin were killed? Wakan could only begin to imagine the power that the dwarf might unleash in anger from his flying machine; he could not conceive that such a machine would not have godlike weapons like those of legend.

With all these factors and possibilities churning in his mind, Wakan knew he had to make a decision immediately, ensuring that neither Mother nor the other Sister princesses knew about Rusk and his Una. *Not yet.* And also how to save Rist. *How do I do all of that?*

First, he had to hide Anklya, keeping her very presence a secret until at least after The Game. This he did by calling in a guardsman of his longtime acquaintance, one owing loyalty to him by virtue of Wakan's covering up the man's past indiscretions, some particularly perverse sins that Mother Herself would yet punish by death or worse were she to find out. He ordered this man to take Anklya to another set of rooms that had been assigned to ShadowFall courtiers, but with instructions that she be dressed in plain slave livery and kept incommunicado.

"You understand, Anklya," Wakan told her, "that your life is in danger should either the Princess or Mother know you are here. After The Game I will come and free you and we will find your Rusk and his machine. But for now you must remain hidden."

"Wakan Kech, I understand. But you must let Rist know that the Una could tell that there were emus under that huge blue godscloth tent, even though we couldn't see Rist through it. Surely that's where Rusk will be looking for him." With a slight bow toward the priest, she left with his trusted guard.

Rist, Wakan thought. *I will tell him; and we will figure a way to contact his twin.* He departed for the training corral, sincerely hoping that Rist could help in this life-or-death situation. And he was thinking, *That machine can see things through godscloth? Is there anything it can't do?*

CHAPTER THIRTY-NINE

*U*nder the concealing godscloth tent, Rist and his combat team exercised their tactics for The Game. "I will run out first, on my emu," he told his crew, "springbow at hand, arrows enough to kill all of the chiefs I can get to. As soon as I make a few shots, you three push the other emus out in the other directions. With their needle spurs they can injure or kill, maim, making it easier for us to finish them off." He indicated which of the other Sisterdom teams that Wakan wished to avoid for as long as possible. "Wakan has some kind of arrangement with Three Rivers and a few others he will tell us about. But if it comes down to them or us, then…" He left the statement unfinished. Every ShadowFall warrior knew going in that they might have to kill all of the other teams, and they were prepared to do it.

As the ShadowFall fighters talked calmly to the emus, placing harmless ankle weights on them that on the morning of The Game would be replaced with needle-spiked spurs, Rist noticed Wakan motioning to him from the one doorway. "What do you want, Wakan?" he asked. "We are still in training. Big times, day after tomorrow."

Wakan said quietly, "Rist, I have just had word from ShadowFall. Your twin, Rusk, is here in Mother's City, looking for you." He closely observed his warrior's reaction. Would little Rist believe such a thing? Would he believe about the Una machine?

But he was surprised as Rist broke into a wide grin. "I expected my twin to be here to see my great victory! Will you give him a good seat to watch it?"

"Rist, there's more that you need to know," Wakan said. "Can we have this arena to ourselves, get your men and birds out for a while?"

"Of course, Wakan, but *why*?"

After they were alone, the priest filled him in, again surprised that Rist accepted the flying Una machine as a matter of fact.

"The Colds told us they had found other gods in The Ice, and a god-machine. I am happy that Sire and Rusk were able to fetch it. When do I see it myself?"

Wakan assisted Rist in untying some of the underwebbing that was holding up the godscloth cover. As their tent gently wafted to the sandy floor, they rolled it up and left half of the oval training arena exposed to the sky.

"And Rusk will just fly over here and come down?" Rist asked. Wakan nodded, assuring him that it would happen. He hoped.

ABOVE THE ENTRANCE TO MOTHER'S PALACE, RUSK WAS GROWING impatient. He'd seen Anklya taken to a side room, and much later a tall dark man in red robes enter that room and take her inside the palace. But an hour later, he'd seen nothing, heard nothing. "Una, return to that courtyard that was covered with godscloth. Maybe Anklya was able to go there."

A minute later Una hovered over the place the emus were detected, but now half of the godscloth tent was down. "Rist! She must have found you!" Thinking about possible problems, Rusk asked, "Una, is there any risk to land inside that courtyard, away from the godscloth? Do you still see springbows or 'phene arrows?"

"Sire Rusk, there is no 'you' here. Scanning shows that the springbows and arrows are stored, not in active use. So long as this craft remains outside of the borophene complex fabric, there is little risk."

"Take us down, then, Una, slowly."

Looking up, Rist and Wakan Kech first felt a slight downdraft breeze coming from above, then a slight tingling of their skin as when lightning strikes close by during a thunderstorm, and then the smell of that same strange after-lightning odor. Standing back under the tent-roof they could make out a slight greenish sheen in the air, a shimmer that settled into the arena, the accompanying wind gently kicking up the fine sand of the training floor. Not knowing what to expect, they watched incredulously as a giant cylinder slowly materialized on the ground surface, a shimmering green object some ten meters long and about three meters across. A nonreflective black blister, an ovoid about a meter in its major axis, sat on its top surface.

Wakan blew out a long breath. "I know it can't be magic, but this is just—*incredible!*" Without comment or visible reaction, Rist waited to see his twin; Wakan was continually surprised at the little man's calmness in the face of the unknown. *Such self-control! ShadowFall has got to import more of these little people! They have a lot to teach us.*

As they watched, a curved door swung open upward and a small dark person stepped out.

"Rusk! It is you!" Rist yelled, running to his twin and hugging him, lifting him off the ground and swinging him around. "So happy to see you!" Letting go of Rusk, he spread his arms toward Una. "And look at this god-machine you found in The Ice! Our Sire must be so proud of you! And I'll bet The Tharn has given you great rewards for such a discovery!"

But Rist was silent, indicating with a nod the presence of Wakan Kech. Rist said, "Oh, Wakan, this is my twin, Rist. Rist, meet Wakan Kech, High Priest of ShadowFall." Not versed in court protocols, Rusk bowed slightly toward Wakan, who returned the gesture.

Rusk said, "Rist, we have to talk. First, can I rescue you now? I will have to find Anklya in this huge palace and then we can return home…" He paused, causing Rist some puzzlement, then continued.

"It's best if I fill you in on what's happened back in The Tharn's Lands since you left."

By the time Rusk finished his story of finding Una, learning to use it, and then the horror of The Tharn's Men burning their home and emus, and his priestly troubles in God's Port, Rist was troubled. "I will help you take revenge on The Tharn, that old fat bastard, killing our birds like that," he said with a grimace. "But I can't leave yet. I have a sworn duty to Princess Perneptheranam, to Wakan Kech, to ShadowFall. I will fight tomorrow, and I will win." He paused. "And I have a duty to myself. I find satisfaction being a warrior. I have a place at ShadowFall; I belong there." Looking at Wakan, he continued, "And Wakan said he wants more of us to live in ShadowFall. Why don't we bring our Sire and our birther there, and maybe some other People, our friends? If your Una machine can land here in Mother's City unseen we can do it in The Tharn's Town, too?"

Rusk said, "But I don't know if I will be welcome back in ShadowFall, Rist." Reluctantly, he told of Una's crash after being shot with 'phene arrows, of his own injuries and then his escape from Rumi Similla. "With Anklya, a handmaiden of the Princess." He looked sternly at Wakan. "She says she may be executed for traveling without permission."

Wakan shook his head; he had long suspected Rumi Similla of insubordination, but now it seemed that she was bordering on treason, if she had been intending to take control of the Una for herself. He was thankful that she had not been able to operate that flying machine, that Rusk was as resourceful as his twin Rist and had brought the Una to him. "No," he said, "I will handle her case with the Princess. She won't be punished. But you can't just abduct the girl again. Let me work on this." He was thinking furiously about how to seize control of the Una machine for ShadowFall without having to confront the little twins from The Tharn's Lands. If not *seize*, then *utilize*? Perhaps a sharing arrangement could be had, maybe permissive immigration from The Tharn's Lands in return for shared use of the Una? He noticed that Rusk had not invited either Rist or him inside the green machine, and had not explained how to fly it. *Or to fuel it. I wonder what makes it fly?* He finally decided just to ask, "May we see inside your machine, Rusk?"

Without comment, Rusk invited them into Una. Both Wakan and Rist showed astonishment that they could see clearly through the invisible walls from the inside. Rusk demonstrated the visual screen at the front of the cabin and had Una speak. Then Rusk said, "Una, fix Rist's eyes." Within seconds it was done.

Rist staggered backwards, almost falling, then looked closely at Rusk and Wakan. "Rusk, how is this possible? To see clearly that which we can touch? It's—it's amazing!" Disbelieving, Wakan put his hands in front of Rist. "You can see my fingers without blurring?"

Tears came to Rist's eyes. "Rusk, I can see your face clearly for the first time now. And yours, too, Wakan. Oh, what we People have been missing since The Beginning of All Things!"

Wakan walked around inside the cabin, marveling at the moving-picture screen, the transparent walls, and the voice of the Una. He had never even imagined the incredible capabilities of the gods' technologies. Again, he didn't believe in magic, but he also couldn't believe what he was seeing and touching, either. *And it flies!* He was determined: *ShadowFall* must *have this machine!* But they all knew that Rusk had to leave before the ShadowFall warriors or any others saw Rusk and Una. Rusk demanded, one last time, that his twin leave with him.

Despite arguments, Rist would not leave, would not abandon his responsibility for fighting in The Game. Wakan wanted Rusk to stay nearby with the Una machine, and for Rist to fight, but was a bit concerned that little Rist was enjoying the warrior life too much. The little man had certainly proven his usefulness and loyalty in stopping the assassins before. But assuming he was successful in The Game, what could the dwarf warrior do with all of his free time after that? *One more thing to consider*, he thought. *Just one of many!*

Wakan promised that Anklya would be reunited with Rusk. "When The Game is over and Rist is victorious," he said, "I will send your Anklya out onto the promenade where I found her, only walking out down the center of it. You will be able to pick her up there. Just don't be detected."

With Rist's assurances that he and his fellow ShadowFall warriors would prevail, Rusk stepped back into Una. Wakan hated to see him leave, especially with the Una, but saw no way out of the complicated situation. From the Una doorway Rusk did say, however, that although he would observe invisibly from above and not interfere with The Game, "If I see Rist being hurt, or about to be, I will land Una and save him." Rist had argued against any such intervention, saying that it would defeat the purpose of the contest and cause certain chaos in Motherland, but Wakan convinced him.

"Rist, you are certain to win. But having a backup plan is always prudent. Always. When Rist grudgingly conceded and agreed, Wakan drew a sigh of relief. *So maybe Rist won't die. And neither will I. One less thing to worry about!*

CHAPTER FORTY

*A*fter a day of rest, Princess Perneptheranam and Wakan Kech were escorted from their temporary accommodations into the vast expanse of Mother's Hall by six armed palace guards. Pernie had not been to her place of birth since departing for ShadowFall five years before, and part of her mind welcomed familiar sights: the high vaulted ceilings, painted in a cacophony of wild colors, each representing one of the conquered Motherless peoples—the blackskins of the scattered tablelands to the southeast, the brownskins of the high dry lands to the west and southwest, the yellow-haired pinkskins of the easternmost highlands and coast. Along with metaphorical representations of their Motherless cultures, accentuating what Motherlanders considered to be primitive rituals and artifacts—time-blunted pyramids, scattered stones of collapsed buildings, barely clothed savages eating their own kind, and the like.

Wakan shivered; at least the High Antis were not yet shown up there as conquered slaves. And if he could help it, they never would be. A lot depended on the outcome of tomorrow's Game—whether little Rist was able to win and survive, or whether his twin Rusk would come through and save Rist if Rist was in danger of being killed. Wakan had seen Rusk fly the unbelievable machine, the Una.

But was the Una capable of landing safely in the arena, grabbing Rist, and flying off with him? *I hope not, for it would cause Motherland-wide wars among the princesses, conflicts that even the Lordess Mother could not control. We shall know tomorrow, one way or the other.* As was his usual wont when a possible situation could not be influenced by himself, Wakan put off that worry until the appropriate time.

Through his soft shoes, Wakan felt the thick, luxurious carpeting of the hallway leading to Mother's Hall itself, where on its high pyramidal dais stood the breathtakingly beautiful Crystal Throne, an outsized sculpture made of a transparent stone-like material, a seemingly magical god-stone that would emit a myriad of colors, but only when a chosen Mother sat on it. Its arched back pointed straight up, toward a vaulted ceiling higher than any other in Motherland, and capped by the largest dome in Motherland. The magnificent ceiling was painted in a realistic portrayal of ancient gods, giant female figures with the purest of white skins, large blue eyes, waist-length, braided red hair, and clothed in flowing white robes. The largest figure, the slender and beautiful Ancient Mother, held in her outstretched hand a scarlet scroll to the present Mother, the latter easily recognizable by her stylized younger face and her long braids of copper-colored hair, a ruler who was accepting Her authority from the Ancient Mother Herself. In the faded background stood some much smaller male figures in gray robes, wistfully observing but obviously ineffectual. Overall, the story the painting told reinforced Mother's god-given power in a manner that even illiterates—*especially* illiterates!—immediately understood.

Wakan had always wondered if anyone had ever kept a painted copy of the faces of all predecessor reigning Mothers from times past. Over the many centuries, untold thousands of years, there had to have been many dozens, hundreds, of them. He let those thoughts go, as his attention returned to where he and his Princess would be standing during the ceremonies to come. To his satisfaction, he found that Pernie and he had been stationed at the center of the semicircular line of Sisters, showing Mother's favor to her youngest daughter. *Our gifts*

of many square meters of tailored godscloth must have had an effect!
he told himself with a suppressed smile.

To their left stood the beautiful light-skinned, silver-haired Princess
Messinex of Three Rivers, herself clothed in a tailored blue godscloth
gown recently gifted from Pernie, and her advisor, Miran Kech, a
fellow captive and countryman of Wakan's, in bright blue satin robes
and hood. They nodded and smiled as ShadowFall's two
representatives took their designated positions. To Wakan's right were
another princess whom he didn't recognize, and her tall blond advisor,
a bearded pinkskin giant. Those two both smiled and nodded
respectfully. Wakan was relieved at the apparently peaceful situation;
he had been afraid that a few of the Sisters might be so hostile as to
launch a physical attack upon him and his Princess on the spot,
regardless of the sure and swift punishment! Such violations of
protocol were not all that infrequent among squabbling Sisters.

Each of the other eleven Sisters, themselves garbed in the most
exquisite and expensive godscloth they owned, was accompanied by
her chief advisor, most of them Kech. But in the center position stood
Pernie, in a finely tailored godscloth gown, comprising her original
swaths of rainbow-colored material now framed by a high collar of
Rist's iridescent offerings and a long, shimmering pale blue train
trailing behind, standing out amongst all the other Mother's daughters
like a noble above a slave. Every eye in the hall, from the hundreds of
Courtswomen and Courtsmen, not to mention eleven envious Sisters,
could not help but focus on the youngest Princess. And her High Priest,
of course—Wakan Kech, himself—draped in many meters of fitted red
satin, standing like a dark carved statue in a solemn, if haughty, stance.
All present had seen the untold hundreds of square meters of curtained
godscloth in Pernie's ostentatious caravan as it perambulated through
the city in the presentation parade.

And now in Mother's Hall, in a profusion of godscloth,
ShadowFall was demonstrating that its Princess alone held the secret of
cutting that unscissable material, driving up the level of jealousy to a
dangerous pitch. Only Messinex, a few meters away, smiled at the
obviously staged display of wealth and capability. Catching Pernie's

eye, she smiled knowingly at her youngest sister. Pernie smiled back, nervous about the precarious political situation that Wakan Kech had placed her in, but appreciative all the same.

Messinex was having mixed feelings about the ceremonies and The Game. She loved Pernie above all her other Sisters, probably the only one of them she truly loved, since their childhood days. But as princess, she wanted her own Three Rivers warriors to prevail in The Game, only her second time as princess to field such a team. As the youngest of the Sisters, Pernie had been her one childhood friend in Mother's Palace. Just four years older than her half-sibling, Messinex had spent considerable time with young Pernie before leaving at age thirteen to become Princess of Three Rivers, now her Sisterdom on the southern border of Motherland. Her domain comprised a vast and fertile lowland savannah and a higher-elevation lush jungle that abutted the Southern Highlands from which, through large canyons, poured the three streams that gave it its name.

Pernie had visited Three Rivers as a child, staying for months at a time, bonding with Messinex, sharing their mutual fear of their biological mother, the Lordess Mother. In subsequent years they had shared continuing correspondence, expressing similar thoughts about how a princess should govern, parallel philosophies about educating their subjects, and sharing various political tactics to protect against their other Sisters' ambitions. Being at opposite ends of Motherland gave them another friendly advantage: they could never war directly on each other, never encroach or covet the other's lands and resources. They both still feared their Mother, while respecting the stability and relative peace She was able to maintain among thirteen princesses of wildly differing personalities and ambitions.

WITH AN EARSPLITTING TRUMPET WELCOME, FROM BEHIND AN enormously high white curtain at the front of the hall, came a hundred armed men, dressed in kilts of Motherland's dominant scarlet colors with matching black leather vestments, their long dark hair braided and tied back, each holding a bow or spear. Wakan discreetly scrutinized the men he recognized as Mothersmen; he had known many of them during his time in court. They and their weapons were not just for show, but could be a deadly force in battle. And their name had other significance as well—as long as they continued to win wars for Mother, they were allowed to keep their manhood. Losing a battle would mean painfully losing what made them men, that threat serving to make them extremely fierce in combat. Wakan winced at the memory of what had happened to some of the losers in a particularly ferocious struggle in the southeast, before new reinforcements finally succeeded where they had failed against blackskin rebels.

As the Mothersmen formed ranks on either side of Mother's Crystal Throne dais, an assemblage of horn and string musicians performed some of the most beautiful music Wakan had ever heard. He had all but forgotten that one wonderful aspect of court life—the artistry of captured Motherless performers not only in music, but also in sculpture, painting and even acting. *Once ShadowFall is truly secure, I need to press Pernie to bring this kind of culture to her realm there.* An unbidden treasonous thought returned, one that would not be suppressed: *Unless Pernie can become Mother herself, and rule all of Motherland from* here!

The musicians faded their ethereal outpourings as a hundred Mother's Maidens entered the hall, singing a lilting song of praise to Mother, with the millennia-old refrain, "Hail Mother, full of grace, Mother of us all." The familiar refrain and melody almost brought Pernie to tears; as a child she had loved her Mother, stern and demanding though She was. That song brought back treasured childhood memories, the loving scenes quickly eclipsed by other reminisces of her own demanding formal education, her strenuous physical training regimen, and worst of all, the sounds of Mother in one of her awful, uncontrollable, shrieking moods. *Like the time she had my nan cut down on the spot by a palace guard just because I showed emotion and cried at the death of my pet dog!...* Followed by other hard recollections of Mother's incessant cruelty to Pernie and her other Sisters. And Her merciless treatment of losers in battle and Her ranting behavior at The Game. Pernie shifted her thoughts away from that turbulent past. Occasionally Mother could be loving, she knew, but could change in an instant to a screaming monster with no regard for anyone. To Pernie's relief, she had never since met another person who acted like that. But of course, nobody else was Mother, with the awesome power of death and life over the millions of people of Motherland!

As Pernie and the others began growing restless, weary from their long trips aboard bouncing wagons, and still standing after two hours of music, songs, and Mothersmen maneuvers, the Lordess Mother Herself entered. Wakan knew that the long, unnecessary standing, the excruciating wait, were intended to weaken the physical stamina of the attendees, so that a rested and fresh Mother would look all the stronger by comparison. As their sovereign walked toward the stairs and then up to the Crystal Throne, Wakan was happy to see that She wore the tailored godscloth robes that he had had fashioned for her. *Hence our favored position here in court,* he thought, smiling. Music swelled, more hymns of praise for the Mother of Motherland, the physical embodiment of their nation, their people. Wakan himself felt a surprising surge of proud patriotism, even for a country that was not his by birth, a lingering emotional bond with the woman whose troops had slaughtered dozens of his own countrymen when he himself had been captured all those years ago.

Recognizing that impressive rituals, repeated at important times, and reinforced by songs and artwork that could influence, *did* influence, the subjects of a realm, Wakan had tried hard not to allow all of the propaganda in front of him to gain entry into his emotional makeup, but only to give it lip service, and thus ensure that his outward reactions appeared to be those expected of a loyal subject. Nevertheless, a decade and a half of court life before ShadowFall, with its daily doses of such displays, had affected him more deeply than he recognized before now. *After five years,* he mused, *all this time gone by, and yet She still commands my loyalty. That is most interesting. I wonder if we, Pernie and I, could educate the people of ShadowFall by using these same techniques—rituals and repetition—not to instill just blind subservience, but also the knowledge of reading and writing and numbers and geoms?*

As Mother scaled the stairs leading to her translucent throne, internal lights illuminated each of the clear steps along the way—green, red, violet, blue—presenting an ever-changing pattern, as if traveling up and down the staircase. Though most subjects thought that Mother was controlling the lights, Wakan knew from intensive study of the throne that the patterns were apparently random and under no human control. He and his fellow Kech had not been able to determine why they lit, why they seemed to move in such a manner, and why they only responded to Mother and no one else. More secrets of the ancients.

Thinking over his observations of the throne from years past, the mysterious moving lights reminded Wakan of the images inside the godsphere that Rist had touched with such amazing results back in ShadowFall, showing the whole round world with moving pictures inside it, speaking in unknown languages, accompanied by other sounds and even music. Did Rist's mere touch have an effect on that sphere like Mother's did on the Crystal Throne? Would the spheres react if Mother touched them? Or would the Crystal Throne respond, if Rist were allowed on it? And how did the throne know that any succeeding female was an offspring of the previous Mother? Was that actually a requirement, or was it merely an invention of a given Mother? He also wondered what would happen if, like the globe lights at ShadowFall, these lights were to fade away while Mother sat up there?

The choral singing ended as Mother seated herself on gilt-edged, padded red pillows on the throne, high above the audience in the hall. Pernie thought, *Oh, she is so much older than I remember! And she looks so pitiful. What has happened?*

Seeing the same sight, of an elderly woman painfully making her way alone up a dozen steep stairs—*stairs obviously made for a taller person!*—Wakan's new vision, of a young Pernie in Her place, would not go away. He studied Mother more closely; in the fifteen years he had spent in her court after his capture, she had gone from a fairly attractive middle-aged woman in her mid-thirties, to a haggard despot nearing fifty. And now, at fifty-five, she was showing her advanced age in a way that even her cosmeticians could not disguise. He wondered if her volatile disposition was any better now, if age had mellowed her erratic outbursts. Involuntarily he recalled many episodes of her screaming at underlings for no reason, of behaviors that alienated her daughters without visible cause. And of sudden tortures or executions of innocents, which actions she often rued within days or sometimes even hours, relying on Wakan's stoic discretion to keep secret her screaming confessions and her sobbing regrets. Not that he had had any choice in the decision to remain quiet; the prospect of losing parts of one's body to a white-hot dull knife over a period of hours or days was quite sufficient inducement for discretion and loyalty!

Mother was also shrinking in height, Wakan saw, from her previous impressive poised stature. Now stooped, she was at least ten centimeters shorter, and weighed much more than she had when he left for ShadowFall, almost bordering on obesity. He figured that the heavy makeup she wore was an attempt to hide the wrinkles and spots on her sagging features. *Stressful years of planning and carrying out expensive and unnecessary wars, of ordering torture and executions, of distrusting everyone, will do that to you!* Pernie's High Priest concluded. Thinking of his happier, more placid and peaceful homeland in the High Antis, Wakan had to concede that *Even a rational, balanced sovereign, totally immersed in running the normal affairs of even a happy nation, ages very quickly. The stress is just too much for one person, even one with a coterie of wise advisors.* He didn't think too highly of many of Mother's actions since he had known her, mostly brought about by her changing coterie of greedy, ambitious advisors. Almost any new group of them would be preferable, but Pernie's picks would be the best. And that all depended on the death match of tomorrow's bloody Game.

Wakan often tried to imagine some other way to organize a country, a way to distribute power in such a manner as to prevent one faction or family—*or gender!*—from using their power to seize control of everyone else and rule in an arbitrary manner, without restriction. The

High Antis homeland of the Kech had a much calmer and gentler, nonhereditary ruling class, but they were almost all of one culture, one language, one tribe. Here in Motherland, the people were so dissimilar and varied in appearance and culture, with so many tribes and clans, and so much more numerous, that Wakan and his fellow Kech kinsmen had not been able to conceive of a system like their own being successful in this vast, troubled land.

IN A TREMULOUS VOICE, MOTHER ADDRESSED HER DAUGHTERS, THEIR advisors, and the hundreds of her guards and court: "Your Mother welcomes you all, beloved daughters and loyal friends." Wakan winced at so many lies in one short sentence; he knew from experience that Mother would have preferred to be left alone, she probably loved none of her offspring, and no friendship of any kind could exist for long in the treacherous environment of Mother's Court. "Your Mother extends Her protection and Her blessings on each of the Sisterdoms. May your realms be prosperous and happy, may your reigns be long and peaceful." The audience was deadly silent, knowing that ancient protocol demanded no interruptions of Mother's speech, not even for applause. "I will counsel with each daughter and her advisor individually and privately, immediately after lastmeal this evening."

Mother looked down, straight at Pernie and Wakan. "I will begin with my youngest, Princess Perneptheranam of ShadowFall, and her advisor, Wakan Kech, my old acquaintance." As the aged woman spoke to him, Wakan remembered the first night of several nights he had spent with her, at her command. She had been a compliant lover, initially totally passive, then becoming most enthusiastic under his guidance, his touch, his new skills.

Knowing what was to be expected of him, after that first time Wakan had secretly commanded that the cook staff sprinkle all of Mother's food with the pregnancy preventative herbal potion used in the High Antis. He did not want Mother to become pregnant and blamed on him, and him possibly suffer the fate of the fathers of the other Sisters. Fortunately for Wakan, she had other lovers immediately after him who had not been so "lucky". And in later years, because he had felt that the baby Pernie would be the best and brightest of all the Sisters, he instructed the cooks to continue with the potions even after he left for ShadowFall. He hoped that Mother never noticed that her food tasters remained childless, too. *So Mother will never conceive again, and Pernie will be the last. As planned.*

In Mother's private meeting chamber that evening after a rather hasty but tasty lastmeal, Pernie tried her best not to show any emotion in her mother's presence, remembering that her beloved nanny had died violently because her charge, the child Pernie, had cried when her puppy was accidentally killed by palace guard dogs. With mixed feelings of both love and fear for Mother, at this time Pernie acted cold and distant, totally unlike her normal disposition. Wakan Kech remained his usual quiet self. To their surprise, Mother laughed, "Pernie, my little girl, I have missed your cheerfulness at court. I hope you haven't let old sourpuss Wakan turn you into an old maid, not at eighteen years old!" Wakan only smiled, acknowledging Mother's humor. He hoped her amiable mood would last. *At least until we have left tonight!* he thought. *After that, such a show would be good!* He figured that one of Mother's unpredictable screaming fits would help unbalance some of the other Sisters prior to tomorrow's Game, all to Pernie's advantage. He also hoped that the one friendly Sister, Messinex, and her Kech advisor Miran, would *not* experience such an outburst.

Pernie cautiously returned the relaxed compliment. "Mother, I saw today that you wore the fitted godscloth I sent to you. It looked beautiful on you."

Mother smiled and said, "I have heard that you have a magic midget from the Dark Highlands who weaves a spell to cut the godscloth. Is that true? Or has our Kech wiseman, Wakan, worked another miracle himself?"

Pernie related a sanitized version of Rist's arrival, neglecting to spell out how the god-scissors could be used by anybody, intimating that only the little man had knowledge of the ancient skills of tailoring the magic material, and that it could not be taught outside his race of little people. Mother shook her head, not smiling this time. "Pernie, my princess girl, Wakan has not taught you to lie very well. I will send some trusted men with you when you return to ShadowFall. I want you, or Wakan, or the magic midget, to show them the process. Let them be trained, and let them come back to me with half of the godscloth windfall that you received through no effort of your own."

Pernie took a deep breath, but smiled and nodded. Wakan had foreseen something like this happening, so he would show the Mothersmen a separate inventory, revealing only one tenth of Rist's treasure. He calculated that, in addition, if those men returned to Mother with all of that godscloth already cut into smaller pieces, some as clothing tailored to fit Mother Herself, others for new draperies for the hall and for her private chambers, with enough for sale to other Sisters and nobles, then Mother would be happy enough, and they would not have to give up the one pair of scissors. If Mother ever had the sole cutting capability, ShadowFall would lose its greatest asset. *Well, that is in the future. I have enough to worry about tomorrow, at The Game.* His growing concern over Rist's possible performance in The Game and over what Rusk might do with the Una machine was threatening to consume all his attention.

Mother reiterated her demand for another ShadowFall secret, that of springbow fabrication. Pernie herself parried this request, saying, "My Mother, I have brought a dozen of those weapons as a gift for you. My guards will train anyone you wish in their use," and again made an excuse of the complexity of ancient knowledge, limited supplies of the source metal, and so forth. Mother nodded and accepted her daughter's lie, both of them knowing it was an untruth. But at the worst, Mother would have new weapons for a few of her most trusted Mothersmen. And She was anxious to see the outcome of tomorrow's Game, assuming that ShadowFall would demonstrate its secret weapon, springbows, to great effect, increasing the demand from the other Sisterdoms. *And raising the price!* Wakan thought.

But he also knew that should ShadowFall not prevail tomorrow, then by ancient custom Pernie and the other losing Sisters would have to grant both Mother and the winning Sister any single request as tribute for failure. Mother and Pernie both knew what tribute would be required of ShadowFall. As did Wakan; which is why he had kept the arrival of Rusk and his miraculous machine secret even from Pernie. The concept of failure tribute itself was a way to limit the introduction of new weapons and tactics to The Game; if you fielded your secret weapons, your tactical innovations, you could end up giving those inventions to all your merciless Sisters to use against you in the next Game or the next internecine war. Wakan had always appreciated that aspect of the ancient traditions, the duty-bound acceptance of limiting near-absolute power. He wished he could somehow translate that concept of constrained power into the ruling structures of Mother's Court and the Sisterdoms. He was also hoping against hope that springbow technology or godscloth cutting tools would be the worst failure tributes Pernie might have to surrender. So far, Rusk's flying Una machine was not even a topic of discussion!

CHAPTER FORTY-ONE

$\mathcal{T}$he morning of The Game, Rist and his teammates were up early, practicing their moves with their emus. "That was a great idea, boss," Thrak said. "Iron anklets with needle-spikes on the legs of the birds will kill anybody who gets close. Better than just a kick." Eddor and Een nodded agreement, though the bare kicks by themselves could be quite painful, as they had discovered during mock combat back in ShadowFall. Rist looked up at the big men, seeing their rugged faces clearly for the first time. *That Una machine fixed my eyes so well. I just hope that my new near vision doesn't interfere with my practiced springbow aim or my bolo throws!*

Standing only as high as their knees, Rusk would not be able to fight the other big men they would encounter today, not hand-to-hand, strength against strength. But by the same measure, no one else in the arena would be small enough to sit astride one of these emus, either. And by the intensive training, a daily regimen of practice fighting, the birds now recognized each of Rist's team as friends, if not as masters. And by the same training regimen, they now considered all strangers as enemies to be killed. Rusk wondered how that would play out against the teams that Wakan wanted to save, if possible.

"An emu's kick can break a man's legs," Rist had told them at the start of their training, "or take out his eyes, rip off his jaw. A kick in the groin or the gut can kill. The iron needle-spike spurs just guarantee the first blow will be fatal." His mates quickly learned from experience how to avoid beaks and feet; now friendly to the team members they knew, the birds would viciously attack any other man who came close. Rist's added weaponry of the spurs just made the outcome of the birds' attacks quicker and more certain. During their weeks of training at ShadowFall, the emus had adapted well to the extra weights on their legs.

"We have a dozen birds," Rist repeated, going over the whole range of tactics once more before they departed for the stadium. "Four of them will be saddled, with three held in reserve for me to ride if the others are killed under me. You all know what to do with the other eight." After the birds were run through their paces the last time, the rest of the team went over details of springbow usage, coordinated spear attacks, and if necessary, the last-ditch defense of fighting together with shortswords and Rist's bolos. After depleting his springbow arrows, Rist would throw his bolos from birdback or afoot. Thinking about his deadly fight with the big velk back home brought the feeling of homesickness to the fore, something Rist knew he could not dwell on while his life was at stake. *I know that Rusk will be up in the air today in his magic machine, watching me. I only wish our Sire Thess were here to see it, too.* A dark thought crossed his mind.

But only if we win.

THE MOTHERLAND STADIUM WAS PACKED WITH ALMOST THE ENTIRE population of Mother's City, with the quiet, reserved nobility occupying the upper tiers all around, and the unkempt mob of jostling, jeering common subjects in the bleachers at the bottom levels nearest the dirt floor, noisily swilling free ale and gorging on free meat pies as they waited for the death spectacle to begin. For good seats and free eats, most people had been there celebrating for the last two days in joyous abandon. Hundreds of serving-slaves mixed among them, passing out Mother's largesse of food and drink. The north end, reserved strictly for the Lordess Mother's favored Courtsladies and Courtsmen, remained calmer, its serving-slaves dressed in finery, passing out exotic snacks and wines. A fifteen-meter-high white stone wall separated the observers from the combatants in the arena, in case any fighter tried to escape or even turn his weapon on the crowd. From past experience, Mother's planners knew that men about to die would sometimes act in dishonorable ways, regardless of certain dire punishments for themselves and their teammates, not to mention the shame of their Sisterdom.

Evenly spaced around the top of the high perimeter wall were draped the colorful banners of the Thirteen Sisterdoms. Beneath each of them, the outline of a large gate revealed where that particular Sisterdom would be fielding its four-man team. Configured as they had been in the hall the day before, ShadowFall's princess and advisor sat above the gate at the north end, immediately below Mother's tall golden throne in the tier above them. Wakan looked left and right. As positioned, on his left sat Princess Messinex and his Kech friend, Miran, in their canopied seats. Smiling slightly, the Keches nodded at each other. Messinex did not smile, apparently absorbed in deep thought, as was Princess Pernie. On Wakan's right sat the Sister he now knew as Princess Jernoma of Ancient Towers, a princess some five years senior to Pernie, along with her fair-haired giant advisor, formerly a captured pirate captain from the Cold Sea. They did not return his look, staring straight ahead. Wakan couldn't make out the faces of the other princesses or their advisors, spaced as they were around an oval stadium two hundred meters along its major diameter. ShadowFall's retinue was privileged to be situated closest to the Lordess Mother's throne.

Wakan was saddened by the imminent loss of life, but knew that for today, at least, The Game would go on regardless of his feelings, and that many men would die, strong men, capable men. *Smart men, too? I wonder if there is another as smart as Rist among them?* he pondered. *Or another Wakan?* He shivered at that thought.

Trumpets sounded; quickly the crowds all became silent, standing as their sovereign entered the stadium, with only the gentle flapping of Motherland flags evincing any sounds of life. But when their Lordess Mother walked in under Her own gold-fringed, scarlet canopy, the crowds began cheering wildly. The Lordess Mother waved to her left and her right, finally sitting down, almost as if collapsing. Wakan figured she must have stayed up most of the night before, if she met with each daughter for the hour she had spent with Pernie and himself. She looked so weary, so worn, aged so much in just the five years of his absence from court.

A sudden realization hit him: what effect might all those years of his baby-preventing potion have had on Mother's health? Back in High Antis, the medicine was only for occasional use, since the nation depended upon a planned replacement birth rate to stay in existence. Might he have hastened Mother's demise? He figured that she must have changed food tasters over the years, but probably not the cook staff, so that possibly any negative indicators did not arise or were not noticed. In any case, Wakan refused to feel guilty. Anything he had done, purposefully or accidentally, that benefitted the ultimate goals of Pernie and ShadowFall—and himself, in the deal—was in accord with the morality and ethics he had learned as a scholar in the High Antis.

Trumpeters sounded the immediately recognizable notes of Mother's Call to Attention, the metallic blasts echoing from the smooth white vertical surface of the surrounding walls. As the reverberations died down, Mother stood behind a conical megaphone and shouted at her loudest: "Let The Game begin!" At that, thirteen large segmented metal doors rolled up around the perimeter, and dozens of fighting men emerged, strutting and swaggering onto the field, cheered on by their Sisterdoms and the local crowds of game-watchers. Wakan paid careful attention to the group of fighters to his left. *Good!* As arranged with his fellow Kech, the four Three Rivers warriors, dressed in green-hued leather armor and armed with swords and several spears each, headed away from ShadowFall's entry gate. Around the perimeter wall, other Sisterdom teams with Kech advisors also began to move away from each other.

So far, according to plan, Wakan noted with some satisfaction. In their location, Pernie and he could not see directly below themselves, not their banner nor the entrance gate, but heard quite a commotion as ShadowFall's fighters emerged. In a moment, he saw Rist astride an emu in front, the big bird with its head covered. A dozen other birds, led by the three other fighters and likewise hooded, rocked from leg to leg, apparently nervous and fearful of the crowd noises and smells. Two of them shat as they stood, Wakan catching the putrid odor from fifteen meters above.

Farther down the wall, other combat teams walked out to their marked positions on the arena ground, awaiting the final signal for the fight to the death. Hearing some shouts near the southern end of the stadium oval, Wakan was dismayed to see four fighters *on horseback*! Who would risk such expensive resources, even for advisors' seats in Mother's Court? He didn't know, and had no far-seer with him to see which Sisterdom was so profligate. In shock, Pernie looked at her priest. "I hadn't known about horses, Princess," he said quietly. "My spies were not that good." But the Princess crossed her arms and squared her shoulders, looking straight out into the arena, obviously highly upset at this development. And at Wakan. "But we have surprises of our own, Princess," he whispered again, not wanting any nearby spies to know the plans. Secretly, Wakan was pleased; the horses would be large targets, easy for Rist to finish off quickly, and no one could complain later about Pernie's emu war-birds.

Trying not to draw Pernie's attention to him, he casually glanced at the sky. The morning was clear and bright, no clouds anywhere. He hoped to see at least a greenish shimmer somewhere above the stadium, a comforting assurance that Rusk would be there to save Rist in case of trouble, but he saw nothing but blue sky, and the sun now risen high.

Where is Rusk?

CHAPTER FORTY-TWO

*U*na's shield was operating; Rusk had seen to that by flying low over the guards who still lined the wide avenue to Mother's Palace. Other than puzzled glances at temporary shimmers as he dropped under ten meters and flew right down the middle of the white walkway, there was no reaction. Then he proceeded to the stadium. Following Rist's earlier directions, he had located the large arena the day before and now hovered some twenty meters above the arena ground, and an equal distance out from the wall, where he could see Wakan Kech and others, including the beautiful wen—*woman!*— presumably the Princess Pernie, to whom his twin had pledged his loyalty. *And his life, if need be,* Rusk thought, *but I won't let that happen!* Nervously, he hefted a spear, keeping his shortsword only partially sheathed in case of quick need. From his vantage point he could see everything below, and had already prepared Una to descend quickly upon a specific code word, directly toward Rist. He watched his twin closely, expecting to have to swoop down and rescue him from some rash action, from disaster.

After a delay, all the combat teams were fielded and at their starting lines, composed of men alone, save for the horsemen at one end of the field and a ShadowFall birdman and his dozen war-birds at the other end; all was ready for the killing to start. Behind her megaphone, with a trembling voice not quite so loud as before, Mother fairly shrieked, "Gentlemen, start your melee!" and then collapsed backward into her throne. Aides ran to help her, but few in the crowds noticed, other than Wakan. Their attention was focused on the field below, where fifty-two men were rushing toward death.

AS PLANNED AND INTENSIVELY PRACTICED, RIST WAS FIRST TO FIRE IN anger. *But not anger*, he thought as his bird lurched leftward out into the arena. *Not anger, but cool calculation, one springbow shot at a time, one kill per shot.* Running to his left, he recalled which Sisterdoms had a Kech advisor, and ignored Three Rivers and a few others, choosing the Kech-less as his initial targets. As he approached the first enemy team—Black Water, from its sigil—one large, armored man stood in front, barking out orders to the reluctant warriors behind him. His companions could not figure out what to do about a dark midget riding a bird! Rist smiled at their confusion, then fired a springbow arrow into their leader's forehead, not waiting around to see his foe fall. He immediately dropped to one side of his emu to present less of a target, but still be able to use the springbow as practiced so many times back at ShadowFall. Along the length of the perimeter wall Rist ran his emu at maximum speed, firing arrows as quickly as he could place them, as quickly as his disbelieving targets presented themselves. At the far end of the stadium, he saw four large, dark shapes coming his way—*horsemen!*

Seeing the large horses and their riders closing on Rist's position and scared for his twin's safety, Rusk had Una drop down to just ten meters above Rist, ready to knock down any attackers and then pluck him out of the fight. But Rist, rather than retreating, was *attacking* them! Rusk decided to stay out of his twin's way, to see what he was planning to do.

Wakan and Rist had not planned on meeting any war-animals during The Game, especially rare and expensive horses. But Rist immediately decided to think of those rapidly approaching beasts as just more velks, evil creatures with more evil riding on them, only not having fangs, but spears and swords. Judging them to be well inside his weapon's range, the little man ran his emu toward the bunched enemies, firing one iron arrow after another at the distant targets, doing as his trainer had insisted, never watching to see which opponent fell. "You shoot, you shoot again, you keep on shooting," the experienced guardsman had repeatedly shouted at him until it took, until his responses were automatic: "You don't watch and wait. You shoot. Or you die!"

After half a dozen arrows, though, Rist looked up to see if anyone was still bearing down on him. No; his arrows had found their targets —the horses were all down, out of the fray for good. He and his men could take care of the riders later. He did quickly note that one of the riders was not getting up from where his horse had fallen. *An expensive day for one Sister!* he thought with an evil grin, hoping that Pernie would not have to feel the same way later, if he himself were so unlucky. Then his bird screeched and jumped; it had taken an arrow in its left thigh, barely missing his leg. "Damn!" Rist yelled, hoping he would not have to fight his way back to his team, not through a forest of rampaging giants!

From above, inside Una, Rusk was shouting for joy: "Damn, Rist! You have earned your man-name today. We will call you *Thist!*" He was able to relax for a moment, newly confident in his twin's capabilities for riding war-birds and for shooting with that springbow device.

But at the north end of the stadium, Wakan was nervous. Though Rist's early attack was hugely successful—*Four horses down! Eight fighters killed!*—and the other Kech-backed teams were prevailing over their lesser-trained foes also with small losses, the priest calculated that soon the only ones left living amongst the tumult on the field might be those of the Sisterdoms of his fellow Kech. That would be the defining moment he had planned, when he would publicly plead with the Lordess Mother to stop the killing and let his fellow Kech-led Sisterdoms share the win; in response, ShadowFall would share its springbow weapons and its training with Mother and those Sisterdoms.

Trying to keep track of the progress of his ShadowFall men, Wakan stood and looked down over the wall. Again, as planned, his other three fighters were crouching in their defensive mode, though it looked as though that might have to change soon. One of the hooded birds was down, croaking, a spear through its kicking body, and the other birds were panicking. *Smelling its blood?* he wondered briefly, *or hearing its squeals of pain?* In the distance, coming back to his starting position, straight down the center of the field, came Rist, aboard his limping bird, shouting. His emu was struggling to keep going with an arrow through its left thigh. Wakan could see that Rist was barely in control of his bird anymore.

"Give me another emu!" Wakan heard Rist yell, as the little man jumped off his injured ride and climbed on another. "And let them all loose, now! This one, too!" It was now time for a ShadowFall offensive; finally Wakan watched as the rest of the flock of war-birds grew alert, their hoods now removed, their fields of vision full of nothing but strangers. "*Go! Go! ShadowFall birds, go get them!*" Pernie's other fighters shouted, following behind them, springbows now in action, finishing off the shocked fighters closest to them.

Eleven angry emus, their beaks sharpened to points, their legs bearing needle-sharp spiked spurs, bore down on the enemy fighters in the arena, wreaking havoc among combatants who had only trained, and expected, to fight other armed men. The other Sisterdoms had chosen the largest men, and those best with weapons, but none of them had considered that their enemies in The Game might not be human, but fierce big *birds*! It had only been five minutes since Rist's unexpected onslaught, and now more of the same creatures were kicking, biting, and stabbing their ways across the field.

Running twice as fast as any man, many of the war-birds caught their prey by a sudden pointed beak in the neck; others clubbed the enemy fighters with their knobby feet, at the same time slashing and stabbing their victims with the iron needle-spike spurs. In ten minutes, over half the fighters were dead or dying, the unluckiest merely eviscerated and screaming their last. Those who tried to wait out the birds, watching as the field of fighters diminished, ready then to attack the survivors, fared little better; the birds still standing turned to attack anybody they didn't recognize as a friend. *Including our Kech allies!* Wakan realized, grimacing. Rist saw that, too, but had no way of calling off the crazed emus. In that instant Wakan knew that his plan for minimizing the slaughter was not going to succeed; other Kech fighters were trying their best to kill the swarm of attacking birds. *No battle plan survives engagement with the enemy*, he had read somewhere.

Several times, ShadowFall's own men had to yell at their birds not to attack them, shouting out the code words that meant "friend." But even then, Eddor, one of Rist's warrior mates, the burly wrestler from Three Rivers, drew a deadly beak in the back from a sudden rush by one of the war-emus from behind him. Wakan groaned at the loss, but ShadowFall's team still had two men standing, and one riding, while none of the other Sisterdoms had more than two left in the fight. Wakan's quick glance at the other princesses revealed a lot of note-taking by their advisors, Kech or not. He knew that five years from now, the next Game would be run a lot differently. *But only* today *counts! In five years, Mother might be gone, or I might be gone. Or The Game might be gone!* That thought cheered him for a brief moment, until screams from Pernie beside him brought his attention back to a horrible reality.

Rist had lost another bird; though his arrows had now accounted for twelve foes, those who had been rattled by the suddenness of his first attacks had regained their senses. It looked to him as though the entire remaining contingent of enemy fighters was now concentrating on killing *him*! As Rist had done in the velk attack near The Ice, as he was used to doing when hunting rabs across the peat fields back home, he pulled the reins left and right, loosening and tightening them, causing the bird to jump left and right, frontwards and backwards, turning in tight circles or running in wide ones. Up in Una, Rusk watched the development closely, ready to land and crush his twin's attackers, if needed, to save him.

The enemies with spears, Rist knew, were the most dangerous, able to reach him from a distance. And with the constantly shifting bird, he couldn't draw a springbow bead on those far targets, or use his spiked bolos against them. People up close, those with swords and knives, were not so much a concern since his bird could take them out with a slashing kick or a pointed beak. Running out of arrows, Rist aimed his ride back toward his starting gate, hoping to pick up more ammunition there.

But suddenly a tall, bloodied fighter appeared in front of him, a spear at the ready. Without thinking, Rist swung and threw his bolo at the man, but could not see if it hit the mark, because his two-leg jumped to one side without warning, almost tossing him from his saddle. At the same time, a stabbing pain erupted in his left ankle and he fought to remain on his bird. But his emu would not respond to the reins; what was happening? And his left leg, it wasn't working! Stunned, Rist saw the sky spinning around, and his teammates Thrak and Een backing in close to him, slashing back at a larger group of men. What was happening? What—?

"Down, Una, now!" Rusk shouted. "Save Rist!"

"Sire Rusk, this craft cannot approach Sire Rist any closer. An armed springbow and a borophene arrow are present. Their qomps override this craft's."

Pounding on Una's wall, Rusk roared, helpless as his twin lay injured ten meters below him. He did see that two men wearing the lavender leather armor of ShadowFall were still at Rist's side, swords flashing in the sunlight.

———

OVER THE ROAR OF THE CROWD, WAKAN COULD BARELY HEAR HIMSELF think. But next to him, Pernie was the one screaming loudest, "Rist! Rist! They have killed my little Rist!" Panicked, Wakan stood at the edge of the wall, hands gripping it tightly. *Surely not! Not the best man in all ShadowFall! What have I done?* Then: *Where is Rusk and his flying machine? Surely now is the time to rescue his brother!*

In the center of the oval field, all of the remaining fighters—less than a dozen from what he could make out in the tumultuous mass—were hacking and slashing away. Only three war-emus were still standing, the rest now spiked with spears or arrows, dead on the ground or hopelessly kicking their lives away. But those three kept running into the melee, knocking out this fighter or the other; Wakan heard more men yelling, some shrieking in pain.

Long, eternal minutes ticked by, slower than the sands in a desk-clock. Wakan and the other Kech had originally planned to eliminate all the other competitors quickly, then to request of Mother that they be allowed to surrender without further slaughter, that they would be willing to trade themselves among the other Sisterdoms, there to share weapons and to train other fighters for Motherland's armies. It would have been a noble effort, showing forgiveness and mercy to each other on the field of combat, and an opportunity for Mother to pardon those who were honorable warriors, for an honorable cause. At the least, Wakan had hoped that a fellow Kech-backed fighter's Sisterdom, along with Pernie's and his, would prevail at the final moment, all the united fighters killing off the others to reduce the threat to themselves until the last few remained standing. But with the unexpected onslaught of the unpredictable and vicious war-birds, that possibility had vanished. Wakan wondered if he had fallen in love with his own ideas, had risked little Rist unnecessarily. Pernie might have his head if the little man died. Or other body parts. He gulped. *Where is Rusk? The Una?*

———

IN THE MIDDLE OF THE FIELD, FIGHTING MEN FURIOUSLY HACKED AND stabbed with knives and swords. Dazed by a spear slammed flat against his temple, and by something painful and unknown affecting his left foot, Rist had fallen off his war-bird, almost unconscious, onto a pile of dead men. Seeing their leader go down, and his bird's head hacked off with a sword, Thrak and Een had stood around him, fighting back the others. During the melee, Rist awoke to the stench of death-loosened shit, disemboweled bodies, and entangled intestines, the odors making him gag. Then the noise registered: the grunts and yells of half a dozen men, savagely fighting right above him. *They're coming after* me*!* he realized dimly. *I've got to get up!* But with several large dead men now draped on top of him, their blood and effluents covering him, he couldn't see or move, could not even pull out his shortsword from its scabbard. *I'm in deep shit again*, he thought, *but worse than in God's Port!* As Rist moved, he felt ever more pain in his left ankle, more of a shock or a bruise than anything else. As he pulled up his leg harder, something down there—*separated*...the pain was incredible, but he willed himself not to pass out.

With supreme effort, ignoring the increasing pain in his leg, Rist was able finally to free his hands and rub the blood from his eyes, at which time he saw one of his mates, Een, still standing, fighting off four attackers. *Where are the rest?* he asked himself. *Dead, already? Thrak? Een?* He began to wiggle out from under the blood-soaked weight above him, moving slowly so as not to get the attention of the foes. Maybe they took him for dead? He shifted his hips, easing the first dead man off of his scabbard and drawing out the weapon. At least he would die fighting, not just under a pile of dead men! But he didn't intend to die that day, or any time soon. Furious at his plight, he yelled as loud as he could, commanding any birds able to hear to come and attack! Were there any left? He didn't know, couldn't see from flat on his back and weighed down with dead meat. The pain in his left ankle suddenly throbbed, getting worse. What was going on down there, anyhow?

A chorus of loud curses erupted around him, painful grunts and vomiting, *whacks!* and *oofs!*, burbles and groans—sounds slowly dying out. Then silence. Wiping blood and shit from his eyes again, Rist saw no movement, though he felt twitching from another weight that had fallen on him, movement that ceased after a groan and a whimper. It was Een, his throat still oozing blood, his unmoving right hand holding tight onto a sword that was plunged into an enemy's chest. Looking upward and slightly to the side as far as he could see, Rist was gratified to see two emus strutting around the pile of people on him. No other movement, no other sounds were evident, so he made a struggling effort to dislodge the bodies on top of him, finally succeeding. Rubbing his sore left temple, his vision blurry, even the far vision, Rist looked around the field, his sword ready to hack and slash if need be, to stay alive, to survive. But all around him, all over the field, were only motionless bodies. *And blood, so much blood!*

One of the emus still had a saddle and reins. As it stood over him quietly, Rist grabbed the reins and painfully pulled himself up slowly, avoiding putting any pressure on his increasingly painful left ankle— what *was* that pain, anyhow?—then goaded the bird toward the north end of the field. A silent crowd suddenly erupted into loud cheers, the unexpected noise startling his ride, which began a rapid gallop. Fighting the reins, Rist succeeded in stopping his bird only two meters from the wall, directly under the canopy where Wakan and the Princess stood, clapping, cheering and grinning widely. The noise deafened him, numbed him.

Not believing his luck, dazed and blood-soaked, Rist raised high his bloodied shortsword in salute. Only then, looking down at his left foot, he saw it crushed and mangled, dangling by a thin red thread of bleeding skin and shreds of gray muscle, above it a white bone protruding from his bleeding leg. Vomiting, he fell from the war-bird.

Unseen, meters above him in Una, a screaming Rusk kept demanding that the god-machine swoop down to rescue Rist, but it would not.

PART EIGHT

FATE

CHAPTER FORTY-THREE

*R*ist heard voices coming from afar. They sounded familiar. Was it his birther, Mell? His Sire, Thess? His twin, Rusk? Had Rusk come down out of the sky and saved him? Or was all of that just a dream? He tried to speak but could only mumble. The voices grew nearer, clearer. Amidst the confusion, a quite severe pain made itself known, an unbearable throbbing near his left foot. *But what*—?

A man's deep voice emerged from the jumble of sensations. "Mother died during The Game," the man said. "Rist, can you hear me?"

Rist tried to place the voice, the commanding tone, the—the —"*Wakan!*" he yelled. "Where am I? Where are you? And, Mother, she—?" Finally able to open his eyes, which were caked with something dried on them, Rist made out the priest sitting beside a wide padded bench where the little man lay. Wakan had traded the gaudy red satin robes of the day before for a coarse, peat-brown toga-like garment with no hood.

"Yes, Rist," the priest said, "the excitement of your apparent death, then your miraculous resurrection, your survival, the last man standing on the field, apparently caused Mother to have a severe stroke. She passed out shortly after you did, and she died last night."

Rist stayed silent, trying to absorb the news. He was not used to so much happening in such a short time, not used to the pain in his leg. Seeing the bandages on that left leg, he asked, "What kind of injury did I get down there, Wakan? That leg seems shorter—" In horror, he pleaded, "Oh no, Wakan! Not my foot! Is it—*gone?*" The pain intensified, requiring his entire effort not to scream. Rist knew that he had his answer right there, in the shortened bandages over the stub of his leg.

"I am afraid so, little Rist," the priest said solemnly. "I had to remove it, amputate it. You received a spear-thrust in your ankle that all but severed your foot, and there was no way to reattach it."

Fighting back tears of pain and shame, Rist gulped. "Will I be able to—to walk?" Then, with a gasp: "Will it ever stop *hurting?*"

Wakan pulled a vial of red liquid from a pocket. "Take this, Rist," he said, uncorking the tube. "I had to wait for you to awaken to give you another dose. This will take the pain away." Rist swallowed the sweet fluid and instantly passed out. He had no dreams.

RIST AWOKE, ALONE ON HIS PADDED BENCH. FROM THE EASTERN position of the sun in the curtainless window, he knew it was midmorning, probably the next day. Just two days ago, he and his teammates—*Oh, damn, they are all dead!*—had arrived on the arena field, there to do battle with all those others. *And now, fifty-one other men, and all those emus, and those beautiful horses, are dead, probably cremated by now, and only I have lived to see this day. And without my left foot! What a waste!* Hardly able to contain his sorrow at the deaths of his teammates and his birds, and in mourning for his lost foot, Rist broke down, sobbing. He hoped nobody would see him this way; back home crying in public was a shameful act, almost unforgivable. Genetics meant that his eyes couldn't shed tears; the rest of his body didn't know that. But he was far, far from home, and very alone. *Where is Rusk? Why didn't he help me?*

A few minutes later Wakan walked in, putting an arm around him.

"That is life, Rist. What we were born into, what we have to do to survive." Rist shook his head bitterly. *He* wasn't born to lose a foot in a battle in these insane worlds outside The Tharn's Lands, crazy lands where thieves were incinerated by sunlight, or where you had to kill total strangers just so your rich and powerful Princess could get richer and more powerful. But he kept those dangerous thoughts to himself. Whoever the new Mother was going to be, treason was treason, and the punishments for it gruesome. And for the moment, regardless of his feelings, he must be Pernie's hero, her mighty champion. He wanted to vomit. And did.

After a firstmeal break, Rist asked for more painkiller, which Wakan obliged. "A smaller amount this time," he warned. "This potion can be addictive. You must apportion it according to the amount of pain. In a week or so, your natural healing and my ointments should bring it down to a tolerable level." Wakan did not volunteer when Rist might be able to walk again, and how. Rist recalled that some Old Men back home in The Tharn's Lands sported wooden feet, prosthetics carved to replace appendages lost to Ice-bite overexposure. Grimacing, he figured he would have to come up with one for himself, if he were ever to get back onto two feet. Would it affect his riding ability? He hoped not.

Groaning, Rist sat up in bed and asked Wakan about what would come next. "I don't know, Rist," the priest replied. "I had always hoped that our Princess would be the next Mother, but she is so young, and she has already declared in front of the other Sisters that she does not want to be considered." That Wakan was dismayed, Rist could tell from the priest's slumped shoulders and the set of frown wrinkles that furrowed his dark face. "I hope it will go to Messinex. At least she is not insane, and has never been at war with Pernie," he said sadly. "I just hope she will be able to converse with the gods on the Crystal Throne." Rist thought it curious that Wakan had not mentioned Rusk and his flying machine. Had something happened to his twin and that Una? But when he asked, Wakan motioned for him to shush. "Not now, Rist," he whispered. "Too many spies. But later, we will meet him."

CHAPTER FORTY-FOUR

*P*ernie was nervous; a convocation of all thirteen of the Sister princesses was gathered in Mother's Hall, at the base of the stairs leading up to the Crystal Throne. Arranged as when they had appeared before Mother just days ago, Pernie in the center, Messinex to her left, Jernoma on her right, five others on either side of those, they were uniformly dressed in black to mourn their biological mother and their Lordess Mother. Nobody spoke. Incense burners laced the still atmosphere with rare fragrances, those reserved for funerals. Pernie welcomed the odors as they seemed to tamp down the usual dampness of the hall, for some reason.

Chinqe Kech, favored advisor of their deceased Lordess Mother, stood at the first landing, addressing them. "Honored Sisters," he began, tears streaming down his brown cheeks, belying his formal black dress robes and diffident stance, an appearance honed to perfection during his years of service to Lordess Mother. "By millennia-old tradition, our next Mother will be chosen by the Crystal Throne." His upswept hand pointed toward that nearly transparent chair-like carving at the top of the stairs ascending the pyramid.

"By the magic of First Mother and Her successors, the first indicator of a chosen princess will be the colors of the stairs as she walks up, barefoot. If the moving colors cease to appear or if they do not appear to travel upwards, that candidate is dismissed." As he spoke, a spectrum of subdued pastels on the stair risers throbbed, but did not move. Chinqe nodded and smiled, as if communing with those colors himself.

"The next test," he continued solemnly, "is when the candidate sits on the Crystal Throne, her bare buttocks touching the crystal surface itself. This skin contact is necessary for communicating with the gods. An acceptable new Mother is chosen when the voices of the gods speak to her, and to her only." Several Sisters began murmuring among themselves, anxiety bubbling to the surface. Pernie noted that several even seemed to be afraid.

"One final word, if you please," Chinqe said. "Any princess who does not wish to be tested, may raise her hand now. Though Motherland may prefer that the choice be made solely by the Crystal Throne, you will be voluntarily dismissed from consideration."

Pernie and half a dozen others raised their hands. Messinex just smiled, whispering, "Thank you, Pernie."

The selection process began at one end, where Princess Weemol of Four Peaks, Pernie's nearest neighbor (*Who tried to assassinate me!* Pernie sniffed) was the first to fail, when the stair colors did not move as she began ascending. Pernie almost laughed out loud, unsuccessfully stifling a chuckle. The next choice was at the other end of the assembled line, likewise a failure. Princess after princess walked up the stairs, which, despite their screams, sobs and curses, did not change colors or appear to move toward the throne. Pernie could tell that Chinqe was worried, with sweat now overriding his earlier tears. *What if* nobody *gets chosen?* she wondered. *Has such a thing ever happened?* Though she and Wakan had never considered that particular possibility, they had discussed how to do a rapid evacuation back to ShadowFall should any Sister or group of Sisters attempt an armed intervention in the selection process. Wakan had been coordinating with Miran Kech, Messinex's advisor, for joint action in such a contingency.

Then came Messinex's turn. *The last choice,* Pernie thought, *since I turned it down.* She hoped that Wakan and Miran had their warrior escorts and wagons ready should Messinex fail, too. Messinex took off her slippers and began climbing the stairs. At once, the colors of the stair risers became brighter, moving slowly at first, as if in invitation, a moving carpet of lights leading upward to the Crystal Throne. Pernie breathed a sigh of relief. *One more step to go!* Messinex turned her back to the throne, lifting her robe and sitting her bare buttocks onto the cold crystal. As her hands tightened on the chair arms, Pernie saw shock in her Sister's face, then her head tilting backward, eyes rolled up. Messinex began speaking, but Pernie could not hear the words, only that she seemed to be responding to an unknown entity. This "conversation" continued for several minutes until Messinex lowered her head and stopped talking.

Chinqe bowed deeply and spoke out loudly, "The Crystal Throne has chosen! Mother Messinex, your subjects applaud your selection!" Pernie was quickest to her feet applauding and cheering. Many of her other Sisters, she noticed, were not so quick and not so cheerful. She made mental notes of the unhappiest. *Messinex might have trouble with those.*

ALL THE OTHER SISTER CANDIDATES HAD FAILED TO AWAKEN THE Crystal Throne, and Pernie had voluntarily passed on the opportunity, for what reasons Messinex didn't fully understand. *Who wouldn't want to be chosen as Mother? The eternal honor, the chance to make a difference. The power!* So Chinqe Kech had called on her, his deep voice echoing through the vastness of the hall. "Sister Messinex of Three Rivers. Will you be tested by the Crystal Throne? Will you dedicate your life to our Motherland?"

Helped up with a hand from her advisor Miran Kech, Messinex had slipped off her sandals and approached the intimidating staircase. *Only thirteen steps*, she thought. *Thirteen steps into glory and fame. Will I be chosen?* Hesitantly, holding her breath, she placed a bare foot on the first step. *These are high risers. Meant for taller people?* To her delight, the entire staircase grew brighter, its unknown illumination source suddenly throbbing as if in anticipation. *It is working for me! Oh, yes, please!* As she took further steps upward, the spectrum of stair colors began changing, a pattern of lights that seemed to be ascending with her, an invitation to the throne. Behind her, Messinex heard words of surprise and happiness from Pernie, from Miran, from Wakan, from Chinqe. And some moans and snarls from her other Sisters. At last she reached the throne.

Per the instructions, she had lifted her robes and exposed her bare buttocks to the crystalline chair. Her first thought was, *Whew, it's so cold!* Sitting completely down, her feet not touching the floor around the throne, she placed bare arms on the armrests. And waited.

For a minute or more, nothing happened. *Am I not chosen?* Messinex had thought in panic. *What will happen if I don't—* But then the Crystal Throne began to speak. To her alone.

At first there were meaningless noises, almost like a person talking, overlaid with crackling noises like green tinder burning in a fireplace. Messinex could *feel* that it *was* someone speaking to her, a woman. She could not understand the words, but knew they *were* words. "Goddess, I hear you, but I do not understand you," she said aloud, hoping the Goddess would hear her. The voice answered in nearly recognizable Motherspeak, but in inflections carrying no meaning: *"—translation algorithms—" "—accommodating tonal shift variables—"*

Confused, Messinex asked, "Goddess, what language are you speaking?" The other voice went silent for a minute, piercing whistling noises and sounds like rushing waterfalls resounding in her ears. Had the Goddess broken off communication? But then more words came through, in the midst of a staccato series of broken phrases, obviously not in human voices, but more like priestly chants echoing in a closed chamber *"DNA compatibility established for—"* then *"—adjusting for q-comm protocols—"* and finally: *"No operator at local lunar terminal. Extreme variation of Diníglish at Earth terminal."* Messinex heard the sounds of the words, but the Goddess's message was not understandable. Then more screeching and crackling noises, and then silence. Messinex was so shocked she was shaking.

With an effort of will, Messinex stood up from the Crystal Throne, shaking her head, her arms trembling. What had she just heard? Was her communication actually with a Goddess? Looking down on the fawning audience at her feet, she determined not to mention anything about her experience on the Crystal Throne. *It is I who have been Chosen,* she mused, *and even though I don't yet know what the Goddess is saying or asking, I am certain that I will learn.* Casting her gaze upward to the painting of many of her predecessor Mothers, she thought, *If* they *learned wisdom from the Goddess, then so will I!* Collecting her composure before descending the color-changing staircase, she saw that all her Sisters and the Kech were bowing in her direction.

Messinex smiled.

WAKAN HAD SUPPOSED CORRECTLY CONCERNING THE NEW MOTHER. Later that day, Princess Pernie came to visit Rist in his hospital bed, accompanied by a retinue of armed bodyguards who waited outside his room. She gave them both the news. "My Sister Messinex has sat on the Crystal Throne, and the gods have spoken to her there! She is the one Sister I feel closest to, so I am happy for her. Now we can go back home to ShadowFall and live our lives in peace!" *For five more years, at least,* she thought.

Wakan shook his head sadly. "Princess, I always wish for your contentment, your happiness, your success, above all else. And I wish the same for all of ShadowFall and Motherland. But—"

"But what, Priest? But *what?*" Pernie demanded angrily. Rist thought that Wakan would apologize immediately to appease her sudden wrath, but he didn't.

"Princess, all of our planning, our training, the loss of our other fighters, the birds, and"—he pointed at the recumbent, injured little man in front of them—"risking Rist's life, even giving up a part of his body, in that melee yesterday, it all came to nothing. You won The Game with your new champion. Coming off such a great victory in

The Game, with your Mother gone, becoming the new Mother was yours for the taking, your Highness."

Shaking her head, Pernie said, "I am a little disappointed in your feelings, Wakan Kech. First off, the Crystal Throne may not have chosen me. And it was *not* for nothing. As a result of Rist's great victory, in spite of his injury, I have appointed ten of my ShadowFall advisors to work with Mother Messinex, trusted men and women I have known for years; they will have much influence over Mother's decisions, along the lines you and I have discussed all this time. And I have received failure-tribute gifts from all the other Sisters—more godspring material, some ancient artifacts with unknown writing, lots more of those strange godspheres, many other interesting things. All that is payment enough."

She reached down and touched Rist on his forehead, gently. "I do wish that little Rist here had not been hurt and that our other men had not died, and I do regret the losses." She held her head up regally, *almost diffidently*, Wakan thought. "But by ancient tradition we had no choice." She smiled sweetly at Wakan and Rist; they knew she was being sincere, but Rist still was in shock at the casual murders and mutilation he had witnessed—*had performed himself!*—even though he had voluntarily chosen to stay and fight rather than abandon the Princess with Rusk and his flying machine. He might never agree with Motherland's savage customs, but he had had little choice. *Until now*, he thought. *No more fighting! Never again!*

Pernie went on, "Was it not you, High Priest, learned one, who taught me that political power always leads to corruption, that more power and more riches just help people get there quicker? That the knowledge of the world, of the heavens, of the past, of the Ancient Gods, that is what is truly important?"

Wakan put his head in his hands, trembling. Finally he looked up and said, calmly, "Yes, Princess, you are correct. I said those things, I taught them to you, but in the preparation and the scheming and the fighting and the excitement of The Game, I let my goals be—eclipsed." He stood, breathing in deeply. "I am certain that Messinex will make a kind and benevolent Mother, one who will lead our Motherland in a new direction toward peace and happiness. Especially with your advisors assisting her." He bowed deeply at Princess Pernie, and then again at Rist.

"Rist, my little man," Pernie said, "Wakan tells me that it will take several weeks before you are able to walk about on two legs." Rist frowned and started to object, but his liege said, "Hush, hero of ShadowFall. I am having a new foot carved for you, of the rarest ivory from the tusk of the skeleton of an Earth-trembler. Mother Messinex has her artificers already working on it, and they will be here a few days from now to begin fitting it on you. You will remain for some time as—as—a *guest* of Mother Messinex in Mother's Palace itself." Wakan noticed her sly smile that indicated Rist would be *extremely* welcome, most likely at Pernie's personal recommendation. The priest smiled, too. Every alliance with the Mother, in whatever form, would strengthen ShadowFall and improve the chances for his and Pernie's plans. He trusted that Messinex, whom Miran Kech said was a habitual user of the High Antis anti-pregnancy herbs, would not be following in the tradition of the deceased Lordess Mother in regard to her lovers.

"Meanwhile, Wakan," the Princess said, "you and I need to return to ShadowFall as quickly as we can, immediately after Mother Messinex's coronation ceremonies in two days. Some of my more jealous Sisters may want to take the opportunity of our absence to try yet another foray against my Sisterdom. There are rumors that some may wish to seize the 'vast hoard' of godscloth some say we have there." Wakan could tell from her wrinkled brow that Pernie was already preparing plans to defend ShadowFall. *If only I can get to Rusk and his flying machine, that will never be a problem again, Pernie!* But he could not tell her anything about it, not while they were in Mother's Palace. *Too many spies, too many eyes*, he thought.

The Princess went on, "Rist will remain here. Because he will be somewhat—incapacitated—I have asked Mother Messinex to provide him with two strong litter-bearers, so that he can have easy access to the Motherland libraries. That will be his assignment, to learn ancient secrets that will help us. Some of those vaults haven't been opened for centuries, I am told. Maybe he can learn more down there than others have, something that can help ShadowFall change the ways of this world, as you and I desire. All knowledge is useful, you know." In a swirl of color and fragrance she exited the room, motioning for her waiting cadre of bodyguards to follow, leaving the tall priest and the short warrior alone with their thoughts.

After everyone had departed, Rist was lying back on his bed, not yet asleep from his latest dose of potion. Wakan whispered, "Rist, I will send the maiden Anklya down the front steps onto the promenade now. Hopefully your twin Rusk will be there to take her. Here is what I will tell her to say."

CHAPTER FORTY-FIVE

*D*ressed again in her ShadowFall godscloth finery and relieved to be leaving Mother's Palace, Anklya strode down the wide front steps and out onto the promenade, walking briskly. *Before anyone changes their mind*, she thought. *All these rumors about the new Mother scare me.* She prayed that Rusk would be nearby to see her leaving, to let her back into that marvelous Una machine, and fly her away from this place! She kept walking, seeing nothing in the sky, no shimmering green haze, feeling no slight warm breeze. *Where is he? I will soon be at the end of this wide boulevard, and out of the palace grounds. Where do I go then? What do I do?* Her fate was totally within another's hands; she hoped Rusk would keep his end of the bargain that Wakan Kech had made with him.

Then like a welcome breeze from the gods, from behind her back Anklya felt a downdraft and a crackling in the air. She didn't look back, but knew it was Rusk. His voice confirmed that.

"Anklya," Rusk said. "Stop, turn around, and look at me." As she slowly turned, Anklya could see that the bulk of Una blocked out some of the view of the palace. "It's all right," Rusk said. "From the palace they can't see us, just a shimmer in the air as if from hot stone. But hurry!" She ran through the open side door, Rusk closing it and ordering Una up fifty meters.

Catching her nervous breath, Anklya said, "Rusk, that Wakan Kech, that priest, told me that we need to go to the first oasis on the road to ShadowFall, and wait there for the Princess's caravan to pass, a few days from now."

But Rusk was more interested in Rist. "What about my twin? Is he all right? How injured was he? Where is he? Can we go get him out?" He was almost shouting, and Anklya reached down to pat him on the head.

"Rusk, calm down. He is recuperating at a room in Mother's Palace. He...he..." She hesitated and frowned. "Wakan Kech said that Rist lost his left foot in the final minutes of the battle. A spear almost cut it off at the ankle." Sitting down in one of Una's large seats, she looked down at Rusk. "Wakan Kech did wonder why you didn't rescue Rist when he was hurt."

Rusk grimaced. "I was there watching the grisly slaughter of all those men. Those horses. Those emus. When Rist was hurt, Una could not approach the springbow and all those metal arrows. Don't ask me to explain, but somehow Una is forbidden to get too close to them." He gulped. "Remember what they did to it when I first landed at ShadowFall."

Not understanding the workings of the god-machine, Anklya just nodded. She knew from Rusk's devotion to his twin that only the Una's obstinance, from wherever it arose, could have stopped the rescue. But having listened to Wakan, she understood that any such interference in The Game would have created chaos in Motherland. "Probably the worst of civil wars," the priest had said, obviously with mixed emotions. "The appearance of such a wondrous machine would have made the other Sisters berserk with jealousy and fear. They all have contingency plans for wars against each other, anyhow. Only the threat of each other's retaliation keeps them from it now. I am sure that Mother Messinex right now is assuring that Her armies are on high alert for attacks against our Princess as we depart back home. Just because Rist was victorious and won for her the advisor appointments and the failure tributes."

Then he had instructed Anklya what to tell Rusk. "We must keep the Una machine hidden from view until I am able to explain it and reveal it to Princess Pernie. It will be the most momentous discovery in the long history of Motherland, and will stimulate some attempted internecine wars at first. But I am sure that, with the proper guidance and advice, the Princess will know best how to reveal its existence to Mother Messinex. And what to do with it after that."

Rusk was surprised at the instructions from Wakan, but remained silent and thoughtful. Una was *his* property and his Sire's, not this Wakan Kech's, and not any princess's! But he kept his reaction cool and unemotional, so that Anklya would not suspect what she might consider treason. First, he had to get Rist aboard Una. Then the two of *them* would decide how to proceed. His mind was in turmoil; he would prefer to live out his life in the warmth and comfort of ShadowFall, but only after bringing his Sire and birther there. And some hundreds of his own People from The Tharn's Land, as this Wakan apparently also wanted. But he expected retaliation from Rumi Similla for escaping with Anklya; he would have to depend on the priest and the Princess to prevent that. And then the brutality of The Game he had just witnessed, the wanton slaughter of so many men—and emus, and those beautiful horses!—had made him violently ill. He would not lend any kind of support to such a system. Even The Tharn's Men had been relatively gentle by comparison. But he was also growing tired of his own comparisons; nobody should ever have to endure any such treatment at all!

But then, remembering what those Tharn's Men brutes had done to his familial home, the suppressed thirst for revenge against The Tharn surfaced yet again. Rusk was also thinking that he and Rist and his Sire perhaps should return to The Tharn's Place with Una, and make the old man surrender and leave. *Or die!* Rusk was momentarily disgusted by his own treasonous thought, but he had just witnessed dozens of men dying for their princesses in defense of a cruel, ancient means of deciding power over others. If it were necessary, he could see that the violent removal of The Tharn might work the same way. But who would come next? He didn't even know how Tharns were selected; there had always been one, back millennia, supposedly. *That will have to take care of itself,* he thought. *People might welcome a new Tharn. Maybe...Sire Thess? Tharn Thess?*

From watching his twin's warring in The Game, Rusk knew that Rist would be capable of another horrendous murder, should it be needed; how many large men *had* his twin killed in that stadium with springbow and armed emus? At least a dozen. Surely, removing one old Tharn would be a lot less of a task for Rist. *If he can even walk now!* Such new, wild visions and concepts seemed to be accessing parts of Rusk's mind and personality he hadn't known existed. He did not care to explore such dark and dangerous caverns of his own soul. Could he himself become a killer of men, as Rist had done so efficiently? He needed time to think.

"Una, stay invisible and take us to the first oasis on the road back to ShadowFall. Now."

"Sire Rusk, yes."

CHAPTER FORTY-SIX

Three days after The Game and the death of the Lordess Mother, Mother Messinex announced that a public immolation of her predecessor and biological mother would be held, after which her own coronation ceremony would ensue. All subjects of Mother's City were requested to attend, along with those visitors who had come for The Game. *Curiously enough*, Wakan Kech thought, *she is using the same stadium where so many died in The Game. Does She intend this to be a signal about her new reign and the old one?* He met with other Kech advisors, old friends of his, to assess how Messinex might rule.

"She's like an older and wiser Princess Perneptheranam," offered Miran Kech, now Mother's chief advisor. "Less brutal, more intellectual, than our Lordess Mother was. Yet wise in the ways of the world. And as you all have heard, she alone among the Sisters was chosen by the Crystal Throne. No one else even came close."

Wakan noticed a slight air of arrogance from his fellow High Antian, a slight verbal put-down of the other princesses and by inference, the other Kech advisors, including Wakan himself. In the previous Mother's reign, that statement alone to a superior could have meant retribution or torture. Thinking on Miran's words, Wakan realized that, however benevolent Mother Messinex might be, her Kech advisor was beginning to make sure that all the other Kech understood her absolute power. *But all that is unimportant, now,* Wakan thought. *I am just happy that no word of Rusk's machine has made it into Mother's Court.*

For his part, Miran Kech *was* feeling slightly arrogant. The Lordess Mother's chief priest, Chinqe, was now retired in the Kech monastery located on the grounds of Mother's Palace, in company with several other Kech whose lieges had passed on or been deposed by the Lordess Mother. As High Priest to the new Mother, Miran was now the most powerful Kech in all of Motherland, and in his own mind was close to eclipsing even the vaunted Wakan himself.

Thinking back over those twenty years to the time when the Kech explorers and their small band of soldiers had met the invading Mothersmen at the crystal-dome-enclosed Chi'a pyramid, Miran did feel some gratitude that Wakan alone, with his mastery of many of the tribal languages of the Dry Highlands, had sufficiently impressed Mother's officers that he and his countrymen were educated wisemen, not mere savages to be enslaved—and castrated! Miran unconsciously touched his groin. *For that, Wakan, I am most grateful!* And Wakan had also convinced the late Lordess Mother to take on all twenty-five Kech captive researchers as librarians, historians, architects, and eventually policy advisors on a variety of subjects. Over the years, Wakan had also inculcated into the minds and souls of his fellow Kech the means of defending their High Antis homeland, by virtue of rumors of its distance, its location within protective boundaries of swarms of savage tribes and inaccessible mountain ranges.

And I do appreciate all of that, Master Wakan. But over the years Miran had come to enjoy the privileges of being in the upper classes of Motherland, something not extant in their homeland's nonhierarchical, tradition-bound society. *But now that I have Mother Messinex's ear, I think the time may have come to send a troop of* emissaries *to the High Antis.* He knew that the High Antis possessed some technologies that

Motherland did not have. As a mere scribe he had always envied Master Wakan's more comprehensive knowledge of the practical sciences—mechanical devices, biology, botany, metallurgy. *Why not send our people to the homeland and* persuade *those secrets out of the priests there for the benefit of Mother Messinex. And me?*

WAKAN HAD NOT WANTED TO WAIT FOR THE IMMOLATION CEREMONY OR for the inevitable and lengthy coronation rituals being planned for Mother Messinex; he was anxious to leave Mother's City and for the Princess to meet up with Rusk and the Una machine. He could barely contain his excitement over how ShadowFall would utilize the Una's fantastic abilities. *We can explore the Dark Highlands where Rist and Rusk come from, that strange God's Port, even that backward Tharn's Land! I might even fly back home!* Another vision arose: of himself returning to the High Antis after twenty years, there to tell the Elders of his unbelievable adventures in Motherland. *But Mother Messinex can't ever know the details of my homeland. None of us Kech have ever broken faith on that taboo subject. Though I'm sure that my people can easily defend themselves against Her conventional armies, the Una machine might make the difference in victory or defeat.* As per his usual mental practice, he set aside such possible future worries to concentrate on immediate issues.

Wakan was able to arrange to send an advance contingent back to ShadowFall under the concern for keeping tabs on Rumi Similla, whose competence and loyalty he convinced Princess Pernie were not all they could be. "Very well, Wakan," the Princess replied. "In fact, if you feel Rumi is plotting, perhaps it is better if *you* take a few armed men and go back quickly. Use my four horses and travel lightly.

"I will be involved in our late Mother's funeral immolation and in Mother Messinex's coronation," she explained. "As well as conferring with my appointed advisors to Mother." Wakan hoped that those advisors would follow through with all of the policies that Pernie and her priest had worked on over the years: more freedom for the citizens, more nearly just laws and regulations, more education for everyone, fewer executions, and much less torture. Each one of those reforms would face fierce resistance from the other Sisters, but with a firm and dedicated new Mother, some progress might be made in the next five years. *And that doesn't factor in what power ShadowFall might be able to bring to bear with the Una!*

"HALT HERE!" WAKAN KECH SAID, AND THE THREE OTHER HORSEMEN pulled up their reins. Over to their right, eastward, a dirt road led off toward a small village surrounded by palm trees punctuating the vast grasslands that stretched in all directions.

"Priest Kech," the horseman said, "We still have daylight, and can make another fifteen kilometers before nightfall."

Wakan Kech shook his head. "No, we will go to the village now and find accommodations. We will save our camp resources for a longer trip tomorrow. I have business over there." He knew that the Princess would have at least one spy among his troupe, someone who would report every detail of the trip. Wakan would find some manner of excuse for this stop, and for his planned absence as well. *Tomorrow; I'll handle that tomorrow.* He was hoping that he could tell Pernie everything about Una and Rusk first, with the excuse that such a secret could not have been shared while they were in Mother's Palace. He anxiously looked in the sky above the oasis to see if Rusk had waited for him, but saw no shimmer, no sign of the flying Una...

IN THE GRASSLAND BEYOND THE OASIS VILLAGE, RUSK WAS WAITING, but impatiently. "*Days!* Anklya. We have waited *days* for this Wakan Kech and your Princess Pernie to arrive. And yet all I can see is the village and the palm trees. What could have happened to them?"

Anklya, watching moving pictures on Una's front screen and

learning about the wonders of the ancient world of gods, shrugged. "Why worry, Rusk? We have all we need here, and there is so much to learn. The history of the whole round world. Did you know that—"

But Rusk cut her off. "I have learned more about the history of the so-called 'gods' than probably any person alive. I had nothing else to do while you were in Mother's Palace, waiting for Rist, waiting for you to get out. I am tired of ancient wars, ancient magical machines, of storms from the Sun, glaciers forming suddenly, of what the world once looked like. I am tired of *learning*! I am tired of waiting; I want to *do* something!" Visions of landing at the Tharn's Place, of Una smashing through its roof and wreaking havoc, of The Tharn's head on a spike, kept roiling through his mind. "Maybe we should just go back to Mother's Palace and grab Rist and—"

But Anklya left her seat and came over and leaned down to hug him. "Rusk," she cooed, "we have other ways to spend our time, you know." As usual, the fragrances she seemed to always have about her, the smoothness of her skin, her overwhelming beauty, made Rusk quieten down and accept her embrace. But shortly afterward, at a most inopportune time, Una's voice interrupted.

"Sire Rusk, four horsemen are approaching the village. One scans to be the High Priest, Wakan Kech."

Groaning, Rusk cursed the interruption, but stood up, dressed, and readied to meet the priest. Anklya was not pleased but understood the urgency. "Later, Rusk?" Breathing heavily, he nodded, mouthing *Yes!*

"Una," he said aloud, "I expect Wakan Kech to leave the village and the oasis and to come searching for us. When he does, please stay at ten meters and make the green shimmer a little more visible. Then land in front of him, with the doorway away from the view of others."

Ten minutes later, Rusk opened Una's door and admitted Wakan Kech into the cabin. Wakan stood in awe, again amazed at the spacious volume inside the invisible craft, the near-magical moving pictures and symbols on the front screen, and the smooth beauty of the cabin's inner finish. He repeatedly rubbed his palms lightly over the walls. "Just amazing, what they could build. Anklya," he said, "thank you for passing on the message that allowed me to find you." To Rusk, he said,

"Your twin Rist has a new carved ivory foot and is learning to walk on it. In answer to his question, and yours, yes, he will be able to ride your birds again." Accepting Rusk's invitation to sit, he said, "And now you must show me all the wonderful things your Una can do, and how I might be able to fly it myself."

Rusk replied, "Wakan, like those godspheres that Rist found at ShadowFall"—he looked at Anklya, who nodded—"this Una only responds to commands by me. Something called *Dee-Enn-Aaa* makes it possible. I think that is the reason only we People can awaken these ancient machines." He had already decided that this was the cover story he would tell Wakan and others. He did not want to share any of Una's powers with anyone else. In fact, after the first meeting with Rist and Wakan Kech the day before The Game, he had quizzed Una on just who could give it commands.

"Sire Rusk, you and your Sire, Thess, are authorized to issue commands at present. With your authorization, any other competent adult person may be permitted to command this craft."

"So if I say that no one else than my Sire and I may issue commands, then that will be true?" He quickly added, "And my twin, Rist, too, of course."

"Sire Rusk, if that is your command, that shall be the protocol." Rusk so instructed Una. He had not told Anklya. *Secrets,* he thought. *Always necessary!* No one else would ever be able to use Una.

"Wakan," he said, returning to the present, "your horse is tied to a palm tree and should be safe for a while. What would you like to see?" The priest broke into a grin.

The next hour was the most astounding one in Wakan's entire life: a flight at a hundred meters altitude to Mother's City in just five minutes, skirting down to five meters in the desert, kicking up dust and scaring rabs and skinny velk-like animals, listening and watching as Una's screens showed ancient cities and technologies. "My gods!" Wakan exclaimed more than once. "Travel up beyond the sky? Those colored beads on the Moon were *cities*? And people once lived on the *Red Warrior* planet? It's more than I ever imagined, more than I *can* imagine!" Trembling, the priest sat back in the bare frame of a seat, eyes shut and breathing hard.

Rusk returned Una to their point of departure. "See here now, Priest," he said vehemently, "how much different the world used to be in ancient times? The gods were able to do all of this, and we can't! And from this Una we have learned that they didn't *leave* us, they *became* us! So we can do anything they did; we have the brainpower. It's just been lost to millennia of The Ice cover that destroyed their world." Pointing an index finger at the priest, he continued, "I don't think I want today's world to stay the way it is now, not anymore. Not any more slaughter, no more bloody Games, not for any Mother, or for any princess!" *Or any Tharn!* he added mentally.

Wakan couldn't immediately object to Rusk's treasonous statements; he wasn't even processing everything the little man was saying. Even knowing intellectually that the ancients—or the gods, or whoever they were—had possessed fantastic technologies, he had not fully realized before what all that truly meant—seeing over vast distances in actual time, communicating with and traveling over the whole wide world rapidly. What a vaster and more complex world it had been! And even reaching out to the Moon and other celestial bodies! All of this achievement, this incredible *machinery*, was difficult enough to comprehend, but to hear that it was all done *without* a Mother or a Motherland in charge, without a vast central authority planning and controlling it all—*that* was near blasphemy!

The concept of citizens organizing themselves without a hierarchy, unheard of! Even in the High Antis, the well-qualified and elected Elders made all the decisions for planting, for research, for defense, and all the rest of a nation's needs. No, Rusk's vehement assertions had to be analyzed. The stupendous revelations of the physical world were one thing; but the implications for a totally different kind of society, those were something else entirely!

Collecting his thoughts and controlling his emotional responses with some difficulty, Wakan Kech finally decided upon a course of action, a definite action that would solve some more immediate problems. He asked a practical question: "How quickly can we fly to ShadowFall?"

Una answered Rusk's repeated question. "Sire Rusk, at top speed, less than fifty minutes." Wakan gulped; Rusk smiled. "Do it, Una, but stay away from the springbow guards."

Wakan thought a moment, smiling. "I know a safe place there; we can land on top of the palace."

CHAPTER FORTY-SEVEN

$\mathcal{W}$akan stepped out of the still-invisible Una onto the roof of Pernie's palace, at a lookout position near the location of the far-seer device he had once demonstrated to Rist. Nobody else was around; there had never been a need before to defend from an attack from the skies. *But that will change,* he thought. *Especially if any other princess finds another Una machine. Or takes this one.* "Anklya, Rusk," he said quietly, "you should stay hidden for now. Based on the story of your escape, I am not certain that Rumi might not have you killed on the spot if she sees you." He made for a secret entrance door known only to himself, and disappeared. Rusk watched him, then closed Una's door and stayed inside. He had seen that Wakan was armed with the shortsword he always carried when not in the presence of the Princess.

Rumi Similla was working at her desk in the throne room when Wakan Kech spied on her through a concealed hole in the wall. *My secret passageways and spy-holes have saved the Princess—and me!— more than once,* he thought. Rumi was working by an open window, the afternoon sunlight casting shadows from her tall, silent guard. *I trust that this guard will obey my orders,* Wakan mused. *I'm not certain I can disarm him, should he resist.* Deftly and quietly sliding open a concealed panel, he stepped into the room behind both Rumi and her guard.

"Good afternoon, Rumi," he announced, walking around in front of the desk. "I hear you had an interesting guest out of the sky a few days ago." Thankfully, her guard only stood stiffer at attention. Wakan smiled and nodded at him. *Good, I don't have to fight him! Her treason, if any, hasn't been shared or fully developed, it seems.*

But Rumi Similla sat back in her chair, shocked, gulping. "Wakan Kech, I didn't know you were coming," she choked out, eyes wide in fear and surprise. "I didn't have any word—*how* did you arrive? The border guards have not reported any individual arrivals, nor any caravan. I didn't expect you back for another month." She seemed to be calming herself, Wakan cynically observed, as she stood defiantly, asking, "And *where* is our Princess?" That last question, a challenge.

Wakan did not answer the question. "Guard, you are dismissed," he commanded, waving the man away. With only a slight hesitation the guard bowed slightly and left the throne room, leaving Rumi and Wakan alone facing each other over her document-strewn desktop.

"Tell me, Rumi, about your little dark visitor and his escape," Wakan said, motioning for her to sit as he pulled up a chair from near the wall. "What do you know about that incident?"

His inquisition took an hour, Rumi studiously avoiding sharing any information about Rusk's origin or the observed capabilities of the Una flying machine. *She's trying to hide information, but why?* he wondered. *Maybe she hopes to get possession of Una for herself? But for what end? A fugitive has no chance in all of Motherland, unless... unless she plans to take it to another Sister. Or directly to Mother?*

Finally, concluding that the woman couldn't be trusted, he would leave her fate up to the Princess. But he wouldn't share any information, either. "Let's just say, Rumi, that I am aware of everything that occurred here when that little twin of Rist's crashed here, and when he ran away in his flying machine." Rumi gasped loudly, but Wakan motioned for her to stay quiet. "You are not to mention any of this to any who did not witness it. Our citizens are henceforth forbidden to discuss it with travelers, traders, or anyone else. You and they know the penalty for such speech." He stuck out his tongue and made a scissors motion with his hand. "This shall remain a ShadowFall state secret." Then he walked out of the throne room and into a dark hallway, leaving a shocked Rumi Similla behind, standing and staring and wondering who had told the priest the story of Rusk and his machine. And—how had he gotten back so quickly, and without being seen? *Did he fly in that machine?* She pulled an alarm cord, calling out her palace guards. *If Wakan has that machine here in ShadowFall, I'll take it from him!*

"Guards!" she commanded as they assembled. "There is an imposter here in the palace, one who claims to be Wakan Kech. Apprehend him if you can; kill him if you have to. But seize any kind of god-machine he may be flying!" Puzzled, the guards nodded and ran to search for whomever it was, each one hoping it would not be himself who had to make the decision to kill someone who looked like the awesome Kech.

Back on the rooftop, Wakan approached Una, hoping that Rusk would see him, sighing with relief when the side door tilted up and admitted him into the cabin. "Rusk, I believe that Rumi Similla will remain frightened enough for now that she will not be a threat to our Princess." He gestured toward the transparent wall, indicating the expanse of the Sisterdom, its vast crop fields, the nearby river, and the distant Dark Highlands. "Now, until we can go fetch Rist and our Princess, why don't you ask your Una to show me more of this whole wide world?"

As Una lifted off from the rooftop, palace guards erupted from rooftop doors. Several springbow arrows bounced off its extended borophene shield. This time, Una was prepared.

"Motherland is about thirteen hundred kilometers in width, east to west," Wakan said, pointing out the shape of the empire on the colorful image at the front of Una's cabin, "and close to six hundred, north to south. We have known that and mapped it for many years now.

But this amazing drawing on this 'screen,' as you call it, shows it differently than I have ever seen it." He looked at Rusk. "And you say that this 'Una,' this flying machine we are in, was able to draw this map from knowledge imparted to it in ancient times?" Puzzled, he asked, "If Motherland didn't even exist all that time ago, how would the Una know?"

Rusk said quietly, "Priest, let me tell you what I have learned from my weeks with Una. First, what you see is not a drawing but an image, something that we would see from way far out in the sky, above the air, a place called 'Space.' I don't know how the image was made, but that's what it is. As for it being a map of Motherland, it is not. Back in The Beginning of All Things, or at least before The Ice came, what we now call Motherland was the bottom of a vast sea called the Gulf of Mexico. As The Ice formed, the sea level dropped hundreds of meters, leaving a great basin. Where we are today."

Wakan sat back hard in one of the cabin seats, causing a swirling cloud of fine dust to rise. "I see. But that was so long ago, it makes no difference to us now. I am sure that in the thousands of years to come, other seas will form, other ice will thaw or freeze. The whole wide world changes but we have to live in what is here now."

In spite of Wakan's desire to travel all over Motherland, to see Sisterdoms he had never visited, Rusk refused to take Una anywhere but back to the oasis where Wakan had boarded. "Wakan, I have to go get my twin before doing anything else. I took you to ShadowFall to demonstrate my Una's capabilities and to let you handle that Rumi Similla, but I don't know how long Una will continue to fly," he lied, "and if it does stop or crash, I want to be on this main road where we can at least find other transportation." Regardless of Una's claims of reliability, he was wary; he could still envision its location at the bottom of kilometers of The Ice where he had first seen it, after a crash thousands of years before.

Having little choice, Wakan agreed. He returned to his other men from the oasis that evening. The next morning, grumbling and snapping at his riders, he continued on his arduous weeks-long journey back to ShadowFall by the primitive means of *horse. What a marvel it is to fly anywhere in mere minutes! What a world we could make!* He had no idea what he was going to tell Rumi Similla about his first visit, other than that she had to keep it secret for her own sake, that he had other means of travel she would never know about. He didn't know what to think about the springbow attack as they were leaving the palace; had Rumi ordered that? By that one action, he knew she was not dependable, so he *had* to get back with Rist and let Pernie in on the facts about Una and Rusk. If she found out from anyone but himself, the Princess would not be happy. *But how to do that,* he wondered. *How?* This time, he was not able to compartmentalize his problem, to put it off until later. His very life depended on Rist's and Rusk's cooperation.

CHAPTER FORTY-EIGHT

*R*ist hobbled along on his new ivory foot, now and then pausing to increase the pressure on it, easing off the T-shaped underarm crutches a bit at a time. After weeks in rehabilitation at Mother Messinex's palace, he was beginning to feel comfortable walking alone. The litter-bearers had been a necessary nuisance when he was completely immobile, but he had discarded them as soon as he could. He still had one companion, Swarch, a tall, dark-skinned Mothersman guard, outfitted with sword, chest armor, and all. *To protect me or to spy on me, I don't know which. Maybe both? Surely inside Mother's Palace there is no need for weapons?*

He knew he was going to have to be able to walk on his own without crutches before trying to meet up with Rusk and his flying god-machine. *However it is that we are going to be able to do that, with no way to communicate face-to-face like we did when he swooped into the training area on the day before The Game.* Thinking back on The Game, he still wondered why his twin had not rescued him during the finale of the melee. *But I am just as happy he didn't; I enjoyed being Pernie's champion, and Wakan said that all of Motherland would be at war if Rusk had interfered. But I do wish I had not lost that damned foot. And didn't have this continuing pain!*

Rist was making his way to yet another of the palace's musty old catacombs, a place hinted at by librarians in the palace proper. "There are tunnels and hallways deep below," said an ancient wrinkled wen —*woman!* he corrected his thought—"that nobody has visited for centuries, I suspect." When Rist had asked why, the reply was a shrug and a brush-off: "Mr. Rist, we librarians are duty bound to collect, collate, and keep the current records of all activities in Motherland, from the Northeastern Highlands to the Cold Sea, to the Deep Blue Southern Sea, and all the reports coming in from all Mother's armies now operating in the Western High Dry Lands." She sighed.

"There is never enough copper to pay for all the local paper scribblings of interest that we would like to possess, and not enough Mothersmen to seize all of them, much less describe and inventory all the carved artifacts and inscribed ancient stones that Mother mandates we must collect." Rist thought that such a rich empire as Motherland should have had legions of scholars studying everything, people like Wakan Kech, just like Pernie's advisor had talked about existing in his homeland of the High Antis. *Even in The Tharn's Lands we had the Old Wen who studies such things.* But apparently Mothers had other priorities. He would never understand the thinking of these strange tall people!

Rist had finally pried out of the old woman an inscribed beezt-skin map—she called it by an ancient name, *bloop-rint*—allegedly showing the way into possibly abandoned stores of knowledge far below the palace. Following the orders of Princess Pernie and Wakan Kech before they departed back to ShadowFall, Rist was trying to discover other totems or godspheres that might give him information about the whole wide world and all the things that had happened before his own birth.

Of course Wakan had also taken him aside with information about Rusk and the Una machine. The priest had looked around them in all directions, ensuring that there were no listeners. "Rist, we plan for the caravan to meet with Rusk at the first oasis on the road back home. I will explain to the princess about Rusk and his machine. I for one want to fly in it and I may be able to persuade her to fly, as well. Una will be a marvelous tool, a revolutionary advantage for ShadowFall, and the Princess will be most grateful to Rusk for bringing it to her."

Startled, Rist started to object, then kept silent. *That machine belongs to Rusk. And my Sire. And, hopefully, to me,* he thought. *The Una saved itself and my family from The Tharn's Men, and enabled Rusk to escape from God's Port and from ShadowFall. Why do these nobles from ShadowFall think we would give it to* them? But having lived among these people for several months, having fought for them— killed *for them!* he recalled, sadly—he knew that power over others seemed to be their prime motivation. He would have to get back with Rusk and their Sire first; only then would *they* decide what Una would be used for. He himself wanted to explore the rest of the whole wide world; Rusk and his Sire might want to do something else. He would keep counsel to himself in the meantime; killing came too easily for princesses and Mothers. *But not for myself?* A small voice seemed to whisper, *Not for the bloody victor of The Game?*

Putting aside plans for a quick reunion with his twin, Rist wanted to satisfy his own curiosity; he was determined to find the oldest Motherland archives first, the deepest ones down. If any records had the *history* of the whole wide world, then the first ones, being closer to The Beginning of All Things, would be the place to begin his search. He hoped the ancient records would not be bound in those collections of bound leaves called *books*; even with his newly corrected vision he could not read the meaning of those symbols, being literate only in the carved spindles of The Tharn's Lands.

Memories of that homeland flooded his mind as he hobbled down one set of stairs after another, further and further into the deep recesses below the palace, his guard Swarch often having to sweep away thick curtains of cobwebs that blocked passageways. A few times, that worthy even used his broadsword to hack away at frameworks of wooden timbers strewn haphazardly in their way. In the absolute darkness of the deep tunnels they were traversing, Rist was happy that he'd had the foresight to have his guard bring a bandolier of Mother's strike-lit torches. *Those self-igniting torches are another interesting development,* Rist thought, *one worth a fortune in coppers back in The*

Tharn's Lands. If I ever return! But after Rusk's revelations of The Tharn's atrocities, he doubted he ever would go back there. *Maybe for revenge? After killing so many for Princess Pernie, adding one more dead body to the score might be easy. And effective. But who would rule as the new Tharn? How does that even work back home?* Those were not thoughts he wanted to pursue at the moment.

Memories of his home and travels seemed to emerge from the echoing darkness and the musky dampness of the ancient tunnels. In the past months, Rist had left his homeland, that cold, Misty Sky patch of ground at the foot of The Ice at the End of the World. He had ridden an iceberg downRiver where he was awed at the beautiful architecture of God's Port, its elegance offset by the fierce cruelty of its reigning Solar priesthood. He had climbed down on a godscloth web from the Dark Highlands to the woman-ruled Motherland, where he killed assassins; and right here in Mother's City, he had fought heroically for ShadowFall and for Princess Pernie, slaying a dozen strangers. *And losing three fighting friends and too many emus! And my damned foot!* At that recollection, memories of the pain returned, too, throbbing reminders of his serious loss. *It does not pay to remember too much!*

Eventually, the pain caused by his T-crutches becoming unbearable, Rist swallowed his pride and asked Swarch to carry him, attached to the big man's voluminous backpack. Hours later, kilometers later it seemed to Rist, having passed dozens of old doors, the two men reached an actual dead end to the passageway. "Sire," Swarch said in his deep voice, "it appears as if we have reached natural rock here, an end to the passageways. Shall we go back?"

Disembarking from Swarch, Rist took a torch from the big man and struck its base against the stone floor, inspecting the adjacent walls carefully. *Surely this long tunnel must have led to a destination nearby?* Under a thick layer of wall dust he finally spotted what appeared to be the outline of a wooden door, reaching from rough-hewn floor to polished stone ceiling. He had Swarch kick it in, breaking loose centuries of dirt and cobwebs, causing a musty cloud of dust and dirt to erupt around them.

Coughing, both men entered the dark, cavernous rooms beyond.

Swarch ignited his own torch, its flames illuminating sconces along the wall. "Light them up, Swarch," Rist said. "But save half your torches for the trip back." The man did as instructed, being surprised that some of the torch supports still had candle material remaining. After a dozen were lit, he positioned himself outside the door. Rist was surprised that the vast room was almost odor-free, as if some kind of ventilation system was keeping the air fresh. *It must be well-sealed*, he mused, *or insects and vermin would be crawling all over the place.* He was grateful that the ancients, whoever they were, had been responsible caretakers of their repository of knowledge.

Now if only you, too, could read anything, Swarch, he thought, *we might get this done a lot quicker!* Rist made his way around the room, avoiding what appeared a few thick and dusty biter-webs untouched in centuries. As he had discovered months before at ShadowFall, most of the contents of this library were also bound books that he was unable to read as yet. But Rist was looking for carved totems like those used back home for recording and reading information. Lacking those, then the strange glassy balls called godspheres promised new information, though Rist had found them to be inconsistent and ofttimes unintelligible.

Brushing away some minor webs, Rist found an array of shelved godspheres, hundreds of them, the shelves stretching back along the walls far beyond the reach of the light from the torches, all covered with the dust of many years, perhaps centuries. Maybe even older? He whistled. "This library might go on for kilometers down here!" Looking around the endless room at the sheaves of aisle-wide biter-webs, the centimeters of dust, the rough stone walls streaked with thick lines of mineral-containing water deposits, anyone could have easily thought the place was shut up before the gods left Earth.

"And when was that, huh?" Rist said to himself. "And what were they, those ancients? Real? Stories?" Having been introduced to *religion* by a priest in God's Port, Rist had been thoughtful, skeptical, about the very concept of gods. Yes, every day he saw the sun up above, a disk so bright he could not view it directly, convinced that it was the same god called Pursuing Dimness back home, the god behind the Misty Sky. And yes, most nights he could also witness the necklace of colored lights across the face of the beautiful, scarred disk of the Moon, which back home was called the Wen of the Mist, again seen through the veil of the Misty Sky. But he could not make the connection between those luminous round things way up in the sky, and himself and other people here on Earth. And Wakan had not been able to convince him that those bright disks were actually other worlds. Or for that matter, that Earth itself was round, like a gigantic godsphere. He wasn't convinced. Anyone could see that the world was flat!

Rist leaned his T-crutches against a shelf and lifted one of the dusty spheres. Wiping grimy dust off the surface, it was like all the others he had handled—twice the size of his own head, smooth, glassy, cool, yet possessing a lot of a vibrancy within, as if it were a living thing. He didn't think godspheres were actually alive, even though some of the ones at ShadowFall were full of moving pictures and spoke in strange languages that neither he nor Wakan could understand. No, a living creature would die if closed up in a dark place like this for years and years without food, without water. Glancing at the stone floor, clean but for a thick carpet of dust, he thought, *a living thing would leave poop all over the floor, too!* He was happy that he was not knee-deep in godsphere excrement.

As Rist held the globe in both hands, he saw a faint red light in the center, almost a flicker. After a minute he was rewarded with another of those strange bright colorful scenes of—*what?* The scene seemed to fade, grow brighter again, show yellowish streaks, finally stabilizing. It was a person, a pink-skinned man like some of those he had encountered at God's Port, wearing a white jacket or robe of some kind. And the man had a voice, although crackly and intermittent. *"... global cataclysm. The WorldNet has collapsed. We who survived have produced millions of these informational globes and distributed them by air and sea, in caves and caverns, all over the accessible...different languages...sunlight powered...random DNA sensing to ensure diversity...quantum technology...thousands of years..."* The light faded into blackness again, the voice dying away as well.

Surprised, Rist almost dropped the globe. This godsphere was strange, but unlike the few at ShadowFall that he had touched and activated, he could actually understand many of the words from this one. He repeated them aloud. "*Air, caverns, languages, years.* I know these words, they are what we say in The Tharn's Lands, Peoplespeak, but what are all those other words, and what do they mean?" He replaced the silent sphere on the shelf and picked up another. He wondered if any of the many hands of hands of hands (*hundreds?*) of other godspheres could explain everything. But though he touched one after another, none responded. And he found no carved totems at all.

HOURS LATER, HUNGRY, TIRED AND FRUSTRATED, RIST HOBBLED ON HIS T-crutches to the door and told Swarch he was ready to go back. This time, he allowed Swarch to transport him the entire way; he was too exhausted to hobble back on his crutches. He carved on his personal totem all that he had learned, and determined to return to this library as soon as possible, with other guards and many porters and wheeled carts, and a litter bearer. Not just for himself, but to remove all of the godspheres they could carry out. Recalling his experience at ShadowFall, he wanted the globes placed outside in a courtyard, in the bright light of the sun, there hopefully to receive power and knowledge from the heavens.

CHAPTER FORTY-NINE

With the Lordess Mother's public immolation performed and her own coronation ritual completed, Mother Messinex was sitting on the Crystal Throne again, as she had every morning for two weeks now. Lifting herself from the massive carved chair, once again confused and disoriented, she held onto one chair arm until the daily dizziness wafted away. *Is it always to be like this?* she wondered. *Meaningless noises, unknown words? And today, not even that girl goddess's voice? Why didn't any other Mother record Her experiences? I can't ask Miran or Chinqe or anybody else. If they or anyone suspect that the Crystal Throne is a fraud of some kind, I might lose my Chosen authority—and my head!—and plunge Motherland into chaos and civil war.* She sighed. *So I will just keep trying, every day, to learn what the Goddess intends for me.* Balance restored, she descended the high stairs carefully, the cascade of colors following her down.

She noticed that her new handmaidens were cheerful as they draped her white godscloth robe over her shoulders and carefully slid her slippers onto her feet. *And why shouldn't they be happy?* She, Messinex, their new Mother, would not be the fickle, cruel, demanding tyrant her own late Mother had been. As she passed, she smiled and nodded at the Mothersmen standing guard in the hall, and continued into the adjacent room where her golden throne awaited. *At least on this chair,* she thought as she sat on golden satin cushions, *no goddess is listening to me and speaking gibberish!*

Though Messinex knew she would have to exert careful control and a necessary level of discipline over her maids and Mothersmen, she wanted to be fair and even-tempered. *Unlike my late Mother!* She hated the thought of having to order any kind of torture or execution—but her Kech priest, Miran, had already presented her with long lists of her late Mother's supporters and lackeys, all of whom should be considered dangerous and disloyal. His suggested individual punishments—typically evisceration or vivisection followed by beheading—made her physically ill. He had not been so vindictive back when he was her adviser in Three Rivers. *Has his new power gone to his head? Or was it just that back home we had very few enemies?* Messinex realized quickly that running a huge Motherland, with its thirteen conflicting princesses, was going to require a different set of skills than merely administering a single peaceful, prosperous Sisterdom. She would have to take Miran's recommendations seriously whether she approved or not. *I inherited a lot of enemies from Mother, and now all of my Sisters, too. Save Pernie. I truly hope not Pernie.*

Most of Miran's suspects were already locked away in dungeons, she knew, so thankfully those few hundred decisions could keep a few more days. Among other more immediate things, she had to choose and appoint a Sister to take her place as princess of Three Rivers. She had asked Miran for a list of suitable candidates from among the Sisters' daughters. On that fateful policy decision, she would also ask for advice from other people more experienced in Motherland's political dynamics. But she strongly suspected that some of the advisors she needed were in one of Miran's dungeon cells.

Messinex had actively welcomed her own advisors from Three Rivers and those that Pernie provided from ShadowFall. She had convened them all shortly after her coronation and together they had begun to establish new rules for Motherland. *And hopefully, enable me to grant more merciful treatment for my own Mother's innocent supporters. If any. Maybe exile?* she wondered. *Or perhaps I should set up a new colony up on those distant Western Highlands, near some of those old domed pyramids? I'll have to ask Miran if any of those places can grow enough crops to sustain a population. I may as well expand Motherland, maybe make room for additional Sisterdoms? And put some of those fat bureaucrats here in the palace to work in the fields! They might prefer that to the dungeon. I'm sure that Miran will have some ideas.*

All her life Messinex had wondered why her Lordess Mother exhibited such extreme swings of emotion, some fierce hours or even full days in which she had lashed out—*literally!*—for no seeming reason. Miran had not been able to provide an answer to that, except that it was a personality disorder, and nothing in the court recorder's notes gave any indication either. Messinex most often had chosen just to hide away somewhere in the palace until Mother's emotional storms blew over.

Could such insanity have come from the stresses of being Mother to millions? Messinex was finding the responsibilities she had inherited to be overwhelming, and even contradictory. She was glad that Pernie's little brown warrior, the bird-riding killer, had won The Game for ShadowFall, even if her own four warriors—her lovers, all—had died in those battles; for now Pernie's calm and moderate advisors would be assisting her, and she was able to keep those people she would have sent to aid Mother had her own men won. Pernie's experienced people would be of great help in administering the vast governmental complex that was Motherland. Those advisors and her Sister Pernie had made ShadowFall a wonderful success story, second only to her own tropical domain of Three Rivers. She hoped that, like Pernie, she could remain in control of herself and not descend into madness and cruelty, like their Mother.

My own Mother will always be a mystery to me. Sighing, she hoped there wouldn't be any treason trials or torture sentences to be handed out today. If there were, Miran Kech might have to handle them; she herself needed more time to contemplate what had happened on the Crystal Throne yet again.

But Miran Kech met her as her retinue entered Mother's Court. "Mother," he said, bowing gracefully, his dark blue silk robe draping majestically over his short, if well-muscled, brown body, "our visitor from ShadowFall, Mr. Rist, desires an audience with you." At the rear of the court, arrayed in a rainbow of dress, dozens of applicants, supplicants, and courtiers were anxiously standing, some hopeful, others trying to hide their impatience after hours of waiting for Mother to preside over court. But they waited quietly and carefully, because they did not yet know the new Mother's personality or foibles; no one wanted to lose their head or their entrails by appearing to behave disrespectfully.

"What a pleasant surprise, Miran," Messinex replied sweetly, taking her place on a red-pillowed golden throne. "Of course, I will welcome Pernie's champion at any time. Right now, in fact." Miran jerked his head back, as if to object, but simply smiled and bowed again. "As you wish, Mother." The murmur of the couriers subsided; *this* smiling Mother was going to be different—*She is polite!*

Miran clapped his hands once and a side door opened, revealing the little warrior now bedecked in a fashionable mauve satin robe, but supporting himself on padded crutches. After weeks of trying to adapt to the unending, grueling and detailed administrative duties in the support of her empire, Messinex was genuinely happy to see a hero who was free of all such nonsense.

To the tittering bemusement of the dozens of courtiers present, Rist hobbled in on his padded T-crutches, bowing to Messinex, as low as his devices would allow. "Welcome, hero," Mother said. "You are always welcome in our court."

"Mother Messinex, thank you for your hospitality," Rist said, awkwardly rising from his bow, "and for your support of my studies in the old libraries below the palace." Since Mother had not mentioned his injury, he decided not to discuss it, either. *Though the damned stub still hurts from all my traipsing in those tunnels these weeks!* He was hoping that the other Kech wise man here—Miran?—might have some healing potion or painkiller Rist could use. He knew that Wakan would have! He missed his Kech friend from ShadowFall for more than just his painkillers, however; the priest was off somewhere with his twin, Rusk. *And I want to leave for ShadowFall as soon as I can walk on my own.* He wanted to be with Rusk again, to fly in that magical Una machine, maybe return home to The Tharn's Lands, to see his Sire and birther. And, yes, to deal with The Tharn. After his rampage during The Game, the vision of putting a springbow arrow into The Tharn's forehead would not go away. And his memories of the nights at ShadowFall in the arms of the wen, Anklya, stirred yet other neglected needs.

"Yes, Rist. And how go your—studies? Do you have all the support you need?" At Rist's positive reply, she asked, "And just what do you expect to find in our ancient libraries? If they have been sealed for centuries, as Miran tells me, if we have indeed done without them all this time, of what possible use could they be?" She was being friendly, but truly wondered at Rist's insatiable curiosity, something she had seldom encountered anywhere else in Motherland. She herself had found very little time—or inclination—to speculate or fantasize; reigning over even a Sisterdom required almost whole immersion in mundane daily affairs, and being Mother took more than that! Obviously, though, Pernie had recognized something of value in such studies and thought them to be useful. "Do you think you can find something of immediate value, or merely curiosities for amusements and entertainments? Stories, perhaps? Brave deeds by Our Mothersmen in olden times, heroic tales we can tell in court and you in the pubs? Or something else?"

Still standing, and with an aching stub pressing down on an ivory foot, Rist endeavored to keep his answers short. "Mother Messinex, Princess Per—er, Pernepthperanam"—he corrected quickly, knowing that a violation could mean his tongue, honored guest or not—"has a much smaller library of godspheres under her palace at ShadowFall. But even there, Wakan Kech and I discovered that at least one of them could speak to us, and—"

Messinex cut him off with a raised palm. "*Speak* to you?" she asked, bringing to mind her own strange experiences on the Crystal Throne. "What did it say, Warrior Rist? Did you respond? Did you understand its language?" Seeing that Rist was struggling to stand erect, she motioned for a guard to provide him a chair, moving him much closer to her throne. Rist sank into the soft cushioned silver chair with relief.

"Mother Messinex," Rist replied, "that globe spoke in a language we did not understand at all, but it did show us little moving images within. Strange sights, of vast watery areas and people and even flying machines." He waited for Mother's reaction to that, but she exhibited no particular interest. *Good! She still doesn't know about Rusk or his Una machine.* "Then it died." At this news, the courtiers began murmuring, Miran successfully hushing them by having the Mothersmen raise their spears threateningly. Court suddenly quietened. On his own volition, Miran had the guards usher all of the courtiers out of court, leaving only herself, Rist, the guards, and himself.

Messinex chewed her lip. She had not experienced quite the same thing as Rist had, but in her case, there had be no recognizable visions, certainly not anything of ancient machines. She thought she knew the language being spoken, but not all of its words, and the gibberish-like communications were always broken off. Were those godspheres and the Crystal Throne all talking to the same gods? The same way?

"But, Mother Messinex," the little man continued, "the first sphere I picked up in the deepmost library below your own palace, it said words I could make out. Words like 'language,' 'years,' 'disaster'; they were dark words, disturbing ones.

"The next day, I took a whole expedition down there and over the next week we brought out wagonloads of materials—hundreds of godspheres, along with statues, paintings, and cartloads of those bound volumes of flat pages that Wakan Kech calls 'books.'" He was smiling broadly now. "And I had all of the spheres placed out in a courtyard in the bright light of the Sun, to absorb His energy and His guidance."

Messinex let out a sigh. "Please go on, Rist. What have you learned that Motherland can use *now*?" She was growing impatient; the little warrior-scholar was intriguing, but her schedule in court was already going to take all day. *All those people waiting out there!* Running an empire was exhausting work, and she did not have enough time for merely interesting conversation.

Somewhat chastised, Rist gulped and said, "Mother Messinex, the Sun recharged the godspheres, and now some of them talk to me and show moving pictures. And they speak to me in words that I know. I believe they are revealing how the whole wide world came to be, and what was here in this place"—he waved his arms around, encompassing the throne room—"before there *was* a Motherland. Once, in the past, all of Motherland was a vast sea of deep water. Right here where we are standing! Before The Ice destroyed the world!"

Messinex frowned suddenly, the room growing silent as she waved a curt dismissal to Rist and her guards, saying sternly that court was canceled for the day. She grabbed Miran's arm and stormed out, cursing under her breath. They disappeared into her private chambers, her white godscloth raiments and his blue satin swirling, contrasting like clashing storm clouds. Mother Messinex was angry, but no one knew why.

Waiting outside the doorway, her handmaidens were once again thankful that Mother Messinex was totally unlike her late volatile predecessor.

CHAPTER FIFTY

"*M*iran," Mother Messinex said grimly, "I want all of those so-called godspheres collected and locked away. And while you're at it, all the ancient books retrieved from the chambers below. No one, especially that little Rist, is ever to see them again. Do you understand?

"Yes, M-M-Mother," he stammered. "But *why*? They may be of great value to Motherland. The ancient wisdom—" But Messinex's stern face was a rebuttal and she waved him out. "Yes, Mother, it shall be done," he replied meekly, bowing repeatedly as he left Her chambers.

Messinex was trembling, and thought furiously, *No one else is supposed to know about the deep history of Motherland! Only Mothers!* She walked over to a wooden wall panel, pressed a sequence of light and dark squares, and a sliding door opened. Behind that door lay a domed room some ten meters square, at the center of which stood a large golden chest the size of the Crystal Throne, a red velvet covered chair, and a small desk. Messinex stood before the ornately engraved chest and gently lifted a hinged panel, carefully removing a handful of stacked golden plates the size of dinner dishes and placing them on the table like a spread of playing cards. Hundreds more remained in the chest. As she had done every day since coronation, she began reading the strange script on the first of the plates, written in the unique ancient language taught to her and all her Sisters while they had lived with their Mother. Outside the rather childish, mundane, and bland teaching examples presented in the priests' classroom as part of her learning process, she had never seen anything written in it elsewhere.

THE CHRONICLES OF MOTHERLAND.

IF YOU ARE READING THIS, YOU ARE THE CHOSEN MOTHER, FOR ONLY A MOTHER MAY BE TOLD, BY THE PRIESTHOOD, HOW TO ACCESS THIS MOST SECRET OF SANCTUARIES.

THE PRIESTS DO NOT KNOW WHAT THIS SANCTUARY CONTAINS.

THE TEACHER SLAVES MAY NEVER ENTER THIS ROOM OR READ THESE PLATES, NOR WILL ANY OTHER LIVING PERSON.

THIS SECRET LANGUAGE IS TAUGHT ONLY TO THE SISTER PRINCESSES, ONE OF WHOM WILL BECOME MOTHER OF HER REALM.

THIS SECRET ROYAL LANGUAGE IS ONLY EVER WRITTEN. IT HAS NO SPOKEN FORM.

OUR HISTORY

KNOW THIS: MOTHERLAND WAS FOUNDED AT THE BEGINNING OF ALL THINGS, IN THAT DISTANT TIME WHEN THOSE WHOM WE CALL GODS WERE STILL LIVING IN THE WIDE WORLD.

THE FIRST MOTHER, BORN OF THE SKY GODS, CAME

DOWN AND CALLED TOGETHER ALL THE WILD AND
SAVAGE TRIBES LIVING ON THE PLAINS BELOW THE
FORBIDDEN HIGHLANDS. SHE, FIRST MOTHER, PROVIDED
THEM WITH THE KNOWLEDGE OF AGRICULTURE, ART,
ARCHITECTURE, AND EDUCATION.

FIRST MOTHER ESTABLISHED THE CLASS OF LESSER
NOBLES, WHOSE SOLE FUNCTION IS TO CARRY OUT THE
WISHES OF THE MOTHER.

SINCE FIRST MOTHER, EACH SUCCEEDING MOTHER HAS
EXPANDED THE AREA OF MOTHERLAND UNTIL IT
ENCOMPASSES ALL OF THE LANDS BELOW THE FORBIDDEN
HIGHLANDS, WHICH REMAIN SAVAGE PLACES FIT ONLY
FOR PROVIDING FOOD, MINERALS, AND SLAVES.

MOTHERLAND HAS ALWAYS BEEN THE CHOSEN LAND
OF MOTHER'S CHILDREN, A PLACE FOUNDED IN PEACE
AND MAINTAINED BY THE POWER OF THE MOTHER.

MOTHERLAND HAS NATURAL, UNRELENTING ENEMIES,
LESSER CREATURES THAT INHABIT THE HIGHLANDS ON
THREE SIDES AND THE COLD SEA ON THE OTHER. IT IS THE
DUTY OF EACH MOTHER TO MAINTAIN THE INTEGRITY OF
THE LAND AREA OF MOTHERLAND, TO KEEP OUT THE
SAVAGE INVADERS FROM THE HIGHLANDS AND THE
COLD SEA.

UNCIVILIZED MEN FROM THE FORBIDDEN HIGHLANDS
OR THE COLD SEA OFTEN ATTACK MOTHER'S PEACE. THEY
MUST BE KEPT AT BAY TO PREVENT SUCH RAIDS. ALL SUCH
CAPTIVES MUST BE RENDERED INCAPABLE OF BREEDING
UNLESS THE REIGNING MOTHER HAS OTHER USES FOR
THEM. ONLY IN THIS FASHION WILL THEIR NUMBERS BE
KEPT SMALL AND MOTHERLAND SAFE.

UNCIVILIZED MEN FROM THE COLD SEA OFTEN ATTACK
THE EASTERN COAST AND MUST BE KEPT AWAY BY OUR
WARRIOR SAILORS. THESE EVIL MEN CLAIM THAT THEIR
SEA ONCE COVERED OUR MOTHERLAND AND THAT THEY
THEREFORE OWN OUR LAND. THESE FALSE STORIES ARE

SPREAD TO WEAKEN MOTHERLAND. MOTHERLAND HAS NEVER BEEN ON THE BOTTOM OF ANYTHING. OUR SACRED DRY LAND WAS CHOSEN BY THE GODS TO BE MOTHERLAND.

EACH MOTHER SHALL BIRTH OR SELECT SUFFICIENT SISTERS TO MAINTAIN THE SISTERDOMS AND TO SUPPRESS ALL ATTEMPTS TO WEAKEN MOTHER'S POWERS BY SUBVERSION, BY FORCE, OR BY TREACHERY.

A MOTHER MUST BE STERN WHILE LOVING, BUT CRUEL WHEN NECESSARY. ORDER AND DISCIPLINE ARE ABSOLUTE NECESSITIES FOR THE SURVIVAL AND PROSPERITY OF MOTHERLAND.

EACH MOTHER SHALL INSCRIBE A SIMILAR GOLDEN PLATE WITH HER THOUGHTS AND ACCOMPLISHMENTS FOR THESE CHRONICLES, AS A GUIDE FOR ALL WHO FOLLOW.

MESSINEX SIGHED. THERE WERE HUNDREDS OF SUCH PLATES IN THE golden chest, each numbered sequentially but not dated in any manner she could deduce. *They must go back thousands of years! Will I ever have time to read them all?* Her cursory glance at the most recent few, those with the highest numbers, didn't seem to offer any great wisdom, mostly only administrative statistics. Further back, there were interesting (though obviously biased, she could tell) stories of conquests in the Highlands, of wars between Sisterdoms, of palace intrigues and betrayals, of various lovers and victims, and of course, the outcomes of the five-year Games that had been established millennia ago. Even near the bottom of the stacks, in the records of First Mother, other than raw numbers of subjects, how many slaves were brought back from raids, and the volume of crop harvests, she found nothing of particular value.

Thousands of years of mundane doings, she thought angrily, *but nothing more about the ancient sea! Nothing more about the gods and where they went, and when. And nothing at all about the voices in the Crystal Throne!* She was almost of a mind to have all the plates just melted down into gold coins, maybe use them to pay for improving the irrigation systems around Mother's City, or to contract for stone-paving more of Motherland's dirt roads. Pernie and others had complained about the rough state of the so-called highways. *Another detail to attend to!*

But in any event she was determined not to let that little Rist dredge up forbidden ancient history, stories that could threaten the security of Motherland. *Those damned godspheres, anyhow!* Once they were just mere curiosities, the source of much conjecture and apocryphal tales of moving images and sounds. But if it were true that little Rist or others really could understand what they were saying, and if those voices had anything to do with what she was hearing each morning on the Crystal Throne, they represented a direct threat to her rule. Who could allow a dwarf savage from the Dark Highlands to listen in on messages intended for the Mother Herself? *Even if they are meaningless?*

A dilemma. She herself liked the little man, respected Rist for his uniqueness and for his amazing victory in The Game. On top of that, Rist was Pernie's champion, and as a result insanely popular with the citizens; she couldn't arbitrarily have him imprisoned or killed. And sending him back to ShadowFall would not solve the problem entirely either: he had mentioned that Pernie's palace library possessed godspheres that talked to him, too. What was it about a dark dwarf that made those globes talk to him but not to other people? A few of the golden Chronicle tablets had briefly told of others who accessed evil legends in such spheres, people who were quickly put to death. But nobody had ever been able to destroy the globes, not by cutting, smashing, or burning. Maybe that was why they were buried deep in the deepest tunnels?

Back in her chambers, with the secret sanctuary door safely closed and sealed, Messinex rang for Miran. Blue robes swirling, he made a grand entrance, a slight whiff of exotic scent about him. "Mother, your wishes are being carried out as we speak. Those spheres that Rist brought up are being collected by the wagonload. What do you want done with them?"

"Miran," Messinex said, "I want you to send Rist back to ShadowFall immediately, with a contingent of Mothersmen. Once there, they are to confiscate all of the godspheres and return them to me. Rist may remain there, but those globes come back here. And send out orders to all of the other princesses that their godspheres must be returned to me, as well." She thought for a moment, then said, "And all those ancient books, too. No telling what heresies they may contain.

"Once gathered, you will arrange for all of them we can find in Motherland to be buried in the deepest dungeons under the Palace here, and then covered in hundreds of meters of the hardest stone-setting material that exists. They will never be touched again, not by man or dwarf!" Miran was making notes on a small pad, but looked puzzled.

"Mother," Miran almost mewed, "shall I offer them a reason *why*? Your Sisters may wish to know, or else they may not comply." His face lit up in a half grin. "May I offer that since your new position is not yet concrete in the minds of all Motherland, that some jealous Sisters may feel that you are trying to acquire properties of theirs that they may not wish to surrender to you."

Messinex said, very slowly and with force, "Tell them that their Mother commands them to send all of their godspheres and ancient books to my palace, without exception and without delay, do you understand, Miran?"

"Yes, Mother," he replied, sincerity almost oozing from his words. "And may I make a suggestion?"

"Do."

"Mother, should any of the Sisters prove obstinate or defiant, this might be your first opportunity to demonstrate your, ah, *absolute* power?"

"*That* again, Miran? Will you not be happy until I have executed one of my own blood half Sisters?"

"Mother, such an event, were it in your best interest, would be very unfortunate, but it *would* show your subjects that you will go to any ends to preserve Motherland and to protect *them* from chaos and anarchy." He drew in another breath and added, "And it is a way to cull some of your more, shall we say, *ambitious*, Sisters?"

Messinex stayed quiet for several minutes. Miran was right, of course; many of Motherland's subjects—and *all* of the Sisters, save one—respected only the threat of force. Those two Sisters who had tried to assassinate Pernie—Jernoma and Phraseent—they were likely good candidates for Miran's kind of deposing. And though she had had no daughters despite trying for years, she did have several very loyal and accomplished servants in Three Rivers whom she could appoint out of hand as new princesses to replace them. And a list that Miran was drawing up of other candidates from other Sisters' daughters.

As to the effect of such royal punishments on Motherland's common subjects—*My slaves, actually!*—she had not yet had her own Mother's decades in which to instill unthinking loyalty and obedience to herself. She would prefer imprisonment or some kind of exile for her unfavorable Sisters, but circumstances might require public executions. Having had almost no interactions with those two much older Sisters during her childhood, she felt little guilt regarding their fates, and the stability of her new Mothership had to take priority.

How sad all of this is, Messinex thought. *Is there no other way to run Motherland, some other way to rule, another method of administering justice? I've had enough killing; even my own four brave warriors died at the hands of other Sisters' teams.* She paused in her thinking. *Did* Rist *kill any of them himself? I couldn't keep track of all the slaughters that day. I'll have to ask the chroniclers.* She sighed again. Being Mother was much harder than she had anticipated.

Nevertheless, she had her priorities, and controlling forbidden knowledge was first. "Miran, send out the command to retrieve all the heretical items, at once." After a long pause she had a momentary flash of anger, then added, ruefully, "And keep track of who responds immediately and who is late. And who dares refuse me." Sighing, she added, "And write up documents with charges of treason against Princesses Jernoma and Phraseent. Together, they once attacked ShadowFall with their armies, and then tried to kill my Sister Pernie with assassins. Those are sufficient reasons." It was strange, but she felt a weird sense of relief at pronouncing death sentences on two of her half-siblings. *I didn't know I could feel that way*, she thought with a shudder, *but I rather enjoyed it.*

With that she dismissed her priest and returned to the hidden sanctuary to read more of the ancient records and to try to determine how the Mothers of Motherland had become so cold and unfeeling. And how she might avoid that fate herself.

PART NINE

FLEE

CHAPTER FIFTY-ONE

$\mathcal{R}$ist was angry beyond belief at what he had just been told. "But Mr. Rist," the Mothersman said apologetically, looking down at the furious dwarf, "I have orders from Miran Kech to pack up all of these globes and these printed materials and everything else, and get them out of the courtyard and back down into the catacombs."

Behind the tall leather-armored man stood half a dozen sweating porters, clad in only breechcloths, and two large oxen-pulled wagons, waiting on the command to begin their tasks. In the heat of the morning sun, they were anxious to put everything in their vehicles and get back into the cool hallways of the palace and the tunnels below it. In the confines of the diminutive open space, some ten meters square, Rist could smell the sweat from the men and the animals, mixed in with the usual odors emanating from the open doorways that led to the catacombs below. *And a kitchen too*, he thought. *Somewhere down there the cooks are whipping up tasty meals for nobles, while I stand here hungry, arguing with a damn soldier about taking away the ancient knowledge of the whole wide world!*

"Wait until I have seen Mother Messinex," Rist pleaded in frustration. "There must be a mistake." The guard hesitated. If he were to contradict the wishes of Mother Messinex, he would literally suffer for it. *If she is anything like the previous Mother!* he thought. *But Miran Kech has given me an order, and this famous little man has given another.* He looked down at Rist before him—the hero of The Game, a very notable personage. *Maybe this one can go back to the priest and ask for additional orders? That would get me off this dangerous hook!*

"Very well, Hero Rist," he said with more confidence than he possessed. "Please go to Miran Kech and request additional details as to the disposition of these, these, er, devices and materials. Tell him we wish to make no mistakes."

The guard blew out a breath of air in relief as Rist stomped off on his crutches, his unbooted ivory foot resounding in sharp echoes inside the hallway. As a Mothersman on duty, he had no choice but to wait and hope that the situation would be resolved soon; sweating under his leather was getting too uncomfortable and smelly, and the oxen and porters in the small enclosed courtyard stank even worse than he did.

But Rist remained upset as he trundled toward the Mother's throne room. And puzzled. How could Mother Messinex want to confiscate the godspheres and ancient books he had worked so hard to bring up from the bottommost tunnels under Mother's Palace? Strenuous days of discovering, sorting, and transporting the mysterious devices up into a courtyard open to the sun. "They have to have sunlight," he murmured. "That's what powers them, makes them light up and talk." He had no idea why they would speak only to him.

HIGH OVERHEAD ABOVE THE OPEN COURTYARD, RUSK AND ANKLYA hovered unseen, Una maintaining its stealthy mode. "Damn," Rusk said, "we've lost him, and after all this time searching. Una was only able to track Rist when he came outside in the open, but now we've lost him. I should have gone down and rescued him when he was out there with all those godspheres and books, right then. Now I don't know where he is, or what's going on with that Mothersman and those wagons." He breathed out heavily. "I can't stand the thought of more weeks of waiting!" Fearful of Una losing its *power,* Rusk had kept it in the air above Mother's Palace for many days now, waiting for the chance to rescue his twin. *If rescue is still the word for it. He didn't seem to be a prisoner, not and argue with an armed guard like that!*

Sharing his frustration, Anklya patted Rusk on his shoulder, knowing that the presence of the Mothersman had been the primary reason for Rusk's reluctance. Short of just landing Una on top of the guard, crushing him, Rusk could not have rescued his twin. An untrained dwarf fighting a professional Mothersman guard with only a spear and shortsword was impossible. And Una's length would have just barely fit into the open space, probably endangering the godspheres and the books, not to mention the porters, the wagons, and the oxen. And she knew that Rusk knew.

"Let's wait here while we can," Anklya said. "Maybe he'll be back."

Rusk cursed again.

THEY DIDN'T HAVE TO WAIT LONG; WITHIN MINUTES A VISIBLY UPSET Rist was back in the small courtyard, saying something to the big guard, gesticulating wildly, finally retiring to a bench away from the ancient books and globes. As Rusk watched, the porters loaded the wagons and left with the guard, leaving Rist by himself, arms crossed and scowling, on the bench.

"Now, Una!" Rusk shouted. "Go down now and reveal yourself. Let's get Rist!"

"Sire Rusk, there is no 'self' in this craft, only a Developing Intelligence program. But your command will be followed." Rusk groaned at the repetitive response. *Maybe I can order Una not to say that anymore? Or teach myself not to use that pronoun?* But his attention was on his twin, who was now standing in surprise looking up as Una's green shimmer grew visible, the flying craft revealing itself and touching down within the courtyard walls with only centimeters to spare.

"Rusk," Rist shouted, "you're here!" Elated to see his twin's magic machine appearing out of nowhere, he walked as fast as he could over the few meters to the opening door. Once aboard, he hugged both Rusk and Anklya.

"Close the door and let's go, Una," Rusk said. But Rist grabbed him by the shoulder, saying, "Wait! What are you doing? Where are you going? I can't just leave—"

Then, as the enormity of his own situation sank in on Rist, he climbed into a big seat and sighed. "You are right, Rusk. I am out of favor with the new Mother; she refused me an audience just now. She has confiscated all those godspheres and books and sent them back down below, probably to be locked away forever." He nodded at his twin. "I am not welcome here in the palace, and that usually means the dungeon or worse." Looking around inside the cabin, he said, "Your flying machine; can it fly us back to ShadowFall? I think Princess Pernie still likes me."

Rusk started to explain that he himself might not be welcomed there by the Princess, certainly not by that Rumi Similla, but only sighed and gave the command. "Una, take us up and away from here. To ShadowFall."

At twenty meters altitude, Una followed the main highway back toward ShadowFall at a leisurely pace, enabling Rusk, his twin, and Anklya to enjoy the scenery. Traffic on the road was light, primarily oxen and wagons, and an occasional lone traveler or family group on foot. But then Anklya said, "Rusk, Rist! I see the Princess's caravan below!"

Rist looked at his twin and smiled. "I know what to do now."

CHAPTER FIFTY-TWO

*P*rincess Perneptheranam was bored. As her godscloth-enclosed coach bounced and jostled its way along the rough gravel road back to ShadowFall, she was trying to stay interested in one of the ancient bound books she had received as failure tribute from her Sister in WaterEdge, the coastal Sisterdom. But reading of incessant battles with big blond pirates from the Cold Sea, in their sailing ships, and about century after tedious century of Motherland's land invasions of various native nations on slaving campaigns, was growing tiresome. "And I'm still a week from home!" she complained aloud, stifling a sneeze from the constant cloud of dust that somehow managed to infiltrate even through the magic material.

And she thought, *With no wise Wakan Kech to talk to, and no little Rist, my brave new champion, to snuggle up with at night!* Ignoring her suddenly attentive handmaids, with whom she never conversed on matters of any importance, Pernie turned her attention to the scrolls of written inventories of other tributes. She was only mildly interested in the four white horses from Four Peaks, the stone slabs from Stone Pyramid with their unreadable markings, and the dozens of godspheres collected from all the rest. *They see no use in dead godspheres, or old books, or strange writings on stone, so they gave them all to me for tribute, thinking they are worthless and that I am just stupid and naive. But wait until little Rist and my Wakan Kech can unlock and understand all the marvels of the gods, and use it to make ShadowFall preeminent in Motherland. Then we'll see who is naive! I expect that—*

"Princess! Princess!" the shouts came. "Please look outside!" The coach stopped with a jerk, throwing two of her handmaids from their seat onto the floor at her feet. Unsheathing a long steel knife from beneath her cushioned seat and indicating to her maids to do the same, Pernie drew back the curtains to access the coach door. Outside the window two of her armed palace guards were dismounting, ready to open the door for her. Nodding to them, she waited until they had opened it, and then stepped down the two steps into the bright sunlight outside.

"What is it, guards? Why have we stopped? We're not even at the white pyramid yet." She had given instructions to take her to that structure en route back home, where she hoped to study the inscribed metal disk located inside it.

"Princess," one guard said, waving a hand toward the North, "there is someone up in front of the caravan we think you will want to see."

"Then bring her to me," Pernie said, tapping her foot in frustration at the unexpected delay. "Or him, whoever it is."

"It shall be done, My Princess." She stepped back up into the coach, irritated. *Who* could *it be out here in the Middle of Nowhere, Motherland?*

Minutes later, Rist showed up at the open coach door. "Rist!" she shouted in surprise, "How did you get here? What kind of horses could catch up with my caravan? I'm so happy to see you! Please step inside, out of that heat!" To the surprise of her handmaids and the onlooking guards, Pernie pulled the little man up into the coach and smothered him with kisses, hugging him affectionately.

Without giving Rist a chance to answer, Pernie repeated, "How did you get here so quickly? You were supposed to be resting for weeks. I didn't expect to see you for months!"

Escaping her arms, Rist sputtered out, "Princess, I did not come by horse. I came…another way. Please come outside and let me show you."

In astonishment, Pernie nodded demurely and walked outside with Rist. She waved her nervous guards back as Rist took her over dusty desert terrain a few hundred meters to eroded mudbrick ruins that had once been a village. Once out of sight behind a high wall, Rist said, "Princess, you remember that I told you I had a twin, Rusk, who stayed behind in The Tharn's Land, there to retrieve more gods and a god-machine?"

"I do recall that Rist," she replied, but waved her hand at the ruins around them. "But what does that have to do with you coming from Mother's City so fast? And why are we standing in an old abandoned ruin, away from my guards?"

"Because, Princess, I want to show you all the answers, but only where others cannot see them." He pointed toward one end of the long wall, where a shimmering green mist seemed to appear out of clear air. As Pernie watched, a large green cylinder materialized, becoming solid inside seconds.

"What—what—what *is* that, Rist?" Pernie said, grabbing him by his shoulders with both hands. "Is that the *god-machine*, a magic tube that comes out of nowhere?" As she spoke, the side door of Una opened and out stepped Rusk.

Pernie almost fainted, but gasped. "Another Rist? Oh, your twin? He came from that machine? How—" Rusk walked up to her and smiled.

"You must be the princess that Rist fought for? *I* am Rusk, his twin. The handsome one." Pernie leaned back against the wall, breathing hard, barely able to comprehend what she had just seen. A magic cylinder? Two little dark men, identical? But her surprise was compounded when Anklya, her handmaid from ShadowFall, walked out of that big green cylinder and rushed to her side, putting an arm around her.

"My Princess," Anklya said, almost in tears, "are you quite well? Is there anything I can do to help you?"

Pernie was overwhelmed. "Anklya, my dear, how did you get here?

In that big green machine? Does it really fly?" Looking down at Rist and Rusk, she asked, "Can you really fly in that thing?" Realization dawned on her: "You all *flew* to meet me, in your god-machine. Now I understand. It's just hard to—to believe."

Minutes later, at Rist's persistent invitation, a reluctant Pernie stepped inside the cabin of Una, where she was overawed at the picture-screens, the moving images, and the concept of a machine that could speak as well as fly. She sat on one of the crew chairs, trying to absorb the reality of everything she was experiencing, attempting to come to terms with technologies so different from anything in Motherland's history. *Only in legends,* she thought, *were gods able to fly and machines talk. But this is real, and I am here in it!* Then, as her responsibilities as Princess came to the fore, she began to conceive how this "Una," as Rist called it, could benefit her Sisterdom. Surveillance of competing Sisterdoms came to mind, as did unimaginably fast travel anywhere in Motherland. *And for war— appearing over an enemy's palace without warning, without opposition!* The usefulness was infinite. *But first I have to have control of it. How?*

Rist demonstrated Una's capacity to lift up quietly and invisibly, and took Una up to look over the adjacent wall, through the transparent fuselage.

"Oh, I can see my caravan over there," Pernie exclaimed. "And we are up in the air! So marvelous, Rist, so amazing." She turned to him and leaned down and kissed him on the forehead. "ShadowFall will be so powerful now! You must let me thank you and reward you with your own estates, your own titles!" Seeing an unsmiling Rusk looking up at her, she added, "And of course, Rusk, you too will share in the best of everything I can offer." Rusk turned away, looking at Anklya with no expression.

Rist sensed the sudden tension, feeling it himself. He knew that Rusk felt as he did, that their discovery was theirs, not ShadowFall's. He wanted to ease any possible conflict before it began. *You don't argue with princesses, no matter how wrong they might be!* He motioned to Rusk, who said, "Una, take us back down." Once they were on the ground again, Rist interceded. "Princess, you really need to return to the caravan now, before your guards come looking for you. It is best if your other people don't see Una or us yet. Who knows what kind of spies have infiltrated your contingent? What they might do to you, to try and capture us and our Una? We will keep an eye on your progress, from above, unseen. Then we can meet you at ShadowFall when you arrive."

Pernie wanted to demand that she be flown to ShadowFall immediately, but knowing what complications would arise if she abandoned her caravan at the moment, she yielded to Rist's request. "Very well, my champion, you are wise to suggest that course of action. I shall return to my coach. But I order you to meet me at ShadowFall within the next week or so. Upon my arrival, I will confer with Wakan Kech, who is already there, about how we will all proceed to make the best use of this most amazing machine."

Rist bowed to her. "It shall be done, My Princess," he said and escorted her off Una, back to her coach. As the puzzled caravan guards watched, he walked back behind the mudbrick wall and stayed. Pernie ordered the caravan to proceed, apparently leaving her mysterious little man alone in the ancient ruins.

CHAPTER FIFTY-THREE

$\mathcal{A}$s Una lifted up once again, Rist said, "Rusk, take us to ShadowFall quickly. If Wakan Kech is already there, I need to talk to him before Pernie arrives. Here is what I think we should do, you and I, and Anklya, before she does."

Within half an hour, Una was hovering above the top of Pernie's palace. Upon landing, Rist found the entrance where Wakan had brought him up to the far-seer, months before. He made his way down into the palace to Wakan's office where he surprised his mentor at his desk. Wakan had just been signing the warrant for Rumi Similla's exile to a remote Mother's Army outpost in the extreme west, and was glad for the interruption of such an onerous task.

"Rist! How wonderful to see you again! Did you come with Pernie? Is she—?" He stopped when Rist put a finger to his lips, then whispered, "How, then—" With a grin, he said, "Did you *fly?* With Rusk and his magic machine?" Rist nodded as Wakan came over and reached down to shake his hand.

"Wakan, let us find a secure place to talk. I have much to tell you." Wakan motioned toward a small adjacent room with a thick wooden door.

Over the next few minutes Rist related how Messinex had

demanded that all godspheres and ancient books be remanded to Mother's Palace at once, no exceptions. "Even all of those I found and brought up from the lowest depths under the palace! I think she means to bury them forever."

Wakan put his head in his hands. "Why? Did she give any reason?" he demanded.

Rist said, "No, when I was telling her about my discovery she had me leave her court. The order came down from Miran Kech an hour later. I was not allowed even to go back and plead my case."

Wakan wondered what Rist had been talking about that upset Mother so, but decided that he probably should not know, either. Instead he asked, "And so, Miran's men will soon be here to abscond with all our own godspheres, our old books?"

Rist nodded. "And we can't let that happen."

Wakan's face grew stern, dutiful. "Pernie will be duty bound to obey Mother Messinex's orders, Rist. There is no way around it." He studied his little visitor. "Why didn't you tell the Princess about the Mother's orders when you met with her on the road home?"

Crossing his arms defiantly, Rist looked directly into Wakan Kech's grim face. "Because, Wakan, I am not going to let that happen. I am going to take all the ShadowFall books and godspheres I can carry on Una, and leave with them. Before Pernie arrives."

Wakan gasped, turning pale. Had he just heard *treason* from Rist? Taking control of himself, he knew that had he heard those words from any other person in ShadowFall he would have immediately called in the palace guards and instituted a well-established regimen of torture and mutilation to uncover all of the details, all of the plotters. But Rist? He couldn't order such a command for this hero of ShadowFall. Surely there was a way to handle this, some compromise that would leave Rist whole and Pernie satisfied. But what?

"Rist," he said, slowly, "you know my first duty is to the Princess, to ShadowFall. I cannot allow you to take our property, nor to violate the specific order of the Mother. Or even to depart without permission." He sighed. "Even if I wanted to, that would result in the death of both of us. Do you understand?' He rose from his chair and paced the room, thinking furiously.

"Not if you leave with us, Wakan," Rist responded. "Come with us, my twin and me—and Anklya. We can go anywhere in the whole wide world. We have thought through this. Here's what we propose: load up Una with all of the ancient globes and books we can carry, and retire to our Sire's cavern redoubt in The Tharn's Land. It is roomy, well hidden, and well supplied, and we can all live there until we make other plans." He walked around to Wakan and looked up at him. "There are ancient secrets we can learn from the globes, from the books, information that we may someday bring back to Motherland." Thinking of the cruel priests of God's Port he added, "Or use it to change things in other places."

Stunned, Wakan sat back down. *Leave ShadowFall? Leave the Princess? Give up my life's work, my favored position, my plans for improving Motherland? I cannot do that. Yet I cannot betray my little friend and his twin, either. What to do?* A niggling memory of his own homeland, the High Antis, started to produce yet other possibilities, other courses of action. *But those, later! Now is now!*

Rist supplied one solution to the dilemma. "Let Rusk and me bring up things from the catacombs right now, quietly. We won't take everything, and nobody even need know we have been here. We haven't been seen by anyone but you. And when the Princess does arrive, you can deny any knowledge that we came back. For all she will know, and all you would know, is that the Una must have crashed and we were lost. Or else we went back home. How does that sound to you?"

Wakan began to breathe again; his little Rist had lately learned deceit as well as killing. Or was fighting in The Game *murder* or only *warfare*? Either way, the little man had changed greatly in just a few months, from an innocent savage to a sophisticated fighter and now, probably worse, a convincing *schemer.* He groaned; *the corruption of Motherland strikes again! What are we doing to the world?*

PART TEN

FINALE

CHAPTER FIFTY-FOUR

*W*hile working outside their cavern complex far north of The Tharn's Town, Mell was first to see Una, becoming aware of a downdraft of cold air, then of a green shimmering in the sky, and finally of a descending *presence.* "Sire Thess! They are coming home!" she shouted, dropping her load of firewood, standing back to make room for the flying god-machine. And hopefully, her twins. Within seconds Reader Thess arrived, placing his arm around his wen and smiling broadly as the craft materialized in front of them.

Rist and Rusk almost tumbled out of the side door, rushing into the embraces of their Sire and birther. Amidst the spectacle of sobs and kisses, the tall blonde Anklya came out of Una, looking around at the craggy stone canyon and its scrub trees, beginning to shiver in the damp cold. Her Motherland garments were made for a warm climate. Thess and Mell cautiously welcomed the tall blonde wen, a person such as they'd never seen before. In his battles with other tall WarmLanders, Thess had never seen one of their wen; and she was attractive in ways he didn't understand at first.

Hours later, after unloading the dozens of godspheres and stacks of leather-bound books from Una and placing them in a dry niche back in Sire Thess' expansive cave complex, the four people sat in front of a wide firepit, drinking peat wine and eating ribs of beezt. Anklya was covered with close-fitting warm velk pelts, courtesy of the skill of birther Mell with scissors and thread.

Sire Thess expressed continuing amazement and satisfaction at his twins' exploits. And approval of their victories. "As Sire of this family," he said, standing with a mug of strong brew in hand, "it is my honor and pleasure to bestow man-names of both of you boys—now men! Rist, for your bravery in the exploration of lands in the South and your victories in that savage Game, by the traditions of our People you are henceforth to be called *Thist*." He poured a libation of drink onto his son's head, wiping it across his face with a grin. Thist bowed to his Sire, his birther, to Rusk, and finally, hesitantly, even to their guest Anklya.

"Rist, for your amazing achievement of waking up the Una god-machine, for flying it through lands and perils unknown, and for rescuing your twin, Thist, by the traditions of our People you are henceforth to be called *Thusk*!" With a wetted head, Thusk bowed to all present. The celebration lasted into the wee hours, Thist and Thusk taking turns relating harrowing details of their exploits on the ground and in the sky and even underwater, much to the delight of the others and to themselves.

After Sire Thess and birther Mell retired to their bedroom in the cavern, Anklya and the newly named men went to another room, where she offered a different sort of reward, one that took much more time, but which culminated in a most satisfying fashion for all.

THIST WOKE FIRST, HIS OUTSTRETCHED RIGHT ARM OUTSIDE THE velkfur covers, chilled in the damp air of Sire Thess' cave. His left arm was covered by warmth and softness—*Anklya*! On her other side slept Thusk, oblivious to the world. Shaking his head to clear the fuzziness left over from last dark's carousing—*and lovemaking!* he recalled with a broad smile—Thist rolled off the thick straw bedding, dressed himself warmly in velkfur robe and hood, and walked outside in fur boots to see the daylight. And to ensure that Una was still there. It was, in all its big green glory. *Almost like a giant tropical fruit from Three Rivers*, he thought irreverently. *One whose seeds may plant our future.*

Thist walked around the craft, rubbing his hands on its perfect warm smoothness, feeling the slight *thrummm* of vibration, almost as if the thing were alive. His twin, Thusk (he found it difficult to think of the new man-name), had told him that although the machine could speak and converse, that it was not truly alive in any fashion that he, Thusk, could understand. Thusk was very familiar with this Una, after flying in it for over a month now, but he himself had much to learn. *This machine, this ancient flying thing; so much of our lives have already depended on it, so much of our future and that of The Tharn's Lands, maybe ShadowFall's—maybe even Motherland's itself?—still depends on it. What we can do with it, what we can learn from it?*

This very day, he decided, *Sire Thess and Thusk and I—and maybe our birther and our ShadowFall maid—we will make a plan.*

We will use Una, and we will change the world!

A FTER FIRSTMEAL, THE TWINS WERE SOMEWHAT SURPRISED AT THEIR Sire Thess. He had reluctantly agreed for them to unload the half dozen springbows and several quivers of metal arrows that they had stolen from the ShadowFall armory. "Wakan didn't know that I was taking them," Thist said, "While Thusk was grabbing globes and books down below. I don't know if they will ever be missed, but I knew we would need them. I will teach you all how to fire them. They are quite effective." Thist didn't mention that Una had required some serious convincing before allowing the dangerous weapons within its cabin. It wasn't physical weapons that their Sire objected to so much, but some of the immaterial items they had been discussing, alien ideas from the Warmward nations.

"I find all of these fantastical inventions acceptable now," Thess said over peat-tea that morning, "having considered that each one of them fulfills a human need: to travel safely, above all obstacles of rivers and mountains and deserts. To travel quickly, in case of emergencies or to deliver goods or even orders. To have spoken records, where even illiterates can understand new knowledge. And the moving, talking pictures in Una's cabin that show things that can't be well described in print or still drawings." He pointed outside toward the black bubble atop Una's fuselage. "I can even understand the need for a human-looking white-thing to pilot Una around; who would want to trust their life to a featureless cylinder, no matter how intelligent it may seem?

"No, all of these things I can understand because people need them. And resourceful people, given enough education, tools, and time, will invent things that people need. But what I have difficulty with, what I fail yet to understand, are the many different ways the societies supposedly work in those lands Warmward. I don't see how anything other than a Tharn-led community can function."

Thist and Thusk had their own ideas about the places they had visited; even Anklya listened in and occasionally spoke up, unasked, something almost never done by wen in The Tharn's Land. The twins were amused by their Sire's reaction to Anklya's interjections. Her pronunciation was not quite what a lifelong Person would use, but the long conversations with Rist and Rusk—*Thist* and *Thusk*!—had made her speech acceptable.

"I've lived my whole life enslaved to a princess," she said. "First to a distant one, then directly for Princess Perneptheranam when she took possession of my village and the lands around the ancient city of ShadowFall, five years ago. My people are *owned* by the Princess, and, I suppose, as she is by her Mother. The class of nobles takes orders from them, and we obey. We attend to their needs. We are never asked, only commanded." She sighed. "Sometimes I think I would like to do other things, like maybe have children, a family." She looked directly at Thusk, pointing down toward him and chuckling, "And sometimes, I would rather just fly away in a magic machine with an exotic little dark man, off to strange lands."

Everyone laughed at Anklya's earnest but humorous complaints, but Thess grew serious. "Even here in The Tharn's Lands, we have no concept of a Person *owning* another. For sure, The Tharn rules his lands by commands, and punishes the recalcitrant with the power and weapons of The Tharn's Men. But most of the time we live and work and do as we wish. We always have."

Thusk popped up, "But Sire, what The Tharn did to our home—"

Thess interrupted, "I am angry that The Tharn burned us out for no reason, and our poor two-legs especially, but for all my rage at that action of his, he doesn't try to *own* us!" Growing more indignant, their Sire sputtered, "See, this is one of those alien concepts you brought back from the Warm Lands that we cannot allow to infect our homeland. Not even the *idea* of this, this, *slavery*!" Mell sat wide-eyed; she had never seen Sire Thess so wrought, so vehement, as now.

Thist spoke up. "Sire, down in God's Port I heard of no Tharn, no Mother, not even a princess, no ruler of any kind." Then the memory of the burned thief came to mind. "But what I did see was the group of 'priests' they called themselves, who had a small cadre of strongarmed men, 'Priests' Men.' Somehow, the priests exert control over their citizens with their stories of the Shining One and the Pale Lady—what we now know as the Sun and the Moon. How those gods in the sky watch all of their activities and punish all of their crimes." He saw disbelief in the faces of his Sire, his birther, and even Anklya. That was a new concept to them all, and he felt that they didn't believe it any more than he did.

"Apparently it works, and their people approve of it," Thist continued, "because a group of those Priests' Men grabbed that poor pier-man who let Cruthar and me into the storeroom to take out my roll of godscloth, then tied him to a post and the priests roasted him alive with their focused sunlight." Thess and the two women cringed at the gruesome vision.

"And nobody stopped them?" Thess asked, unbelieving.

"The crowd cheered it," Thist replied. "So they all must truly believe it."

Thess shook his head. "All this time I hoped that my icebergs were being used by civilized people in the Warm Lands," he groaned. "I knew the WarmLanders were big and could be warlike—I had to fight them many cycles ago, you know." Unconsciously rubbing his left thigh, a gesture his family had seen all their lives, he went on, "But I thought that peaceful trade, after all these cycles—*years*—of it, meant that they were rational men. Now I see I was mistaken."

Thusk said, "But Sire, God's Port has incredibly beautiful buildings, made of cut and finished stone, many times larger than The Tharn's Place. They have unusual lifting devices, and huge sailing ships, and colorful fabrics." Thinking over the attractions that he had enjoyed most, keeping his gaze from comparing the shapely Anklya with that of his birther and other wen in The Tharn's Lands, he said, "And a variety of People we don't have. Most men taller than Anklya, people with skin colors from pure black to pink like hers, to almost pure white. People with hair the color of foxfur, the colors of peat, and some men with even *no* hair, bald heads." Nervously, Thess and Mell laughed out loud at that ridiculous statement; baldness was unheard of in their land. But it did indicate some of the strangeness of those foreigners.

"What I'm saying, Sire," Thusk continued, growing more intense, walking around and gesticulating, "is that there must be useful knowledge in God's Port, and some reasonable people we can deal with, like the smart people who can cut and stack those stone buildings, who make those godscloth nets and ropes, even those who made the big reflectors that burned up the poor warehouseman that Thist saw. After all, they *do* buy our Ice. Maybe we should trade for their *knowledge* instead of their *copper*?"

Then Thusk thought of all the wonders that Una had already revealed. "Or maybe, now that we have Una, we can trade some of *our* new knowledge for whatever of theirs we might want?" *Maybe hire some of their stone-builders?* He kept thinking of how impressive those big buildings would look in The Tharn's Town. On the other hand, Mother's City outshone God's Port to the same extent that that city outdid The Tharn's Town. But how would Thist ever be able to talk to Mother Messinex again, after running away, or himself to Pernie, after stealing her property? *Well, those people will just have to get used to dealing with us!*

Thist concurred with Thusk's fervent ideas, excitedly picking up on his unspoken thought. "And Mother's City itself exceeds God's Port in buildings and vastly more in population and everything else. We could get a lot more trade goods from down there, if we can negotiate. It *is* ruled by a Mother with absolute powers, but she has a council of advisors that are usually changed every five years, after The Game." He grew silent after that, vividly recalling his life-and-death melee in the stadium. *Fifty-one men, ten emus, four horses! How many did I kill by myself? At least a dozen. And for what?* At that moment of reflection, his guilt returned, his self-hatred started to boil over again; right then he wanted nothing more than the destruction of Motherland, even ShadowFall. *And all of the princesses—even Pernie!* The chilling thought hit him full force: *Una might make all of that possible!*

Calming himself while shaking, Thist put away those thoughts and just said meekly, "I don't think we want that kind of reign here at home, nothing like Motherland, or like God's Port." Thess and Thusk looked at him with sympathy; Mell and Anklya wanted to take him in their arms and hold him and comfort him until his dark mood passed, but in the presence of the several unexpected demonstrations of male fury they had just witnessed, now feeling like mere wen in the male-ruled domain of The Tharn's Lands, they did nothing.

CHAPTER FIFTY-FIVE

*A*fter lastmeal, Sire Thess, Mell, Anklya and the twins all sat around the makeshift table as dying flames eked out their last dance in the firepit, leaving burning embers to illuminate the somber faces of the people. Sire Thess blew out a breath of resignation. "So it is agreed, all present, that we possess a force of unimaginable power, far greater than any other ever known since the so-called gods left—actually destroyed by The Ice that enveloped the whole wide world." Nods all around, he continued, "And we can't live in this cavern forever, nor do we want to. We have too much to offer to all humankind."

Holding up one gloved hand, Thess pointed upward with his index finger. "But one, we can't go back to our burned-out home in The Tharn's Town, because the brutal chief of ours is a tyrant. Ordinary people can't live under arbitrary rules that I now see as the whims of an old drunk, however courageous he once was, however just he seemed to be in cycles—*years*—past." He almost whispered, "And The Tharn's Men number near...near"—he tried to think in terms of the new number system he had learned from Una—"at least one *hundred*, with most garrisoned around The Tharn's Town plus a few northern outposts."

He held up his middle finger and said, "*Two*, although from your reports the Warm Lands climate sounds better than our perpetual bitter cold to just uncomfortably cold, you both may not be welcomed back to that ShadowFall. Your Princess and your Kech priest by now have surely found out the extent of your understandable theft of their books and globes, even though we have not been able to bring any back to life, if that's what it is. The ShadowFall Sisterdom, you say, Thist, has a few hundred men already armed with those springbows and spears?"

Thist answered, "Sire, that is correct. And Wakan Kech can put out the order and have thousands more ready in another one to two days depending on the urgency the Princess commands."

"*Three*," Thess went on, carefully registering the facial responses of his family and guest, "The Motherland has thirteen Sisterdoms that can raise their own armies, and add to that, the many thousands of armed guards and Mothersmen you all saw in Mother's City."

Thess concluded, then sat down, dejected. "There is no possible way, then, that we could ever hope to do direct battle with those Motherlanders, who could crush the entire population of all of The Tharn's Lands, should we attack."

Thist spoke up. "Sire, I have had enough of killing. I won't do it again, unless it's to protect all of you here." His wave included Anklya, who managed a wan smile. Thist continued to be amazed at what his improved vision meant; being able to see the maid's smooth face, her high cheekbones, the faint blush when she approved of his words. "But if we are not to die of old age here together in your cave, we have to take some action. But no killing."

Thusk stood, putting down a beezt-rib and wiping his lips with his hand. "But with new knowledge, and Una, maybe there is another way. Sire Thess speaks the truth—we are too few in numbers to fight like the rest of the whole wide world does, so we need to think *differently*." The looks on Sire Thess' and Thist's faces told him that they were waiting for his different ideas.

"Obviously we should begin at home; we truly don't need The Tharn. After I saw what his men did to our home, and our poor emus, I just wanted revenge, to kill him." He saw Thist shaking his head at that. "But after being in God's Port, in ShadowFall, and at The Game in Mother's City, I have tried to figure a way to remove The Tharn without destroying our nation while doing it. And a way to change ShadowFall and all of Motherland without war."

"We're listening, Thusk," Sire Thess said.

"We will enlist other people," Thusk said, "people who stand to gain from a change in the way things have always been done. That includes a huge percentage of citizens in every one of the places we know about. They just have to realize it. And we start at home—The Tharn's Town."

THE DARK WAS VERY DARK, WITH NO LIGHT FROM THE ABSENT WEN OF the Mist, as Thist walked quietly toward a group of humble straw huts. *Thick as Dark,* he recalled the old aphorism. *I can almost taste it,* he thought, *but it's probably just the smell of the fish in the River here, or maybe even the perfumes of my old friends from the iceberg crew.* In the abodes just ahead, Cruthar, his Sire Strether, and the rest of berg-crew were sleeping off a night of pubbing near the New River dockyard. Thist went up to an open doorway—no netting against the flying biter-bugs, he noticed—and said quietly, "Cruthar, are you home? This be Thist. Er, Rist."

A minute later his old berg-mate stumbled to the door, holding one hand to his sweaty forehead and a club in the other. "*Yer* who? *I don't know no—*" Rusk held up a candle to light his face, and Cruthar broke out into a grin. "Be damned! Rist! Ye made it back! Been a whole season since I left you, all covered in shit!" He grabbed Thist and pulled him into the hut, hugging him and pounding him on the back. "I can't wait to tell ever'body that ye're well and good!"

"Cruthar," Thist whispered, "keep it quiet. I don't want anybody to know I'm here—yet." Cruthar indicated a rickety table and chairs near a crude fireplace. "I have a deal for you, Cruthar, so please listen. If you like it then you can tell it to all the other berg-men, even the fishermen—everybody who works with their hands in The Tharn's Town."

"I hear you," Cruthar replied, equally quietly. "I knowed the rest of your family was burnt out by our chief." Wiping his face with a towel and water, he said, "Nobody says anything about why that went on, but let me tell you—the stories that are told about your Sire and Rusk, they are jist unbelievably wild."

"Probably not wild enough, Cruthar," Thist said. "You wouldn't believe where I've been, what I've done..." He tried, unsuccessfully, to suppress memories of his killing rampage at The Game. "Just let me say that the whole wide world is fixing to change, and I would like you to be part of it, to profit from it."

Thist opened his palm toward the beg-man, as if asking for coppers, for money. "My first question is how much do you pay in tributes, Cruthar, when you wait at the lift to get back into The Tharn's Lands from the Warm Lands? Before you answer, how would you like that to be zero, nothing? You and the crew keep it all for yourselves?"

Sobering up, Cruthar put on a serious face and began to listen. After their discussion, Thist said, "Cruthar, come outside with me. I will show you something that will open your eyes."

———

A LITTLE LATER, ACROSS TOWN AT A LARGESTONE HOUSE, SIRE THESS and Thusk similarly awakened Broker Thenuss, chief Ice broker of The Tharn's Town, with whom Thess had dealt for many hands of cycles, selling berg information that the man used when securing possession of down-coming ice. After expressing surprise that Thess was back in town—The Tharn having offered rewards for his capture—Thenuss offered them black peat-tea and sat down to hear his old friend's urgent request. "Thenuss," Thess asked in a whisper, "how much do you pay to The Tharn every time you buy a berg? And in all the other business transactions in town—buying and selling peat, beezt, rabs?"

Thenuss sat, puzzled. No one had ever asked such a thing before. The Tharn's thirty percent tribute tax applied to everything, to every business, every transaction. There were hundreds of craftsmen, smiths, weavers, not to mention higher-level brokers like himself who paid at every step of their work activities. And the peat farmers Coldward paid half of their crops to The Tharn's Men. *Does Thess have something new to offer? What is better?*

Thess knew he had his friend's interest, and continued, "Have you ever asked why The Tharn gets any money from all of us who do the work? And what does he do with it, other than support his men? Keep a harem of wen? Buy the best peat-wine and -beer? The best food?"

Then Thess supplied the hook: "Thenuss, what if you paid zero tribute tax, nothing? And kept it all for yourself and your family, to buy what you want?" Thenuss couldn't answer; he was thinking of the possibility of an immediate thirty percent more income.

"What can I do, Thess? What are you saying?"

"Come with me then, and prepare to be surprised. I will truly open your eyes."

BACK IN UNA, THESS AND HIS SONS MET TO REVIEW THEIR NIGHT'S work. "Sire," Thist said, "I think we will have the berg-men and the dockworkers on our side; Cruthar was pretty convinced."

Thusk chimed in, "And from your conversation with the broker Thenuss, the higher-level businessmen and all of the workers they finance should support our plans, too."

Thess appeared to be glum. "But it all depends on the timing, and whether The Tharn will step aside for this Council of Elders we are proposing, and go quietly into retirement. Or if he will fight." He pointed at the springbows lining the wall of Una's cabin. "Will we have to use those, do you think?"

Thist shook his head. "Sire, I am very good with them, but unless you two are threatened, I will *not* shoot first."

Frowning, Thusk looked at his twin. "But *I* will, Thist. I personally saw what his men did to our home, and our emus. This plan is worth The Tharn's life, if it has to be that way. It will save our land." But

Thist turned away; his twin had no idea what it mean to take a life. *In my own defense,* he thought, *I will have to say that shooting at the large men, even the horses, during The Game, was different than it would be shooting at one of our People.* He finally realized what he was dreading: killing a Person, one of his own kind. *I shouldn't be thinking that, but I am! But Thusk has never killed, so he can't make a distinction. Yet.* He hoped that his twin would never feel the guilt he was experiencing. *Even though they were only WarmLanders…*

Thess then said, "Boys, we have one other stop to make before our plan begins. The Old Wen must be with us…"

THREE DIMS LATER, PURSUING DIMNESS—*THE SUN!*—STOOD AT ITS highest point in the Misty Sky. For The Tharn's Town, the temperature was as high as it ever would be this time of year, a dawn crispness yielding to an ever so slight melting of rime. The plaza of The Tharn's Place was filled with mingling crowds of People, all waiting in anticipation of some important announcement rumored to be revealed at noon.

A nervous Thenuss and a dozen other prosperous businessmen— brokers, bankers, even wealthy shopkeepers—stood in their finery furs, while behind them milled hundreds of ordinary folk and workers of all kinds, in costumes from drab to mediocre, cloth aprons and leather, each one trying to get a decent vantage point from where to view whatever it was that was going to happen, many shopworkers and laborers just enjoying a rare opportunity to get away from mundane tasks and hopefully to see something exciting. Thenuss and a few of his friends kept looking at their hands and nervously smiling, anxiously shaking their heads. Back in the crowd, Cruthar and his Sire Strether and their berg-crew were doing likewise.

As usual, half a dozen Tharn's Men, axes across their backs, spears at their sides, stood at guard under the timber portico of their chief's largestone palace, nervous at the apparent bravado of the noisy crowd filling the plaza at the bottom of the stairway. Selected for their height and strength and blind obedience, known for their brutality, for the first time in their cycles of service they did not cow their fellow citizens, feeling uneasy at being so outnumbered. The crowd reciprocated the feeling; something new was happening, something historic—or maybe horrific?—was about to occur. And citizens of The Tharn's Town knew it had to do with them. Tensions were building. Where was The Tharn? What would he say?

The wide wooden doors slammed open, and an obese drunken Tharn stumbled out, his gold fur robe open, his belly exposed, and shouting, "What in the name of the gods is going on out here? Who called this gathering?" He stumbled into the nearest guard, jerking the spear away. "Who is leading this mob, this collection of—of—of —*trash?*"

The crowd grew quiet, only the muted rustling of *What? Metal? Tools?* could be heard from the mass of workers behind the front row of businessmen. As The Tharn watched, a rivulet of people stepped aside, one old wen being helped through the crowd until she stood at the front of the assembled people. Recognizing who she was, even The Tharn became quiet as she stepped up on the stairs, unaided, and turned to face the mass of people.

"Everybody here knows me," the wen said in a deep croak of a voice. "I am the Old Wen, the keeper of the carved records of our land." Smiling broadly she said, "And as you all know, I was blind. But then, an old student of mine, Thess, showed me a miracle—and now I can See!" Waving her hands at the astonished crowd, she said, "I can See my hands, I can See your faces, I can See any place I can touch!"

Cheers broke out, and a chant: "Old Wen! Old Wen!" As voices died down, someone shouted, "How did it happen, Old Wen? Can anybody do it? Is it only a miracle for you?" Back behind her, The Tharn was unsteady, holding tightly onto the guard whose spear he had taken; he looked like he might vomit, but said nothing at the spectacle unfolding in front of him.

The Old Wen spoke, louder this time. "Reader Thess, whom you all know, has a big green flying god-machine that removed thick dark layers growing on my eyes—*cataracts*, he called them—and he says he will do the same for all of you! All of you can See!"

Cheers broke out again: "Old Wen! Reader Thess! Old Wen! Reader Thess!"

At this chant, The Tharn regained some stability and shouted, "Old Wen, go home! Shut up about Thess, the traitor. I burned down his house because he is a thief, a dirty thief! Now shut up and go home before I—" He hoisted the spear as if to throw it at the Old Wen, when a voice from the plaza yelled, "Do that and you're dead, you fat drunk!"

As The Tharn hesitated, his men lowered their own spears as if to charge the crowd, but put them down when a strange crop of metal implements seemed to grow among the tight assembly of People: dozens of long crowbars, tall rakes, iceberg poles, even shovels and picks, sticking high above the crowd. The Tharn looked at his men, and they at him, nobody knowing exactly what they should do next.

Then out of the sky came the strangest thing anybody in The Tharn's Town had ever seen.

CHAPTER FIFTY-SIX

*A*board Una, the companions Thess, Thist, and Thusk prepared themselves for the climax of their plan. Thess said, "Una, become opaque, and land carefully, right at the bottom of the stairs. And let me talk through your loudspeaker."

"Sire Thess, it shall be done. No borophene weapons are detected. The shield is contracted. You may speak when ready."

Appearing in the air thirty meters above them, the crowd saw a large green cylinder materialize out of nothing, then descend slowly, touching the ground lightly as everyone, even The Tharn and his men, drew back in fear and curiosity. One of the guards said something to The Tharn, but his voice was drowned out by the collective gasps of the hundreds on the plaza. The Tharn said something back to his men, but they apparently refused, holding back their spears and not unleashing their axes. The Tharn began screaming at them, but to no avail. The guards had encountered Una before, not knowing if it were a living creature, and now were fearful of its possible revenge for their earlier attacks.

"People of our land," Thess' voice boomed out over Una's loud-speaker system, "this is Reader Thess, whom you all know. I am flying inside this god-machine that I recovered from The Ice many hands of dims ago. With me are my newly man-named twins, Thist and Thusk, heroes renamed for their man-actions down in the Warm Lands." Through Una's one-way transparent walls, Thess and his twins could view the agitated collection of The Tharn's Town people, some brandishing tools as weapons. On the portico, The Tharn was red-faced and screaming incoherently, shaking a spear up at Una.

Thess' loud announcement continued, "As you know, The Tharn deliberately and without cause burned down my home and killed my two-legs." He let that sink in and then said, "In fact The Tharn has done many evil things for many years, all without any reason other than to increase his own wealth and power. This god-machine I am in has more power than does he. With it, my twins have flown to the Warm Lands and to other nations that are much more populous than our land, much vaster in size, and with comforts, amenities, and riches that we have only dreamed of."

Thist motioned to Thess to hurry up. He knew that his laborer friends from the bergs and docks would not be impressed by mere rhetoric and history, but only by action. If his plan didn't get implemented soon, only chaos and anarchy would follow. And death, more death. Thist worried that their plan of peace might work no better than had Wakan Kech's plans during the vicious Game. Reluctantly, he reached for springbows and quivers of arrows, giving one set to Thusk. *Time for action, if needed,* he thought. *But I pray not!*

"Friends and fellow citizens," Thess' voice resounded through the plaza and beyond, where even more people were swarming in from the town to see the flying green thing from the sky, "my twins and I have spoken to many of you already over the past few days. Here is what I am offering: in this machine we can fix your eyes to see everything both close up and far away, as we did for the Old Wen. We will offer education, too—the answers to what lies above the Misty Sky, what happened before The Ice came, and much more. And a new way of doing business—no more tribute taxes on your sales and transactions. You will get to keep everything you earn!"

The reaction was unexpected, some people shouting, "What about The Tharn? He is our leader, who are *you*?" And a slow, steady chant began, building to a crescendo: "The Tharn! The Tharn! The Tharn!" Seen through Una's wall, The Tharn began to strut about on the portico, spear in hand, even as others began shouting, led by the Old Wen, "Reader Thess! Reader Thess! Reader Thess!" Sides were forming, and a serious fight was brewing.

Thess and his sons dropped their jaws at all of this. Thist whispered, "Not at all what we wanted is it? Let me talk to them. Una, open the black dome and let me speak through the white-thing."

Atop Una's fuselage, the black cockpit slowly opened, pivoting all the way back. The white-thing turned its faux-eyes toward both sides of the imminent mobs, then toward The Tharn and his men. The manlike appearance of the white-thing scared everyone into silence. Then Thist's voice came through it. "Everyone, this is the man Thist, formerly the boy Rist," he said, even louder than Thess had, his voice echoing from the largestone walls of The Tharn's Place and down the streets of The Tharn's Town. "I am speaking through the pilot of this craft. Everybody, please put down your weapons. This god-machine we are flying is all-powerful, and we don't want anybody hurt." At that, many of the raised implements and weapons sank back down, out of sight.

Thist continued, "If you want your eyes to be able to see as does everyone down in the Warm Lands, all those countless numbers of people, and as the Old Wen does now, if you want true knowledge of the whole wide world, you will listen to me.

"What is going to happen is this: The Tharn is going to give up all his titles and his powers, and will be exiled to a comfortable cave home we have prepared for him far up north. Our nation from now on will be called The People's Lands, and our town, The People's Town. All government decisions will be made by a Council of Elders, led by the Old Wen, with its first members my Sire Reader Thess, Broker Thenuss, berg-man Strether, and others to be selected by the council." Thess cringed at that; he had offered Thenuss and Strether together his entire ice business as a final inducement to join in the challenge to The Tharn. *I have suffered a great loss. Of course, if we lose this battle right now, their skulls will be decorating the palisade along with ours!*

"Those named council members, please assemble on the steps here. And the person formerly known as The Tharn, please step forward and peacefully await your transportation." At that, the white-thing rotated slowly around, as if assessing each person's status, and what to do with them if they disobeyed. Each person stood rock still, unable to assess what might happen if that strange creature were to find fault with them. The white-thing faced The Tharn and stopped rotating.

Una's door opened and its three passengers stepped out, two of them carrying strangely curved metal devices with rods strung across them. Reader Thess walked around the green god-machine and up the steps next to the Old Wen. A hand of man-lengths away, The Tharn stood defiantly, upraised spear in hand. "Thess, you traitor, you thief!" he yelled, stepping forward. "And your peat-rat twins, just as bad. What are they carrying, music-makers for your funeral?" Thess could smell the peat-wine on the fat man, almost as if he had been bathing in it. A part of his mind noted that this was the first time in cycles that he'd seen the fat old man without young wen hanging all around him. *They must have known what was about to happen,* he mused. *All wen seem to know instinctively when to stay out of the way. Or maybe, just which side will win. And it's not that old fat guy, not this time.*

Thist and Thusk raised their springbows, but Thess motioned them down. They didn't obey, but kept sweeping their weapons, keeping their aim at The Tharn and his nearest guards. Thess said, "Please, old friend from the war days. Your time is over; you can go and rest now, no more responsibilities. Put down your spear and let me take you to safety." Then he added softly, unheard by the others, "You can even bring some of your wen, if they want to come. They will be comfortable."

"Thess," The Tharn said solemnly, moving forward and lowering his spear as if to go quietly.

Thess said, "Thank you, we can—" But the fat man suddenly lifted his spear horizontally, lunged forward and thrust it into Thess, the sharp iron point entering his chest and protruding out his back. Thess tried to speak but blood gushed from his mouth. Gurgling, he grabbed the spear in his chest and fell forward.

In shock, Thist stood still, unable to move, as his Sire collapsed in front of him.

Without thinking, in a rage, Thusk released a springbow arrow into The Tharn's right eye, following it quickly with another one to the face of the nearest guard. Both men collapsed to the ground without a sound, their blood quickly spewing down the stairs. The other guards, seeing the impossible fact that The Tharn was dead, threw down their spears and backed off, hands up. His fury assuaged, Thusk regained his senses, waving the guards away into the crowd that was now swarming around Una, up toward the portico. He briefly noticed that two of the escaping guards went down in a flurry of fists and axes. *No loss there!* He hoped they were the emu-killers.

On his knees now, Thist cradled his Sire in his arms, wiping blood from his mouth, as Thusk knelt down to assist. But it was too late; Thess was no more. During their adventures down in the Warm Lands, they had both seen tall people crying when in pain or sorrow. At that moment, they only wished they could shed tears, too.

CHAPTER FIFTY-SEVEN

*T*husk finished off his large mug of peat-beer and burped loudly. Wiping foam from his mouth with a furred sleeve, he stared into the raging fire in the large fireplace of what had been The Tharn's Den, now The People's Room. Dark, heavy wooden furniture, covered with plush stuffed pillows fringed with gold weave, stood like monuments all around the perimeter of the space. Thusk apologized to the others, "That was fine beer; the old man kept the best for himself." They had agreed that the title of the deceased ex-chief —*Killed by me*! Thusk thought, proudly—would never be spoken again. Thist had wanted to erase that evil man's name from the Old Wen's archives as well, taking him out of history entirely, but the Council of Elders decided that his memory be kept as a record of how *not* to run a land.

To Thusk's left, his birther Mell sat silently, in dark mourning veils. To his right, Thist sat, sipping his own mug of brew. Next to him sat Anklya in a large chair made especially for her height. "The Old Wen does not want to move into The People's Place," Anklya said, "and I can understand why. I visited her caves yesterday, and they are marvelous to behold. What treasures must be there, and she wants to look after them."

Thist nodded. "Nobody wants to move into this place, it seems. Not even Strether, Cruthar, or their crew. You'd think"—his wave encompassed the vast room, the fine furniture, the drapes and carpets and finery—"that this would be better than their huts."

Thusk said, "I think that nobody has any good memories of this place. We might ask the Old Wen to propose tearing it all down and using the materials to build some houses for the poor."

Mell said quietly, "Maybe I can stay here until we can rebuild our family home, that the evil man burned down?" Everybody agreed that the new council should take up that as a first order of business.

Cruthar walked into the room, the berg-man looking his finest in new velkfurs liberated from the ex-chief's large wardrobe. He spoke with respect, "Sire Thusk, Sire Thist, it is all prepared."

Then Thusk rose, saying solemnly, "Birther, Anklya, Thist, it is time." They walked silently outside to the plaza where two large pyres stood, waiting for a signal. A hushed crowd of People stood back a ways from the wooden structures, their bent heads expressing grief.

Thist wondered which of the two deceased men they were grieving, *The murdered or the murderer?* He whispered to his twin, "Anklya's suggestion that we immolate our Sire and his enemy together, acknowledging their old friendship and their service to the Lands, was a good one. Now, supporters of the old man and the new martyr both get to demonstrate their loyalties." He spat to one side. "You know I wanted to feed that fat old man's carcass to the dock-rats and then stomp their shit as he passed through them." He sighed. "But at least I will now get to see his ashes float away. What a tyrant, what a murderer!"

Thusk nodded, but kept silent. It was a good idea, a way to erase the past. He was sure that People would eventually lose all respect for The—the *old man's* memory.

The Old Wen raised her hands, and the fires were lit. Mell wailed openly, but physiologically, like all other People, no tears could flow. *I wonder if Una can fix that, too?* Thusk mused.

Goodbye, Sire, Thist thought. *I hope that one of those gods in the sky will take you.*

CHAPTER FIFTY-EIGHT

Three weeks passed as the People of The People's Lands adjusted to their new ways of life. After firstmeal one morning, Thist and Thusk sat alone in the People's Room, talking over their plans. "I have just restocked Una," Thist said, "as we discussed. There are provisions for a month, and weapons aplenty for us both." His twin nodded, sipping a cup of peat-tea.

The large fireplace was putting out good peat flames, taking the chill off the cool Fall air that seemed always to circulate a bit too much in the drafty People's Place. The twins sat for a moment in relative silence, barely aware of the pleasant background noises from the kitchen, where Mell and Anklya were supervising meal preparations for the poorer citizens of The People's Town. *That is a good idea I brought from ShadowFall*, Thist thought. *A "safety net" for the disadvantaged*, Princess Pernie had said. "A hungry belly foments rebellion," as Wakan Kech put it more bluntly. *I think a few other decent things about ShadowFall and Motherland, maybe even God's Port, can teach us how to live better here in our country.* He and his twin envied and respected the fine and massive architecture of those Warm Lands, and wondered whether their People's Lands would ever be able to have such fine buildings.

About other ways of life, though, they had different ideas. After hours of reviewing ancient history on Una's moving pictures, Thist and his twin didn't think the old "gods" had much to offer in that respect. Certainly, the ancients had developed wonderful, magical technology —flying to the Moon and Mars and building cities there!—but the many centuries of never-ending strife, wars, drugs (whatever *those* were), and even worse problems, were not to be envied. Their own homeland, The People's Lands, now calm and peaceful once more, was much more technologically primitive than those past civilizations, amazing as they must have been, but even Motherland's princesses and the cruel God's Port priests didn't kill people by the millions!

Nodding his head toward the kitchen, Thusk said, "I think that Birther Mell sitting in with the Old Wen on the new Council of Elders is working well, and together with Strether's berg-men, the craft laborers, and the businessmen, they can work together to figure out how to run things in the new ways, without a tyrant for a chief.

"After all, with none of his hangers-on and thugs to support, no tribute taxes are needed anyhow, and everybody is happy about that. I *am* carving up a totem list of other items they might want to think about doing as a community, like paving some streets of The People's Town with flat stones, for example, like those in Mother's City or God's Port. Maybe paid for by voluntary contributions from the businessmen and shopkeepers and farmers who use them? And some fair way for those returning traders to pay the guards down at the Warm Lands lift for their services."

Thist stood up and stretched, walking around in front of the fireplace. "And all those godspheres and printed books we brought down from our Sire's cave, those can go to the Old Wen; Anklya wants to see if any other People can get the globes to talk, like you and I did." He held up a totem spindle, eyeing the many cuts and marks around its curved surface. "You know, *we* all need to learn how to read those printed words, too. According to Anklya, a lot more information can be put on one of those pages than on our totems. And they're a lot easier to carry around, too. What do you think?"

Rising, Thusk chewed his lip. "Anklya can continue to live here in

The People's Place, with our birther, until they tear it down, if they decide to do that. And she can set aside some rooms where she can teach People how to read those printed books." He gestured toward the front door of The Place, where Una's bulk loomed large, still surrounded by amazed, respectful citizens. "You know, in the last weeks, Una has corrected the eyesight of—of—*hundreds* or *thousands* of People that marched through it," he said, trying to adjust to Una's numbering system.

"So now they ought to be able to *see* the print in the books. If the older People can't change their reading and writing habits all that quick, I think maybe at least the younger children should be introduced to it right now—let them learn *both* ways to read and write and then decide which one to use. And everybody needs to learn Una's decimal number system, too. That is incredibly efficient for counting, and for accounting." He smiled. "You need to carve that suggestion for the council, too."

They both grew silent, only the crackling fire and the noisy bustle from the kitchen providing any sound. Each man's face was grim, their wrinkled brow shadows flickering in the firelight. "You know—" they both said at the same time. Laughing, Thist nodded to his twin. "Yes, I know. We have been putting it off for days now. But our new People's Lands can get along without us." He looked around the room. "There's nothing more for us here. And besides, it's getting cold again, days away from the Season Cold 'solstice,' as Wakan calls it. You know, speaking of him, down in Motherland it will be a lot warmer than here."

Thusk said, "So we are in agreement: We have to return and do something about Pernie, and Wakan, and ShadowFall. We need to go back and settle accounts, earn their respect again. Maybe apologize for our lies and theft?"

"And maybe do something even in Motherland itself? Try to help Mother Messinex understand that all that ancient knowledge is too important to hide away?" Thist was wary of attempting to try arguing against the Mother and her slimy chief advisor Miran Kech, and it showed in his sneer. He shrugged.

"You do know that we may not have *any* friends left down there, not even Pernie or Wakan."

"And in Mother's City we may have a whole town full of enemies." Thist was hoping that his celebrity status as The Game champion might help his case with Mother Messinex, but he was uncertain of that.

Thusk spread his arms. "So, twin, what are our chances of changing those lands as much as we have changed our own?"

"Poor to none. But we do have Una. And each other."

Grinning widely, they shook hands. In the kitchen they said their several sad farewells, then walked outside to the god-machine and lifted off.

To fly South.

Printed in the USA
CPSIA information can be obtained
at www.ICGtesting.com
LVHW060152090124
768377LV00047B/305/J